George Augustus Sala

The Life and Adventures of George Augustus Sala

Vol. II.

George Augustus Sala

The Life and Adventures of George Augustus Sala
Vol. II.

ISBN/EAN: 9783337056155

Printed in Europe, USA, Canada, Australia, Japan

Cover: Foto ©Raphael Reischuk / pixelio.de

More available books at **www.hansebooks.com**

THE

LIFE AND ADVENTURES

OF

GEORGE AUGUSTUS SALA

WRITTEN BY HIMSELF

In Two Volumes

VOL. II.

NEW YORK

CHARLES SCRIBNER'S SONS

1895

CONTENTS

CHAPTER XXXVI.

PAGE

Over the Mont Cenis Pass—Venice—A Battle between a Crab and a Rat—At Trieste—Over the Semmering to Vienna — The Kaiser — Turner's Venice — Padua — Milan — H. M. Hyndman—" Viva Verdi ! "—The Salas of Milan.

CHAPTER XXXVII.

A Badly Provisioned Army—An Interview with Garibaldi —His Career—What he did with his Uniform—His Lady Devotees — His Ingenuousness — Daniel Manin — Legend of a Special Correspondent—I recognise my Overcoat—Edward Dicey—Lord Ronald Gower—Garibaldi at Stafford House— Compulsory Peace.

CHAPTER XXXVIII.

Mr. Frederick Hardman—The First War Correspondent— Peter Finnerty and the Walcheren Expedition—M. Plantulli —At Padua—Marshal Haynau and the Caffé Florian—Shakespeare's Familiarity with Italian Cities—Ferrara : Haunted by the Ghost of Lucrezia Borgia—Donizetti's Opera—I Rejoin my Wife—An Incident at Mestre—A Reminiscence of Niagara—Venice on the Eve of its Liberation—Good-nature of the Venetians—The Fenice Re-opened—Popular Enthusiasm— Enter the King.

CHAPTER XXXIX.

Perugia—Rome in 1866 and in 1894—Papal Warriors—The Colosseum—Cardinals in State—The Holy Father on the Pincian Hill—Papal Money—Guido's Beatrice Cenci—Pompeii— From Naples to Marseilles.

CHAPTER XL.

Paris—Napoleon's Interest in the Exhibition—The Imperial Commissioners—"Old King Cole" and his Panorama of English Literature and Journalism—The late Lord Houghton—The Commissariat—The "Test House" and its French Nickname—Baron B—— and his Variegated Career—The Distribution of Prizes—Napoleon III. and Ferdinand de Lesseps as Prize Winners—Vicissitudes of Fortune.

CHAPTER XLI.

Mr. Felix Whitehurst—Arrival of Abdul Aziz at Toulon—In the midst of Flunkeys—Attempt on the Tsar Alexander II.—Trial of Berezowski—Maître Arago's Defence—News of Berezowski in 1886—Frightening a Sentinel—A Galaxy of Royalty—The First German Emperor.

CHAPTER XLII.

An Execution at Maidstone—Lord Mayor Allen and his Chariot—The Queen's State Carriage—The Clerkenwell Explosion—The Boat Race of 1868—Buckstone and Toole and the Old Cognac—The Tichborne Claimant and his Friends.

CHAPTER XLIII.

A Feat of Memory—St. Martin's Hall: The Queen's Theatre—Mr. and Mrs. Labouchere—An Invitation to Write a Play—Watts Phillips: a Neglected Dramatist—Edward Sothern—At Home again—The Strand Music Hall—Mr. Lionel Lawson—Mr. John Hollingshead—*Wat Tyler* at the Gaiety—Miss Nellie Farren, Mr. J. L. Toole, Miss Rose Coghlan.

CHAPTER XLIV.

Prince Pierre Bonaparte's Stormy Career—The Slaying of Victor Noir—Maître Floquet—Incidents of the Trial—M. Henri Rochefort—M. Paul de Cassagnac—An Acquittal—A *Solatium* to the Victim's Kindred.

CHAPTER XLV.

" Kit " Pemberton—Military Linguists—Correspondents to keep in the Rear—Paris before the War—An admirer of *la grosse Cavalerie*—Crowded Churches—A Thoroughly Popular War—At Metz—A Musical Colonel—Nicholas Woods—Henry and Athol Mayhew—Augustus O'Shea—Mr. Simpson —Sydney Hall—" Azamat Batouk "—O'Shea in Trouble—An Insubordinate Aide-de-Camp — Mr. Simpson's Tent — A Bullying Commandant—Meeting the Commandant again—Metz Demoralised.

CHAPTER XLVI.

Panic in Paris—Spy Fever—I am Arrested—Mobbed by Prisoners — At the Préfecture—A Remand—A Friendly Gaoler—Lord Lyon's Intervention—A Fit of Hysterics—My Narrow Escape from being Butchered—Tales of the Prussian Uhlan.

CHAPTER XLVII.

The Lyons of 1870—In Straits at Geneva—A Friendly Chemist—To Rome—Cadorna takes the City—The British and Foreign Bible Society to the Fore—Thomas Cook—My First Acquaintance with him—Frugal Box Book-keepers— Cornelius O'Dowd's Attacks on Mr. Cook—Departure of the Papal Garrison—A Mass Meeting in the Colosseum—The *Plebiscitum*—A Review in the Campo di Marte—Might and Right.

CHAPTER XLVIII.

A Libel—My " Extravagance "—A Question about my
Nose—Mr. Friswell, my Assailant—Heavy Damages—How
the Money went—At the Opening of the German Parliament
—A Tobacco and Beer Symposium—Among the French Prisoners at Spandau.

CHAPTER XLIX.

The Prince of Wales's Illness—The Thanksgiving Service
—The Tichborne Claimant again—His Coolness—Funeral of
Napoleon III.—Illness—A Resourceful Doctor—Walking
over One's own Feet.

CHAPTER L.

Dr. Kenealy's Career—The End of Sir Alexander Cockburn's Summing Up—The Verdict—A Parting Glance from
the Claimant.

CHAPTER LI.

My Acquaintance with Three Kings of Spain—A Call
from Don Juan de Borbon—A Parlour Maid's Comment on
Royalty—The Duke of Aosta—Madrid in Winter—Colonel
" Howsomever" and his Stories—Antonio Gallenga, Then
and Now—Archibald Forbes—Roger Eykyn—King Alfonso's
Entry—A Journey to Zaragoza—Left Behind—Washing with
Candles.

CHAPTER LII.

Barcelona—A Train attacked by Carlists—Levying Tribute
—Another Attack : the Tables Turned—Cordova and Seville
—Don Arturo of Bobadilla introduces himself—Gibraltar—A
Charge of Insulting the Sons of the Rock—The King of the
Monkeys—Algeria.

CHAPTER LIII.

PAGE

Death of Shirley Brooks—His Editorship of *Punch*—Lord Beaconsfield as a Patron of Men of Letters—The Difficulty of Saving on £2,000 a Year—Demolition of Temple Bar: *Daily Telegraph* Victory—The Griffin—To Russia again—The Flower of Russian Society—Denounced as a Turkish Spy—An Ill-tempered Courier and his Peculiarities—The Monotony of Russian Life—The American Minister—The Russian Climate—Adelina Patti and her *Chasseur*—Odessa.

CHAPTER LIV.

The Black Sea—The Bosphorus—Campbell Clarke—Harems on the Tramway—Plundering St. Sophia—Mosaics and Jujubes: a Widow Lady's Penetration—Dancing Dervishes—The Dogs of Stamboul: a Story of them—Alexander McGahan—Eugene Schuyler and his Smoking Party—Frank Scudamore—Hobart Pasha—Baker Pasha—Colonel Burnaby—British Diplomatists at Constantinople—Mr. Consul Reade—The Son of Napoleon the Great's Gaoler.

CHAPTER LV.

M. Barère—Mr. Hormuzd Rassam—General Ignatieff: a Reminiscence of his Father—Sir William White—Christmas at Constantinople—Proclaiming the Turkish Constitution—Moslem Toleration—Athens—Story of a Deaf Judge—Syra—At Monte Carlo: more Ill-luck—Captain Cashless—Madame La Baronne Unetelle and her Indignation.

CHAPTER LVI.

Breaking into my own House: Story of a Caretaker and a Haunch of Venison—In " Society " again—Mr. Disraeli and Miss Braddon — Presented to the Prince of Wales—The Grosvenor Gallery—" Paris herself Again "—A Dinner to Archibald Forbes.

CHAPTER LVII.

At Richmond, U.S.A.—The Carnival at New Orleans—
A Cock-fight—Chicago—Over the " Rockies "—San Francisco—The Palace Hotel—The Streets—Chinese Festivities
—The *San Francisco News Letter* and Mr. Frederick Marriott—Edward Sothern.

CHAPTER LVIII.

Another Russian Mission—Irish Stew in St. Petersburg—
The Ill-conditioned Courier again—The Earl of Dufferin and
Lord Frederick Hamilton—A Recognition at the Beefsteak
Club—An Inopportune Attack of Lumbago—Lying-in-State
of Alexander II.—A Memorial Service.

CHAPTER LIX.

Permission to wear Court Dress—An Offer of Free Quarters
declined—Entrance of Alexander III. into Moscow—A Brilliant Scene—The Coronation—The Tsar at Dinner—A Run
for the Telegraph Office—A bit of Journalistic Smartness.

CHAPTER LX.

A Lecturing Tour—Mr. Chauncey Depew—An Interview
with President Arthur at Washington—General Butler—
Failure and Success—At the Royal Palace, Honolulu—King
David Laamea Kalakaua — Auckland — Mr. Dalley — Melbourne—" The Land of the Golden Fleece "—Wagga-Wagga
—A Snub at Mudgee—New Zealand—Tasmania—A Christmas Dinner of Boiled Mutton and Turnips—My Wife's Death.

CHAPTER LXI.

Calcutta—Smitten with Fever—The Queen's Jubilee—An
Urgent Note from Mr. Labouchere—Introduction to Pigott
the Forger—His Confession—My Second Marriage.

THE LIFE AND ADVENTURES

OF

GEORGE AUGUSTUS SALA

CHAPTER XXXIII

SOME NEWSPAPER MATTERS

IT was shortly after the death of the Prince Consort
that I became aware of the presence of a new leading
article writer in the columns of the *Daily Telegraph*.
Members of the staff of great daily papers do not, as a
rule, see much of one another. I had my own room at
the office ; and although I occasionally met Horace St.
John, I never conferred with him on journalistic matters. With respect to the articles I was to write I saw
only my editor, Mr. J. M. Levy, or his son Edward. I
was most forcibly impressed by the style of the new
leader-writer ; replete as it was with refined scholarship, with eloquent diction, and with an Oriental exuberance of epithets. Some of the leaders—giving expression to the universal feeling of sympathy for, and
condolence with, Her Majesty in her bitter bereavement—struck me as being about the most pathetic utterances in poetic prose that I had ever read. But it
was the Eastern aroma of these articles which most attracted my attention and excited my admiration. It
occurred to me one day to ask Edward Lawson who
the gentleman might be who wrote so sumptuously

about the Nilotic butterfly and the sacred rivers and temples of burning Ind? He told me that the writer was a gentleman newly arrived from India, and that gentleman is now my very good friend, Sir Edwin Arnold, K.C.I.E., C.S.I.

Shortly after this discovery I was dining with the late E. M. Dallas, of the *Times*, and his wife, who had been the gifted *tragédienne*, Miss Isabella Glyn, at their residence in Hanover Square. Among the guests were Sir Edwin Landseer and James Hannay; and in the course of the evening the conversation turned on a leader in the *Daily Telegraph*, in which—alluding to some exceptionally scandalous divorce case, which was then the talk of the town—the writer observed that comments on such a case would best be made, not in the English language, but in Latin. James Hannay, who was really a very competent Ciceronian and Horatian scholar, had a craze that no journalist save himself was entitled to claim any familiarity with the Latin tongue; and observed, with a chuckle, that the " dog "—meaning the author of the article in question —might, if he essayed to deal with the speech of old Rome, experience some difficulties in connection with the subjunctive mood. The article was none of mine, but I conjectured, I know not with how much reason, that it was from the pen of the gentleman who wrote so eloquently about the Nilotic butterfly; and I somewhat hotly told Hannay that, to the best of my knowledge and belief, the author of the essay at which he was sneering was a Master of Arts of Oxford, the winner of the Newdigate prize for his English poem on the Feast of Belshazzar, and who had been subsequently appointed Principal of the Sanskrit College at Poona and Fellow of the University of Bombay; and that in all probability he had forgotten more Latin and Greek than Hannay ever knew.

Dallas and Landseer were highly amused by my taking up the cudgels in defence of a colleague, concerning whose identity I was not at all certain. Nor have I ever known, to this day, whether Sir Edwin did or did not write the impugned leader. If he did not I beg his pardon. In any case, I have never ceased to entertain the sincerest appreciation of the genius, both as a poet and a prose writer, of Sir Edwin Arnold. The dullest, hardest-headed of prosers myself, I love the divine art of poesy with passionate devotion ; and after I am dead the world will see, I hope, the commonplace books which I have filled with extracts from the greatest masters of poetry in ancient and modern times. Thus, as a humble professor of prose, but as one whom Providence has blessed with the faculty of admiration, and who has never been envious of his superiors in letters, I deliberately place Edwin Arnold, as a poet, next after Algernon Charles Swinburne ; next to him Alfred Austin ; next, Lewis Morris, and next William Morris. Concerning the poetesses it would be invidious to say anything. The remainder of the bards or would-be male bards are, to my mind, only so much leather and prunella.

Talking of Alfred Austin, I smile when I remember my first meeting with that elegant *littérateur*. It must have been some time in 1862. *Temple Bar* was paying its way, but was not making a mint of money ; and Mr. John Maxwell, its proprietor, was not indisposed to sell the copyright of the magazine for a round sum. I had finished my novel of " The Seven Sons of Mammon." Maxwell had relinquished his rights of " deadlock " on the re-publication of the fiction for £100 ; and Tinsley Brothers, of Catherine Street, had given me £500 for five years' right of issuing the romance. But that sum was not enough to purchase the *T.B.* Edmund Yates was in the receipt of a handsome salary at the General Post Office; but he needed all his income, and all he could earn by assiduous literary labour besides, to keep up that which he considered to be proper state and dignity. Edmund liked luxury, and kept his brougham and pair, with a groom and coachman in buckskin and "pickle-jars," to say nothing of a sleek hack for riding in Rotten Row, long before age and infirmity induced me to hire a humble *coupé* from a jobmaster. My friend and sub-editor, therefore, suggested that young Mr. Alfred Austin was just the kind of gentleman to come forward with a portion of the necessary funds for buying *Temple Bar*. He was talented, he was prosperous, he was energetic. So a little dinner party was got up at Yates's residence, which was then somewhere in St. John's Wood. I know it was in that district, because he fell into a mighty rage with me when I hinted that the morals of St. John's Wood were not, in those days, wholly free from reproach. Some months afterwards, when he moved into other quarters, he incidentally told me that his next door neighbours at St. John's Wood had been, on one side, Mesdemoiselles Lais, Phryne, and Aspasia; and on the other side a gentleman deprived of his reason, and who was occasionally wont to escape from his keeper, and dance wild sarabands on the lawn in a costume which the Spaniards call *en cuerpo*, and the Red Indians "all face."

Mr. Alfred Austin, when we came to talk business, treated me in what I considered to be a rather *du haut en bas* manner. I half thought that he was of opinion that I had borrowed my suit of evening dress from Messrs. Blackford, in Holywell Street; and then it suddenly occurred to me that I had been reading a poem of his called "The Season," in which I was alluded to as the inhabitant of a garret, "wrapping my rags around me as I wrote." Considering that at the time named

I had an income from one source or another of at least
£40 a week: that I had been elected a member of the
Reform Club, and was, after a manner, a country squire,
I need scarcely say that the allusion to the garret and
the rags was the cause of much laughter in the domestic
circle at Upton Court. How little people know about
one another, to be sure! There was brilliant, whole-
souled Matthew Arnold, who was so very fond of snarling and sneering at the journalists whom he called the
" young lions of the *Daily Telegraph*." Bless us and
save us! When he was jibing, some of the writers
whom he assailed were growing middle-aged lions ; and
three of us at least, who yet continue to roar daily in
the columns of the *Daily Telegraph*—Edwin Arnold,
Francis Lawley, and myself—are rather ancient lions.
Many years afterwards I met Matthew Arnold at the
house of Mr. George Russell, now Under-Secretary of
State for India.

As regards the negotiations with Mr. Alfred Austin,
they had no practical issue. Him also I did not meet
for a very long time ; but when I did have the pleasure
of renewing my acquaintance with him I had read
" The Human Tragedy," " The Golden Age," " Young's
Widowhood," and many other of his enchanting poems.
Naturally, my mind reverts sometimes to the lines
about the garret and the rags in the satire of " The Season," which contained, by the way, a line which might
have been signed by Pope, or Swift, or Churchhill. It
was a description of a fashionable dinner-party, and the
arrival of the gentlemen when they joined the ladies in
the drawing-room was thus tersely summed up—

" Then the half-drunk lean over the half-dressed."

Gentlemen took their wine, and a great deal of it, in
1862. Not all the two and three bottle men had passed
away ; but I attribute the pleasing advent of after-

dinner abstinence from port, sherry, and claret at the conclusion of the repast to two causes. First, the introduction of the service *à la russe*, which absolved hosts from the obligation of carving, and led to the introduction of light and elegant dinners, in place of the heavy feeds which required to be washed down by potent beverages. If you will look at Richard Doyle's cartoon of a dinner-party in the " Manners and Customs of the English," in the *Cornhill Magazine*, published in 1861, you will see that the host is carving; and more than that, when the whole of the dishes were placed on the table other guests were expected to carve the viands nearest to their hands. This led to much overeating on the part of the company, to much fatigue on the part of the carvers, and the subsequent recruiting of exhausted nature by swilling an excessive quantity of wine before the gentlemen joined the ladies. But a far more important agent in abolishing the brutal custom of drinking wine after dinner, was that patronage of smoking, which we owe to the Prince of Wales.

CHAPTER XXXIV

MAINLY ABOUT A WEDDING

EIGHTEEN HUNDRED AND SIXTY-THREE was to me a very eventful year. I had left Upton Court and taken a house in Guildford Street, Russell Square. Early in March the Heir Apparent of the British Crown was married to the Princess Alexandra of Denmark. His Royal Highness went down to Dover to fetch his bride elect, and we journalists had a hard time of it when the Royal pair entered the Metropolis. We breakfasted at Guildhall, where the City authorities were very kind to us, and agreed that a couple of carriages, in which eight of us were bestowed, should form part of the civic procession which was to meet the Prince and Princess. Henry Rumsey Forster was, of course, to the fore, as the representative of the *Morning Post;* and, in the interest of some other paper—the name of which has escaped me—was the Rev. J. M. C. Bellew, who had been one of my contributors to *Temple Bar.* A noticeable personage the Rev. J. M. C. Bellew, father of the extant, talented, and well-known actor. He had, I believe, for a time, performed sacerdotal functions at Calcutta, where his congregation was very fond of him, and presented him with a life-sized portrait of himself. Returning to England, he was for a while minister of a church in Regent Street, near Verrey's; then he had another cure of souls somewhere in the Regent's Park; and at the time of the marriage of the Prince he was officiating at a proprietary chapel in Bloomsbury.

Subsequently he joined the Roman Catholic Communion : possibly with the idea of becoming a priest of that church ; but he overlooked the circumstance that although the Church of England recognises Romanist Orders, the Church of Rome does not reciprocate that theological courtesy. Ultimately Mr. Bellew became a public lecturer, taking Shakespeare for his theme, and illustrating his lectures by means of scenery, costumed groups, and choruses. He was a born actor ; and had he seriously adopted the stage as a profession, would have attained, I should say, considerable repute. Supremely handsome, of commanding presence, with a dulcet, yet sonorous voice, and perfect enunciation, he had every requisite for the making of a tragic actor. He was, withal, an excellent fellow, full of mirth and *bonhomie*.

We duly entered our carriage on the eventful morning, and proceeded at a snail's pace towards London Bridge ; but our progress was so tedious that Forster and I agreed that but for the dignity of the thing—as the gentleman said, who was the occupant of a sedan chair, of which the bottom fell out—we might as well have walked ; and, by the time we reached the end of King William Street, we bade farewell to dignity altogether, and being both provided with police passes, made the best of our way across London Bridge, which was splendidly decorated for the occasion, and sped towards the " Bricklayers' Arms " goods station, where the Prince and Princess were to arrive. Never did I behold such an astounding multitude as that which crammed every foot of ground on the line of march when Albert Edward and Alexandra of Denmark entered the City. At the Mansion House the Royal and the civic processions were mingled in hopeless confusion ; nay, there were even black isthmuses of loyal subjects between one batch of carriages and another.

In vain did the escort of Life Guards and strong bodies of City police do their best to keep at a reasonable
distance the thousands upon thousands of cheering,
shouting, hat-waving people who were pressing round
the Royal carriage. They came so close that I saw
the Princess lay her hand caressingly on the shock
head of a little dirty brat, whom his mother, possibly
to save the urchin from being suffocated, was holding
up. Thus pounding and plunging and surging through
the thoroughfares went the *cortége* from the Mansion
House, through Cheapside, and Ludgate, and Fleet
Street: the mob roaring loud enough to blow down
the walls of half-a-dozen Jerichos.

At Temple Bar a curious diversion took place.
There the civic procession left the Royal party; and a
strong body of the Metropolitan mounted police having seen the Royal carriages and the Life Guards
safely through the Bar, proceeded to charge, with the
intention, so it seemed to me, of trampling under the
hoofs of their horses the long-suffering group of journalists, of whom I was one. I remember that one of
our number was Mr. John Leighton, well-known as a
capital caricaturist under the pseudonym of " Luke
Limner," and the author of an amusing little book on
the caprices of fashion, called " Madre Natura." I
don't know whether Mr. Leighton had anything to do
with any newspaper of the period, or how he came to
be one of the journalistic crew; he had, apparently,
been hunting that morning, for he was got up in a
grass-green coatee, and cords and gaiters, and flour-
ished his hunting crop; and this odd guise seemed so
to exasperate one mounted constable that he went
specially for Mr. Leighton, and essayed to goad him
violently back into Fleet Street. Fortunately, I had at
the time the questionable advantage of being "known
to the police;" and a friendly inspector linked his

powerful arm in mine and piloted me through this slightly too active squadron of cavalier constables.

We followed the procession on foot as far as Pall Mall, but not without one final mishap, which occurred close to the equestrian statue of George III. Up came riding a very consequential Assistant Commissioner of Police—one Captain Labalmondiere—who, in a high-handed and authoritative manner, ordered us off, saying that His Royal Highness did not like to be followed about by newspaper men. We told this glorified " Peeler " that we had all permits to pass between the lines ; and I added that my own pass had been given me by Mr. Commissioner Mayne, one of the Chief Commissioners, to whom I was personally known. Then the lofty " Bobby " proceeded to slang me, and I slanged him in return with interest ; and it is possible he might have given me into custody for high treason or arson, for trying to pass bad half-crowns ; only, fortunately for me, the friendly inspector was again to the fore, and whispered something to the captain in blue and silver ; whereupon he gave me a farewell scowl, and rode away in a huff. I " took it out of him," as the saying goes, in the next number of *Temple Bar*. Farewell, Labalmondiere ! Life, a philosopher has somewhere observed, is not all beer and skittles. Similarly, I may observe that the path of that very useful servant of the public, the journalist, is not altogether a highway of roses. He is continually liable, while in pursuit of his vocation, to be snubbed or insulted by Jacks in office, dressed in a little brief authority.

I have mentioned this little episode because I wish just to give a glimpse of the difficulties which journalists have to encounter in the execution of the arduous and responsible duties of their profession ; but it is only fair to add that in most instances the constituted authorities show the greatest kindness and courtesy to the representatives of the Press; this is particularly the case at the Guildhall, where, on the occasion of any important civic function, ample accommodation is afforded for those who have to chronicle the proceedings for the newspapers. Perhaps the functionary who takes the best care of journalists is the Lord Chamberlain, for the time being. I am unable to remember the name of all the Chamberlains to whom I have had the occasion to offer my thanks for politeness and generally obliging conduct shown to my fraternity at Royal weddings and funerals; but the last Lord Chamberlain to whom journalistic thanks were due was Lord Carrington, who looked after our comfort and convenience most sedulously at the marriage of the Duke of York and the Princess May. And, goodness knows! Lord Carrington had enough to do on that memorable day in his official capacity.

In the second week in March I went down to Windsor by the last train from Paddington, to attend on the morrow the marriage of the heir to the Crown and the " Sea Kings' Daughter from over the Sea." My travelling companion was W. H. Russell, who had been commissioned by Messrs. Day and Haghe to write the letter-press for an *édition de luxe*, describing the Royal wedding, to be sumptuously illustrated by means of chromo-lithography. Shortly after ten the next morning we were admitted at the south door of the Chapel, and ascended the somewhat rickety stairs to the organ-loft. I don't think that W. H. Russell was in the organ-loft, or that he wrote the narrative of the wedding in the *Times*. I think he was away from us, near the altar, in Court dress; as was also Mr. W. P. Frith, R.A., who was to paint a large picture of the wedding.

Mark the difference that had taken place in levée

dress since March, 1863. The painter of the most graphic scenes of English social life which we have had since the days of Hogarth was in shorts, silk stockings, a snuff-coloured coat, with cut-steel buttons, a brocaded waistcoat, a black silk bag without a wig to it, and a *jabot* with ruffles. It is still permissible to wear that preposterous costume; but the vast majority of gentlemen who periodically wait upon the Prince of Wales, at St. James's Palace, if they do not chance to be officers in the army or navy, or deputy-lieutenants, wear either a very handsome and becoming suit of black velvet, with black silk stockings; or a sort of uniform coat, with a little gold lace at the collar and cuffs, a gold stripe down the seams of the trousers, cocked hat, and dress sword. There were just a dozen journalists in the organ loft, and among them was a gentleman who, possibly, was somewhat inexperienced in the art of special correspondence, and had been summoned in a hurry by his editor from the reporters' gallery in the House of Commons. It is a droll fact that this gentleman at one stage of the proceedings fell to stenographing the Order of the Solemnisation of Matrimony, and was quite grateful, but not at all abashed, when a colleague hinted to him that the Marriage Service would be found, *in extenso*, in a volume entitled the Common Prayer Book.

Of another occupant of the gallery I have a pleasant recollection. This was a highly respectable journalist, the late Mr. James Grant, editor of the *Morning Advertiser*. He had been a long time in the reporters' gallery in Parliament, and had earned considerable literary repute by a book entitled, "Random Recollections of the Houses of Lords and Commons." Mr. James Grant was, however, something more than an excellent reporter and a capable editor. He was a theologian of extreme Calvinistic views; and was the author of many devotional works published anonymously, among which was one entitled, " Heaven our Home." He inveighed very bitterly while we were waiting for the bridal procession, against the sinful conduct of the Corporation of London on the day of the entry of the Prince and Princess into the metropolis, in permitting Mr. Eugene Rimmel, the perfumer, of the Strand, to erect his bronze incense-burning trophies on London Bridge. A sad and gloomy day would it be for England if incense was to become one of the institutions of this Protestant land. " There has been too much of this sort of thing lately," he remarked ; " a stop must be put to it, the public pulse must be felt; the public voice must be heard." He was only appeased when I pointed out to him that Her Grace the Duchess of Inverness (Lady Cecilia Underwood, the second wife of the Duke of Sussex), with a tartan mantle thrown over her form, had just been conducted to her seat in the choir. His Scottish patriotism was aroused; his ire was appeased, and the incense grievance was temporarily dismissed.

Dear old " Jemmy Grant !" He was of very humble origin, and was originally, I think, a baker in some small Scottish burgh ; but his tastes were literary, and an article which he had written in connection with his native town being accepted by the editor of *Blackwood*, or some other influential magazine, Jemmy was led to try his fortune in the great metropolis, where his pluck, his hard-headedness, his intelligence, his unswerving truthfulness and integrity, raised him to an important position in that world of journalism of which he was to be afterwards the historian. There is a droll story, whether apocryphal or not I do not know, about the first magazine article of Jemmy's writing. The tale was to the effect that when the paper was published the editor sent Jemmy a cheque ; and he considered the amount of the draft so splendid, he determined to regale three of his cronies with a bottle of port wine at the village hostelry. So he, with the miller, and the provision-dealer, and the flesher, went off, say to the "Waverley Arms," called for a bottle of the best port, and speedily consumed it. A second, and a third bottle followed; when one of the convivial party observed, that he should like a pint of "yill," or ale, as the port, although doubtless of first-rate quality, had made him somewhat thirsty. The order was given to the landlord, who rushed into the room in a state of great consternation. "What, gentleman!" he said; "ale after my red port wine? It is shocking; such a thing cannot be tolerated." There was a little liquid left in one of the bottles; he poured it into the glass and tasted it, uttering at the same time a shriek of mingled wrath and amazement. "That gowk of a waiter," he exclaimed, "has been giving you anchovy sauce."

When Jemmy became editor of the *Morning Advertiser*, he was too often the dupe and the butt of wicked wags at the Universities of Oxford and Cambridge. He really had a taste for antiquarian research; only, as ill-luck would have it, he was altogether ignorant of the classic tongues; and irreverent undergraduates used to send him sham inscriptions in Latin and Greek which they declared to have been copied from ancient stone tablets recently excavated. These inscriptions, when translated into English were found to be so much silly or idle rubbish; and it was not until the editor of the *Advertiser* had been "sold" at least half-a-dozen times, that he thought of the expediency of consulting one of his reporters, who was a good classical scholar, before he inserted the contributions of his young friends at the Universities.

About the wedding itself, I need say but little: the pageant having long since been considered as an historic one which has passed into the chronicles of the land. One surprise indeed was in store for the spectators; and that surprise was one most heartily relished by them. Beyond the general impression that the youthful bridegroom would wear some military uniform, nothing was known of what his costume would be like, and a murmur of satisfaction rang through the chapel when in the bridegroom's procession the Heir Apparent appeared in the scarlet and gold of a general in the army, but wearing also the dark blue robes of the Garter and the Collar of the Most Noble Order on his shoulders.

Only one more lifting of the curtain of the past. Directly over against the organ-loft, at the south-eastern extremity of the chapel, there was a pew or closet high up in the wall by the altar—a dusty, musty nook, first built, I have heard, in Henry VII.'s time, but swept and garnished and hung with tapestry for this grand pageant of the joining of the hands of two happy and handsome young people. In that closet, in widow's weeds, sat Her Majesty the Queen. It was eleven o'clock at night before I had finished writing my account of the wedding for the *Daily Telegraph*. The next day I wrote for *All the Year Round* another article on the subject, but in a wholly different key, suggested by Vinny Bourne's dainty little poem, "The Jackdaw." You know the first verse of that tenderly humorous production—

> There is a bird that by his note,
> And by the blackness of his coat;
> You might suppose a crow,
> A strict frequenter of the Church,
> Where bishop-like, he finds a perch,
> And dormitory too.

and the last—

> He sees that this great round-about,
> The world, and all its motley rout,
> Church, army, physic, law,
> Its customs and its bus'nesses,
> Is no concern at all of his,
> And say—what says he?—CAW!

The philosophic, bishop-looking black-coated bird was sitting at the top of the church steeple whence he surveyed the bustle and the raree show beneath him. He summoned it all up in the monosyllable "C-c-caw!"• and I thought that I might as well "Caw" in *All the Year Round*.

CHAPTER XXXV

ACROSS THE ATLANTIC

VERY early in the 'sixties there had come to the front
a young lady author whom I had known from her girl-
hood, and whose friendship I hope that I still retain.
This was Miss Mary Elizabeth Braddon, for many
years past the wife of Mr. John Maxwell. She and
her mother were neighbours of ours, living in Guildford Street, and then in Mecklenburgh Square. One
of Miss Braddon's earliest fictions was called, I
think, "The Black Band; or, the Mysteries of Midnight;" but it was "Lady Audley's Secret," a novel
which Mr. Maxwell was publishing in one of the many
serials of which he was proprietor, that first brought
its accomplished author into real celebrity, and when
the work appeared in three-volume form, Messrs.
Tinsley, who published it, and the writer herself, made
a very large sum of money by perhaps one of the most
powerful romances which, to my mind, has ever been
penned since the appearance of Godwin's " Caleb
Williams." It is customary in this pre-eminently tol-
erant and grateful age, when an author has taken the
liberty to live beyond the period which the critic
thinks propitious to his consignment to oblivion, to de-
clare or to insinuate that he or she has written himself
or herself out, and that his or her writings have become
utterly and intolerably stale, flat, and unprofitable.
Miss Braddon has been one of the few instances of
practically proving to the critics that they lie in their
throats. No single trace of decrepitude or of lack of

invention and dramatic energy can be attributed, even
by the most malevolent, to the very latest of her novels.

I began to write a novel myself in the summer of
1863 ; it was called, " Quite Alone," and was mainly a
study of character : the heroine being a French lady
whose profession was that of a circus rider, and who
was afflicted by a most diabolical temper. Dickens
was very pleased with the idea, and secured it for *All
the Year Round;* and my name was to be attached to
it, so that my sole grievance associated with *Household
Words* was now amply compensated. Mr. Frederick
Chapman, of the publishing firm of Chapman and
Hall, heard of the forthcoming fiction, and secured the
copyright on handsome terms. It was about three-
parts finished when there came to me, quite unexpect-
edly, an offer from the proprietors of the *Daily Telegraph*
to proceed as a special correspondent to the United
States, then in the midst of war. For many months
prior to the outbreak of the great contest between the
North and the South, the English public resolutely refused to believe that Federals and Confederates would
come to blows. There had come to England a very
curious type of American character, a Mr. George
Francis Train, who had scarcely been out of his boyhood ere he made a large fortune by mercantile transactions in China and Australia. His object in visiting
this country was to start in the metropolis and in large
provincial towns a system of tramways, such as were
then common in American cities.

We are plentifully endowed with tramways at the
present day ; but Mr. G. F. Train, as a benefactor in
this particular direction, came a little too soon ; and it
is usually the fortune of premature benefactors to be
reviled, spat upon, and driven out of the cities which
they wish to benefit. Mr. Train began to put down a

tramway at the corner of Oxford Street and the Edgware Road ; but the parochial authorities soon made him take it up again. He was indicted for causing a nuisance, tried at the Croydon Assizes, convicted, and fined £500. Prior, however, to this convincing proof of British appreciation of his merits being given to him, he was suffered to entertain the nobility and gentry and the representatives of literature, science, and art at a series of very grand banquets. He was the readiest of speakers ; and at one of these symposia he emphatically declared his belief that not one drop of blood would be shed in the United States. It was a case, he observed, which might be likened to Edwin Landseer's picture of " Dignity and Impudence "—the North was the great calm, powerful Newfoundland ; the South was the fussy, yelping, but plucky little Scotch terrier. Only a few days after George Francis Train had made these utterances, Fort Sumter was fired upon by the Confederates, and in an instant the States, from the Atlantic to the Gulf of Mexico were ablaze.

Frequent and protracted were the conferences between the proprietors of the *Daily Telegraph* and myself as to how my mission to America in the midst of war was to be carried out. They knew perfectly well that as the son of a West Indian lady and the grandson of a West Indian slave-owner, my sympathies were on the side of the South ; indeed, I may say that with the exception of the *Morning Star*—an able journal long defunct—the North had very few friends among the organs of public opinion in the metropolis. Antonio Gallenga and Charles Mackay had been successively the representatives of the *Times* at New York. Gallenga was not actively hostile to the North ; but he gave mortal offence to the Manhattanites by calling New York itself "a city of one street"—Broadway.

Then out came W. H. Russell, as special war correspondent of the *Times*, who so unmercifully bantered
the Federals for their stampede at the first battle of
Bull Run, that on the opening of the next campaign
the correspondents of the English press were not allowed to join the headquarters of the Federal Army.

Then the *Standard* had a wonderful correspondent
in New York who, under the signature of " Manhattan," roundly abused the North, its generals, and its
statesmen three times a week; and altogether the
prospects of the representative of an English journal
proposing to chronicle the events of the day in an
English newspaper were the reverse of inviting.
However, I was full of youth and of love of adventure,
I was burning to see what the Americans were like;
and I counted the days before I could complete all my
arrangements and take my ticket for Boston, where
it was settled that I should land. My wife, womanlike, was bitterly opposed to my going to America at
all; and the idea of my travelling in a country convulsed by war so preyed upon her mind that she became positively ill, and my departure had to be post-
poned for a week till she got a little better. One circumstance, however, conduced in an eminent degree
to soothe her in her sorrow. I had as a travelling
companion my old friend John Livesey, a son of one
of the earliest leaders of the teetotal movement. In
1863 Mr. Livesey was interested, to a large extent, in
some iron mines in Nova Scotia. He had crossed the
Atlantic many times; and from Halifax the exigencies
of business took him frequently to Boston, New York,
and Philadelphia. The *Daily Telegraph* made me an
offer of £1,000 for a six months' tour in the States,
in the course of which time I was to write two articles a week. I had a dim idea that America was
rather an expensive country to travel in: so I con-

sulted John Livesey on the point. He reflected for a time, and then made answer: "On the whole, I should say, yes; with the letters you have got, you will have to go a good deal into society and to entertain as well as to be entertained. But you cannot take your wife with you. A thousand pounds would not hold out for four months." My wife, I am glad to say, also had a companion during my absence; this was the widow of Robert Brough, who, with her dear little daughter Fanny, came to live with Mrs. Sala in Guildford Street, and abode there some months.

It was at eight o'clock on a dark November night that John Livesey and I departed by the express commonly known as "The Wild Irishman" for Holyhead. My wife, who, poor woman, could scarcely move, insisted on coming to the railway terminus with me; and a party of my friends were on the platform to give us a parting cheer. I shall never forget a burly, bearded guard at Euston, who, when I had parted from all that was dear to me in the world, and had flung myself in a very limp and boneless manner in the corner of the carriage of the mail, thrust his head into the window and whispered: "Excuse me, sir; but you have another three-quarters of a minute before the train starts, and you can get out and give the lady another 'hug'"—the which I did. I am sure that guard must have been a family man, and had given some one a hug before he went on duty that night. God bless him, any way, and I hope that all his journeys have been as prosperous as mine.

It is not necessary that I should go into extended detail touching that which I saw and that which I did in the United States; my sojourn in which country, allowing for a few weeks which I passed in Mexico and the Spanish West Indies in the spring of 1864, extended over a period of nearly thirteen months; so that I received from the proprietors of the *Daily Tel-egraph* more than £2,000 for my journey. Livesey's prediction that I should not be able to have my wife with me in the States was not altogether verified. As I incidentally mentioned in the precursor of this book, " Things I Have Seen, and People I Have Known," gold was at a tremendously high premium in America in 1864. It rose sometimes to cent. per cent. Now, I drew on my bankers, Messrs. Duncan, Sherman and Co., for gold, or, rather, the value of gold as repre-sented in Government greenbacks ; thus, for a hun-dred pounds, of which the normal value would have been five hundred dollars, I used to get from seven hundred to a thousand. The prices of articles of daily life varied according. to the rate of exchange. I did not live in New York on what is called " the Ameri-can system," by which everything, except alcoholic liquors, is included in the weekly charge for board. These charges had gone up since the war ; and I think that at the first-class hotels, the St. Nicholas—long since defunct—the New York, and the Fifth Avenue, board was $4 a day. I lived at the Brevoort House, on Fifth Avenue and Eighth Street, close to Washing-ton Square, an establishment of which the proprietor was a Mr. Clark, a most courteous and obliging gentleman.

The hotel was conducted on the European system. You paid so much a day for your room, and an addi-tional four or five dollars if you wanted a private par-lour—a supplement which was to me more a neces-sity than a luxury, as I was obliged to have a good many books and papers about me for journalistic pur-poses. There was a first-rate restaurant attached to the hotel, where you breakfasted and lunched and dined *à la carte*. On the whole, my bills at the Bre-voort House were rarely under £20 a week in English sterling ; but when I travelled far afield, to Boston, to Philadelphia, to Baltimore, to Washington, and to Niagara, I experienced the full benefit of the high rate of exchange. Railway fares had not risen; nor were the charges for expressing your luggage increased. The price of board at the best hotels was slightly, but not seriously, enhanced; and I lived at hotels conducted on the boarding system. I had brought with me a very large wardrobe, and I had need to have done so, since gloves were sometimes $3 a pair, and boots $15— in greenbacks.

Somehow or another I so managed matters that I always had a round balance at Duncan and Sherman's; and I remember one day my kind friend, James Lorimer Graham, who was an ardent partisan of the North, saying to me at the end of a lively political discussion, " You've no reason to grumble, any way ; why, confound it, you're living on your exchange ; " and so to a certain extent I was. I had in April sufficient spare cash by me to take a trip to Havana and Mexico ; and again, in June, when the *Daily Telegraph* credited me with another thousand pounds, I sent home for my wife, who came out to New York and travelled with me to the chief northern cities, to Niagara, to Montreal, Quebec, and Toronto, and to the watering-places of Newport and Saratoga. She used often to say, laughing, that our first conversation, when I had brought her from the wharf at Jersey City, was of a somewhat prosaic nature. She immediately began to overhaul the contents of my wardrobe, and in a voice in which sweetness was mingled with severity, observed, " You are twenty-four pocket-handkerchiefs short; and what have you done with your socks ? " To this, I believe, I made the wholly unpoetical reply, " Bother my socks ; have you got any gold ? " It was so long ere I had gazed on the blessed effigy of Her

Majesty on a golden disc. Sometimes, however, I was constrained to buy gold down town before making a trip to Canada. The Canadians would have nothing to do with greenbacks: their currency was in dollars and cents; but it was a metallic one; and if you brought any greenbacks with you, it was only at a ruinous discount that you could get them cashed.

Livesey and I spent Christmas, 1863, at Montreal, in Lower Canada, taking Niagara on our way; and on Christmas Day we dined with a hero of the Crimean War—Sir William Fenwick Williams of Kars. I also remember meeting at Montreal a very genial naval officer, Admiral de Horsey; and it was also at Montreal that I had the honour to make the acquaintance of Major Wolseley, now Field-Marshal Viscount Wolseley. Some weeks afterwards, at Washington, and subsequently at New York, I made the pleasant acquaintance of a young gentleman named Malet, who is now Sir Edward Malet, Her Majesty's ambassador at Berlin. I do not mention these trifling circumstances in any spirit of vanity or conceit. I merely cite them in proof of what is to me, in my old age, an extremely gratifying fact. The friends I have made I have been fortunate enough to keep; and the great folks whom I have known during a very long and, I hope, a modest and undemonstrative career, have not dropped me.

I found Montreal a highly interesting city, but not quite so picturesque a one as Quebec. It was not French enough for me, although I was hospitably received in a good many French houses; and the Archbishop of Montreal was so polite as to ask me to come and taste his hothouse grapes, of which his Grace cultivated no less than eighteen varieties. By the time that I had got to the twelfth, I am afraid that I meekly suggested that a small quantity of the juice of the grape in its fermented condition—that is to say, a glass of dry sherry—would not, under the circumstances, be unacceptable. Another friend whom I made in Montreal was Colonel Earle, who had recently exchanged from the Line into a regiment of the Guards; and, as General Earle, afterwards met his death, valiantly fighting in the Egyptian campaign. I had a letter of introduction to him from Mr. Young, the editor of the *New York Albion*, a brother of Mr. George Frederick Young, the noted advocate of Protection, who once had a furious newspaper passage-of-arms with the present Sir Robert Peel on the question of Protection *versus* Free Trade.

Finally, through whose introduction I know not, I was introduced to an officer in the Scots Guards, who afterwards became one of my dearest friends, and whose premature death I bitterly lamented and still. lament. This was Captain, afterwards Colonel, James Ford, the son of a Canon of Exeter, to whom students of Dante are indebted for an admirable translation of the " Inferno," and a nephew, if I mistake not, of the Ford who wrote the " Handbook to Spain," and a large number of essays on Spanish subjects, in the *Quarterly Review.* Montreal, early in 1863, was full of British troops and fugitive Confederates. The Scots and the Grenadier Guards were stationed at Montreal; the Rifle Brigade were at Hamilton; and I still occasionally meet and talk over old times with one of the then officers of the Rifles—Lord Edward Pelham Clinton.

I have said that Montreal was full of Confederates, ladies as well as gentlemen; and one night, dining at the mess of the Scots Guards—I think that they were Scotch Fusiliers in those days—I found another civilian guest, whose name was Brune, a very wealthy merchant from Baltimore, but whose political proclivities being strongly Southern had impelled him to cross

the Anglo-American frontier in a hurry. There was
such a prodigious quantity of first-rate claret consumed
on this memorable evening that the feast was known
in the annals of the regiment as "the great Brune
night." "Secesh" sentiments were the rule, and sympathy with the North the exception. The fun became
very fast and furious; and about midnight these jocund
sons of Mars persuaded me to sing, as a compliment to
Mr. Brune, the famous Confederate song of "Maryland, my Maryland!" I had just concluded the stirring verse :—

> " Thou wilt not yield the traitor toll,
>   Maryland, my Maryland !
> Thou wilt not crook to his control,
>   Maryland, my Maryland !
> Better the fire upon thee roll;
> Better the shot, the blade, the bowl,
> Than crucifixion of the soul,
>   Maryland, my Maryland !"

The exquisitely beautiful melody of this stirring song
is that of the German Volkslied, "O Tannenbaum!
O Tannenbaum!" (Oh fir-tree); and of the German
Studentenlied "*Gaudeamus igitur Juvenes dum Sumus.*"
I say that I had just finished this verse, and was pro-
ceeding to attack the concluding stanza, beginning :

> " I hear the distant thunder hum,"

when we became aware of the melodious sound of
female voices outside the mess-room. Upon my word,
the Confederate ladies, who had retired to rest at a
comparatively early hour, had arisen from their
couches, wrapped themselves in cloaks and dressing-
gowns, and were singing the chorus of " O Maryland,
my Maryland !" The Grenadier Guards had a mess
of their own in Jacques-Quartier Square; and among
the officers of that gallant corps were the Duke of

Athole and Lord Abinger; the last-named nobleman was married, during his stay in Canada, to Miss Magruder, the daughter of the well known Confederate General.

It was not until the summer of 1864 that I visited Quebec. Travelling, in the first instance, by steamer, on the beautiful river St. Lawrence, and by the Thousand Islands, the romantic, old-fashioned aspect of the old capital of Lower Canada pleased me hugely. Quebec was then the residence of a Governor-General of Canada, Viscount Monck, and we were hospitably entertained at his Excellency's summer quarters near Quebec. I specially remember these viceregal dinners, for two very different reasons. Lord Monck's butler had been the proprietor of the original Industrious Fleas, and his talented troupe, including the flea that drew the cannon, the flea that rode in the sedan-chair, and the flea that impersonated Napoleon Bonaparte's charger, Marengo, had all been burnt— poor little insects!—in a terrible fire at the Governor's country seat. The next reason why Lord Monck's hospitality still dwells in my mind is, that I met at his table the illustrious Gordon, without being, in the slightest extent, aware of the fact; indeed, I did not know it until a very few years ago, when a lady—a relative, I believe, of Lord Monck—in some Reminiscences which she published of her sojourn in Canada, enumerated Gordon and my humble self among the guests at this particular banquet. I venture to think that the lady was rather pleased with me than otherwise, 'for she incidentally mentioned, in her book, that when I was presented to Lady Monck, " I bowed like a courtier." Goodness gracious me! How did the lady expect me to behave? · Did she think that I ought to have entered the drawing-room on all-fours, or that I should have hopped about on one leg, like the burglar in Mr. Gilbert's comedy?

Animated debates were going on in the Legislature at Quebec on the subject of the Federation of all the British North American colonies; and one of the most animated speakers on the subject of the proposed Dominion of Canada, was the late D'Arcy Magee, a singularly gifted, accomplished, and amiable native of the Sister Isle. Good-looking, eloquent of speech, and a ready writer, he had been in his salad days, when he was green of judgment, a Young Irelander; but emigrating to Canada, had become a staunch Loyalist, and when I knew him, he was Minister of Agriculture. It was his mournful fate, ultimately, to be murdered by a Fenian. D'Arcy Magee and I were great cronies; and I am indebted to him for one of the drollest electioneering stories that ever I heard. It was at Montreal, at the height of some electoral contest for the representation of the city, that one of the candidates had convened a meeting of negro electors, who, in the early stages of the evening, seemed far from favourable to him. He went on speaking, however, and dwelt over and over again on the then burning tariff question, telling his hearers that what they chiefly needed was a carefully-adjusted system of *ad valorem* duties.

Now it chanced that there had just entered the hall a young nigger-waiter from an adjacent restaurant, who held under one arm another waiter—but a dumb one—a japanned tin tray, in fact. The negroes are very fond of rhythm; they like sound, without troubling themselves much concerning sense, and somehow or another the words *ad valorem* tickled the ears of the young darkey from the restaurant. " Ad valorum, ad valorum, ad valorum !" he repeated in rapid *crescendo*, rapping meanwhile the japanned tin tray with a doorkey. It was as though he had sounded the loud timbrel in Egypt's Dark Sea. " Ad valorum, ad valorum !" the whole audience began to shout, to scream, and to yell, clapping, meanwhile, their hands, and stamping their feet on the ground ; and then there arose an aged negro of great influence in political circles at Montreal, who thus addressed his hearers : " My brudders, we must all vote for old Ad Valorum —bully for you, Ad Valorum." The candidate was returned by a thumping majority, and was ever after known in darkey circles as " Good old Ad Valorum."

There was a Dominion dinner, if I mistake not, during my stay in Quebec, and I had to make a speech. Then one of the regiments of the line at the citadel asked me to mess ; and there I met dear Hawley Smart, then a captain in the 5th Foot ; he had gone out, I think, as an ensign, to the Crimea, and had won his commissions of captain and lieutenant on the field of battle. Already, in 1864, he was thinking of literature, and showed me a capital sporting article which he had written, called " Saratoga Races." He and James Forde, of the Scots Fusiliers, came down to New York in the course of the year, and stayed with us at the Brevoort House. Hawley Smart was a nephew of the renowned racing baronet, Sir Joseph Hawley, at whose house, at West Brighton, I was enabled, through the kindness of my friend, the Hon. Francis Lawley, to pass many pleasant hours. I was nervous at first about accepting Sir Joseph's invitation ; since—although I have long studied the history and the anatomy of the horse, and can draw the animal tolerably well—I am as ignorant as a Pottawottomi Indian of all turf matters. But, to my agreeable surprise, I found Sir Joseph Hawley's house full of rare books and splendid specimens of the Old Masters, among the last of which I recollect a magnificent full-length life-sized portrait by Sir Anthony Vandyck, of a Doge of Genoa, whose robes of crimson damask

seemed absolutely to flow over the frame and reach
the carpet. It was as agreeable to find that the racing
baronet was well versed in literature, old and new, and
that he was an expert connoisseur and critic in art;
nor during the day did he once make mention of such
a quadruped as a race-horse.

There was one drawback to enjoyment of life at
Quebec. The hotels were few, and not good; so that
we put up at a boarding-house, kept by a lady by the
name of Steele, where we were really very comfortable,
and experienced the greatest attention and courtesy
from our hostess. I was praising her to an American
gentleman staying in the house, whose terse comment
on my panegyric was as follows:—" Kind, clever lady!
I should say so. Why, sir, she was raised on Piccadilly." Yes, there is something in " being raised on,"
or born, or educated in Piccadilly. It gives one some
kind of a social *cachet*. Of course, we visited all the
sights of Quebec; and I went out to the Plains of
Abraham, to see the monument erected by the pious
care of Lord Aylmer, when Governor of Canada, to
the memory of the two heroic foes—the French
Marquis de Montcalm and the English General
James Wolfe—who, on this never-to-be-forgotten bat-
tle-field, " met a common death, and inherited a common glory."

We made an excursion to a village on the banks of
the St. Lawrence, called Indian Lorette; and thence
proceeded to see the picturesque Falls of Montmo-
rency, much smaller than those of Niagara, but, to my
mind, surpassing them in beauty. Indian Lorette was
one of the queerest half-French, half-Redskin town-
ships that I met with in Canada. In some respects,
when you alighted from your carriage, you seemed to
have landed right in the middle of the eighteenth century. There was a *seigneur du village*, who, the day

being Sunday, was driven to church in an old-fashioned yellow chariot, hung upon very high springs. He was an old gentleman, and I did not ask his name; because I was resolved to believe, for the nonce, that he could not possibly have any other name than that of the Marquis de Carabas. He had a pew in the church large enough to hold twenty worshippers, and although I would not swear to the fact, I think that the officiating priest prayed for him as well as for the Queen and the Governor-General.

But I must return to Montreal on my way back to the States. It was at Montreal that I first met the late Sir James Macdonald, one of the ablest statesmen that Canada has produced; and the place of my meeting him was the office of the Grand Trunk Railway, Canada, just after a Board meeting, at which one of the directors told me they had had to consider an application from one of the switchmen on the line, who happened to be an American citizen, for three weeks' leave of absence, *in order that he might attend to his duties as a member of the Legislature in the State of Vermont*. There's labour-membership for you, if you like! and we seem to be coming rapidly to a similar condition of things in this country. Sir James, then Mr. Macdonald, was, facially, wonderfully like Lord Beaconsfield; and when in Ministerial uniform, the resemblance of the Canadian to the British statesman was so close as to be almost comic. Another distinguished politician whom I met at Montreal was Sir George Brown, the proprietor of the Toronto *Globe*, who was destined, poor gentleman, to die by the hand, not of a Fenian, but of a vindictive workman.

The heat of a New York summer proved too much for my wife; although I was revelling in perpetual sunshine. We tried a *villegiatura* at Saratoga, and another at Newport; but at the end of July my wife de-

clared that another month in America would kill her;
so I sent her home by one of the splendid steamships
of the Cunard line, under the command of that excellent master-mariner and Commodore of the Cunard
Fleet, Captain Jenkins. He was the politest of skippers,
and his name was a household word among the ladies
in the upper circles of Fifth Avenue and Washington Square. He was a wag, too, and I know not now
how many times has been related his retort to the lady
who persistently asked him "whether it was always
foggy off the coast of Newfoundland." "Blame my
cats, ma'am!" he replied; "do you think I live there?"
The Commodore was always an adept at improvisa-
tion; and some of his patter songs were as humorous
as they were spontaneous.

I came home by the Cunard steamship *Asia*, in December, just in time for Christmas in Guildford Street,
but ere, for the present, I part from the great Republic, I may be allowed to say a few words touching two
of the closest of my many American friends. The two
gentlemen I allude to are the late Samuel Ward and the
still living William Henry Hurlburt. Samuel Ward,
or Uncle Sam, as he was popularly known, was, when
I knew him, in the prime of life. That life he had begun under highly favourable auspices, coming, as he
did, of an ancestral New York family, and having enjoyed, as he had done, a thorough classical education.
He was, furthermore, a fluent French scholar and a
poet of no mean calibre. He began his career as a
partner in the great banking firm of Prime, Ward, and
King, in Canal Street, New York; and afterwards had
been concerned in all kinds of commercial, financial,
and mining adventures in Mexico and California. I
have not the slightest idea as to what business " Uncle
Sam " carried on in 1864. Throughout the Legislative Session he was generally travelling between New

York and Washington, and interviewing, or being interviewed by, leading politicians, for conference with whom in the Federal capital he had a mysterious little house of his own, somewhere near Pennsylvania Avenue. Whether he rolled logs, or ground axes, or pulled wires, or was a lobbyist, or a mugwump, or bull-dosed anybody, it is no business of mine to inquire. I only know that he always seemed to have plenty of money, that his conversation was delightful, and his hospitality inexhaustible. His first wife, I think, had been a daughter of the house of Astor. His second spouse was a Miss Zenobia Grimes, of an old family in Massachusetts. "Uncle Sam" was a consummate gastronome; although, like most genuine epicures, his appetite was a very moderate one.

We used to dine much better than I can dine at this time of day in London at Delmonico's, which had then two branches "down town," one in Beaver Street, and another at the corner of Chambers Street; and a third at the corner of the then fashionable East Fourteenth Street and Fifth Avenue. Then there was another very splendid restaurant "up town," called La Maison Dorée; and finally, there was an excellent house for dinner in Lafayette Place, where Sam Ward always kept a stock of rare wines. The other intimate friend of mine, whom I first knew in 1864, was William Henry Hurlburt, who was then, as he is now, a distinguished journalist. At the time of which I speak he was a leader writer in the New York *World*, of which the editor was Mr. Manton Marble. I have rarely known a man so varied in accomplishments as Hurlburt. He was one of the most brilliant conversationalists I ever met with; and he could judge things from an English as well as from an American standpoint. A scholar, a linguist, a traveller, a brilliant writer, a fluent public speaker, with a singularly melodious, yet forcible voice.

All the fairies, save one, seemed to have been present at his christening. Many years after we became
friends, an American lady in Rome told me that Hurlburt, early in his career, had been an Unitarian minister; and that he won the admiration of the female
part of his congregation, not only by his eloquence as
a preacher, but also through the circumstance that he
was accustomed to ascend the pulpit stairs " with a
true polka step."

The friendship which I conceived for William Henry
Hurlburt remains undiminished to this day. I am not
one of those who desert old friends when they are
under a cloud. He was defendant in an action for
breach of promise of marriage, and the jury returned
a verdict in his favour; but there were some mysterious
features in the case which have never been, and probably never will be, cleared up; and I am wholly at a
loss to understand the *acharnement* with which Hurlburt has been pursued. I was subpœnaed as a witness,
to testify as to his handwriting in certain letters which
were submitted to me; but I told the plaintiff's counsel,
Mr. Candy, Q.C., that I could not possibly swear that
the calligraphy of this correspondence was Hurlburt's:
inasmuch as I had not received a letter from him for
full twenty years; that I had to read, every year, thousands of communications from all sorts of people from
all parts of the world; and, finally, that I was more
than half blind. So the learned counsel affably told me
to go about my business.

Soon after returning to England I published the
article which I had written in the *Daily Telegraph* under
the title of " My Diary in America in the Midst of War,"
and I dedicated the two volumes to W. H. Russell with
the simple legend " Crimea, India, America." Is there
a British journalist who has done more for his country,
for the Republic—I mean the term in its true sense,

La Chose Publique, the Public Thing—than William Howard Russell? When our heroic soldiers before Sebastopol were half starving, in rags, and decimated by sickness, Russell, as war correspondent of the *Times* newspaper, recorded their sufferings and denounced the carelessness, the stupidity, the crass imbecility of the Government and its officials, who had been the prime cause of the misery and the mortality in the ranks of the British Army. No history of the war, into the undertaking of which England was cajoled by the tortuous policy of Napoleon III., would be complete without the amplest of justice being done to not only William Howard Russell, but to the heroic Florence Nightingale, the " Lady of the Lamp " of Longfellow.

> " On England's annals, through the long
>   Hereafter of her speech and song,
>   That light its rays shall cast
>   Through portals of the past.
>
> " A lady with a lamp shall stand
>   In the great history of the land,
>   A noble type of good
>   Enduring womanhood."

By the way, Alexis Soyer, who, during his stay in the East, did yeoman's service in the hospital kitchens at Balaclava and Scutari, told me a story about Miss Nightingale, which I have not seen in print. A soldier who had been severely and shockingly wounded was in such dire agony that, after the manner of his kind, he burst into a frenzy of cursing and swearing, for which he was sternly rebuked by the surgeon, who was bandaging his wounds. "How dare he," asked the medico, "use such language in the presence of a lady." Miss Nightingale was standing close by, and she said quietly to the surgeon : " Please to mind your own business. Can't you see that the poor man is in fearful pain, and does not know what he is saying?"

"America in the Midst of War" was published by Tinsley Brothers, of Catherine Street, who paid me £800 for the copyright. Thus, contrasting the financial results of my American tour with those of my Russian journey seven years before, I think that on the whole the balance was much in favour of the Transatlantic expedition. I went back to my old business of writing six leaders a week in the *Daily Telegraph*, quite unconscious that another most stirring and eventful year was before me. In April, 1865, the Emperor Napoleon III. was preparing to make a progress through Algeria; and my proprietors suggested that I should follow the Imperial party, and send home letters descriptive of what I had seen in North Africa; so I once more bade farewell to my household gods in Guildford Street and started for Paris *en route* for Marseilles and Algiers.

Before, however, I recount my experiences of a trip to Barbary, I may mention a somewhat ludicrous adventure which happened to me in connection with that excellent American comedian, Mr. Joseph Jefferson, the unrivalled impersonator of Rip Van Winkle. One Saturday I saw an advertisement in the papers stating that on the ensuing Monday Mr. Jefferson was to make his appearance at the Adelphi Theatre in Dion Boucicault's strikingly romantic *Rip Van Winkle*. It seemed to me that I had often met Mr. Jefferson in society in New York, and that we had been on friendly and, indeed, intimate terms; so I wrote to him at the Charing Cross Hotel as follows: "Dear Old Hoss,— Pork and beans to-morrow at seven. Come on." The letter was duly sent to the hotel; but early on Sunday morning the terrible truth broke on my mind that the actor who had been so friendly to me in New York was not named Jefferson, but had an entirely different appellation; and that I did not know Mr. Joseph Jefferson of *Rip Van Winkle* fame from the Man in the Moon. How the astounding aberration had come about I cannot tell. I passed the day in moody perturbation. At 7.30 p.m., lo and behold! Mr. Joseph Jefferson, in full evening dress, duly made his appearance, " I wasn't going to miss a good chance," he said, as he took his seat at our humble board, and we spent a delightful evening.

I may also in this connection remark that just before I went to the States I had the honour to make the acquaintance of Miss Kate Bateman, a young and beautiful actress, who took the town by storm by her pathetic and impassioned performance of Leah in the drama of that name, which was played for I know not how many months in succession at the Adelphi. Horace and Augustus Mayhew, Charles Kenney, and I used to go at least three times a week to the stalls at the Adelphi for the express purpose of weeping bitterly over the woes of the persecuted Hebrew maiden, and of being thrilled by the terrific curse which she uttered. I remembered the charming actress as having, when quite a little girl, played in conjunction with her sister as " The Bateman Children " at the Surrey Theatre, and also at the St. James's. Their papa was a highly typical American gentleman whom we used to call Colonel Bateman. Eventually, he became lessee and manager of the Lyceum; and it was under his spirited management that Henry Irving made his earliest and most brilliant successes.

Colonel Bateman had one curious physical peculiarity; he had a head of hair as bushy as Henri Rochefort's; but it was rebellious hair, hair that would not be either parted or smoothed. There was a story told about this head of hair and clever little William

MacConnell, the artist, which will bear relating. There was a dress rehearsal at the Lyceum one evening, and the stalls were very full. Little MacConnell was sitting just behind Colonel Bateman, who had his hat on. The artist could see nothing of what was going on; and he touched the manager on the shoulder, saying: " Will you be kind enough to take your hat off?" " Willingly," replied the always courteous and obliging colonel. Off went his hat, but suddenly up sprang his rebellious hair like so many quills of the fretful porcupine. *" For Heaven's sake put your hat on again,"* cried little MacConnell in dismay.

A very good fellow, an "all-round" one, was Colonel Bateman; he had a varied experience as a theatrical manager in the States, and was full of droll stories of theatrical vicissitudes; among which I remember one of his having taken a company touring in a barge down the Mississippi. Times were bad and audiences scanty. One evening when the colonel was playing King Lear to a sadly exiguous audience, in the middle of the storm scene, the actor who played Edgar rushed on to the stage and exclaimed, " By Jove ! Colonel, Cordelia has got a bite." Cordelia, who was not wanted from the end of the first to the fifth act, had been busily engaged, at the stern of the barge, in fishing.

Colonel Bateman may also be credited with having introduced into London conversational circles the capital anecdote of the two Virginians who thought that they had been grossly overcharged for the refreshments which they had consumed at a saloon in New York. After much wrangling with the saloon-keeper, one of the friends whispered to the other, " Jem, pay the bill for the honour of old Virginny ; but shoot the beggar behind the bar." The New Journalist may very probably scout this story as a chestnut; but I have always liked to study the genesis of jokes and to give due credit to those persons who have first set them a-foot.

I remarked that I went to Paris in April. I found at the Grand Hotel William Russell, who had come to see a daughter who was at school close to the Porte Maillot. We were at breakfast on a furiously hot morning, the 20th or the 21st of April, when we read in *Galignani* the news of the assassination on the 14th at Ford's Theatre, Washington, of Abraham Lincoln, President of the Republic of the United States, by John Wilkes Booth. I had known the assassin at Montreal, in Canada. He was a strikingly handsome man, dark, with a piercing gaze; but to me he appeared to be in a chronic state of " whiskey in the hair" and verging on *delirium tremens*.

I am under the impression that on the night on which I took my departure for Algeria the first performance of Meyerbeer's opera *L'Africaine* took place at the Académie Impériale de Musique, but I cannot be exactly certain of this point, inasmuch as in that very compendious work called " Celebrities of the Century," it is stated that *L'Africaine*, which had been off and on in rehearsal since 1838, when Scribe first placed his libretto in the composer's hands, was brought out at the Grand Opera in 1861 ; whereas I am now referring to 1864. At all events, I know that a certain number of tickets for representatives of the London press had been granted by the Director of the Opera, and these gentlemen, comprising Mr. James Davison, the musical critic of the *Times*, Sutherland Edwards, and Augustus Harris, the father of the present knightly *impresario*, together with your humble servant, dined very comfortably at the Café Riche. A little before eight my musical friends went off to their *stalles d'orchestre ;* and I departed for Barbary.

I had, however, to wait a couple of days at Marseilles to witness the arrival of the Emperor and his suite. Some years had passed since I had visited the Phocæan city; and I was fairly amazed at the changes for the better which had taken place at Marseilles since the establishment of the Second Empire. The town, as I knew it first, was about the dirtiest and most evil-smelling mass of houses, inhabited by a population as unwashed and as malodorous as could well be conceived. At least Cæsar had cleansed Marseilles. At least he had sanitated it. At least, under his sway, magnificent new streets had been built, and the historic Cannebière endowed with palatial hotels in lieu of the filthy and comfortless inns of yore, reeking with the fumes of garlic and bad tobacco. The Marseillais professed to be very grateful to Cæsar for what he had done for them, and they actually built and presented to the Empress a handsome palace on the sea shore, where, as they put it, their Imperial Majesties "could always have one foot in the sea."

When the Empire collapsed the good city of Marseilles forgot all the benefits which had been conferred on it by Napoleon III.; and after the ex-Emperor's death the Municipality of Marseilles contested the right of the Empress to retain the palace, which was her own personal and private property. A lawsuit followed; and the Municipality, in the course of the legal proceedings, had the exquisite good taste to style the Empress Eugénie, "the widow Bonaparte." Her Majesty won the day; but with quiet disdain she renounced her rights to keep possession of the palace.

Most thoroughly did I appreciate my trip to Algeria; it was the first taste I had had of the East, and although the lower part of the city of Algiers does not differ very much from an ordinary French seaport town, the upper part, or Kasbah, was, in 1864, alto-

gether Moorish. Strangest of sights to me were the
Moorish women, gliding about the streets in what
appeared to be white muslin clothes-bags and pillow-
cases, and their features, all save the dark and piercing
eyes, concealed by the white *yashmak*, or veil. Algiers, however, has become during the last quarter of
a century such a favourite winter resort for English
people that I do not propose to bore you with any
detailed description of the place or the people. My
business is with His Imperial Majesty Napoleon III.,
and his progress through Cæsarian Mauritania. I had
brought with me letters of introduction to the Prefect
of Algiers, to General Fleury, the Imperial Master of
the Horse, and to M. Pietri, the Emperor's Private
Secretary, and at seven o'clock one morning I had an
audience of Napoleon III. himself. His Majesty was
fresh from his bath, and was wrapt up in what seemed
to be a railway rug, girt round his waist by a silken
sash. He was most condescending, and gave me permission to follow the Imperial *cortége* to the borders of
Kabylia : adding laughingly, the tour would be rather
a costly one, but that English newspaper correspondents had so much money. I replied with the lowest
of bows that it was the newspaper proprietors who
had the money, but that the correspondents were generally in a state of the direst indigence. The Emperor
spoke French, and smoked a cigar during the audience. It was not till 1868 that he finally abandoned
the Havana for cigarettes, the fumes of which he was
almost incessantly inhaling. A more dazzling progress
than that of Cæsar through his Algerian dominions I
have rarely seen. One remembers the old historians'
account of Alexander's progress through India. The
dazzling uniforms of the Imperial staff contrasted
strangely enough with the white burnouses of the
Bedouin chiefs who came in from the desert on their

grey steeds, and very often with their coursing grey-hounds in leash.

It was at a place called Boufarik, after an Agricult-ural Show, that I came across a gentleman of whom history should make some mention. I found him sitting on a stone in the middle of a courtyard of an Arab house; he had a large umbrella over his head, and he was perspiring profusely. There was nothing strange in those circumstances; still my curiosity was awakened when the gentleman told me that he was of Swiss nationality, that his name was Dunant—he was waiting for an audience with the Emperor—and that he was the promoter of the Geneva Convention, or Red Cross Ambulance system, than which, I suppose, a more humane and Samaritan undertaking has not been known since the foundation of the institution of Sisters of Charity by Saint Vincent de Paul.

I journeyed to Oran, the capital of the westernmost department of Algeria, on the Mediterranean. A performance was given at the theatre, at which the Emperor was present; but, visiting the house on the following evening, I noticed an exceedingly droll incident. There was an opera troupe at Oran, and the piece played was *L'Italiana in Algieri*—the heroine being an Italian damsel, who had been captured by Algerine pirates. Next to me, in the stalls, was sitting an immensely fat old Turk, one of the orthodox old-fashioned types of Osmanlis, who had not yet relinquished his huge white turban, his caftan, and his baggy breeches for the red fez and single-breasted black frock-coat of the modern Turk. Whenever the heroine came on the stage the corpulent old Turk began to laugh, and continued laughing till his very sides shook. It was not a noisy laugh; but a series of subdued chuckles, similar to those in which we read that the elder Mr. Weller was wont to indulge. I asked

the friend sitting next to me, who was the editor of a
newspaper, what on earth the corpulent infidel was
laughing about. "The opera tickles his fancy so,"
replied my friend. "Thirty-five years ago, just before
the capture of Algiers by the French, he was one of
the wealthiest slave dealers in Oran, and his brother
was a notable pirate, who, I warrant you, had kid-
napped many scores of Italian and Greek ladies in his
time."

When, after visiting Constantine and other places
too numerous to mention, the Emperor and his brilliant followers returned to Algiers, a grand banquet
and ball were given at the Palace of Mustafa Supé-
rieur at Algiers. The scene in the palace gardens, in
which all the trees were festooned with coloured
lamps, and in which the mingling of Oriental and
French military costumes was curiously picturesque,
was like a dream in the Arabian Nights, grafted on
the vision of some grand festivity at the Tuileries or
Saint Cloud. I preserve, nevertheless, one very disagreeable reminiscence of the supper at Mustafa Su-
périeur. The *menu* comprised ostrich eggs, boiled
hard, cut in slices, and served with a piquante sauce.
I tried a slice ; I never tasted anything so abominably
nasty in my life. There is a memory of tastes as of
everything else ; and while I am writing, the hideous
savour and odour of that slice of ostrich egg distinctly
recurs to me.

I left Algeria shortly after Midsummer, and came
home in a sufficiently leisurely manner. Being at
Marseilles, I naturally proceeded to Nice, which was
unbearably hot, and spent a couple of days at somewhat cooler Monaco, where there was a little bit of a
gambling house in the upper town itself. Then I
travelled to Paris ; and so took the train to Strasburg,
wandered up and down the Rhineland for a week or

two, and then wooed Fortune at the Kursaal, at Homburg. I backed the red steadily, and won a good round sum ; prudently avoiding, for some time, any speculation on the numbers at roulette. But a non-professional gamester is sure to make a fool of himself at some time or another, before he bids farewell to the tables. Just for fun, you know, I backed thirty-six, my own age, at the period named, with a gold Frederick ; and thirty-six won. Then, of course, I took to plastering the *tapis vert* with gold pieces *en plein*, *à cheval*, and so forth ; always "insuring," as the silly term goes, on zero ; and in a day or so I was very comfortably *décavé*, or "cleaned out." It was ten o'clock at night ; and having, as I thought, lost the whole of my available cash, I was turning in deep disgust from the table, when a friendly croupier called out to me, " But, Monsieur, you had a louis on zero." Yes, I had "insured" on zero, and I thought that I had lost it ; but as it turned out that zero had won, I left a portion of my winnings on zero, and zero came up again. Then I gathered up my winnings ; went off to the *trente-et-quarante* tables, and won more money before the Kursaal closed than I had ever won in my life. My luck continued for an entire week, and it appeared to me that it would be a very excellent thing to invest a portion—the major portion—of my booty in jewellery for my wife. Every afternoon when I returned from Homburg to Frankfurt, to dine at the Hotel de Russie, I used to buy valuable bracelets and necklaces, rings and chatelaines, at the principal shops in the Zeil ; and it was positively delightful at night to open the nice little morocco jewel cases, lined with white or blue satin, and gaze at the sparkling baubles within.

My luck turned, and away went the balance of my winnings. Then, naturally, I had recourse to the good offices of Herr Hirsch, Herr Wolf, Herr Kohn, Herr

Hahn, Herr Fuchs, etc., etc., dealers in second-hand jewellery, and I punctually lost the proceeds of my sales. I kept the morocco cases, however; and when I returned to Guildford Street, Russell Square, I turned those incomplete symbols of conjugal affection out of my travelling bag; and related, half laughingly and half groaning, the story of my discomfiture. At least the empty cases showed that my intentions had been, in the first instance, praiseworthy. But the road to a certain place, we all know, is paved with good intentions, and empty morocco cases which have once contained gems may be among them.

By this time the autumn was far advanced. But my friends in Peterborough Court thought that another foreign tour would do me good, and themselves no harm; so we arranged a lengthened Continental journey, in which I was to be accompanied by my wife, which was to begin at Brussels, and terminate at St. Petersburg, and Moscow. My proprietors knew perfectly well what they were about; they wished to continue my training as a journalist, and as special correspondent, so that when I was at home, and leading articles on the institutions and manners of foreign countries were required, I could write *en pleine connaissance de cause.*

We left England in November; stayed awhile at Brussels; did the field of Waterloo, and, by some odd caprice of Fate, went out of our way to the city of Cassel, as dull and dreary a German town as could well be met with, but which had, to me, an odd attractiveness, due, I should say, to my having frequently read that wonderfully vehement and superbly phrased pamphlet of Mirabeau :—the " Avis aux Hessois." His Highness Frederick II., Elector of Hesse-Cassel, embellished the capital of his dominions with several very handsome public buildings, art galleries, and so forth:

the expenses being defrayed out of his own private purse. His wealth had been acquired by trafficking in the flesh and blood of his subjects, whom he lent, for a consideration, to the King of Great Britain, to fight his battles in America and elsewhere. Five thousand Hessian troops were hired to fight against the Pretender in Scotland; and the English Government paid twenty-two millions of dollars for twelve thousand Hessians who were sent to America between 1776 and 1784. It was this system of dealing in white human flesh and blood that incited Mirabeau to pen his furious tractate, which I have always considered to be one of the principal portents of the Revolution of 1789.

Then we visited the historic gardens and palace of Wilhelmshöhe, the North German Versailles. That palace was to be, only five years later, the residence of Napoleon III. as a prisoner of war. We went to Hamburg, and thence to Holland, passing a very pleasant time at Rotterdam, at Amsterdam, and at The Hague. At the handsome Opera House, at the last-named city, they were playing Halévy's opera, *La Juive*. Many of my readers may be aware that the great majority of the chorus singers at Dutch theatres are always Jews; and it was extremely funny when the Jewess—who was a Christian young lady, with blue eyes and auburn hair—made her first appearance in the piece, to find her pursued by a howling mob who were lyrically supposed to be Christians, but who were in reality Israelites, and who passionately demanded that the accursed Jewess should be drowned, or hanged, or burnt.

Coming out of Holland, we returned to North Germany; and so, passing through Cologne, took up our quarters at the comfortable Hotel de Russie, hard by the Schloss Brücke at Berlin. There we spent our Christmas; and I was making arrangements to proceed to Konigsberg, *en route* for St. Petersburg, to see what the Tsar's capital looked like in winter, when I received a telegram containing only these words :—" Revolution. Spain. Go there at once." The instructions were certainly vague ; still I understood them at once, and thoroughly. It was a bitterly severe winter ; but there was otherwise no impediment to my journeying to Madrid at once. My wife accompanied me as far as Paris, whence I sent her back to England. I only stopped three hours in the French capital, and then, travelling night and day, took the railway to Bordeaux, and thence across the Pyrenees to Madrid. There were no *wagon-lits* in those days. I had left my slippers behind me while hurriedly packing at Berlin, and I never took my boots off till I reached the Spanish capital. Even then it could scarcely be said that I took my boots off ; since they had to be cut from my swollen feet. The revolution in Spain turned out a sorry "fizzle" ; there had been a military *pronunciamiento* against the government of Queen Isabella in one of the regiments in garrison near Madrid ; but after a few courts-martial had been held, a few officers and soldiers shot, and a few deputies deported to the Balearic Isles, confidence was restored and order reigned in Madrid. I had a letter of introduction from the Foreign Office to Sir John Crampton, Her Britannic Majesty's Minister to the Court of Queen Isabella, who, like all the British diplomatists with whom I have come in contact in the course of my wanderings, treated me with the utmost cordiality. But I was even more fortunate in finding at a stately mansion the playfellow of my childhood, dear " Vicky " Balfe, now become the Duchess of Frias, the wife of a grandee of Spain of very ancient lineage, whose father had been Ambassador Extraordinary at the Court of St. James's at the coronation of Queen Victoria. Balfe, the composer, was also staying with his daughter and son-in-law. I was continually at their house, and met there the youthful Duke of Alva and a number of Spanish nobles of the *sangre azul*, the portraits of whose ancestors looked down on you in the deathless canvases of Titian and Valasquez. The kindly Duke of Frias was much pleased with the interest which I told him that I had long taken in the work of the Spanish painter and etcher, Don Francisco Goya y Lucientes, whose " Bull-fighting " and " Prisoners " series of engravings I had already acquired. It is to the generosity of the Duke of Frias that I owe the addition to my collection of Goyas the " Desastres de la Guerra," the " Caprichos," and the " Proverbios;" together with copies in monochrome of the two famous studies of an Andalusian belle, " La Maja," one draped and the other undraped ; the model it has now been ascertained having been not by any means, as was commonly asserted, an eccentric Duchess of Alva, but a once popular Spanish actress.

There was just one little embarrassing circumstance attendant on my knowing Her Majesty's Minister Plenipotentiary as well as the Duke and Duchess of Frias. The first husband of Victoria Balfe was Sir John Crampton himself; but the marriage had been annulled for reasons which it is perfectly unnecessary to specify here, but which reflected no moral discredit on either party. Now, I used to go with tolerable frequency to the Embassy ; and his Excellency would often ask me how the Duchess of Frias was looking. There was scarcely a day, on the other hand, that I did not see either the Duke or Duchess; and my former playfellow would usually ask how Sir John Crampton was looking. Have I not said, and more than once, that this is an extremely funny world, if we only took care to keep our eyes open to the comic episodes ?

In Madrid also did I gain the friendship of a still living and revered journalistic *confrère*, whom the *Times* had sent out as special correspondent to describe the incidents of the revolution which turned out to be a fizzle—Antonio Gallenga, and his devoted, accomplished, and still living wife; and I remember Mrs. Gallenga summing up the Spanish character thus tersely and vividly: "We went to Toledo," she said; "and there were seven men in cloaks gathered under an archway, close to the hotel, and smoking cigarettes. We spent five hours sight-seeing in Toledo; and, returning to the hotel to pay the bill, and return to the railway station, we found the same seven men wrapped in cloaks, and smoking *papelitos*, gathered under the archway." The man in the *capa* or cloak—which, by the way, he arranges in precisely the same manner that the ancient Romans disposed their togas—is a permanent institution in Madrid. He is all over the city; but it is chiefly in the great Square, the Puerta del Sol, with a fountain in the middle, where converge the principal streets of the city, that the man in the cloak congregates with other mysterious *Madrileños*, in more or less shabby mantles. You may see something of the same kind every afternoon in the Piazza Colonna at Rome; but the Spanish loafer hangs about the Puerta del Sol from ten in the morning until late at night. It may be assumed that at early morn he has taken the national breakfast of a cup of chocolate made very thick, with a glass of cold water—the Spanish drinking-water is the most refreshing in the world—and a slice of bread; but whether he ever lunches or dines, I am not prepared to state; nor, again, can I certify that he has any other wearing apparel underneath that cloak. What is he? Some say that he is a *cesante*—an ex-Government clerk, who for reasons of economy has been eliminated from the service without

any pension. There he was, however, in the spring of
1865; there he was the next time I returned to Madrid,
more than ten years afterwards; and there he is, I
have not the slightest doubt, in 1894, in apparently the
same cloak, wearing the same *sombrero*, and puffing at
the same *papelito*.

It was in Madrid, too, that I renewed my acquaintance with worthy Mr. James Ashbury, then a young
millionaire, whom I had first known in the United
States, and who had come to Spain on some matter of
a railway or a mining concession. In company with
Mr. Ashbury, I visited that astonishing monument of
art and devotion, the Escorial, which English people,
for some reason unknown to me, persist in spelling
Escurial; just as they say *auto da fe* instead of *auto de
fe*, and *guerra al cuchillo* instead of *a cuchillo*. The last
was the terse reply of Palafoz at Saragosa to the
French general who summoned him to surrender.
Guerra a cuchillo answers in Spanish to our " war to the
knife;" but *guerra al cuchillo* would mean " war against
the knife." I can see now the gridiron-planned palace
monastery rising from the foot of the jagged Sierra in
gloomy, almost savage, state. We did the Escorial
thoroughly, but as a museum of curios there was not
much to behold. The monastery was stripped of its
treasures by Napoleon's legions, and most of the good
pictures have been removed to the Museum at Madrid.
A few old monks were pottering about, and showed us
the rare coloured marbles and the prodigious frescoes
by Luca Giordano, commonly called " Luca fa Presto,"
or " Luke in a Hurry." Chiefly in connection with
this dreary edifice there dwells in my mind the Panteon, or royal tomb-house, in which are deposited,
among other defunct Spanish sovereigns, the ashes of
Charles V. The friars showed us also the black marble shelf on the edge of which Queen Isabella of Spain

had, with a pair of scissors, scratched her name, as indicating the spot where, in the fulness of time, her remains would rest. We declined an invitation to visit the adjoining Panteon de Los Infantes, commonly called " El Pudridero," where, among other members of the royal house of Spain, moulder the bones of the unhappy Don Carlos.

We returned to Madrid just in time for the Carnival, which, at the time of which I speak, was quite an important festival in aristocratic Madrid society. The streets throughout the day presented a veritable masquerade; there being a great many more masked and fancifully-attired persons in the street than individuals in ordinary costume. Of course I except the loafers or mooners of the Puerta del Sol, who, wrapped in their *capas*, gathered as usual round the great fountain, and regarded the brilliant scene around them with stale and accustomed looks, puffing their *papelitos* meanwhile. In the Prado the cavalcade was marvellous to behold in its variety and splendour. All the equipages of all the grandees in Madrid seemed to be passing up and down the great drive; but the armorial bearings on the panels of the carriages were carefully concealed by many-coloured draperies; and the coachmen and footmen, as well as the occupants of the vehicles, wore masks and dominoes. The very horses were veiled, and, save to eyes long experienced in carnavalesque proceedings, it was almost impossible to identify the turn-outs of even one's most intimate friends.

In Italy they have a saying :—

> " In carnevale
> Ogni scherzo e legale."

In carnival time all practical jokes are justifiable. Whether they have a kindred saying in Spain, I know not; but I prudently bore the Italian one in mind when a tall gentleman, dressed as a Crusader, quietly removed from my mouth the cigar I was smoking and trampled it under foot. I knew what was coming. He produced a handsome morocco cigar-case, with a monogram in gold, opened it, presented me with a superb regalia imperiale of Cabanas make, and, making me the gravest of bows, departed. A friend told me the same morning, that as he was writing a letter in the coffee-room of his hotel, a perfect stranger, masked, of course, too, came up to his table, took the letter from him, and to all appearance proceeded to read it. He had not, however, done anything of the kind, for in an instant he returned the half-finished missive, and showed my astonished friend that he had been holding the letter upside-down. In the evening we went to a grand mask ball at the Opera. Very few of the ruder sex were masked or in dominoes; the vast majority were in evening dress; and the fun of the evening was for the ladies, who were all masked up to their eyes, to say impertinent things to you in a shrill falsetto. I think that ere midnight I was told that I was a monster of ugliness, that I had run away with the wives of several of my most intimate friends, and that I had taken refuge in Madrid because Great Britain had at that time no extradition treaty with Spain, and because I was "wanted" at home for burglary, incendiarism, forgery, and an attempt to poison my grandmother.

The Spaniards have an exquisitely keen scent for the foreigner; although he may minutely conform to Castilian manners and customs, and speak the language with irreproachable fluency, they will at once spy him out as an *estranjero*. A French lady whom I had the advantage to know, the wife of a Spanish officer of rank and a Roman Catholic, told me that when she went to matins at the church of the Atocha at Madrid she always adopted the Spanish custom of wearing a black mantilla; and she flattered herself that after long practice and with the help of her maid she had succeeded in looking, so far as her head and shoulders were concerned, altogether Castilian. But it was no good. One morning a ragged street-urchin "spotted" her; and, pointing at her with the forefinger of derision, cried to an equally tattered brat, his companion, "*Mira la Frances!*" "Look at the Frenchwoman."

The *Pronunciamiento* which had brought me in the depth of winter from Berlin, having ignominiously collapsed, Gallenga judged that it was time to return to Printing House Square. We resolved, however, ere he departed to make a trip across the Sierra Morena and see what Seville, Cordova, and Granada were like, and we purchased tickets entitling us to occupy a *coupé* in a train leaving Madrid for the South the next morning; but that self-same afternoon the *Times* recalled Gallenga by wire; and he liberally gave me his ticket, by means of which I made the first part of the journey in great comfort. In the matter of travelling, as indeed in most other things, the Spaniards are a peculiar race. In Germany they used to say that only crowned heads, Englishmen, and madmen travelled first-class. In Spain, in my time, it was the second-class and not the first one that was the least patronised. The really poor used the third-class; but everybody with the slightest pretensions to gentility travelled first; and I usually found the first-class carriages inconveniently crowded, although the occupants thereof frequently look as though their circumstances were not precisely of a nature to warrant their paying first-class fares.

I remember a typical instance of an entire family at a wayside station entering a carriage of which hitherto

I had been the only occupant. There were apparently a grandmother, a mother, a wife, and a young lady of eighteen, the daughter, perhaps, of an ancient hidalgo with white hair and moustache. The ladies were not precisely in rags, but they were desperately shabby; as for the *caballero*, he had to all appearance selected his attire from one of the old clothes' shops hard by the Plaza Mayor. Such a shocking bad hat as he had, I have rarely beheld. Stay! there was a boy about eleven, as seedy as his sire. The family brought with them a prodigious assortment of bundles and brown-paper parcels emitting a faint and not altogether agreeable odour. These they were carrying with them; no doubt for the purpose of not having to pay for the conveyance of their luggage, the charges for which in Spain are very high; and when I meekly protested against the bundles and parcels being scattered all over the carriage, and even behind my seat, the small boy rose, and addressing me as " *Usted*," the conventional abbreviation of " *Vuestra Merced*," "your worship," proceeded to tell me in a fluent oration that I ought to think myself honoured by travelling in such company. Where the honour came in I failed to see, but I was subsequently considerably amused by the transformation which took place in the garb of my travelling companions just before we reached Madrid. The shocking bad hats, the greasy mantillas, the patched and faded cloaks gave way to quite spruce and smart garments; and when we reached the capital I found two stalwart footmen in handsome liveries waiting for the family, and who, after assisting them to alight, proceeded to gather up all the bundles and parcels. I suppose that the head of the house was a Don with the longest of pedigrees, and I hope that he drove a coach-and-six, and was the owner of a palatial mansion in the Calle del Alcázar.

My experiences in travelling from Madrid in the direction of the Sierra Morena were widely different and not on the whole so pleasant. We travelled without any incident to speak of throughout the night; and at dawn we had entered the province of La Mancha: an arid, barren, treeless land, swept by blasts in winter and scorched by sun in summer; but imperishably memorable and intensely interesting to all students of Cervantes. For this is the country of Don Quixote. After passing the gorge of Despenaperros we came to a little rickety village called Venta de Cardenas. The " Handbook of Spain," reminds us that, in a *sierra* close by, the Knight of the Rueful Countenance began his penance, and that near Torre Nueva he liberated the galley slaves. In fact, there is scarcely a rood of ground in this region that does not remind you of the immortal company of men and women made palpable, visible, and vascular by the genius of Don Miguel de Cervantes y Saavedra.

I was in no mood, however, to dwell upon the beauties of Don Quixote that February morning; since, at Venta de Cardenas, the train for Madrid broke down. La Mancha is mainly table-land, and is said to be two thousand feet above the sea level; but although apparently a plain, it is very undulating, and in the dips an occasional streamlet creates something like verdure. The great want of the region is, as a rule, water, and in the present instance Venta de Cardenas, like poor Ophelia in *Hamlet*, had too much water; the streamlets had been swollen into torrents, rolling down from the neighbouring *sierra*, and the country for miles and miles around was flooded; so we were forced to leave the train and wait until the waters had subsided. This was misery number one. Misery number two arose from the circumstance that there was nothing to eat at the Venta de Cardinas. " *No hay nada* " (there is nothing whatever) is a common reply to any questions you may ask as to the condition of the larder at a Spanish inn; save and except only at the time of *puchero* or boiled fresh beef garnished with *garbanzos* or chick peas, and sausages highly impregnated with garlic: which national dish is usually served in the provinces at noon. It was seven in the morning when our breakdown occurred; and there was not even the morning chocolate and bread to be obtained. I had had nothing since seven on the preceding evening, and was desperately hungry. *No era nada!* There was positively nothing to eat; and although I thoroughly believe that tobacco allays the pangs of hunger, even a confirmed smoker does not care about smoking more than three cigars before breakfast. I had had no breakfast at all at the time when my third weed had been consumed; and to add to our woes, it was bruited about that it was extremely uncertain whether the quantity of *puchero* available would suffice to feed even a third of the passengers. Thus famine-stricken and shivering with cold, the *desdichados* ejected from the water-logged train were grouped on the summit of a hill, and using, I am afraid, in many instances language unfit for repetition in polite society.

At length there came splashing through the water from the south of the Venta a *diligencia* or stage coach drawn by eight mules. There had evidently been floods in another part of the district, and these freshets had stopped another train. The occupants of the *diligencia* appeared to be excellently well victualled and were munching sausages, bread and cheese, and cakes with great gusto. In particular, I took note of a stoutish gentleman with a black closely-clipped moustache, who, notwithstanding the plaid ulster which he wore, together with a Glengarry cap, I at once set down in my mind as a French commercial traveller. In his right hand he carried a black bottle, and under his left arm he bore, somewhat ostentatiously I thought, a long, thick loaf of bread with a lovely crust to it. I went up to him, addressed him politely in the French language, told him that I had had nothing to eat for fifteen hours, and begged him to let me have for prompt payment a portion of his crusty loaf. He replied very brusquely that he had not yet had his breakfast, and that he had ample use for the provisions which he was carrying. Meanwhile, I was measuring him very carefully; and observed that he was rotund of stomach, and could, if occasion demanded it, be easily winded. So I took the crusty loaf from him; broke it in half; gave him back one moiety—not the largest one—and handed him at the same time a silver dollar. How he raged! how he stormed! what opprobrious names he called me. *Malhonnête !—excessivement malhonnête*, were the mildest of his powers of eloquence. But in the end he pocketed the affront and the silver dollar even as ancient Pistol pocketed the groat that Llewellyn gave him to heal his cudgelled pate withal.

We abode at the Venta de Cardenas till nightfall, but gangs of navvies had been despatched both from the north and the south; dams had been thrown up; the waters, also, were subsiding; and after travelling a few miles in mule carts, we touched dry land again, rejoined the rail, crossed the mountains, and found ourselves in the lovely city of Cordova. I had already made the acquaintance of a Cordova in Mexico; but the Andalusian Cordova is infinitely more interesting than the fourth-rate Mexican town. No more winter after you have crossed the Brown Mountains. It was only mid-February; yet we were in the midst of orange and olive groves in full bloom. We found, too, a really comfortable *Fonda* or hotel, which was positively as clean as a new pin; and in this connection let me say,

that much of the old Mahometan cleanliness is still to
be found in Andalusia; it is only in the north that dirt
reigns with almost unrivalled sway.   Seville is as clean
as Cordova; Cadiz is spotless; I saw nothing objectionable in the way of sanitation at Granada, and the
only really dirty town that I have lighted upon in the
south of Spain is Malaga.

Naturally, my first visit was to the famous cathedral,
which was anciently an Arab mosque, and is still popularly known as " La Mezquita ;" just as at Stamboul,
even the Turks will sometimes speak of the largest of
their mosques as "Santa Sophia" (*Agra Sophia*, the
Holy Spirit—not a feminine saint as the Franks usually assume).   There are so many naves and transepts
crossing and recrossing each other in this astounding
edifice that the interior has been called a forest or
labyrinth of pillars, and the strangeness of the sight is
enhanced by the circumstance that the columns are in
no way uniform or of the same length; they are of
jasper, porphyry, verd antique, and other precious
marbles; and have been adjusted to fit in between the
arches and the pavement by the Procrustean process
of either sawing off a portion of the shafts when they
were too long, or piecing them out with huge, dispro-
portioned capitals.

The Carnival was in full swing at Cordova; and in
a peregrination of the city I was enabled to witness
one of the prettiest Spanish variants of that festival, in
what are called *escuelas de baile*, or ambulatory dancing
schools.   One sat in the courtyard of the *Fonda*, or in
the *patio* of some friend's house; when suddenly, about
eight or nine in the evening, there would come the
shining apparition of a bevy of children, boys and girls,
in full ballet costume, who proceeded to execute, with
fairylike grace and dexterity, a series of national
dances, such as the *chica*, the *fandango*, the *guarachua*,

the *zaronga*, the *trapola*, the *seguidilla manchega*, and
the *zapateado*. These small performers, who were
under the guidance of a wrinkled old gentleman in a
cloak, who played on the guitar while they danced,
never asked for any backshish; but if you slipped a
dollar in the old gentleman's hand he did not refuse it,
and incidentally expressed his hope that you might
live a thousand years.

It was not, however, until I had left Cordova, and
gone further south, to Seville, that I saw the Carnival
in its full glory. The enchanting city! Over and over
again have I been there since 1865; but in Seville, as
in Rome, you discover something new and something
delightful every time you revisit the town. This
work, however, does not profess to be in any degree
of the nature of a guide-book; and for that reason I
will not say anything more about the curiosities of the
capital of Andalusia, save just to mention that on
Shrove Tuesday, at Vespers, in the cathedral, I witnessed the unique spectacle of the little choristers
dancing before the Altar. The urchins are dressed
up in slashed doublets and trunk-hose, with ruffs en-
circling their chubby faces, short mantles, and little
toy rapiers; and at a given stage of the service, they
dance a slow and solemn measure, which gradually
quickens into quite a joyous *fandango*, clacking, meanwhile, their castanets. Some English ladies who were
with me began to cry while the little fellows with the
ruffs were footing it. At what will not tender-hearted
women weep? I know one lady who always sobs
when she is at a review, and witnesses a musical ride
of the Royal Horse Artillery. I intended to have
gone on from Seville to Granada and to Malaga, but
Fate said no. The cruel wire brought me, one morning, a despatch—the usual brief despatch—running
thus: "War between Italy and Austria imminent.

Go to Venice." So I retraced my steps, and bidding farewell to that land of Spain I love so well, I made haste to reach Paris, and went down to Calais to meet my wife, with whom I travelled to Italy by the Mont Cenis route.

CHAPTER XXXVI

You ladies and gentlemen of England, who live at
home at ease, and take, it may be, your autumnal holiday on the Continent in August or in September, have
little idea of the discomfort, and occasionally the danger, of a journey from France to Italy thirty years
ago. We chose the Mont Cenis route—the pass, you
will remember, selected by Horace Walpole, who,
while crossing it, had the misfortune to see his little
lap-dog run away with by a wolf. In these days the
tourist is conveyed swiftly, securely, and comfortably
in a saloon carriage, with very probably a restaurant-
car attached to it, through that extraordinary monument of engineering skill, the Mont Cenis tunnel : the
run from Savoy into Piedmont lasting less than five-
and-twenty minutes; but in 1865 you had to crawl
from Lans-le-bourg to Susa in a diligence drawn by
fourteen or sixteen mules.

The road was a very fine one, constructed between
1802 and 1811 by that great benefactor and scourge
of the human race, Napoleon I. At the culminating
point, some ten thousand feet above the level of the
sea, there was a tolerable hotel, where you could get
delicious lake trout and remarkably good cheese ; but
it was the length of time consumed in the lagging diligence, and the horrible jolting and creaking of the
machine itself that reduced you to a condition approaching despair. It was more amusing crossing the
mountain in winter time ; when the diligence was

placed on a sledge. Then came the Fell railway over the mountain, which did its work very well, although you usually emerged from your railway compartment as black as a sweep, from the smoke of the locomotive.

I had already been to Venice, in the early days of *All the Year Round*, but the City of the Sea was new to my wife, and the place gave her never-ending pleasure. It was during this, my second visit, to the Queen of the Adriatic, that I witnessed a very curious encounter between a crab and a rat, a description of which I gave to my friend, the late Frank Buckland, the naturalist. The battle of which I speak came off in this wise. We were staying at the Hotel Victoria, a very comfortable house, on a canal branching from the Canalazzo. It was a late spring afternoon; the tide was out; and at that time of the day the side canals of Venice do not smell very sweetly. I happened, however, to be looking from my window, when I became aware of a large water-rat, nearly as large, I should say, as my old friend, Marshal Blücher, at Upton Court, who—pardon the misuse of the personal pronoun—was, to all appearance, going out to tea— that is to say, he was running swiftly along the stone ledge of the basement of a palace opposite, and was obviously on pleasure bent. On his way he met a crab—a fine spiky fellow, who had been washed up on to the ledge, and was thinking of tumbling himself into the water again. But it apparently occurred to the rat that undressed crab would be a very nice dainty at the tea party to which he was bound and he forthwith attacked the crustacean. "Oh Lord!" the Yankee bear-hunter is said to have exclaimed, when he came in contact with the animal. "Don't you help the b'ar, and don't you help me; but just stand clear, and you'll see the biggest b'ar fight that ever was." Persons of sporting proclivities should have seen that fight between the crab and the rat. The rat's policy was to turn the crab over on his back; but the crustacean so firmly gripped the rodent in his claws that he won the victory, and tumbled over with his captive into the canal. Possibly his brother crabs had a high old time of it that evening on marinated rat.

I have often seen the smile of incredulity rise on the lips of my friends when I have told this story; but Frank Buckland told me that there was nothing phenomenal in the encounter, and that it was quite within the margin of probability that the crab should win the fight. All I know is, that I saw the rat and the crab, fast locked in an inimical embrace, disappear in the waters of the Adriatic. We only remained a short time in Venice. A further despatch bade me go to Vienna; so we crossed to Trieste, where there was a horrible north wind, called the *bora*, blowing. " It is so strong, sir," remarked the affable cashier of the banker on whom I had a letter of credit, "that you might place your hat and stick on that wind and accept half-a-dozen bills on it without any of the objects reaching the ground." We reached Vienna by that extraordinary railway over the Semmering, the "corkscrew" railway, as it has been called, and the only one in Europe—according to a facetious engineer—on which the traveller can see the back of his own neck, so continually winding is the line. There is a railway closely resembling the Semmering between Sydney and the Blue Mountains of New South Wales.

It was early in May when we arrived in the Kaiserstadt, and alighted at that comfortable hotel, the " Archduke Charles," in the Kärnthner-Strasse. I had a letter from the Foreign Office to Lord Blomfield, Her Britannic Majesty's Ambassador at the Court of Vienna, and experienced the usual diplomatic kindness and hospitality. Vienna was in a tremendous state of excitement, a rupture between Austria and Italy being expected every day. The excitement took a religious as well as a political aspect. There were pilgrimages to the shrine of Maria Hilf, and the devotional agitation of the masses culminated on the Feast of Corpus Christi—a glittering pageant, to witness the passing of which a friend obligingly procured for us a window in a house in the Graben. I saw His Imperial, Royal, and Apostolic Majesty, the Kaiser Francis Joseph, walking in the procession, with a bevy of Archdukes, just before the Cardinal Archbishop of Vienna, who bore the Pyx, with the Host, under a sumptuous canopy.

Again did I behold the Kaiser, in the garden of Schönbrunn, whither we had repaired to see the Palace picture gallery, and the room in which the poor young Duke of Reichstadt, the only son of Napoleon the Great, breathed his last. The Emperor drove up to the great door of the Schloss in a light victoria, accompanied only by a single aide-de-camp, and without any escort. He was in the white-and-gold uniform, and crimson trousers, with plumed cocked hat, of an Austrian Field-Marshal, and that uniform is, to my mind, the handsomest and tastefullest in the whole world, excepting always that of our own Household Brigade. Francis Joseph, in May, 1866, could not have been more than six-and-thirty years of age; but not often have I seen a countenance of a comparatively young and good-looking gentleman so deeply marked by an expression of sadness and anxiety as that which appeared in the lineaments of the Emperor that day at Schönbrunn.

All the walls and all the *cafés* of Vienna were placarded with appeals to the patriotism of the subjects of Kaiser Franz Josef. "*Das Vaterland Ruft,*" was the heading of these posters; but I had got my travelling instructions by telegraph, and made as much haste to get out of the Kaiserstadt as ever I possibly could. We came down again by the Semmering to Trieste, and took the Austrian Lloyd steamer late at night for Venice, reaching the Lido at daybreak.

Very many are the aspects under which I have beheld the beautiful city. You know there are at least half-a-dozen notable painters, each of whom has his own particular Venice—I mean his own peculiar way of treating the city, chromatically. Canaletto's is an eighteenth-century, matter-of-fact, surprisingly faithful, but somewhat prosaic, Venice. So is that of his almost compeer, Guardi. Among English painters, Holland made us familiar with a Venice soberly rich in colour. Cooke, the Royal Academician's Venice was full of atmosphere, but rather frigid. Clarkson Stanfield's Venice was breezy and cheerful; but Turner's was, and always will be, the Venice after my own heart, although he gave on canvas a scheme of colour applied to Venetian pictures *en permanence;* whereas, in reality, the Turneresque Venice only fascinates your sense at certain periods, usually in April and May. It was into the Canalazzo of Turner's Venice that the Austrian Lloyd steamed on a golden May morning. The city presented, as we neared it, a rainbow appearance. The Ducal Palace, the Piazza San Marco, the Molo, the Zecca, the Basilica—all so many " harmonies " in pink, and blue, and gold, and white, seemed to dance in the water. When you landed you were welcomed as usual by the pigeons that haunt the domes and buttresses of the cathedral; on the broad bosom of the Grand Canal, the sable gondolas flitted hither and thither, or emerged from the minor canals, the gondoliers uttering their customary—and, to the stranger's ear — incomprehensible cry. That evening, on St. Mark's Place, there was the customary popular gathering to hear the Austrian military band play; and the officers, in their white tunics, sauntered up and down, ogling the grisettes and such foreign ladies of comely mien as were present; but the upper classes kept sulkily aloof from the Piazza; the Venetian ladies rarely left their palaces, and when they did venture abroad were invariably habited in mourning; and the great Opera House, La Fenice, had been closed for years; notwithstanding the offer of a liberal subvention on the part of the Austrian Government. Patrician Venice, educated Venice, cultured Venice, would have nought to do with the loathed *Tedeschi*.

The next day war was declared between Austria and Italy; but three days' grace were allowed to all foreigners who wished to leave the Dominio Veneto. My people in Fleet Street had telegraphed me: "Garibaldi in the Tyrol in force; join him. Letters to him waiting Milan." Not an instant was to be lost. I conjectured that the expedition would be a somewhat hazardous one; so I could not take my wife with me. The manager of the Albergo Victoria, Mr. Robert Etzensberger, a highly intelligent German-Swiss, kindly undertook to see after my wife, and provide her, if needful, with funds, should her supplies run out; for on the morrow Venice was to be placed in a state of siege. Then I betook myself to the British Consul-General, Mr. Perry, the brother of a well-known English judge, Sir Erskine Perry, and a grandson, I believe, of the celebrated journalist, Perry, of the *Morning Chronicle*. The Consul-General told me that my wife should have every assistance in case of need, and that although she would be the only English lady left in the besieged city, there was no reason to think that any disturbances would take place, the Austrian garrison being formidably strong.

It was as well, however, Mr. Perry added, to be

careful; and the need for caution had also struck the Ottoman Consul, who had incited his Government to send up a Turkish corvette to the Lido, for the protection of the good old monks of the island convent at San Lazzaro, who are Turkish subjects. How often have I been rowed out to the island to converse with the excellent friars!—who are still as proud as ever of the visit paid to them by Byron, and who make a modest revenue by selling strangers a curious product of their printing press, the prayers of St. Narses in thirty-seven languages.

It was not with the lightest of hearts that I left my only treasure in the world in a foreign city, and took the train which, on a long causeway, crosses the lagoon to Mestre, whence I hastened to Padua. That city the Austrians were holding, and they were also in strong force at Verona; but they had evacuated Vicenza, which city had at once been *imbandierata*, or hung with banners bearing the national Italian colours, by the exulting inhabitants. Presently I reached Verona; and, after considerable trouble, obtained from the military authorities a permit to cross the frontier at Peschiera. The railway had been monopolised for military purposes; so that we were fain to make the journey to the shores of the Lake of Garda by diligence. At Milan I found letters to General Garibaldi, to several members of his staff, and to Mrs. Chambers, who, with her husband, Colonel Chambers, were warm and generous friends of the Hero in the Red Shirt. Also, in the city of the Duomo, did I find several of my brother special correspondents, among whom I may mention Mr. George Henty, then, as now, a member of the staff of the *Standard* newspaper; Mr. Bullock, who represented the *Daily News;* and Mr. Henry Hyndman, who had come out in the interest of the *Pall Mall Gazette.*

In 1866, Mr. Hyndman was about as brilliant a young gentleman as I have ever met with; an Oxonian, a noted cricketer, somewhat given to sporting, full of life and gaiety, a ripe scholar, and some hopes of being able, at no distant period, to formulate a Universal Theorem; and, finally, a staunch Tory. I very rarely see him now. I am told that he is the same Mr. Henry Hyndman who has achieved considerable notoriety as a Social Democrat, and mixes himself up with people whom persons of culture would, I should say, be as a rule somewhat chary of associating with. But stay; Mr. William Morris, decorator, poet, and translator of the Odyssey, is likewise, I am told, a Social Democrat; and I must not talk politics. I have long ceased to have any of my own. But whether my old friend Henry M. Hyndman be a Conservative or a Radical, a Legitimist, an Imperialist, or a Bonapartist, a Know-nothing, a Copper-head, a Protectionist, a Free-trader, a Young Czech, or an Old Czech, a Clerical or a Liberal, a Chauvinist or an Anti-Semite, I am convinced that he can never be anything else than the genial and high-minded English gentleman that he was in 1866.

Milan was in a ferment; the newspapers teemed with patriotic leading articles; the music-sellers were selling thousands of copies of a specially composed martial hymn called the " Grida di Guerra," and " Garibaldi's Hymn," and another stirring melody, " Va Fuori d' Italia, Straniero," were ground on every street organ. A grand performance was given at the Scala, in aid of a fund for the benefit of the Italian wounded. The last time that I had been in that superb Opera House was in 1859, just before the war between France, Italy, and Austria, which terminated in the evacuation of the whole of Lombardy by the last-named Power. The Milanese could not bring themselves to dispense with the Scala, as Venetians had dispensed with the Fenice; but they partially consoled themselves for their subjugation by the *Tedeschi*, by whistling and cat-calling all the singers and all the dancers who were applauded by the Austrian officers in the stalls ; while at the close of the performance there was usually a shout from the pit of "*Viva Verdi !*" which was a covert way of acclaiming "Vittorio Emmanuele Re d' Italia," the first "V" standing for "Viva," and "V, E, R, D, I" for the remaining letters.

At the outset of this Autobiography I mentioned there were three distinct branches of my family in Italy, and that I was a humble scion of the Roman branch. I am somewhat glad to have set forth the fact, since I found in Milan no less than three Salas, none of whom were members of the Brahminical classes. There was a Sala who was a baker; while another followed the useful, but plebeian calling of a tinsmith ; the third, I think, was a carriage-builder, and was rich, which slightly increased my respect for him, and I should have liked to claim him as a brother Roman. When I got down to Como, on my way to join Garibaldi in the Tyrol, I found yet another Sala, a lady, whose Christian name was Caterina, and who sold sausages and tripe. I do hope that the worthy lady did not belong to the Roman branch.

CHAPTER XXXVII

I FOUND Garibaldi in a miserable town somewhere in the Northern Tyrol; his army of red-shirts had eaten and drunk up everything that was edible or potable; and the solitary *caffè* of the place bore an announcement over the door that it was closed "*per mancanza di tutto*"—for want of everything. I suppose that there was never an army in the field, except, perhaps, in some South American Republic, so sorrily supplied as was Garibaldi's host of *camicie rosse*. There was some kind of commissariat; but the provend was irregular and insufficient, for the reason that the commissaries were unable to procure the provisions they wanted. The red-shirts were brave enough, and were leavened to some extent by veterans who had formed part of the Thousand of Marsala, who, under their heroic leader, captured the Two Sicilies; but the mass of the Garibaldini were raw youths, patriotic clerks, and shop assistants, who scarcely knew their drill. They did not plunder; and besides, as you may surmise, immediately war was declared all the available poultry seemed instinctively to hide themselves in remote holes and corners, undiscoverable by marauding parties.

Such looting as did take place was probably more among the officers than the rank and file; since I remember a Marquis, commanding a body of mounted Garibaldini, sending me a note in which, with his compliments, he stated that he had got some friends to dinner. A salad was to be included in the repast, and could I lend him an egg? He added in a postscript that he hoped to be soon able to reciprocate my courtesy; as, this being Tuesday, he had every reason to believe that his servant would be able to steal a chicken by Sunday, at the latest. The idea of the faithful orderly laying siege, and opening the trenches, and storming the citadel in which the fowl was ensconced was mirthful.

I had a long interview with Garibaldi on the afternoon of my arrival at headquarters. He received me in the friendliest manner; and told me that there was not the slightest need for me to have brought a letter of introduction to him, as he was well aware that the newspaper which I represented had always been a firm friend of Italy. He added that he would do what he could for my colleagues and myself, but that he was very badly off for stores and for munitions of war; in fact, he said with a smile, he was almost in the same position as the proprietor of the *caffè*, who had been fain to close his establishment in consequence of a "*mancanza di tutto.*" I could not help reading between the lines as he spoke; and fancying that he was somewhat sore at what he considered to be either the indifference or the animosity of the Italian military authorities to the irregular force which he commanded.

There are innumerable portraits, busts, and statuettes extant of Giuseppe Garibaldi; and it would be wholly useless, not to say impertinent, to give a detailed description of this heroic man. Still, it must be remembered that he has been dead twelve years; that the public memory is fleeting; and that the young British adolescent, fresh from school or college, was a small boy when Garibaldi died. He was verging on sixty years of age when I first beheld him. Of middle height; somewhat spare, moderately full short beard and moustache; hair still auburn although beginning to be flecked with grey, and a wonderfully lucid blue eye. He was clad in the *camicia rossa*, or red woollen shirt, which is so closely associated with himself and the brave fellows he led; and in connection with this historic garment, it may be mentioned that this red shirt was simply the article of attire worn at that period in the American merchant service. Garibaldi had followed a great many callings while he was in the United States. Among other things, he was foreman to, if not in partnership with, an Italian manufacturer of soap and candles at Staten Island, New York; and early in the 'fifties he was a skipper of a vessel trading between Philadelphia and Genoa. It is a matter of history that the authorities of the last-named seaport forbade him to cast anchor in the harbour, and sent him away, packing. A soldier, a sailor, and a patriot, one quality was certainly lacking in Giuseppe Garibaldi—there was nothing of the statesman, in the Machiavellian or Talleyrand sense, about him. He could not tell lies; he knew not how to negotiate, to cog, to finesse, or to cajole. His own convictions were unswervingly Republican; but, recognising the fact that Italy was in the main monarchical, and that the country yearned to be united under the constitutional sway of a Prince of the House of Savoy, he cheerfully yielded to the general wish of his countrymen; and after his magically swift conquest of Naples and Sicily, he quietly handed them over to Victor Emmanuel II., whom he knew to be as courageous and as truthful as he was: and on his way to attack the fortress of Gaeta, the last stronghold of the Neapolitan Bourbons, he hailed the King of Sardinia as King of Italy. Practically, it was by Giuseppe Garibaldi that the "*Re galantuomo*" was crowned.

It is amusing to remember an anecdote told me by one of Garibaldi's secretaries, M. Plantulli, touching Garibaldi's uniform as a General in the regular Italian army. The uniform itself is a very handsome one, including large gold epaulettes of loose bullion strands. This imposing costume, together with a plumed cocked hat, General Garibaldi wore only on two occasions. He donned it when he boarded a British man-of-war to tender thanks to the Admiral, who had protected the landing of the Thousand at Marsala. He wore the uniform again at his interview with Victor Emmanuel, after the conquest of the Two Sicilies; but when he returned to his island home at Caprera, it is a comical fact that he presented his General's much-gold-laced panoply to his cowherd, who gravely drove cattle about the fields of Caprera in this gorgeous martial panoply. Exposure to wind and rain and a scorching summer sun very soon reduced the stately garb to a lamentable state of tarnished seediness; and the cowherd, who preferred freedom of action to being tightly buttoned up, always wore the coat open, so as to display a coarse canvas shirt, with a red woollen sash round the waist. It was the delight of Garibaldi and his friends, when they met this cowherd, gravely to salute him in military fashion, and acclaim him as "*mio Generale*."

Menotti Garibaldi, the General's eldest son, was not with us at the outset of the campaign; but his younger brother, Ricciotti, was serving as a private in one of the regiments of red-shirts. Two English ladies were also in our company, and eventually did much Samaritan service to the Garibaldini. First, there was Mrs. Chambers, who had come out with her husband, Colonel Chambers, to look after Garibaldi's personal comfort and see that he was well provided with pocket-money. It was the singular lot of this singular man to be platonically loved and cherished by a noble gathering of English ladies, who seemed to regard him as a Fighting Brother who must be taken care of. His life was as pure as the cause for which he fought, and the voice of calumny was never for an instant raised against the devoted Englishwomen who tended him with love and devotion. Another of his lady-adherents was Madame Jessie Merriton White Mario, whom I remembered as having been, in her unmarried days, a sedulous student in the reading-room of the British Museum, but who in 1866 had become the wife of an Italian gentleman and friend of Garibaldi.

I have said that he was no statesman; he was too blunt and too simple-minded to practise any of the devices of statecraft. Although the co-operation of Napoleon III. had enabled the Italians to wrest Lombardy from the Austrians, he never forgave him for not redeeming his promise to emancipate Italy from the Alps to the Adriatic. He always alluded to the Emperor as "*ce Monsieur;*" and disdainfully spoke of the cession to France of Nice and Savoy as a "*mercimonio*"—a vile, illicit, and contraband transaction. Our brief campaign was not a very glorious one. We were badly off for a field-train, and it was difficult to procure mules to drag the few mountain-howitzers that had been doled out to Garibaldi by the Italian Government. Expert marksmen did not abound in the ranks of the Garibaldini; whereas the Austrians had a plentiful supply of Tyrolese sharpshooters, who could be seen through our field-glasses systematically "potting" the red-shirts at long range; while sergeants and corporals stood behind to score the results of each volley.

As to the special correspondents, their means of locomotion were various and the reverse of comfortable. Sometimes we managed to hire a light carriage

for a few days; sometimes we got about on mule or
donkey-back; and sometimes we were forced to walk.
Dr. Maginn once observed that for duelling purposes,
any one might be considered a gentleman who wore a
clean shirt once a week. I am afraid that during the
Garibaldian campaign I entirely lost the qualification
of a gentleman in respect to duelling. One of my colleagues had been fortunate enough to purchase a rickety little open shandrydan, drawn by two miserable
screws, one of which he christened Homer because he
was blind, and another General La Marmora because
he manifested a chronic disinclination to advance. At
night-time these lamentable Rosinantes were tethered
to some convenient underwood; and then, my colleague, having carefully arranged the harness under
the carriage, placed over it a waterproof-sheet and
slept the sleep of the just; at least, he knew that the
harness would not be stolen; and as for the screws
they were scarcely worth stealing. The weather—it
was now June—was delightful—not too hot during
the day, and not too cool at night; and as most of
the journalists were young and strong, it was rather
diverting than otherwise to have to rough it. There
was little to eat beyond some dreadfully distasteful
and hard meat, which purported to be salt beef, but
which I am the rather inclined to believe was salt
horse, together with some mouldy biscuits; but one of
us had laid in a good store of chocolate in tablets at
Milan; and chocolate, when savoury provisions run
short, is a capital stay or hold-fast.

Garibaldi was the most abstemious of mankind; still
he could, on occasion, be festive; and by the camp
fire at night I have seen him smoke his little Cavour
cigar and sing his little song. Of his utter unworldli-
ness, his singleness of mind, and his childlike belief
that a large proportion of mankind were as virtuous as

he was, I remember, a striking illustration in a remark
which he made when someone in a mixed company at
the bivouac was dwelling on the necessity of reforming
the Italian Criminal Code. "I would reform the code,"
observed Garibaldi, "and the codes of all other nations
into the bargain, with this *scatola* of *zolfanelli*;" and
as he spoke he held a box of lucifer matches. Most
marked, indeed, was the difference as a politician between Giuseppe Garibaldi and another of his contemporaries, as patriotic, as devoted, and as upright as he,
I mean Daniel Manin, the chief of the short-lived Republic of Venice, in 1848.

When the Austrians regained their sway over the
Dominio Veneto, the President of the Republic of
Saint Mark took refuge in Paris. He had been bred
an advocate; but there was no employment available
for him at the Parisian Bar. He was very poor; and
as a means of subsistence he obtained an engagement
to give lessons in Italian to the daughters of the celebrated French dramatist Ponsard. Or, perhaps it was
Legouvé. Week after week did he toil and moil in
attempts to drum the conjugations of the Italian irregular verbs into the heads of the young ladies; but one
afternoon, losing all heart, he quietly remarked: "I
am good for nothing but to be a ruler over men;" and
so made his pupils a low bow, put on his hat, and departed. Garibaldi was the born soldier, or rather the
born chief of partisans; he was another Hofer, another
Schill, another Tell—if there really was ever such a
personage as William Tell—but he was not a director
of policy or a framer of laws.

We had a bit of a battle with the Austrians at a
place called Montesuelo; and in connection with this
engagement, which was not wholly advantageous to
the red-shirts, a ludicrous story is told of one of the
special correspondents. I suppose that in every camp,

from that of the Tenth Legion of old down to those of the armies of modern times, there are always current a large number of more or less apocryphal stories which, in campaigning parlance, are known as "shaves." I know not how much truth, if there be any, there is in the little story which I am about to tell, for I did not witness the incident to which it refers myself; still, as "shaves" went, it may be considered as a sufficiently humorous one. At the time when the battle was at its height one of the Garibaldini battalions, decimated by the fierce fire of the Austrian Infantry, was wavering, and seemed in imminent peril of being hopelessly broken.

The special correspondent of whom I speak was a tall, thin, good-looking gentleman, who habitually dressed in a light brown-holland suit, and enhanced the picturesqueness of his white pith helmet by attaching thereto a white muslin pugree. His only weapon was an alpenstock, and his usual means of locomotion was the open shandrydan with the two bandy-legged ponies, of which I have already spoken. Suddenly—I tell the tale as it was told to me—there appeared in front of the half-routed battalion of red-shirts this notable journalist, mounted on a white horse. He had a light paletot over his brown holland ; and waving his alpenstock wide in air and the pugree streaming from his helmet behind, he shouted in a stentorian voice, "*Avanti, ragazzi, Avanti !*" And the story went on to say that his appearance so stimulated the martial energy of the wavering red-shirts that they re-formed their wavering line, charged the enemy, and repulsed them with serious loss. Whether they took the rider of the white horse for "Garibaldi's Englishman," or for one of the Seven Champions of Christendom, or for one of the Great Twin Brethren who fought in the battle of the Lake Regillus, I cannot tell.

An ancient Roman writer, however, has observed that there is no falsehood so flagrant but that it has an element of truth in it. For the accuracy of one portion of the " shave " touching the correspondent on the white horse I can vouch. I had the pleasure of meeting him when the fight was over; and immediately perceived that the overcoat he wore, a drab summer paletot, was mine own; and I remembered that I had left the garment at Peschiera just before the Austrians had entered that town in force. My friend said that he had annexed the coat, as lawful booty of war, having found it on the body of a slain Austrian officer; but that as he knew the coat was my property, he now laughingly restored it to me. But mark the caprice of Fate! In those days I always wrote with the dark blue ink which Dickens invariably used, and which most of his young men also made use of out of liking for their Chief. I had brought to Italy a tin flask with a screw top, and holding about a pint, and I had left this flask, about three-parts full, at Peschiera. In the other pocket I had left a memorandum book. When I came to examine the pockets of my coat, I found my tin flask, sure enough ; but the ink had been poured away ; the bottle had been washed out, and it was half full of rum; my notebook had disappeared, but in its stead was a pack of playing cards. The mystery of the white horse I was never able to clear up. Was the Austrian officer who came to grief a mounted one ; and did my friend also annex his horse as lawful booty of war ?

About this time came to the front another English war correspondent, my good friend Edward Dicey, now a Companion of the Bath. A Cambridge man, he had travelled extensively in Italy, and knew Garibaldi very well. He had long been a colleague of mine as a leader writer on the *Daily Telegraph;* and I suppose that he was one of that band of "young lions" about whom the late Mr. Matthew Arnold used to write such very smart things.

There was yet another visitor to Garibaldi's camp who has honoured me from that day to this with constant and thoughtful friendship. This was Lord Ronald Gower, a younger brother of the late Duke of Sutherland, whose mother, the good and beautiful Duchess of Sutherland, was, as I have said more than once in the earlier part of this book, one of my mother's most steadfast and most generous patronesses. The Duke, her son, was an enthusiastic admirer of Garibaldi, and was his host at Stafford House on the occasion of the visit of the Liberator of the Two Sicilies to London—a visit so magnificently begun in the popular enthusiasm which it excited, but which was brought to a sudden and mysterious termination. Lord Ronald Gower shared his brother's admiration for Garibaldi. I shall have something to say later on touching his lordship's accomplishments as a draftsman, a sculptor, and a writer on art and *vertu;* but I should like him to tell me, should he chance to read this page, if there be any truth in the following little story which I heard in Italy touching Garibaldi's visit to the Duke.

It is to this effect. When Garibaldi, after a protracted and triumphant progress from the east to the west of the metropolis, arrived at Stafford House, he was exhausted by fatigue; declined to partake of the banquet prepared for him; and said he should like to have some bread and cheese and a bottle of pale ale, and then retire to rest; which he presently did. The next morning, at eight, the servant came to his door to ask if he lacked anything. There was no Garibaldi in the room. The domestic came again at ten; but the quandam Dictator of Naples was still absent. Being

diligently sought for, he was found in the great picture
gallery; where he was quietly sauntering and admiring
the masterpieces of painting on the walls. Breakfast
was ready, he was told. The General expressed his
thanks, but said that he had already breakfasted.
" Breakfasted !" exclaimed in astonishment his interlocutor. " Yes," calmly replied the frugal hero, " I
get up at six; I feel hungry; there was a little bread
and a little cheese left, I eat him, and there was also a
little beer remaining, and I drink him." If this be a
"shave," it is a tolerably close one as an illustration
of the Spartan simplicity of Giuseppe Garibaldi in all
things.

We had another fight with the Austrians some days
after Montesuelo, in which the Garibaldini remained
masters of the field; and, indeed, it may be said that
although Garibaldi had won no striking victories in
his campaign, he had at least continued to advance
into the enemy's country, and had well planted his foot
on the soil of the Southern Tyrol. After the engagement, of which I have spoken, the Italian troops halted
at a village where there was a small poverty-stricken
tumble-down little church; and there being no hospital
nor convent available, the wounded were carried into
the church. There was adequate surgical aid at hand,
and there was a miserable deficiency of hospital ap-
pliances, especially of bandages; and it is a fact which
the humane, the merciful, and the compassionate
should lay to heart, that the two noble Englishwomen,
Mrs. Chambers and Madame Jessie Meriton White
Mario, tore up every rag and stitch of their under-
clothing to make bandages withal, and came out of
that church with nothing but their gowns to cover
them.

After another successful brush with the enemy,
Garibaldi believed that he would be able to push on

as far as Trent and occupy that important town ; but, alas !—did not Mr. Kinglake remark, in "Eothen," that, alas ! was an ejaculation which everybody wrote and nobody uttered ?—there appeared at head-quarters an open barouche and pair, in which was seated an Italian staff-officer, in a dark blue uniform and gold bullion epaulettes, who turned out to be an aide-de-camp of King Victor Emmanuel. The Prussians had routed the Austrians at Königgrätz ; there was to be peace between the two Powers ; and Italy, much to her disgust, was instructed by her French friend—Garibaldi's *ce Monsieur* — to make peace with the Kaiser. As a consolation, however, the Dominio Veneto was to be given up to her ; and thus the Emperor Napoleon practically was to redeem his promise of freeing Italy from the Alps to the Adriatic. Rome only, and the States of the Church, were excepted from the stately kingdom conferred on the whilom Sovereign of Sardinia : — the luckiest monarch, I should say, that has lived for centuries. Still, although the glittering prize of Venice, Verona, Padua, Vicenza, and Mantua was dangled before their eyes, the Italians felt sore with the peace which had been concluded without giving them Rome. They were sore at having been worsted by the Austrians in the Quadrilateral ; since, although the *Tedeschi* did not pursue the Italian army, but re-entered Mantua at nightfall, the Italian army had been forced to fall behind the Mincio, and though they vehemently declared Custozza to have been a drawn battle, there was a general consensus of European opinion that Austria had won the day on the 24th June, 1866.

They were sorer at having been signally defeated by the Austrian fleet, commanded by Admiral Tegethoff, at Lissa, in the Adriatic, and although the Italian Commander, Admiral Persano, stated somewhat vaingloriously in his despatch, that the Italians remained masters of the scene of battle (*noi siamo padroni delle seque di Lissa*), it is certain that Tegethoff rammed and jammed the Italian warships into a cocked-hat, as the Americans would say, and sunk one huge ironclad right out. As for Garibaldi, he was more than sore; he was enraged; and made haste to throw up his command, and return to his island home at Caprera. At the conclusion of this—well, let us say, equivocal— campaign, the little band of English special correspon- dents broke up. Hyndman and the present writer re- turned to Milan; Henty left for Ancona, in the har- bour of which he witnessed the fearful catastrophe of the foundering of the ironclad *Affondatore*, a disaster which took place just as the enormous vessel was en- tering the port.

CHAPTER XXXVIII

THE LIBERATION OF VENICE

AT Milan we found the late Mr. Frederick Hardman, a well-known travelling correspondent of the *Times*, who afterwards represented that journal in Paris. Mr. Hardman may be considered as one of the pioneers of that peculiar class of journalists of whom William Howard Russell has been for a long time the acknowledged *doyen* and chief. Hardman had served the *Times* during the Carlist and Cristino war in Spain, in which there did good service for another journal the late Mr. Charles Lewis Gruneisen—another pioneer of special war correspondents. He was on the Cristino side ; had been captured by the Carlists, and was about to be shot, when he was rescued from his impending fate by the intercession of the late Lord Ranelagh, who had taken service in the cause of Don Carlos de Borbon. There was, as we are all aware, no special war correspondent at Waterloo ; although I have heard it stated that an agent of the house of Rothschild, and an English commercial traveller, were on the field on the 18th June, 1815.

So far as I can make out, the first recognised war correspondent of a newspaper was a gentleman—I have never heard his name — who represented the *Times* at the siege of Antwerp, in 1831. Much earlier in the century the Walcheren expedition was joined in an informal and unrecognised manner by a journalist named Peter Finnerty, who, on his return, told the British public a great deal more about that unfortunate naval and military blunder than the British Government of the day cared to have published :—

> "Lord Chatham, with his sword drawn,
> Was waiting for Sir Richard Strachan ;
> Sir Richard, longing to be at 'em,
> Stood waiting for the Earl of Chatham."

Who wrote this epigram? There are many variants of the lines which I have quoted. In one version, Lord Chatham is the waiting earl, and his sword is a "sabre." In another, Sir Richard Strachan is not "longing," but "eager." Peter Finnerty, at some period of his career, managed to get in prison, if not into the pillory, for libel ; and he always ascribed his prosecution to the maleficent influence of Lord Castlereagh. Peter was a humorist ; and the revenge he took on his potential persecutor was peculiar. Whenever he met his lordship in the street he always took off his hat and made him a series of profound bows, which Lord Castlereagh, who had not the slightest idea of who Peter was, never failed to return with true patrician courtesy. Peter was at one time art-critic for one of the London daily newspapers, and whenever a portrait of Lord Castlereagh came under his notice at any picture exhibition, he took care to describe the effigy of the noble lord as that of one of the loveliest of mankind, insinuating, however, before he had got to the end of his critique, that his lordship was an embodied counterpart of Old Nick.

The autumn was demoniacally hot at Milan ; and I longed for the seaside. Another motive impelled me towards the shores of the Adriatic. Peace was concluded, but the Convention by which Venice was to be ceded to the Italians was not yet signed. The city was still in a state of siege, and my wife was still shut up there. Half-a-dozen times I ran down to Mestre

on the main land; and a friendly milkwoman, and an
equally obliging laundress used to fetch and carry our
correspondence in their barges across the lagoon.   It
was announced, however, that in another fortnight or
three weeks the siege would be raised ; although Venice would continue to be garrisoned by the Austrians
until the beginning of November.   Meanwhile, civil-
ians from the outside would have free ingress to the
place.

The interval I passed in travelling in the company
of M. Plantulli, Garibaldi's whilom secretary, or aide-
de-camp, through the liberated Dominio Veneto, which,
with the exception of Verona, had been wholly evacuated by the *Tedeschi*.   M. Plantulli was a lively, festive
little gentleman, a quondam student, I take it, of the
University of Naples, and an *Italianissimo* of the *Ital-
ianissimi*.   He worshipped Garibaldi ; and, young as
he was—he was scarcely thirty—he had done good
service in the cause of his beloved country.   At the
age of sixteen he had served that country both in meal
and in malt; for, at the early age I speak of, having
been implicated in a political conspiracy against the
Government of King Bomba, it was Signor Plantulli's
patriotic, but scarcely agreeable, lot to be condemned
to hard labour for life and in chains.   He got out of
durance, however, with one of the Thousand of Marsala, and entered Naples in triumph with his Chief.
"We at once," he used to say, "proceeded to the
Royal Palace of Capo di Monte, and apartments were
assigned to all the members of the General's staff.
They put me into an immense bedroom, with crystal
chandeliers hanging from the ceiling, and candelabra
carrying twenty wax tapers each, *all of which I took
care to light*.   There was a huge four-post bedstead,
with pillars of the Corinthian order, with gilt capitals,
and draped with sumptuous damask.   I did not un-

dress, but I threw myself on the bed, which was covered by a quilted counterpane of eiderdown, covered with silk and gold brocade; and, lying on my back, dug both my spurs into the bed with the exultant fancy that I was digging them into the corpse of the prostrate and vanquished Bomba, or rather his effete son Bombina."

Plantulli and I visited Padua; where I made at once for the historic Caffe Pedrocchi, a place of entertainment which, so it is said, had never been closed for a single night in the course of three consecutive centuries. There is another *caffe* at Venice that has a similar social record—the Caffe Florian. When Marshal Haynau was in command in the city he issued a general order, directing that all the *caffes* should be closed at midnight. The proprietor of Florian's waited on His Excellency, and represented that Venetian social life did not virtually begin until midnight. " I care nothing for that," the Marshal sternly replied ; " if you don't have your shutters up by twelve o'clock, I shall send you to gaol." " But, Excellency," submissively urged the *caffe*-keeper, "I have not got any shutters; and Florian has never had any since the days of Marino Faliero." He had brought down, it is true, that unfortunate Doge by rather a long shot; but Haynau, who was in the main not altogether inhuman, laughed, told the landlord to go about his business, and promised that he should not be molested.

I have no desire, as I have already hinted, to pad out my Autobiography with guide-book notices of different towns, at each of which I made a few days' sojourn ; still I cannot help dwelling briefly on just two subjects. Wandering from Milan to Mantua and from Padua to Verona and Vicenza, there grew up in one, day after day, a stronger and stronger impression —an impression which has become an unalterable conviction—that Shakespeare knew every rood of ground and every building in the cities, the scenes of which he had laid in the *Merchant of Venice* and in *Othello*, in *The Two Gentlemen of Verona*, in *Romeo and Juliet*, and in *The Taming of the Shrew*. Few tourists who have visited Northern Italy have escaped being pestered by *ciceroni*, who have offered to show them the tomb of Juliet at Verona; the shop of the apothecary at Mantua; and the Palazzo del Moro, on the Grand Canal, at Venice; but it was the constant study of ostensibly petty details in Shakespeare's Italian plays that led me to the full and fast belief that he was familiar from actual experience and observation with the Northern Italy of his time.

There is not in his works the slightest indication that leads a reader, who is as familiar with the Peninsula as he is with his own country, to think that the Bard of all Time knew anything personally about Rome; whereas the plays which I have mentioned seem to me to bear the strongest testimony to his thorough knowledge of, among others, the cities which I have cited.

Next you will pardon me if I venture on yet another brief excursus, not at all of a guide-book character, on Ferrara. I don't wish to talk about the gloomy, unhealthy city, either from an artistic and architectural, or a historical point of view; but, during the three days, Plantulli and I abode in an imperfectly sanitated, hotel, about fifty times as large as it should have been to meet the requirements of its average number of guests, I was haunted by the ghost of Lucrezia Borgia. Not by her historic phantom. Those who have read the late Mr. Gilbert's admirable monograph on Lucrezia, know that the much maligned Duchess died in her bed in honour and fair repute. She had had, it is true, four husbands; but

where is the harm in that circumstance? How many
spouses had the Wife of Bath?—and did not another
lady, when she espoused her fourth consort, cause to
be engraved inside her wedding ring this sweet little
posy—

> " If I survive,
> I will have five ? "

It may be true that Donna Lucrezia's early married
life may have been a little breezy ; but if she *did* cause
to be stabbed or murdered a few people whose room
she preferred to their company, it must be remembered that the application of cold steel under the fifth
rib of objectionable people was an integral part of the
manners of the epoch ; and the cup of cold poison was
very plentifully administered, and that the science of
chemical analysis was in its infancy.

For the rest, Lucrezia was a very good wife to her
fourth husband, Don Alfonso d'Este. She patronised
literature and the arts; she favoured, it is said, the
cause of the Reformation in Italy; she corresponded
with Bembo, and she pensioned Ariosto. The dame
who haunted me was the Lucrèce Borgia of Victor
Hugo's tragedy, and the Lucrezia of Donizetti's opera,
which was nearly the first that I ever witnessed. I
can hear now, in my memory for melody, Grisi as
Donna Lucrezia, Rubini as Genarro, and Brambilla as
Mafio Orsini ; but I forget who was the Don Alfonso,
and who the Gubetta. There came back to me at Ferrara the strains of " Com' e bello," the dulcet melody
of " Di pescator ignobile," the terrific denunciation of
the masked lady by Genarro's companions at Venice,
and the glorious *brindisi* in the last act, " Il segreto per
esser felice." Why is it that *Lucrezia Borgia* is never
played in England, nowadays? Is it that modern hy-
per-criticism deems the glorious opera too puny for

modern ears, depraved and distorted by Wagnerism;
or is it because we have no *prima donna* at present who
could do justice to the part of the heroine? Why
have we no impersonators of Norma, of Semiramide?
Is it that we have no operatic singer who is equal to the
requirements of "Al dolce guldarni" or of "Qual mesto
gemito?" Tell us, Sir Augustus Harris, tell us why.

Not alone, however, was I pursued by the apparition of Donizetti's Duchess. I had visions of the
fierce, passionate, much-hating, much-loving woman.
I knew Victor Hugo's tragedy by heart, since, as a
boy, I read it in secret at night or at early morn. Its
resting-place was between the mattress and the pail-
lasse of my bed; for *Lucrèce Borgia* was a play which
had been sternly placed in the domestic *Index Expur-
gatorius*. With what grave joy did I find myself in
desolate, evil-smelling Ferrara, which is too vasty, not
only for the guests in its hotels, but for its inhabitants,
so that you can hire a palace with scores of rooms in
it, each as big as a barn, for about £75 a year. But
the Ferrara which revealed itself to me was the city
of Victor Hugo. First, I mentally strayed to Venice,
and saw the masked lady bending over her sleeping
son; I watched the young nobles enter and virulently
denounce the guilty daughter of Pope Alexander VI.
Then I came back to Ferrara, and conjured up the
scene in which the reckless young patrician, headed
by Genarro, hacked out of the escutcheon over the
ducal palace, the first letter of Borgia—leaving it OR-
GIA. Then that quaint conversation in the street between *les deux hommes vêtus de noir*, Gubetta and Rus-
tighello; the stormy interview between the Duke and
his wife; his indignant apostrophe to her, beginning,
" *Tenez, Madame, je hais votre abominable famille*," and
her famous retort, "*Prenez garde, Don Alfonse d'Este,
mon quatrième mari.*"

And so on to the last act—the banquet at the Princess Negroni's, the glorious *brindisi,* followed by the Penitential Psalms, chanted in lugubrious strophes by the sable-clad friars bearing torches, who, drawing aside, reveal seven coffins. Then enters the implacable Donna Lucrezia. " *Vous m'avez donné un bal à Venise,*" she says, addressing the poisoned nobles, "*je vous rends un souper à Ferrare.*" They are all dead men, but Genarro lives long enough to slay his wicked mamma. Curtain. End. Thus it is in the play, at least; but there was no end to the tragedy, to my mind, while I sojourned in the fatal city. There seemed to me to be an uncomfortable number of *farmacie,* or druggists' shops, in Ferrara; and a dozen times a day I used to fancy that I saw the brougham of Donna Lucrezia standing at the door of one of these establishments. I was, in truth, glad enough to get away from the gloomy old place; since Ferrara had begun to work upon my nerves. I distrusted the food at the hotel—it was normally very nasty food—and half suspected that the Baleful Duchess had been putting arsenic into the *risotto,* or *nux vomica* into the wine.

But the state of siege at Venice was raised; and I was suffered to rejoin my beloved partner in life. She had got on, during my absence, tolerably well, and had been comforted during the last few weeks of her virtual beleaguerment by the letters transmitted to her by the friendly milkwoman and the obliging laundress. Mr. Etzensberger, the manager of the Hotel Victoria, had stood by her manfully, and there was an account of somewhat alarming proportions to be paid; a bank post-bill—are there any bank post-bills now? —which had been transmitted to her on my account from London, having either been stolen, or gone hopelessly astray on its way through Southern Germany, whence, in due course, it should have reached Venice.

I must recall a rather interesting incident which I witnessed at Mestre, the station where I took the train which rattles over the railway causeway across the lagoons. I had to wait a considerable time; whiling which time away with a cigar, I became aware of a four-horsed drag, or four-in-hand, splendidly horsed and splendidly "tooled" by a gentleman in a grey box-coat with mother-of-pearl buttons as large as cheese plates, and collar and cuffs of fawn-coloured velvet. He wore a white silk hat with a black band. The two grooms in the dickey sat rigidly upright, folding their arms like a couple of statues ; and by the driver's side was a handsome lady, fashionably attired. The gentleman rose, pointed with his whip in the direction of the lagoons, said to the lady, "Venice is over there, I reckon," and straightway turned his team, and drove composedly back along the narrow road. Let us not accuse him too hastily of indifference to the beauties of the Queen of the Adriatic. Possibly he had driven that drag right through France, down south to the Riviera, and then along the marvellous *Chemin de la Corniche* to Genoa, whence he would go, without much difficulty, to Mestre. But what could he have done with a four-in-hand at Venice?

I do not remember that the Grand Canal, even in the severest of winters, has ever been frozen over. There was something, however, especially whimsical in a gentleman driving such a long distance and contenting himself with what may be called a Pisgah view of the Italian Palestine. At least, four English Grenadiers, whom I was aware of once at Niagara, saw more of the Falls than the gentleman in the box-seat of the four-in-hand saw of Venice. It was in this wise. I was at Niagara, on the Canadian side, in the winter of 1863. Four strapping sergeants of the Grenadier

Guards, then in garrison at Montreal, in their warm grey great coats, had got leave to visit Niagara. I saw them emerge from the railway station; I watched them proceed, with military deliberation and exactitude of step, to the Table Rock; they took a view—a brief, but comprehensive one—of the Horseshoe falls, immediately following it by the simple evolution known as right-about-face, and marched back to the railway station again. Julius Cæsar tells us, in his "Commentaries," that he came into Gaul "with summary diligence;" but he stayed there somewhat longer than the four sergeants did at Niagara. Typical British soldiers were they. They might have been brethren of the famous Four Sergeants of the Indian Mutiny, who, with the sacks of powder on their backs, marched across the open and blew up the Cashmere Gate at Delhi.

We had the merriest of autumns in Venice; although there was still a strong Austrian force there, and the Austrian Governor-General, Baron Alemann, periodically issued alarming proclamations forbidding the display of what his Excellency ambiguously termed "*stoffe colorate*," which coloured stuffs were, indeed, banners and pennants of the Italian tricolour, which certain *caffe*-keepers had prematurely hoisted, not outside, but inside their premises. Still, everybody in Venice knew that Baron Alemann's sway was destined to be a very short one; and the sewing together of *stoffe colorate*, and the making of tricoloured cockades went on in secret, but briskly. Great preparations were also made for re-opening the Fenice Theatre, which splendid house—the successor of the theatre once glorified by the scenery painted by the illustrious Antonio da Canal, commonly called Canaletto—had been closed for many a long day during the Austrian domination. It was also understood that the lessees of the Teatro Malibran, where the principal amusements used to consist of rope-dancing and sword-swallowing, together with the Teatro Apollo and the Teatro San Samuele were also putting their houses in order.

The Hotel Victoria was full. Henty and Hyndman had joined us to witness the liberation of Venice from foreign rule; while from Milan had been despatched, as representative of that important journal *La Perseveranza*, a certain Dr. Carlo Filippi, a profound but versatile scholar, and a skilled musician, who used to fascinate the ladies—especially two charming daughters of a Prebendary of St. Paul's, who were travelling with their uncle—by the grace and vivacity with which he would sing, accompanying himself on the pianoforte, songs in that Venetian dialect which has been made attractive, and even fascinating, to Italian scholars in some of the comedies of Goldoni. The Venetian dialect is one of the softest and sweetest forms of patois which I know; and contrasts very favourably with the harsh *minga* of Milan and the guttural Bolognese. In the local speech of Venice nearly every word is mellifluous, and consonants are discarded as much as possible. Thus "*padre*" is "*pare*," and "*madre*," "*mare*." The Venetians, too, have a passion for making all nouns feminine, and I have even heard a gondolier speak of Victor Emmanuel as *la Rè*. The poor fellow might, to be sure, have pleaded that in pure Tuscan, as well as in French and German, Majesty is always of the feminine gender.

On the 3rd of October Venice and Venetia were surrendered by Austria to the French Government, to be handed over to Italy—Kaiser Francis Joseph being too proud to cede directly this splendid appanage of his Crown to a Power which he had twice beaten in battle. The formal transfer of the city took place on the 17th October, at noon, the Commissioners of Napoleon III. being presided over by that General Leboeuf, who, as Marshal Lebœuf, played a not very brilliant part in the Franco-German War of 1870. The Convention was signed at the Hôtel de Ville, and the cession proclaimed to the whole city by a salute of a hundred guns. The Italian colours were run up to the summit of the three tall masts in front of the Cathedral of St. Mark. The Austrian *schwarz-gelb* was hauled down; and General Baron Alemann—a stout little gentleman, of pleasant mien — was absolutely cheered by the crowd as he embarked at the Molo on board the gunboat which was to convey him to Trieste. The Venetians, notwithstanding all that English people read in "The Bravo" and similar romances, have always been a kindly, affectionate, and placable folk. When Fra Paolo was stabbed, in consequence of some theological controversy connected with the Council of Trent, he knew full well that the stiletto which wounded him was not held by a Venetian hand; and as he sank swooning to the ground, he murmured "*stilo Romano.*"

I have been told that during the long occupation of Venice by the *Tedeschi*, it was with the greatest rarity that Austrian sentinels were ever assaulted, or that attempts were made to assassinate them ; and if there be a city on the face of the globe most favourable, in a topographical sense, to the perpetration of midnight murders, that city is assuredly Venice. You have only to stab your man and tip him over into one of the side canals ; and away the tide carries the corpse into the Adriatic.

The moment that the Austrian Governor had taken his departure, the Italian troops, who had been massed at the railway terminus hard by the Papadopoulo Palace and gardens, were quickly shipped on board roomy barges, which were towed by four steamers down the Grand Canal to the Molo. The first barge was crowded with "Guardie Civili," or gendarmes; and the people who filled the gondolas and wherries on the Grand Canal cheered these gallant police-constables in their cocked hats, and red, white, and blue plumes, uproariously. It is not often the gendarme's lot to be cheered. A few days after the entry of the Italian garrison a plebiscitum was taken; and the result was that 651,758 votes were cast for the annexation of the Venetian to the kingdom of Italy. There were only 69 votes recorded against union. Venetian Deputies at once proceeded to Turin to communicate the result to Victor Emmanuel; and meanwhile the Italian officers at the garrison of Venice proceeded to make themselves as comfortable as possible in their new quarters. They crowded Florian's and the Specchi *caffès;* but the proprietor of an establishment which hitherto had been mainly patronised by the *Tedeschi*, hastened to take down his sign, which was that of " L'Imperatore d'Austria," and to put up something Italian and patriotic instead.

A few discontented Venetians, suspected of " *Austriacante* " sympathies, complained in an undertone that the Italian military bands, which discoursed every evening sweet strains on the Piazza San Marco, did not play half so well as had been done by the Austrian military bands, whose instrumentation was simply perfect; but these grumblers were soon frowned out of countenance. Then the Italian officers loudly demanded that the Fenice Theatre should be opened. The *impresario* wanted to wait until the arrival of His Majesty; but the military gentlemen would brook no delay. Then the unhappy manager urged that he had no company, either operatic or choregraphic: in answer to which plea he was bidden to send for a company from Vicenza or Rovigo, which he presently did ; and the company speedily arrived and alighted at the Hotel Victoria. A queer troupe they were. I hesitate to say that the *prima donna* was fifty and one-eyed, or that the *basso profondo* had a wooden leg ; but they were certainly not artistes of the calibre, either physical or artistic, that English Opera-goers were accustomed to see at Her Majesty's Theatre in the Haymarket, or that they see at present at the Royal Italian Opera, Covent Garden.

There arose, moreover, a slight difficulty in the circumstance that the *prima mima*, or leading dumb-show actress, and the *prima ballerina* insisted on doing the washing of their gauzy draperies at home, and on hanging them out to dry from the upper windows of the hotel, which in the Middle Ages had been a stately palace. But this is an incident which very frequently happens in the towns of provincial Italy, when even marchionesses and duchesses not unfrequently do their light washing at home, and convert the window-sills of their mansions into drying-grounds. Mr. Etzensberger, however, politely but firmly set his face against the practice, and he was also obliged to tell the manager that he could not tolerate the proceedings of the company in ordering their dinners from a neighbouring and cheap "*trattoria*," or cook-shop, instead of partaking of the principal meal of the day at the *table d'hôte*.

The English guests from the Hotel Victoria filled two rows of the stalls at the Fenice on the night when the theatre was reopened. I cannot recall the name of the opera performed, because it was interrupted at least twenty times by the audience shouting for the " Marcia Reale " to be played, or for " Garibaldi's Hymn " to be sung ; and when the over - fatigued artistes could no longer sing, the pit and gallery howled the hymns themselves. Then they called for *vivas* for the *Rè Galantuomo;* then there was a shout of " *Rè Eletto in Campidoglio !* " meaning that they wanted to see their elected King installed as Sovereign of United Italy at the Capitol of Rome. ' *Vivas* for Amadeo, Duke of Aosta ; *vivas* for the Italian Army and Navy then resounded from the auditorium ; one waggish occupant of the pit crying, " By all means bring the cavalry to Venice ; " while another facetious gentleman in the gallery, pointing to the red and silver shield of the House of Savoy, which cognisance was displayed in the centre of the arch of the proscenium, called out, " *Sale e tabacchi,*" in allusion to the Royal escutcheon placed over the doors of all Italian shopkeepers who are licensed to deal in the Government monopolies of salt and tobacco. But the most frequent, the noisiest, and the most enthusiastic *vivas* of the evening were those thundered for " *La Perla di Savoia.*" " The Pearl of Savoy " was and is the good and beautiful Margherita, Queen of Italy.

The King made his entry into Venice on the 7th of November, accompanied by a brilliant staff, and escorted by his own special body-guard in cuirasses, plumed helmets, and jack-boots; but who had obviously not brought their horses with them. His Majesty entered one of the State barges, which for weeks previously the municipality of Venice had been decorating for the use of their Sovereign and his court. When the King stepped into his barge at the railway terminus, a great roar went up from the multitude. " At last," quietly observed Dr. Filippi to me, " the Venetians are satisfied ; they have got their King in a gondola." As for the people in the gondolas and open boats, it is no exaggeration to say that, without much difficulty and at twenty different points, you might have crossed the Grand Canal on foot—so prodigious and so closely wedged together were the *em-barcations*. But the Prefect of Venice with a boat full of *Guardie Civili* preceded the Royal flotilla; and with inimitable dexterity the gondoliers managed to make a lane or water-way for the King to pass, the boats closing up behind him immediately afterwards.

There was a *levée en masse* of the old Venetian nobility, many of whom were not in gondolas, but in large " barchi," or barges, the hulls of which were gilt down to the water-line, canopied with crimson and blue and cloth of gold and silver; while there were *faisceaux* of flags at stem and stern, and the rowers were clad in rich Venetian costume. I only wonder that when the King landed at the Piazetta, the people did not catch His Majesty up in their arms and carry him away bodily into the Cathedral of St. Mark. " I have not been to mass," said a Venetian to me, " for twenty years; but I have been to St. Mark's this morning, and I mean to go there every day for a fortnight. You see the King is in our midst." I hope that the gentleman's devotional feelings did not wholly die away at the expiration of fourteen days.

Then there was a rush to the Royal Palace, the façade of which fronts the Basilica, and of course the " *Rè Eletto* " had to show himself at one of the windows to be acclaimed over and over again with volleys of cheers. At night St. Mark's Place was illuminated " architectonically "—*i.e.*, the lines horizontal, vertical, and semi-circular of all the columns and cornices and arcades of the Piazza were traced in threads of fire; as was also done with the lines of the Byzantine façade of the cathedral, the fairy-like little Loggetta, and the two great columns on the Piazetta; the Campanile became a tower of fire; and the horses of St. Mark were outlined with gas-jets.

CHAPTER XXXIX

ERE royalty took its departure, my wife and I, following instructions from headquarters in Fleet Street, bade farewell—but not, as we hoped, a lasting one—to Venice and went south. Our destination was Rome, where we were to remain until the following January. By this time the winter had begun, and in Venice, although the day of the royal entry had been a fine and sunny one, the weather was disagreeably raw and occasionally foggy. It grew worse by the time we got to Bologna ; and we arrived at Perugia in a snow-storm. I had never been in that artistic city before ; I did not know there was a clean hotel there ; and we passed the night at the post-house, one of the dirtiest Italian inns that I have ever met with. The house was very ancient, and in a photograph would have been handsome. Our bedroom was immense, with a curiously-timbered roof, an antique carved wainscot, and walls hung with possibly mediæval, but unmistakably ragged and rotting, tapestry. The landlord and landlady were politeness itself ; and a chamber-maid, who, to all appearance, had not been washed from the time of Perugino, hastened to kindle a wood fire on a huge open hearth. The fumes of the faggots nearly choked us, to begin with ; but when the perils of impending suffocation passed away, we were able to enjoy a capital supper of fish, flesh, and fowl, washed down by some of the rarest old wines I have ever tasted. Whether it was Chianti or Montefiascone, I

am not aware, but it was undoubtedly a vintage of
true " *Est., Est., Est.*" character.

There was a gap in the railway to Rome, owing to
the snow; and we had to leave Perugia in a lumber-
ing old *berline de voyage*, painfully dragged by two
wretched nags, which reminded me of the steeds harnessed to the *calessino* of my colleague in Garibaldi's
campaign in the Tyrol. We found, however, the railway available again at a station called Saint Something or Another, and about six in the evening arrived
at the railway terminus at Rome. The station was a
deplorable one—small, inconvenient, foul, and to all
appearance, structurally tumbling to pieces. In the
dirty Custom House the dirtier Papal *doganieri* gave
us an infinity of trouble : tossing about our belongings
with their unwashed hands, and delving to the very
bottom of our trunks in quest of any books which we
might have brought with us; but I had been fore-
warned of the tricks and manners of these gentry, and
had brought no literature whatever with me. Had I
had any with me, the Custom House officers might,
perhaps, have impounded my " Murray's Handbook,"
and assuredly they would have seized any Anglican
Bible or Testament in a passenger's luggage.

We stayed at Rome till a fortnight after Christmas,
at the Hotel d'Angleterre, in the Via Bocca di Leone,
over against the palace of the Duca Torlonia, and close
to the Via Condotti, the Piazza di Spagna, and the
Corso. I have been, perhaps, twenty times to the
Eternal City since 1866; and I have never even thought
of staying at any hotel there save the Albergo d'Inghilterra. Every day was a new revelation and a new
series of delights ; but I may not be guide-bookish, and
must refrain from saying anything about the public
buildings or the antiquities of the place. It will be ex-
cusable, however, if, for the benefit of the younger

generation, I mark a few of the differences between the Papal Rome of 1866 and the Monarchical Rome of 1894.

At the first-named period the streets swarmed with monks and beggars : the paving was bad, and the lighting worse. The Papal police were lazy and cowardly, and the Papal officials notoriously venal. There was a brigade of Papal Zouaves enrolled for the purpose of defending Rome against the Italians, and which consisted mainly of Frenchmen from the South and of Irishmen. Some of these sacerdotal warriors were very fine fellows of most martial mien. The Papal Zouaves were either succeeded or preceded by another auxiliary corps called the Antibes Legion, which had been raised almost entirely in the southern departments of France. The *caffes* were crowded at night with the Zouaves and the Legionaries, whose principal amusement next to playing dominoes, smoking, and coffee drinking was warmly to shake hands with each other as they entered or departed from the room. The frequency of these amicable salutes was, perhaps, that the majority of the Romans did not care to shake hands with the gallant *condottieri* of his Holiness Pio Nono and preferred to scowl at them ; muttering meanwhile curses, not loud but deep.

The Colosseum, in the last days of Papal rule, had been, in its more ruinous portions, carefully underpinned and buttressed by Pius IX. and his predecessor Gregory XVI.; but the arena had not yet become the scene of the extraordinary excavations carried out during the last twenty years by Professor Lanciani and other erudite antiquaries. Scholars could only surmise the existence of the dens of the wild beasts beneath the arena ; nor had they even surmised that the animals and many of the paraphernalia of the amphitheatre were raised from the subterraneans by means of mechanical " lifts." The vast circular area of the Colosseum, as I first saw it in 1866, was marked at intervals by the Stations of the Cross; and on Sundays sermons were preached there from a pulpit in the centre by Franciscan and Dominican friars.

As for the Cardinals, the Princes of the Church, who at present are very rarely seen in public, and then only in modest coupés, drove about in full scarlet, in open carriages and pair, and carriages and four; the horses decked with gilt and beribboned with scarlet; the Pope likewise often took an afternoon drive on the Pincian Hill. I can recall the venerable and benevolent Pontifex Maximus distinctly in a *soutane* or cassock, with a cape of fine white camlet, and his good old face —from which beamed the sweetest of smiles—surmounted by a shovel-hat of crimson velvet, worn fore and aft. When the weather was fine the Pontiff would, from time to time, alight from his equipage and, followed by a couple of domestic prelates, take a little walking exercise, freely bestowing his blessing on the crowds who, kneeling, lined the sides of the Promenade.

The Papal money consisted of paper currency, which was generally at a discount, and of silver and copper coins of about equal value with the franc and pieces of fifty centimes current in France and Belgium. These had superseded the old *paoli* and *bajocchi*, the older *scudi* or crowns, and *ducati*, which were, gold coins I never saw. Years, too, have passed since the Papal silver has been current in Italy; yet so recently as July, 1894, I found francs and half-francs bearing the profile of Pio Nono current in Brussels. They were shortly afterwards withdrawn by Ministerial decree from circulation in Belgium.

For the rest, we enjoyed ourselves to the full, during our stay at Rome. The charming young ladies who were daughters of the Prebendary of St. Paul's, and were travelling with their uncle, came on to Rome; my dear old friend Rudolph Gustavus Glover, of the War Office, came out from London to spend his winter holiday with us; and what with excursions and evening parties and studying antiquities and attending Pontifical functions, the time passed rapidly and delightfully. During that first Roman pilgrimage I began a practice which, from that time to this, I have made systematic, that of purchasing a copy in oil of Guido's portrait of Beatrice Cenci—I mean the one so called; and it has long since been proved to demonstration that the lovely girl with the white cloth over her head and who is looking at you over her shoulder with eyes, the expression of which you never forget, was not the unfortunate Beatrice, but a young girl, name unknown, who was Guido's model, and whose face appears in at least three of his pictures. Some say she was a Greek and a purchased slave of the painter. The so-called Beatrice is, plainly, not more than fifteen; whereas it has been irrefragably proven that the real Beatrice was at the time of her execution twenty-two, not very good-looking, and a mother.

I have often thought, standing in front of the high altar in the Church of San Pietro in Montorio, where the luckless Beatrice lies buried, that it is a sad thing that hard-headed and unmercifully vigilant and diligent professors—the Italians and the Germans are the greatest offenders in this respect—should devote their erudition and their acumen to the task of turning romantic legends inside out, and showing beyond dispute that they are mainly apocryphal. Why are the lovers of the picturesque to be robbed of their Beatrice as she is pictured, or as they believe she was pictured, on Guido's canvas; or as she moves and breathes and burns in Shelley's deathless tragedy? From this point

of view I can thoroughly comprehend and sympathise
with the thoroughly feminine declaration of adherence
to the belief in a long accepted myth made by an English lady of rank who, when she had read the volume
in which some inexorable professor had shown that the
legend of Beatrice Cenci is in many respects unfounded
on fact, exclaimed: " The book is all very well, but it
is not true; it can't be true, *and it shan't be true*."   That
"shan't be true" was gloriously womanly.

But I have to say something about that practice of
mine in connection with the hapless daughter of the
wicked Francesco Cenci.   I have said that every time
I visit Rome I buy an unframed portrait of the pseudo
Beatrice, never giving more than the sum which I paid
for the first one, and I have now, I think, either fourteen or fifteen of these works of art.   I do not at all
know what I shall do with them; if I have them framed
my friends will laugh at me.   I think that eventually I
shall have them made into a screen, which will certainly
be unique if it have no other good quality.   Most people, I apprehend, have their whims and oddities, which
are pardonable perhaps if they do not do any harm to
anybody.   *Πᾶς ἄνθρωπος ἔχει τὸν τρελλόν τοῦ.* (Every
man has his craze.)   Do you remember the charming
passage in Victor Hugo's " Rhin," where, in a market-
place of a German town, he saw such a pretty assortment of little sucking pigs, that he would have liked,
so he confesses, to have bought the whole lot if he had
only known what to do with the juvenile porkers when
they were delivered at his hotel.

In mid-January we went from Rome to Naples; and
had the pleasure one Sunday of having Pompei entirely
to ourselves, with the exception of a ragged minstrel
of the *lazzarone* order, who, sitting on one of the upper
grades of the ruined theatre, obliged us with "*Addio !
Bella Napoli*," not forgetting to bring in Santa Lucia at

the conclusion of each verse, accompanying himself on the guitar. After that I favoured him with a speech in English on the ancient Roman drama, whereupon he took to flight dismayed, and we were alone—quite alone, superbly alone—in this marvellous city of the dead. We took a Messageries steamer from Naples to Marseilles; the weather was abominably stormy; the captain of the Messageries was not a very adventurous mariner, and we put in to spend the night at no less than four ports, Civita Vecchia, Leghorn, Porto Ferrajo, and Hyères. Altogether, we were six days making the voyage; and when I mildly complained to the captain of what I thought the unnecessary delay, he turned brusquely on me, saying : "*De quoi vous plaignez-vous? Vous êtes nourri.*" Yes, we were nourished, although perhaps there might have been a little less garlic in the cookery and a little more flavour in the *vin ordinaire.*

CHAPTER XL

WHEN we arrived in Marseilles I sent my wife back to England to see her friends and equip herself, if need be, for a fresh journey; while I went on to Paris, and took up my quarters at the Hotel Windsor, in the Rue de Rivoli, where, phenomenal to relate, the obliging landlord let me have a suite of three rooms on the *entresol* at the extraordinary cheap rate of fifteen francs a day. I cite this tariff as phenomenal, because the great International Exhibition of 1867 was imminent. The Second Empire was in its autumnal splendour; and although the Exposition was not to open until May, Paris was already thronged with visitors from every quarter of the globe. To be sure, I told the complaisant landlord, M. Blard, that I intended to occupy the suite of rooms for some months; and, as a matter of fact, I was a tenant of them from May till September. The rooms were very dark, but nicely furnished; and there was happily no *table d'hôte* in the hotel, so you were not expected even to lunch or to dine in the house. Comfortable quarters, *café au lait* in the morning, and for the rest full liberty to do what you liked in the matter of the provand— that is my *beau idéal* of comfort in a continental hotel. I have always hated *tables d'hôte* for two reasons, first, you are often obliged to sit at dinner next to people whom you would certainly not ask to dine with you; and next, because among the rudest and generally the most objectionable people that I have ever met with on my travels, the folks whom I may call English *table d'hôte* trippers are perhaps the most disagreeable.

There was plenty to see in the Champ de Mars even before the Exhibition opened. The building was completed, but as yet only partially furnished. It was a gigantic structure of glass and iron; but there was some ingenuity in the design of M. Le Play, although outwardly, the Exhibition had a mean and stunted aspect. The vast series of concentric ellipses in the Champ de Mars offered all conceivable facilities to visitors for a proper display of their wares. It was perfectly easy both to get into and out of the place, and nobody could lose his way. The radiating streets which converged to the interior gardens, and the great raised platform which ran right round to the machine galleries, were all original ideas, ingenious in conception, and skilfully worked out. The Emperor Napoleon III. took from the outset the liveliest interest in the enterprise, and watched with the deepest solicitude over its development. He frequently visited the Champ de Mars in the early spring; and almost every afternoon during the heyday of the Exposition, Cæsar, leaning on the arm of an aide-de-camp, might have been seen strolling from stall to stall examining, criticising, praising, and purchasing objects of beauty or rarity. To be sure, the Emperor did not think much of the building as an artistic achievement; and when it was completed, he complimented M. Le Play on having built him a "grandiose gasometer."

The management of this gigantic enterprise was entrusted to a body of Imperial Commissioners, presided over in the first instance by Prince Napoleon, who, however, early retired from his post. This was at the outset a heavy blow and sore discouragement, for the

Prince, one of the cleverest of men, was no merely ornamental President; his co-operation, his counsels, and his suggestions had been eminently serviceable in 1855, and might have been of even greater value in 1867.

The Commissioners turned out to be a very rapacious, grasping and greedy body, who were constantly quarrelling with the Foreign Commissioners, and doing their best to extort more and more cash from the *concessionnaires* of the different shows and places of refreshment in the annexes. Foremost among the English Commissioners was Mr. Henry Cole—I forget whether he had been yet knighted—whom I had known ever since the Hyde Park Exhibition of 1851. He was extremely serviceable to me, and introduced me to the whole of the Foreign Commissioners sitting in solemn confabulation. Seldom has there lived a more resourceful, ingenious official than "Old King Cole," as they used to call him at South Kensington; and with surprising skill and alacrity did he respond to the invitation of the Imperial Commissioners to exhibit something which might serve as a comparative history of England during the last five-and-twenty years.

With rare industry, patience and research he brought together that which might be called a complete panorama of English literature and journalism. On an array of screens in the English Department he displayed an almost innumerable series of newspapers, magazines, reviews, and serial publications of every imaginable form, type, character, size and price, ranging from the quarterlies and the half-crown and shilling magazines down to the humble catch-pennies of Seven Dials—all the London and all the provincial papers, the most rubbishing farthing ballads; all the almanacks, all the puffing pamphlets of advertising tailors

and hatters found a place in this unique collection.
Is it yet extant, I wonder, at South Kensington, or
elsewhere?

The Exposition was opened by the Emperor and
Empress in person; and it was pleasant to notice the
cordial greeting given by the Imperial couple to the
more conspicuous among the English visitors present:
especially the late Lord Houghton, with whom both
the Emperor and Empress shook hands. The brilliant, cultured, and amiable peer, whose son is now
Lord-Lieutenant of Ireland, passed the season in Paris,
where he had a charming suite of apartments in the
Avenue des Champs Elysées, where he gave a series of
sparkling *déjeuners à la fourchette* to fashionable, literary, and artistic notabilities. There I met Edmond
About, Taine, Villemessant of the *Figaro*, Albert Wolff
and Gustave Doré. Singular to relate, I did not find
among Lord Houghton's guests either Alexandre
Dumas the Elder or the Younger.

The last had been, as I have already said, a school-
fellow of mine; and I was frequently his companion
when his father took us out for a Sunday outing. The
elder Alexandre did not die until 1871; the younger
Alexandre still lives, a prosperous gentleman, yet from
the year 1840, although I often went to Paris, and con-
sorted with French journalists and men of letters, I
never from my schoolboy days downwards set eyes
either on the author of " Monte Cristo," or on the
writer of " La Dame aux Camélias."

One of the most noteworthy features of the Exhibition of 1867 was its commissariat. There were innumerable *cafés* and restaurants, not only in the annexes,
but in the outer zone of the building itself; where
Messrs. Spiers and Pond had established a great
restaurant for the " exhibition," if I may put it so, of
the much-calumniated art of English cookery. There

was a buffet, too, at which officiated a number of handsome barmaids, who were the objects of enthusiastic admiration on the part of the French visitors, who bestowed a liberal amount of patronage on English roast beef, English legs of mutton, and, pardon the paradox, English Irish stew. There was a Russian restaurant, too, where you could obtain *stchi*, or cabbage soup, sturgeon and *côtelettes à la Pojarski*. There was an American restaurant, where canvas-back ducks, terrapin, gumbo soup, pork and beans, succotash and pumpkin pie were served; and there was even a Turkish restaurant, where sham Orientals from the Faubourg St. Denis brought you sham pilafs and sham kebobs washed down by sham sherbet.

In some of the annexes of the Exhibition grounds the humorous element was pleasantly marked. Mr. Cole, seconded by an able official connected with South Kensington, and whose recent decease as Sir Philip Cunliffe Owen a host of friends have mourned, caused to be erected a strange structure, which was termed by the English Commission the "Test House," where everything that could conduce to the internal decoration and external convenience of a dwelling-house was experimentally exhibited. The French gave this building the sobriquet of " Le Cottage Anglais," or more irreverently they nicknamed it " Le Goddam," and they persisted in regarding it as a typical specimen of English domestic architecture. The irreverent sobriquet just cited is a very old Gallo-Anglicism. Five-and-fifty years ago it was habitually given me by my schoolfellows at the Pension Hénon; but I read that more than four hundred years since Joan of Arc used to allude contemptuously to " Les Goddams Anglais." Thus it would appear that Marlborough's soldiers were not the first who " swore terribly " in their continental campaigns.

The " Test House " was certainly a very grotesquely incongruous pile of chimney-pots, cowls, gutters, drain-pipes, ornamental tiles, terra-cotta mouldings, tessellated pavements, revolving shutters, ventilators, wire fences, improved cooking-stoves, spring latchets, patent bolts, and door handles up-to-date.   But it answered its purpose and was true to its real title, for outside and inside its walls all that ingenious manufacturers could do to perfect the thoroughly British institution known as " comfort " could be applied and tested.

There was not, I think, any German restaurant in the grounds ; but there were plenty of beer *cafés*, the keepers of which were periodically harried and heckled by the Imperial Commissioners, who, on one occasion, to satisfy the greed of the French *concessionnaires* of seats, seized all the chairs in the foreign *cafés* at one fell swoop, so that the unhappy consumers of Bavarian and Lager beer had to drink their liquor standing. An indignation meeting of these and other aggrieved persons was held one evening in the grounds, and I was intensely amused at listening to the impassioned oratory of one of the foreign *brasserie* keepers, a certain Baron B——.   There are persons who, as in the case of the two Alexandre Dumas', have been to me lines running parallel but never meeting, and it has been my fortune to light on people personally almost strangers to me, but whom I have constantly met during a long succession of years.   Baron B——, of Belgian extraction, I had met first at St. Petersburg ; years afterwards I lighted on him at New York.   Then again I found him at Monaco.   On another occasion he turned up at Algiers, and in 1867 I chanced on him in the Champ de Mars.

Since then I have been aware of him at Constantinople and at Monte Carlo, and I am only amazed that

I have not come across him at San Francisco, at Honolulu, in Australia or in India. When I meet him, he
shakes hands, and observing " *Comme on se rencontre !* "
smiles, bows, and departs. He has played many parts;
he has been to my knowledge a scientific traveller, a
glove-buyer for a firm of Manchester warehousemen
in St. Paul's Churchyard, the manager of a music-hall,
an agent for a manufacturer of sewing-machines, and
the keeper of a *brasserie*.

Of the general contents of the Exhibition I forbear
to say anything in detail. Were I to enlarge on the
wonders of art and industry displayed in this colossal
bazaar, I should be writing dismally ancient history;
and besides the glories of the Second French Exposition temple have been eclipsed by those of the Third
and Fourth, all of which I suppose will again have to
pale their fires before the splendour of the next Universal Exhibition in Paris which the world is promised
or threatened with. Still certain things took place between May and October which it was my business to
chronicle, and recurrence to which may not be uninteresting. I was present at the distribution of prizes
by Napoleon III., a ceremony which took place in the
Palais de l'Industrie in the Champs Elysées. In the
exceptionally brilliant company gathered round the
Emperor on this occasion were the Sultan of Turkey,
Abdul Aziz, the Prince of Wales, Prince Humbert of
Savoy, now King of Italy, the Crown Prince of Prussia,
Prince Louis of Hesse, the Duke of Cambridge, and a
son of the Tykoon of Japan. The eldest daughter of
Queen Victoria and of England, the Crown Princess
of Prussia, was also in that superb gathering. There
was a pretty incident during the proceedings in the
tremendous burst of applause which greeted the con-
cession of Grand Prizes, first by His Majesty Napoleon
III. as the designer of dwellings for the working

classes—a prize which was gracefully accepted on behalf of his papa by the Prince Imperial; and next by
the cordial storms of plaudits on the part of the French
which accompanied the bestowal of a Grand Prize on
M. Ferdinand de Lesseps, the enterprising promoter
of the Suez Canal. Poor people! poor people! The
distribution of prizes was to be followed only three
years later by Sedan; and the sequel to Suez was to
be Panama. Is it trite, is it jejune to quote in this
connection the mournful words of Gray?

> Ambition this shall tempt to rise,
>   Then whirl the wretch from high,
> To bitter Scorn a sacrifice,
>   And grinning Infamy.
> The stings of Falsehood those shall try,
> And hard Unkindness' alter'd eye,
> That mocks the tear it forced to flow;
> And keen Remorse with blood defiled,
> And moody Madness laughing wild
>   Amid severest woe.

The ups and downs of man and womankind that I
have seen during the last forty years! Royal, Imperial
crowns won and lost; picked up from the gutter or
pilfered from the right owners; beggars set upon
horseback to be afterwards tilted out of the saddle and
rolled in the mud; speculators hailed one day as benefactors of their species, and the next day denounced as
swindlers and impostors; republics dismembered and
reunited; petty principalities swollen into many mill-
ion peopled monarchies; Crowned Heads and Presi-
dents deified and then assassinated; what political up-
heavals have I not witnessed, what social eruptions
have I not watched? And all this while I have been
tranquilly earning my bread by scribbling "copy" for
a newspaper.

CHAPTER XLI

THE Exhibition was at its height when I travelled
from Paris to Toulon to witness the arrival of the Sultan Abdul Aziz, and in a journalistic capacity accompany the Commander of the Faithful to Paris. Our
resident correspondent in the French capital had been
for some years Mr. Felix Whitehurst, a light and pleasant writer who was always *au courant* with everything
that was passing in the political and fashionable world,
and whose conversation in private life was full of gay
persiflage and pleasant anecdote. He was a man who
always looked on the sunny side of things; his main
pursuit in life was *la bagatelle;* and I remember his
telling me once that his only trouble in the world was
to get the seam of his silk stocking precisely in the
middle of the calf of his leg when he was dressing for
a Court ball. An Imperial Court ball, *bien entendu;*
for Felix Whitehurst was in the best of good graces
both at the Tuileries and Palais Royal and was equally
a favourite with the Emperor and his cousin Prince
Jerome Napoleon. Through Whitehurst's kindly intermediary I obtained permission to travel on board
the Imperial train, and duly witnessed the disembarka-
tion of the Sultan, who was attended by a host of
pashas, beys, and effendis, who for the nonce had relinquished their ordinary plain black single-breasted
surtouts and appeared in gorgeous uniforms with
gold embroidery. The French official to whom the
management of the journey was entrusted was a cer-

tain M. Charles Filon, special travelling courier to the Emperor and Empress, and who, I believe, had been in the service of Louis Napoleon when he was in captivity in the fortress of Ham. I got to Toulon safely, having travelled very comfortably in a coupé with an Imperial Vice - Chamberlain, but the next morning when the express started for Paris, I stayed talking with a friend on the platform and suddenly the train began to move.

" *En voiture ! en voiture !* " exclaimed a guard, giving me at the same time a friendly push. There was an open door ; and through that door I stumbled into a first-class carriage in which there was fortunately one vacant seat. In a few minutes afterwards I discovered, first to my horror, and next to my amusement, and eventually to my edification, that I had fallen among flunkeys.

My seven travelling companions were four Imperial footmen, the body-servant of the Marquis de Gallifet, an assistant cook at the Tuileries, and a Court hairdresser. What would the illustrious chroniclers of the sayings and doings of Mr. James Yellowplush and Mr. Smawker have given to have been the companions, or the interlocutors of these eminent creatures in powder and plush ? There were no second- or third-class compartments attached to the train ; so that was why the lacqueys, the cook, and the hair-dresser travelled first-class.

They were all very polite to me, and in a festive sense were very good fellows ; but never had it been my chance to encounter a squad of such shameless marauders as these flunkeys turned out to be. No charge was made for refreshments at the buffets on the line, and at Lyons, at Marseilles, and at Nice the liveried dacoits swept everything edible and potable before them. They ate and drank as much as ever they could, and carried off with them as much as their pockets and their hands could carry. Bottles of wine, cold pies, cigars, cold roast fowls, cakes of soap, and flasks of eau-de-cologne from the dressing-rooms—nothing came amiss to these freebooters. Their conversation was to me delightful; and ere long I was fain to confess that there was not one touch of exaggeration in the pictures of flunkeys drawn by Dickens and Thackeray.

We left Toulon at five in the afternoon and halted at Lyons at early morning. Our stay was of three-quarters of an hour duration; for a good many things had to be done. There was the inevitable *café au lait* to begin with; and I promise you that my friends the flunkeys did not omit to loot as many lumps of sugar as they could secrete. Then a Turk in a fez ran wildly to and fro on the platform exclaiming that his High-ness the Sultan required a foot-bath. There would not appear to have been such an article available at the Lyons terminus; but a convenient substitute for a *bain de pied* was found in a large soup tureen. Ere we left the station I heard one more delicious utterance of flunkeyism. One of my fellow-travellers asked what had become of "Gallifet." "*Il est en train,*" replied another lacquey, "*de cirer les bottes de son homme.*" Poor Marquis de Gallifet!

Molière was outdone. *Les Précieuses Ridicules* had been improved upon, the man had become the marquis and the marquis a man. Jodelet and Mascarille had come to life again. And so no more of the Sultan Abdul Aziz, whose eventful fate it was to be deposed and soon afterwards to die by his own hand. I never set up as a political prophet; but in the case of this particular Padishah I hazarded a prediction which by the strangest of accidents was verified by the event. When the news of the Sultan's deposition reached

England, I was writing a weekly page of paragraphs entitled " Echoes of the Week," in the *Illustrated London News ;* and in one of these paragraphs I remarked that the misfortunes of Abdul Aziz might possibly culminate in "scissor-cide." It was with a pair of scissors borrowed from his mother to trim his beard withal that the Sultan Abdul Aziz destroyed himself.

Another memorable event took place during the Exposition season. Early in June the Tsar Alexander II. of Russia visited Paris. On the 6th of June while driving in the Champs Elysées, the Autocrat was fired at by a half-crazy Pole called Berezowski, whose weapon was a half worn-out horse pistol. The bullet, however, did find a billet; it wounded in the nostril the horse ridden by M. Raimbault, one of the Imperial equerries in attendance on the Tsar. The would-be assassin was at once seized by a crowd of detectives in plain clothes, who during the Second Empire always clustered thickly round the carriages of Imperial and Royal personages. A four-wheeled cab was hailed, Berezowski was thrust into it by three *sergents de ville*, while at least a dozen police agents hung on behind, sat on the box or sprawled on the roof of the vehicle. I was present a short time afterwards at the trial of the half-demented Pole, which took place before the Court of Assizes of the Seine. Cards of admission were extremely difficult to procure even by journalists ; but Felix Whitehurst made interest with the Minister of Justice and procured me the much-coveted ticket.

The court was crowded almost to suffocation ; and it was a broiling July day. Berezowski was brought into court and seated between two gendarmes on the *banc des accusés.* He was a little, shrivelled, bird-faced man with a cropped head of hair and a yellowish complexion. His interrogatory by the President of the

Tribunal was not particularly instructive; since he spoke very bad French, and in almost inaudible tones. One of his replies, however, I managed to hear. He said that he had been driven to commit his sanguinary crime through *la misère;* that is the reason you will remember that Figaro in Beaumarchais's comedy adduced for turning barber.

But Berezowski's plea in extenuation of his crime did not by any means suit the book, or rather the brief of the prisoner's eloquent although somewhat stagey advocate, Maître Emmanuel Arago, who when his turn came to reply to the counsel for the prosecution delivered a long and violent tirade against the despotism, the cruelty, and the treachery of Russia especially with regard to Poland. He spoke of Siberia, and the knout, of Polish princesses chained to wheelbarrows, and Polish counts slaving in the mines; he dwelt on the red-herring torture, the electric battery torture, the half drowning torture, and other amenities of Russian criminal jurisprudence; and then, drawing himself up to his full height and adopting the trick common at the French bar of pulling up the cuff of his coat until about eight inches of shirt sleeve were revealed, he thundered forth: " Yes, M. le President, yes, *messieurs les jurés*, the wretched man in the dock had two mothers: *sa propre mère* and his beloved native country; and the Tsar of Russia has outraged them both; for Berezowski's mother died of grief, and the ruthless Emperor has murdered Poland." I was sitting close to the jury-box when this startling peroration was pronounced; and I heard one of the jurymen remark to his next neighbour: " *Après ces belles paroles la tête du malheureux ne tombera pas*." Nor after the " beautiful words " uttered on his behalf by his counsel did the head of Berezowski fall beneath the axe of the guillotine. A sympathising jury delivered a verdict of guilty with extenuating circumstances, and the Pole was sentenced to penal servitude for life.

It happened that in 1886 I was telling the story of his trial in a lecture which I delivered at Sydney, New South Wales; and when I came to the verdict of the jury a voice from the middle of the hall cried out: "I saw Berezowski last week: he is employed as an assistant baker at L'Ile Nou." The next day the owner of the voice called on me, and he turned out to be Her Britannic Majesty's Consul at Noumea in New Caledonia. One would have thought that at the downfall of the Second Empire, the Republican Government would have liberated Berezowski; but they kept him in durance from 1867 to 1886; and for aught I know he may be baking bread for the convicts at L'Ile Nou now.

One had to work pretty hard as a special correspondent in those days. It was five o'clock before the verdict was delivered; and it was ten p.m. before without either bite or sup, but with the aid of much tobacco I had got through three columns of copy. I drove down in a victoria to the old General Post Office in the Rue Jean Jacques Rousseau, to post my letter myself; so that it should be in time for the morning mail, and I was in such a hurry to place the packet in the letter-box, and I jumped so suddenly from the carriage that the sentinel on duty was alarmed, and presenting his bayonet at me cried menacingly: "*Qui vive?*" I explained matters to him, but my explanation did not seem to satisfy him; and a *sergent de ville* coming up, the sentinel, a little, stunted creature in a blue great coat and with baggy crimson trousers tucked up under his white gaitered shoes, accused me of assaulting him. I had only frightened him. Fortunately I had my passport and some visiting cards with me; and the *sergent de ville* chancing to be a sensible fellow bade me go about my business, laughing at the sentinel, who looked remarkably like a monkey I had once seen on Richmond Hill bestriding a Newfoundland dog in the charge of a German showman. I wonder that the little man in the red trousers did not charge the *sergent de ville*, but perhaps his musket and bayonet were too heavy for him to make efficient use of those lethal weapons.

"Come to Erfurt," wrote Napoleon the Great to Talma the tragedian, "and you shall play before a pit full of kings." The front row of the stalls so to speak at the Grand Theatre of the Paris Exhibition of 1867 was full of crowned heads and heirs to thrones. In addition to the Royalties I have already mentioned, the French metropolis was visited between May and November by the Kings of Greece, Belgium, and Sweden. Ismail Pacha, Viceroy of Egypt, was also a guest of the Emperor Napoleon. Some years afterwards I dined in the company of Ismail—not bankrupt but deposed and banished—at the Garrick Club, London. The Emperor Francis Joseph of Austria was another potentate who visited this astonishing show and enjoyed the hospitality of Cæsar. I have reserved for the last mention of the visit of the Crown Prince of Prussia, afterwards William I., seventh King of Prussia and first German Emperor. That chivalrous sovereign was born in 1797. He began his military training when he was quite a child; and in his fourteenth year he was promoted to the rank of second lieutenant. In 1813 he was appointed aide-de-camp to his father at the allied head-quarters at Frankfort-on-the-Main. It is not at all unlikely that the young prince caught a distant view of Napoleon the Great at Leipzic.

The late Duchess of Cambridge had a clear remembrance of seeing Napoleon in 1813 mounted on his white charger Marengo. At all events, it is a matter of history that the Prince of Prussia as a lad of seventeen entered Paris with the allies in 1814. Naturally he would have been present at the reception given at the Tuileries by the restored King of France, Louis XVIII. As naturally he would have gazed on the Arch of the Carrousel, then adorned with marble effigies of soldiers of the First Empire and surmounted by the brazen horses of St. Mark, plundered by the armies of the French Republic from Venice ; and most naturally would he have ridden up the Champs Elysées and inspected that Arch of Triumph of the Etoile which Napoleon I. had planned to commemorate the victories of his legions, but which was not finally completed until the reign of the Orleanist Monarch, Louis Philippe. Fate is nothing if not ironical. The Prussian Prince, who in his youth had witnessed the downfall of the conqueror and captive of the earth, and entered his capital with the sovereigns of Prussia, Russia, and Austria, and our own Wellington—who was to be the honoured guest of the Third Napoleon in 1867, was destined in 1871 to ride once more under the proud monument of the Etoile at the head of the victorious German armies, to find the dynasty of the Bonapartes in the dust and to listen haughtily to terms of peace sued for by a Republican Government.

CHAPTER XLII

I HAD been absent from England for nearly two years
when the Exposition ended; and was glad enough to
get back to London, and to the comforts of home and
club life. We did not, however, choose London as
our abode; but took a pretty house on the Terrace, at
Putney, over against the " Eight Bells " Tavern. Both
the Terrace and the tavern have long since been demolished; and the last time that I strolled through
Putney I found the heretofore quiet little village transformed into a bustling suburb of quite metropolitan
brilliancy in the way of shops; and I sought in vain
for an old-fashioned Tudor or Jacobean house, with
many windows, which mansion, it is said, had been
inhabited during the Civil wars by Oliver Cromwell.
Ubiquitous Oliver! If tradition is to be trusted he
must have had as many habitations as he had heads.

I have good reason to remember the late autumn of
1867; since I was sent down to Maidstone to witness
the first execution under the provision of the Act for
abolishing public executions. It is a disagreeable topic
to touch upon, and I am disinclined to recur to it here
at any length. I may just say, nevertheless, that I was
accompanied on this dismal errand by two journalistic
colleagues and old friends, Mr. Edmund Yates and
Mr. Joseph Charles Parkinson. We each wrote a
faithful narrative of the scene at Maidstone, which was
a sufficiently sickening one, and we were all abused for
having simply done our duty. Oddly enough, I re-

ceived in the autumn of this present year of grace, 1894, a letter from an amateur autograph collector, who mentioned, among other things, that he was the possessor of an autograph letter of mine, addressed to the editor of some provincial newspaper, by which, he said, he set some store. I venture to give a copy of it, inasmuch as the document may be considered as a contribution towards this candid, and, I hope (errors excepted), modest Apology for my Life.

MARINE HOTEL, HASTINGS,
Wednesday, 14th August, 1872.

DEAR SIR,—I beg to acknowledge receipt of your note. I am not a reporter; and were such my vocation I could not write anything of a journalistic nature save for the newspaper to which I am exclusively attached—the *Daily Telegraph*. I have seen a great many executions in my time, and, some four years since, wrote an account in the *Daily Telegraph* of the first private execution at Maidstone. I thereafter made up my mind never to witness another hanging : first, because the spectacle at Maidstone made me sick ; and next, because I was very foully abused in the *Saturday Review* and the *Pall Mall Gazette*, on account of the narrative I wrote.

The abuse of which I speak was manifestly prompted by mere newspaper jealousy and spite. Mr. Yates, Mr. Parkinson, and I were dubbed "ghouls," "vampires," "men with mudrakes," and the like, merely because we drew a faithful picture of a novel and ghastly occurrence. But no one had reviled Charles Dickens when, as an amateur, not professionally, he attended the execution of Courvoisier. Nobody quarrelled with Thackeray when, equally unprofessionally, he witnessed an execution at the Old Bailey, and in *Fraser's Magazine* wrote an article called "Going to See a Man Hanged." Finally, nobody was shocked when "Tom" Ingoldsby (the pseudonym of a clergyman of the Church of England, mind you) wrote "My Lord Tomnoddy" in *Bentley's Miscellany*.

I note in my diary two events which occurred towards the close of 1867, both of which call for a few words of comment. On the 9th of November the unusual, and, I should say, almost unique, sight was presented to the multitude gathered together to witness the Lord Mayor's Show of the chief magistrate proceeding from Guildhall to the Law Courts at Westminster in a simple chariot, chocolate in hue. A third of London was amazed; another third was horrified; and the remainder laughed at the elimination of the time-honoured state-carriage from the procession. The Lord Mayor who ventured on this bold innovation was Mr. W. H. Allen, a member of a well-known firm of publishers in Waterloo Place; and his action in excluding the old-fashioned gilded ark on wheels from the pageant was not, I should say, prompted by any feeling of penuriousness, but by the conviction that state coaches, Gog and Magog, men in armour, the banner of the late Countess of Kent, Mr. Common Hunt and the Water Bailiff's Young Man, were grotesque anachronisms which might well be improved off the face of the Lord Mayor's Show. I was not, and am not, of Mr. Alderman Allen's way of thinking. Heaven preserve us from the day when there will be no Lord Mayor's Show, no visits of the chief magistrate and his train to the Law Courts, and no Guildhall banquet! All these paraphernalia may be practically without use, and, to some extent, childish; but they serve to remind us of an historic past, dignified, picturesque, and gaudy; and I would no more abolish Gog and Magog, and the rest of the mediæval properties of the 9th November than I would call for the suppression of the Queen's Beefeaters and the Gentlemen-at-Arms, or give the power of licensing—or refusing to license—the Royal Italian Opera to the London County Council.

By the way, it is worth while marking the fact that such of my readers who have not been favoured with a card of admission for the Royal Stables at Buckingham Palace, and who are not less, say, than thirty-five years of age, have never seen the state-carriage of Her Majesty Queen Victoria. The equipage in which Her Majesty rode from Buckingham Palace to Westminster Abbey on the joyous day of the Jubilee was a "dress" carriage, with glass upper panels, but it was not the Royal state-carriage, which dates from the year 1762, and which was designed by Sir William Chambers, the architect of Somerset House, and painted with allegorical scenes by Cipriani, R.A. This gorgeous coach cost £8,000. Some of the new journalists who described the Jubilee procession, hastened to inform their readers that the Queen occupied the state-carriage, which was drawn "by eight Hanoverian ponies." Ponies, forsooth!—they were horses of the old Hanoverian stud breed; and it should be remembered that Napoleon I., when he seized Hanover, took away a number of the cream-coloured steeds from the Royal mews there to Paris; and that to his state-carriage at his coronation eight cream-coloured horses were harnessed. The Parisians called them *les chevaux café au lait*. Their abduction by the Corsican Usurper so irritated George III. that, until the fall of Bonaparte, in 1814, the King of England's carriage, when he opened or prorogued Parliament, was drawn by black horses.

It was on the 12th December, 1867, that, just as I was about to return to Putney, at the end of my day's work, I was intercepted at the Waterloo terminus by a nimble messenger from the *Daily Telegraph* office, who told me that an explosion had taken place at the Clerkenwell House of Detention, and that I was to repair thither at once. The swiftest of hansoms conveyed me to the prison. It was nightfall when I arrived at the House of Detention. There was a strong *cordon* of police round the scene of the explosion to keep off the mob; but the inspectors on duty knew who I was, and allowed me to pass. My eye lighted on the strangest of spectacles. All the cells in the prison were lighted up; the wall in front was one great black mass, in the middle of which, low down, there was a huge cavity, through which you could descry the gas lamps in the prison yard. The *débris* of that yawning chasm in the wall had formed a high mound in Corporation Lane; and on the top of the hillock of broken bricks stood Captain Eyre Massey Shaw, directing, with his usual coolness and decision, the operations of the firemen.

There was a strong detachment of the Scots Guards on the ground. The explosion was a madcap attempt on the part of the Fenians to liberate a member of their faction who was confined, on remand, in the House of Detention. The only eye-witness of the outrage was a boy, who was standing, about four o'clock in the afternoon, in front of No. 5, Corporation Lane, when he saw a large barrel close to the wall of the prison, and a man leave the barrel and cross the road. Shortly afterwards he returned with a long squib in his hand, which he thrust into the barrel. Some other boys had gathered round, and one was smoking, and he handed the man a light, which the recipient applied to the squib. When he saw that the squib was beginning to burn, he ran away. A police constable ran after him; and when he arrived opposite No. 5, "the thing went off." There were several people in the street at the time, and children playing. The explosion blew down several houses, and smashed most of the coarse glass panes in the windows of the prison; and the result of the outrage to the unoffending in-

habitants of Corporation Lane were most shocking.
Upwards of forty people, men, women, and children,
were more or less severely injured; and seven were
killed, one on the spot; while the remainder died from
their wounds.

I had passed through the *cordon* of police easily
enough; but to get back to Fleet Street was a matter
of considerable difficulty. The crowd was enormous;
and the police, naturally, could not tell friends from
foes, or Fenians from journalists; but cuffed and buffeted all the assemblage impartially. I managed, however, to get close to the detachment of Guards, who
were marching away from the scene of the explosion,
and telling the officer in command who I was, he good-
naturedly allowed me to " tail on," so to speak, to the
detachment, and at the steady pace at which the soldiers were marching, we were soon clear of the crowds,
and I was free to make my way to Fleet Street and
write a description of what I had seen. The Fenians
suspected of having committed, or of being accomplices in the Clerkenwell outrage were not tried until
April, 1868, but all were acquitted; with the exception
of one, Michael Barrett, who was hanged in front of
the Debtors' Door, Newgate, on May 26th. This was
the last public execution that took place in England.
The year 1867 came to an end with a very serious Fenian scare; other explosions occurred, there was great
public excitement, and nearly thirty thousand special
constables were sworn in.

Early in 1868 took place the annual University Boat-
race, and we had a large party of friends to witness
the contest and lunch at Putney. Among my guests,
if I remember aright, were Mr. John Lawrence Toole,
Mr. J. Baldwin Buckstone, then lessee of the Haymarket, and another well-known comedian. The party
enjoyed themselves thoroughly; but on Toole making

his appearance in the balcony to look at the motley
groups crowding the Terrace, he was at once recognised, and loud calls were made on him for a speech—
a request with which, in his usually urbane manner, he
at once, and facetiously complied. Those were days
in which the very old British fashion of gentlemen
drinking brandy and water cold after a substantial
lunch had not entirely vanished; and the two actor-
managers, disdaining to watch the humours of the
giddy throng without, or to join in the perhaps frivolous conversation of the company within, betook
themselves to serious confabulation, aided by libations
of cold brandy and water. It happened that I had
brought with me from Paris a small parcel of very old
and rare cognac. Indeed, it had come from the cellars
of Napoleon I. The bottles were labelled 1812; and
the wine was a present from a dear, deceased friend of
mine, James Lorimer Graham, of New York. Two
bottles of this precious brandy remained; and one I
set, with proper pride, before the two actor-managers.
From time to time they were joined by other guests,
who helped them to dispose of the cognac. Really
good brandy is a very powerful magnet. In about
another hour a second bottle was produced; then the
two empty flasks were removed; and another bottle
was brought, which, however, they did not more than
half empty, and then, quite sober, and without apparently having " turned a hair," they shook hands with
us and departed. When all the customers had taken
leave I asked my wife to explain to me the inscrutable
mystery of the third bottle of rare old cognac labelled
1812.

"You see, dear," she replied, "it was like this. The
first bottle came, surely enough, from Mr. James Lorimer Graham's parcel; but when another bottle was
called for I just took off the label from bottle number

two and pasted it on a bottle of British brandy, of which Messrs. B——, the well-known distillers, sent you a couple of dozen this morning; and I acted in precisely the same manner when I sent them the third bottle. So you see, that you have still one bottle of the rare old cognac left." Now the British brandy of that epoch was what is known in distilling circles as "gin-wash," flavoured with the best French cognac. It is very nice indeed, but not very potent, and that fact may account for the exemplary sobriety of the two actor-managers when they left the Terrace, Putney. Buckstone in particular was—as a friend who accompanied them to the station told me—as right as a trivet. On their way a little boy asked him the time of day; to which query the comedian, quoting Shakespeare, replied, " Time to be honest "—a really striking intellectual effort, I take it, after the consumption of so much brandy and water, even though it were British.

To describe my life during 1868 would be only to chronicle so many days, weeks, and months of hard, but pleasant work; so many hundreds of leaders written; so many public functions described, so many picture exhibitions criticised and books reviewed. We moved from Putney, first back to Sloane Street; and then to a house in Thistle Grove, now Drayton Gardens, Brompton. In Thistle Grove, nearly opposite to our house, lived a family by the name of Bloxam, the head of which was a wine merchant, who was the son-in-law of Mr. Thomas Roberts, a then well-known solicitor in Spring Gardens, with whom I had been for a long time on terms of intimate friendship. Some time in 1868 Mr. Bloxam, whom we frequently visited, and who, with his wife and sister, as frequently visited us, began to tell me of a lawsuit which might be soon expected to come on, and which would make, he thought, a considerable stir in the public mind. A claimant to the ancient Barony of Tichborne, so he informed me, had arrived from Australia, where, at a place called Wagga-Wagga, and under the name of Thomas Castro, he had carried on the business of a butcher.

The Claimant's case was that he and eight of the crew were saved from the wreck of a ship called the *Bella;* that he went to Australia, and lived there for fourteen years under the name of Castro; and that he was married in January, 1868, as Castro, but in July of the same year as Tichborne. In 1867 his claim was recognised by the Dowager Lady Tichborne, who had advertised for her long-lost son, who had formerly been an officer in a cavalry regiment. No other members of the family accepted him ; but Sir Clifford Constable and some of his brother officers did. A select circle of believers in the Claimant was gradually formed ; and I found, one evening, at Mr. Bloxam's, Lord Rivers, whom I had known years before as the Honourable Horace Pitt. His sister, the Honourable Harriet Pitt, had been one of the Queen's Maids of Honour. Another zealous friend of the Claimant was Mr. Guildford Onslow, M.P., who is said to have backed him to the extent of nearly £15,000; and among his other influential friends the name of Mr. Quartermaine East and Mr. Biddulph recur to me. Most of these gentlemen were frequently to be found at Bloxam's. What the last-named worthy party had to do with the business I am unable to say with certainty. Possibly he may have had some share in organising those celebrated Tichborne bonds, the holders of which were to be reimbursed when the Claimant recovered his title and estates.

This bulky litigant I did not see in the flesh until 1869. In 1867 he was mainly in Paris in attendance on

the lady who believed that he was her son. With
regard to Mr. Bloxam, I am fully persuaded in my
mind that he had an entire and implicit belief that the
then corpulent Claimant was not Arthur Orton, formerly of Whitechapel, butcher, and that he *was* Roger
Charles Tichborne, son and heir of Sir James Tichborne, Baronet, who—Roger—was born in 1829, partially educated in France and at Stonyhurst College;
who sailed for Valparaiso, South America, in 1853,
and who left Rio de Janeiro in the *Bella*, which foun-
dered at sea in 1854. I knew Mr. Bloxam very well,
and I had not at any time any reason to doubt his
candour and integrity. That which I subsequently
saw of the Claimant I shall relate in its proper place.

CHAPTER XLIII

THE year 1868 will always be memorable as the one in which I was introduced to Henry Labouchere, M.P. There was a building in Long Acre used as a place for lectures and public meetings, and called St. Martin's Hall. Here, in 1858, Charles Dickens made his first appearance as a public lecturer, in aid of the funds for the Hospital for Sick Children; and here I once had the fortune, or misfortune, to listen to an American called, I think, Mason Jones, who was gifted with an extraordinary mnemonic faculty, and who positively recited " Paradise Lost," without book, from beginning to end. I did not, I confess, hear him right through; but when he had rolled out about three hundred verses following the Invocation and Introduction I went out for a little walk. When I returned the orator was attacking Satan's Address to the Sun. I again strolled out to smoke a cigar and call upon a friend. By this time Mr. Mason Jones had got as far as Eve's Recollections; but when he had reached the Evening in Paradise I stepped over the way to partake of some light refreshment at Mr. Nokes's hotel, opposite the Royal Italian Opera, Bow Street, Covent Garden. But, hurrah! I was in at the death, and with unabated vigour did Mr. Mason Jones spout his peroration:—

> " The world was all before them where to choose
> Their place of rest; and Providence their guide,
> They, hand in hand, with wandering steps and slow,
> Through Eden took their solitary way."

The world knows nothing of its greatest men; and I am not aware of what became of the phenomenally verbose Mr. Mason Jones; but if he be still in the flesh, were I to meet him again, and did he too propose to recite, say Carey's "Dante," or Hoole's "Tasso," *in extenso*, or Spenser's "Faërie Queene," I fear that I should pray to be delivered from Mr. Mason Jones, even as Oliver Cromwell prayed to be delivered from Sir Henry Vane.

There was little *raison d'être* for St. Martin's Hall, which might have been more appropriately called St. Clement's, or St. Paul's, or St. Giles's Hall; and after an unsuccessful series of Promenade Concerts, given by an enterprising individual called Strange, some time lessee of the Alhambra, in Leicester Square, the Hall was reconstructed as a theatre; and late in October, 1867, was opened under the management of the late Mr. Alfred Wigan. In 1868–69 the manageress of the Queen's was a very pleasing actress and sweet singer, long since known and admired by a large circle of friends as Mrs. Henry Labouchere. Mr. Labouchere was actively concerned in the management. He wanted a new piece—he was always wanting new pieces—and my friend, Andrew Halliday, the author, in conjunction with Mr. Frederick Laurence, of *Kenilworth*, one of the best burlesques ever produced in modern times, and who also wrote for Drury Lane, under the Chatterton management, the melodramas of *The Great City* and *King of Scots*, told me one evening that Mr. Labouchere would be very glad to enter into negotiations with me for a drama full of exciting situations.

It is a whimsical fact that repeatedly, during my career, I have been importuned by theatrical managers to write pieces for them; but I have never been able to convince them that, although I know a good deal about

the stage and its ways, I have not within me the stuff
for making a successful playwright; being, as I have
said more than once, entirely devoid of the faculty of
imagination, and incapable of constructing plots. At
all events, the knowledge of my deficiencies in this respect has saved me from the humiliation of having a
play refused. The few which I have written were proposed not by me, but by the managers themselves; and
they were all, in their way, successful. It is true that
even now I see my way to the composition of an historical tragedy; but not a line of it has been committed
to paper. My good friend, Sir Augustus Harris, was
good enough to approve the idea; but as it would cost
about £4,000 sterling to bring out the piece with adequate spectacular effect, Sir Augustus scarcely sees his
way to producing my tragedy at the Theatre Royal,
Drury Lane.

Nevertheless, I thought that there would be no harm
in seeing what Mr. Labouchere was like. An appoint-
ment with him was made to meet Halliday and myself
at ten o'clock one evening, in his private room at the
theatre. He was then one of the Members for the
County of Middlesex. He struck me as being, in all
respects, a remarkable man, full of varied knowledge;
full, withal, of humorous anecdotes, and with a mother-
wit very pleasant to listen to. His conversation was,
to me, additionally interesting; since, when I was in
Mexico, I had gone over most of the ground which he
had travelled; and that I was familiar with the United
States and with Russia, in both of which countries he
had long resided, when he was in the Diplomatic Service.

I know not what it was which prevented me from
writing a piece; still in 1868-69 I was constantly at the
Queen's, generally in the company of Watts Phillips,
artist, satirical essayist, and dramatist. A gifted and

most versatile man was poor Watts, much admired and appreciated by many friends; but, as I have always thought, cruelly and ungratefully ignored and neglected by the great body of the public. He was a pupil of George Cruikshank, and drew vigorously; but the outcome of his artistic capacity did not extend beyond his making a number of facetious drawings for *Diogenes*—in which he also wrote " Thoughts in Tatters, by the Ragged Philosopher "—and for other comic publications, and perhaps the flower of his graphic talent is to be found in pen-and-ink drawings, with which he adorned, almost to exuberance, his letters to his friends. His dramas were singularly powerful and compactly constructed; and singularly enough, although he resided for a long time in Paris, he did not, as far as I am aware, borrow any of his plots or characters from the French. Had he lived in these golden days for playwrights, had he been the contemporary of the Petitts, the Pineros, the Simses, and the Thomas Arthur Joneses, Watts Phillips could have made thousands of pounds from such dramas as the *Dead Heart, Camilla's Husband, The Huguenot Captain, Paper Wings*, and *On the Jury*. As it was, his labours brought him little beyond bare bread and cheese. He was one of the last of the old race of dramatists, who were accustomed to sell their plays to a manager " out and out."

The end of it was that poor Watts went, financially, all to pieces. He had never enjoyed good health, and he died, quite worn out, early in the 'seventies. He was an eccentric, rather difficult to get on with—the same things have been said, I apprehend, more than once, about myself—but I loved the man dearly, and mourned his loss as that of one of the friends and colleagues of my youth, at a period when my own *gioventù* was most tempestuous; but when Watts was enjoying the only prosperous epoch in his life, and was living, a happily-married man, with young children about him, at a pretty villa near Norwood. That must have been about 1855. I am glad to be able to say that among the kindest, the most actively generous of his friends in his last years, was Henry Labouchere; and that after his death that gentleman, in conjunction with the late Mr. Chatterton, then lessee of Drury Lane, did their best to help the loved ones whom he left behind him.

Edward Askew Sothern, the unique impersonator of Lord Dundreary in Tom Taylor's not very powerful comedy of *Our American Cousin*, I had known as early as 1863–64. He had played the character more than a thousand times before coming to England; and he played it four hundred and ninety-six times at the Haymarket Theatre; but the part of the American Cousin himself, Asa Trenchard, fell to Buckstone; and that of the senile old lawyer's clerk, who had been a schoolmaster, was enacted by Chippendale, a rare representative of stage veterans of the Farren school, and whose wife, a competent actress, I afterwards met in Australia. I wrote an article about Sothern's Lord Dundreary in a series of papers called "Breakfast in Bed." The paper was full of impertinences, which I almost wondered that Sothern did not resent; but possibly he saw that through all my *persiflage* there was evident the highest admiration for him as a dramatic artist; and we soon became very good friends. He was something else besides an admirable comedian, a cultivated gentleman, and a good fellow. He was a wag and an inveterate practical joker; most of his achievements in the last-named direction have passed into the "chestnut" stage, and will not bear repetition; and those to which publicity has not been given will be imparted to the public in those reminiscences which I hope that his friend and occasional collaborator, Mr. John Lawrence Toole, is now engaged in writing.

In the early autumn of 1869 I took, as usual, my four weeks' holiday at Homburg; and experienced the usual ups and downs, culminating with having to get a cheque on London cashed in order to be able to return home. I found at the Hotel de Russie at Frankfort the late Mr. Lionel Lawson, one of the principal proprietors of the *Daily Telegraph*, and who had some interest in the then juvenile Gaiety Theatre, Strand. The Gaiety is built partially on the site of Exeter 'Change, a small and gloomy arcade, constructed by the late Marquis of Exeter, the owner of the freehold, with the idea of reviving the glories of the old Exeter 'Change. It was full of commodious shops; but the public declined to patronise it, and the walls of Exeter 'Change were, like those of Balclutha, generally desolate. I mind the place well, since Mr. Pond, the advertising agent, and myself had a house and office there, where we published a comic journal, called *Punchinello*. Exeter 'Change having come, as a thoroughfare for pedestrians, wholly to grief, its site was utilised for a large building, called The Strand Music Hall, which speedily, notwithstanding its most commanding situation, was, as a commercial speculation, wholly disastrous. It was demolished, and in its stead arose the present elegant and popular Gaiety Theatre.

With Mr. Lionel Lawson there came Mr. John Hollingshead, who was the lessee and manager at the Gaiety; and one afternoon " Honest John," who had been an ally of mine for many years, proposed that I should write a burlesque to be produced at the ensuing Christmas. He had got, he said, a capital idea for such a piece. " What do you think," he asked, " of Wat Tyler? Taxes, you know, and all that kind of thing. People always like to listen to digs given at the taxes." At once I hailed the proposal; and simultaneously I settled in my mind—from the slang analogue for a hat, a " tile "—that Wat Tyler should be by trade a hatter, and that he should wear an inordinately tall Gibus. I set to work on the piece immediately I got home ; but I hasten to record that the only merits which *Wat Tyler* possessed, and which ensured it a run of some eighty nights, belonged to Mr. John Hollingshead, the suggester of the title ; to Miss Nellie Farren, to Miss Constance Loseby ; to Mr. Toole, and to the scene-painters, costumiers, and ballet-master. *Wat Tyler* was hastily, inconsiderately, and in many instances stupidly written. I was in bad health at the time, and overwhelmed with work. The doggerel dialogue had to be written at odd times whenever I had an hour to spare ; but I was obliged to devote two or three hours every day to the rehearsals, and my enforced absences from Fleet Street drove my friends there nearly frantic.

Wat Tyler was duly produced at the Gaiety. I believe one gentleman in the stalls regaled himself with a hiss ; and very probably, like Charles Lamb, who hissed his own farce of *Mr. H——*, I might have actively sympathised with the gentleman in the stalls had I been present at the first performance of my burlesque. But I happened to be away busy in writing ; and only reached the theatre in time to be told that the piece, with all its manifest imperfections, had found favour in the eyes of a crowded audience ; and that I must needs respond to a cry for the author, and appear before the curtain. So I presented myself in the not very suitable evening apparel of an overcoat and check trousers ; and I am told that instead of backing out gracefully on the front side, I turned my back upon the audience. I had, however, taken the precaution of leading on Miss Nellie Farren at the same time, and of pointing to her as the lady who had principally contributed to the success of the evening. She played the part of Sir Reginald Plantagenet; was, of course, enchanting in doublet and hose; was arch, *piquante*, and vivacious, and sang to admiration a parody of "*Com' è gentil*," from *Don Pasquale*. A very clever singer — Miss Constance Loseby — was Mrs. Tyler; and Wat Tyler, who was shockingly henpecked, was played with his accustomed drollery by Mr. J. L. Toole. I think, too, that pretty lady named Rose Coghlan was in the cast. I am gratified to say that I never witnessed a performance of *Wat Tyler*. John Hollingshead paid me handsomely for the piece, of which he was really the inventor; and I received in addition, during several weeks, handsome royalties on the sale of the book of the words. Such was my last experiment in dramatic authorship.

CHAPTER XLIV

NOTHING of moment occurred in my career until March, 1870, when I was despatched in hot haste to Tours in France to describe the trial before the High Court of Justice specially empanelled for the occasion of Prince Pierre Bonaparte, the third son of Lucien, the nephew of the First Napoleon, and the cousin of the Third one, for the murder of a Paris journalist, a young man, whose *nom de guerre* was Victor Noir. (His real name was Yvan Salmon.) The career of Pierre Bonaparte had been a stormy, and not a very reputable one. In early manhood he had joined the Carbonari in Italy; he was warned to quit the Papal States, and on his refusing to do so was arrested by a party of Papal gendarmes, or *sbirri*. Armed only with a *couteau de chasse*, Pierre Bonaparte contrived to slay the Captain of Police, and to wound two of his subordinates; but receiving in return a ball in the chest and a thrust from a bayonet he was overpowered and conducted to the Castle of St. Angelo, where he remained for some months in captivity. On his release he went to England, and thence wandered to Corfu. Crossing to Albania he had a fight with some hostile shepherds, or *palikares*, or brigands—the terms are nearly convertible ones—and killed, it is said, two of his adversaries, and seriously wounded a third. He managed to get back to Corfu; and the Lord High Commissioner, thinking him a not highly eligible guest, politely requested him to leave the Ionian

Islands. He subsequently resided a short time in the United States; where, at New York, shortly after Louis Napoleon's abortive *coup de main* at Strasburg, he met his princely cousin, who had been deported beyond the Atlantic by the Government of Louis Philippe.

When the Citizen-King collapsed, Pierre Bonaparte hastened to Paris, where the Republican Government gave him a command in the Foreign Legion. He was elected as Deputy for Corsica, a member of the Constituent Assembly; and although he voted with the extreme Left, he always loyally supported his cousin Louis Napoleon. Then he left France, which was, in truth, rather glad to get rid of him, and took his departure for Algeria, where he displayed considerable courage in divers minor engagements with the Arabs. When the Second Empire became an accomplished fact, Napoleon III. gave his turbulent kinsman the rank of Prince and of Highness, but he was not to be considered as a member of the Imperial family.

The Emperor made him a handsome allowance. He professed to have given up politics, and he lived, indeed, in great privacy in a suburb of Paris; but he seemed to have entirely divorced himself from his Republican proclivities; and his closest ally in a political sense was the ultra-Bonapartist, M. Paul de Cassagnac; while he held in the bitterest hatred Henri Rochefort, and all the contributors to the ultra-Republican *Marseillaise*.

As for the hapless Victor Noir, he had been a journeyman watchmaker, then a florist, and ultimately drifted into journalism: becoming an assiduous contributor to the columns of what the Parisians call *la petite presse*. He had considerable descriptive talent, and a curiously keen faculty for finding out things connected with the upper classes; and from this acquisition he would have proved a valuable member of the staff of an English "society" journal. His mode of procedure was, as he candidly admitted, to begin by making friends *avec les larbins*, or lacqueys of the aristocracy. My Toulon experience taught me that there was a good deal of information to be gained by consorting with flunkeys. He had but recently joined the *Marseillaise*, and he was engaged to be married two months later, when he was on the 10th January, 1870, sent by M. Pascal Grousset to the residence of Prince Pierre Bonaparte to demand reparation for an insult addressed by the Prince to the *rédacteurs* of a journal called the *Revanche*. To Auteuil he consequently repaired, being accompanied by another journalist, M. Ulric de Fonvielle. About four in the afternoon they arrived at Auteuil; sent in their cards and were conducted to the drawing-room. Five minutes afterwards the Prince, in rather a *négligé* costume, entered the room.

They delivered M. Pascal Grousset's message, and handed the Prince a letter from that gentleman. Pierre Bonaparte seemed surprised that the letter was not a challenge from Rochefort, for whom he professed the utmost disdain. He read the letter and threw it on a chair, and then he began to abuse the two journalists.

According to the evidence of M. Ulric de Fonvielle the Prince struck Victor Noir in the face, and then drawing back a pace or two drew a revolver and fired at the young journalist, who, pressing his hands to his breast, rushed from the room and downstairs and fell dead in the street. The Prince fired another chamber of his revolver at M. de Fonvielle, who vainly endeavoured to extricate his own pistol from its case; again the Prince fired, and the scared M. de Fonvielle succeeded in escaping from the house, raising cries of "Murder."

This, then was the weighty affair of which I was commissioned to follow the judicial unravelling before the Haute Cour de Justice. At Tours I found two colleagues representing important English newspapers—my old friend Antonio Gallenga of the *Times*, and Mr. Frederick Boyle of the *Standard*. There was, besides, a host of French journalists; and we Britons availed ourselves of the advice given to us by a friendly Commissary of Police, to visit the court on the Sunday before the trial, and nail our professional cards in the particular parts of the tribune reserved for the press which we desired to occupy. The counsel was sagacious; for the rush for seats the next morning was tremendous; but our French *confrères*, although somewhat grudgingly admitting that possession was nine-tenths of the law, did not molest us during the many days the trial lasted.

I can scarcely say, however, that they were oppressingly polite to us. The scene in the High Court of Justice the next morning was an imposing one; the Judges in scarlet and ermine were ranged at a long table of quadrant form on a high platform; and at one extremity of the table was the *greffier*, and at the other the Public Prosecutor, both in scarlet robes. To the right of the last-named functionary was the dock, a railed-off space furnished with a comfortable easy chair; and to this area was conducted shortly after the court had been formally opened, the distinguished prisoner.

The first time that Napoleon the Great ever saw Godoy, the Prince of the Peace, he described him in a letter to his brother Joseph as *un taureau*. Prince Pierre Bonaparte would have passed very well as a *toreador*. He would, I should say, physically, have been altogether at home in a bull-ring at Seville; and in my mind's eye I pictured him in full *matador* costume, standing, Toledo blade in one hand, and with the other slowly waving the little red flag as a lure for the bull to dash himself at the point of his rapier. As a matter of fact, the prisoner was dressed in a frock coat of the colour known as *bleu barbeau*, with gloves of yellow or *beurre frais* kid. He was perfectly self-possessed; and displayed much argumentative skill while undergoing the interrogatory of the President of the High Court, M. Glandaz. And of this typical Corsican's personal courage there cannot be the slightest doubt. He had a strident and rather harsh voice, but he kept his temper within bounds; save when he made mention of what he called "*l'infâme Marseillaise*," and its editor-in-chief. Then his voice rose almost to a yell; his face was suffused with a deep purple, and his hands convulsively clutched at the portfolio of crimson morocco leather in which the papers necessary for his defence were bestowed.

It is but fair to Pierre Bonaparte to admit that the version which he gave of the tragedy at Auteuil differed materially from that given by M. Ulric de Fonvielle. According to the Prince, he had written to M. Rochefort, challenging him to mortal combat. The next afternoon, after receiving a doctor, who was treating him for a slight attack of influenza, he was informed by a domestic that two gentlemen wished to see him. Under the impression that his visitors were the seconds of the editor of the *Marseillaise*, he directed that they should be shown in without reading the names on their cards. When he found himself in presence of the two journalists, they assumed, according to the Prince's showing, a provoking attitude; and after he had read the letter and had expressed his astonishment that it was not one from Rochefort, the tallest of the two journalists struck him a smart blow with his fist on the left cheek; and at the same time the Prince declared that he saw the shorter of his two visitors, M. de Fonvielle draw a pistol from his pocket and endeavour to cock it; whereupon drawing a revolver which he carried habitually in his own pocket, he fired on the tall young man, Victor Noir, who immediately rushed from the apartment; while the short M. de Fonvielle secreted himself behind an arm-chair, whence he aimed his pistol at the Prince, who returned the compliment by another shot, which, however, did not reach its mark. One of the counsel for the *partie civile*, who, without regard for Prince Pierre's indictment for murder, was seeking damages against him on behalf of the family of Victor Noir, was Maître Charles Thomas Floquet, then an advocate about forty years of age, who had attained some notoriety by shouting, " *Vive la Pologne, Monsieur!* " on the occasion of the Tsar Alexander II. visiting the Paris Palais de Justice. He was practically the real prosecutor; the law officers of the Crown showing, if not an actual prepossession in favour of the prisoner, considerable apathy in pressing the case against him.

The trial lasted several days, and was enlivened by more than one humorous incident. Laughter is not generally a distinctive feature of a trial for murder; yet the High Court at Tours, during the examination for the prosecution of M. Ulric de Fonvielle was more than once convulsed with merriment. Neither the counsel for the prosecution, nor the advocate for the defence, nor the jury, nor M. Ulric de Fonvielle himself were able to obtain a satisfactory explanation of why the last-named gentleman had failed to get his revolver out of its leathern case and adjust the trigger so as to fire on Pierre Bonaparte. The journalist pleaded that he had done his best, but fate seemed to have been against him. The unlucky revolver and case were handed up to the bench; and the President having previously taken care to ascertain that the weapon was unloaded, clicked the lock once or twice, observing in a mildly reproachful tone to the journalist, " *Et cependant, Monsieur de Fonvielle, vous n'avez pas pu armer votre pistolet.*" Simultaneously I heard a growl from the bench immediately beneath mine. The growl emanated from Antonio Gallenga. "No; confound him," he remarked, "he did not cock his pistol. Why he did not take the sword of Harmodius and Aristogiton and stab with steel in myrtle dressed?" I ventured in an undertone to observe that they managed these things better in Italy; whereupon Antonio uttered another growl; but there was a smile on his honest face when, looking upwards, he said that I was always fond of my joke. Yes, such is the fact, I have always been of opinion that this is a very funny world. How runs the old epitaph?—

> " Life is a jest, and all things show it,
> I thought so once, but now I know it."

Only the worst of it is that the wrong side of our mouth is that on which we are sometimes compelled to laugh. On the whole, however, I consider it judicious to follow the advice of Beaumarchais's Figaro and laugh as often as we possibly can, because we never know at what moment we may be constrained to weep.

Then, on another day of the trial, occurred another incident of a serio-comic character. It suddenly occurred to M. Wilfred de Fonvielle, brother of Ulric, and like that journalist an ultra-democratic Republican, to go temporarily stark, staring mad. From the bottom of the court he raised and reiterated once and again the terrible revolutionary cry, " *A mort ! A mort !* " In vain did the friends by whom he was surrounded strive to calm down the excitement of the bellowing journalist. Whom, or what he was denouncing death against did not appear; but as he resolutely refused to hold his tongue, the chief law officer of the Crown eventually rose and demanded that the perturbator should be brought to the foot of the court to be punished for contempt. We English journalists thought that all kinds of dreadful things were about to be done to M. de Fonvielle; but to our pleased surprise the President, M. Glandaz, did not sentence him to imprisonment, but after bestowing on him quite a paternal reproof for uttering a cry which was alien to modern French manners, fined him in quite a moderate sum for his malfeasance.

I should have said that when Prince Pierre heard the first shout of "*A mort! A mort!*" he snatched up his red morocco pocket-book, and with a very agitated expression of countenance, fairly made a bolt for it into the room behind the dock, closely followed by the officer of the gendarmerie who had him in charge. Now as to the personal courage of this typically Corsican personage, there could not exist the slightest doubt. He had braved death time and again; only I suspect that he was under the impression that M. de Fonvielle and his friends were bent on storming the dock, and tearing him to pieces; and when a man thinks that he is within measurable distance of bodily dismemberment, is he to be blamed for showing his exasperating foes a clean pair of heels?

Droller still was the third incident in a trial which, as I shall presently endeavour to show, was fundamentally a farce. At a late stage of the proceedings the advocate for the *partie civile*, who, as I have already said, were doing their best to press home the case against the Prince, called as a witness M. Henri Rochefort. The ex-contributor to the *Figaro*, ex-editor of the *Lanterne*, and then *rédacteur-en-chef* of *La Marseil-*

laise, was undergoing a term of imprisonment at Ste.
Pélage for a violent attack on the Emperor and the Imperial *régime ;* and a murmur of excitement ran through
the crowded auditory when the trenchant pamphleteer
was brought in custody into court and placed in the
witness-box. Questioned as to his name and pre-
names, the journalist, who used formerly to be spoken
of as " the convict Marquis," replied that his name was
Victor Henri de Rochefort Luçay, born at Paris in
1830. His examination both by counsel for the prosecution and the defence was a delicious exhibition on
his part of adroit fencing. He alternately parried and
attacked ; and while professing the utmost respect for
the Court, took occasion to sneer at the moral character of a lady whom he called Lucretia — meaning
Madame Charles Bonaparte, the mother of Napoleon
the Great—and to insinuate that he was the illegiti-
mate offspring of the Comte de Marbœuf, Governor of
Corsica ; while with another skilfully malignant allusion to the Dutch Admiral Verhuel, he induced the
inference that that distinguished Batavian, and not
Louis Bonaparte was the father of the Emperor Napoleon III. This sliest of sly hits aroused the official ire
of the Public Prosecutor, a very tall, gaunt functionary, with a dolorous expression of countenance, who,
when he stood up in his judicial scarlet, was qualified
by Gallenga as *Le grand spectre rouge*. He was in the
middle of a long-winded oration rebuking the witness
Rochefort for his moral turpitude, when a series of
titters, culminating in a burst of laughter, were audible
in court. The editor of the *Marseillaise* had gone
quietly to sleep. It was, possibly, that which is popularly known as "a cat's sleep :" such a factitious slum-
ber, perhaps, as that in which Watts Phillips used to
tell us was once indulged by Mr. Labouchere, M.P.,
while Watts was reading a new drama to the then

Member for Middlesex. But it was difficult to beat the playwright at the game of intellectual tactics. He read the manuscript slowly and more slowly, and eventually subsided into "a cat's sleep" of his own, upon which Mr. Labouchere timeously woke up. The Public Prosecutor, however, found that he could make nothing sleeping or waking of Henri Rochefort, whom, among fresh cachinnations on the part of the public, he sternly bade to stand down. As he was being conducted out of court the occupants of the front row of the press tribune availed themselves of the opportunity to press heartily the hand of the terrible satirist; and then the question was asked how he had come down from Paris. "First-class *coupé* between two gendarmes," he replied. "The *coupé* quite complimentary. *Merci du compliment*."

A few more witnesses were heard, including a dark complexioned, burly-looking gentleman, M. Paul de Cassagnac, who incidentally remarked that he was extremely devoted to the Prince. His evidence, however, could throw no kind of light on the manner in which poor Victor Noir came by his death, and shortly after M. de Cassagnac's dismissal from the witness-box the President summed up fully, and, as I thought, very fairly, to both parties. Then there was an interval for luncheon; the prisoner was taken away; the judges left the bench; and the jury retired to consider their verdict. A whole hour elapsed before they came into court again. "*Que diable!*" exclaimed my next neighbour, a Parisian *feuilletonnist*, "what are the *ganaches* waiting for? Hadn't they made up their minds before they entered the box?" "Not so," replied an equally satirical gentleman of the press, his neighbour. "They are waiting for the verdict to be telegraphed from Paris."

At length, however, you heard that tramping of the

soles of boots which I always consider to be peculiarly characteristic of a jury entering or leaving the box. Of course, the idea is a nonsensical one ; yet, be it as it may, I always fancy that the footsteps of jurymen, who obviously get their boots from all kinds of makers, have a sound of their own, just as the boots of policemen and soldiers, and the shoes of convicts have all their separate reverberations. The jury unanimously acquitted Prince Pierre Bonaparte of the murder of Victor Noir, otherwise Yvan Salmon: thus practically accepting the theory of the defence, that the Prince had only legitimately defended himself under great provocation, both from the deceased and his companion, Monsieur Ulric de Fonvielle. Once more did Pierre Bonaparte make a clutch at his red morocco portfolio ; but this time it was with an air of triumph that he did so ; and, bowing to the court, he was about to retire in joyous haste, when he was recalled by the voice of the Procureur-Général. "Am I not free?" he asked briskly. "No, Prince," replied the law officer ; "the *partie civile* are about to plead." We did not stay to listen to the litigation as to the amount of damages due to the bereaved family of Victor Noir, for we had had no lunch. But while my colleagues and myself were refreshing ourselves, news arrived that the court had awarded against the Prince a *solatium* of twenty thousand francs, payable to the kindred of the dead journalist.

A very curious scene occurred to wind up this strange drama. No sooner was Prince Pierre liberated from the Penitentiary, where he had been confined since the beginning of the trial, than he drove straight to the hotel, where he received what is termed in the absurd modern newspaper parlance an "ovation." The Prince's brow was assuredly not encircled with a wreath of myrtle. He bore no sceptre in his hand ; the proceedings were not enlivened by a band of flute-players ; nor did the ceremonies come to a close with the sacrifice of a sheep: unless, indeed, the acquitted Prince partook at his evening repast of *gigot de mouton à la Provençale*, or *côtelettes à la Soubise*. But a mob of his sympathisers pressed round him, seized his hand, plucked at the skirts of his coat, and exchanged downright effusive embraces with him. He was well out of it.

After the fall of the Second Empire, which brought with it the withdrawal of his own pension, Prince Pierre, I am afraid, fell for a time on evil days. At all events, I have before me a highly-glazed card, bearing the inscription, " Princesse Pierre Buonaparte: Robes." Now I have reason to believe that the plucky Princess, the militant Corsican gentleman's wife, kept the ex-Imperial pot boiling by carrying on the business of a dressmaker somewhere in New Bond Street.

CHAPTER XLV

BACK to England, and back to work. I have nothing to record that would be of interest to my readers touching the winter and spring of 1870; but in the third week of July a series of very momentous things began to occur, some of which I had, in my capacity as a journalist, to chronicle. War with Prussia was resolved on by the French Government on the 15th of July, and the declaration delivered at Berlin on the 19th. On the same day the North German Parliament met, and engaged to support Prussia in the coming struggle; and the next day Wurtemberg, Bavaria, Baden, and Hesse Darmstadt declared war against France, and took steps to send contingents to the Prussian army. It was immediately settled in Fleet Street that I was to proceed to Paris at once; and, after remaining a few days there, endeavouring to ascertain the state of public opinion in the capital, and events as they occurred day by day, I was, so soon as the Emperor left Paris, to go to Metz, in the East of France, which city—*Metz la Pucelle*, as she was then proudly called, as a hitherto impregnable fortress— was to be for a time the Imperial head-quarters. After that, I was to await, as Mr. Micawber awaited, for something to turn up.

We needed, of course, a professionally military war correspondent to do the fighting; and the *Times* had already secured the services of a dashing and very clever Guardsman, Colonel, or Captain " Kit " Pemberton, who had already distinguished himself in literature by a vivacious novel of military life, of the " Digby Grand " type, which he published under the *nom de guerre* of " Leo." But in those days military gentlemen who could write with ease were not very easy to find; and it was even more difficult to light on officers who possessed any marked attainments as linguists. In this last respect, it seems to me, that the valiant warriors who fought under Welling- ton, in the Peninsula, and under other prominent com- manders in the Two Sicilies, were much better skilled in the tongues than the officers of the present genera- tion. Of course, I know what of late years has been done in this direction by the course of linguistic stud- ies pursued at the Royal Staff College. Our contem- porary Sons of Mars often " take up" Russian, and, for aught I know, Arabic and Hindustani. But from the beginning of the century to the crowning victory of Waterloo the candidate for a commission in the British army was not vexed by any literary or scien- tific examination. A young fellow of sixteen or sev- enteen who desired to obtain an ensigncy in the Line had only, under the dear old purchase system, to pay £450 into Messrs. Cox and Greenwood's, and, after a very brief delay, if the medical board certified that he was physically "fit," and his parents or guar- dians, or his parish clergyman had vouched for the respectability of his moral character, he was duly gazetted as an ensign, say in the 150th Foot, joined his regiment, and, naturally, fought as the cubs of the British lion always fight.

This was, perhaps, a rough and ready method of manufacturing officers. Still have I known, in my childhood, scores of Peninsular officers of the highest distinction who, although they had become wholly oblivious of the Greek and Latin which they had learned, or tried to learn, at Eton or Harrow, and were altogether innocent of Euclid, spoke Spanish and Italian with fluency and accuracy. They had become conversant with the Castilian speech during the war in Spain; and they had acquired the Tuscan tongue in Sicily, where, for years, Great Britain maintained a strong military force; while others spoke French, which they had learned at that military school at Angers where young Arthur Wellesley had himself studied. The Prince Imperial, after his father's downfall, graduated as a cadet at the Royal Military Academy, Woolwich. Poor Don Alfonso of Spain was summoned from the military school of Sandhurst, to ascend the throne of Spain. Why, with the precedent of Angers before us, should not English lads be sent for awhile to St. Cyr, to the École Polytechnique, or to Saumur; or, for the matter of that, if they are scions of noble British families, to the École des Pages at St. Petersburg, which is one of the finest military academies in Europe? Can it be that modern continental governments are less liberal in their views of international military training than the old French Bourbons were?

Sprightly Felix Whitehurst again made interest at the Tuileries and the Ministry of War to obtain permission for the not yet famed special war correspondent and myself to proceed to the front. He was met by a courteous but positive refusal from the Emperor himself, who remarked that Prince Gortschakoff had told him that during the war in the Crimea, the War Office at St. Petersburg was always perfectly *au courant* with what was going on at the British headquarters before Sebastopol through the brilliant communications forwarded to the *Times* newspaper by "Monsieur William Russell." Cæsar smiled as he made this remark; but it was a smile that might be,

and was, taken as equivalent to a *douche* of the very
coldest cold water. The only concession which he
would make was that foreign correspondents would
not be molested so long as they kept with the rear of
the Imperial army ; and to this he added, with another
significant smile, that they might from time to time
be furnished with trustworthy information of what
was going on at the front :—which information would
be judiciously conveyed to them by the proper authorities.

As an old journalistic hand I was able to estimate in
advance the probable value of such judicious information. There was a dear old gentleman at the Ministry
of the Interior, the father I believe of the well-known
Bonapartist Deputy M. Robert Mitchell. M. Mitchell
père was in charge of the Press Department at the
Ministry ; and after I had been introduced to him by
his son the courteous anxiety which he displayed to
furnish me from day to day with " trustworthy information " was almost overwhelming ; but I feared the
Greeks and the gifts they gave, and did not trouble
Mr. Mitchell, senior, much. I failed to see the good,
as the French proverbial locution puts it, of seeking
for noon at fourteen o'clock.

Paris during the few days that I remained there was
in the strangest of conditions. The mass of the population were most undoubtedly enthusiastically in favour of the war ; and in society you were freely told
that the guiding spirit in provoking hostilities between
the Emperor Napoleon and King William of Prussia
had been the Empress Eugénie, and that she had triumphantly spoken of the struggle which was imminent
as " *Ma guerre.*" It would have been far better for
herself, her husband, and her son if she had not instigated—if she did instigate—the war which ushered in
l'année terrible.

The streets of the capital on the 23d of July were thickly placarded with copies of an Imperial proclamation in which Napoleon announced that, to vindicate the national honour, he was about, alone, to take in hand the interests of the country. Incidentally, likewise, the Emperor made this statement, "*J'amène mon jeune fils avec moi*"—an utterance the grammatical orthodoxy of which the philosophers at Nice began to impugn; arguing that it was only to the army at the front the Emperor could say that he was bringing the Prince Imperial; whereas to the Parisians he should have said—"*J'emmène mon fils:*" meaning that he was taking his son with him from the metropolis to the seat of war. Then among the boulevard loungers there was current a ridiculous "shave" to the effect that the last telegraphic dispatch wired from Germany by the diplomatist Count Benedetti to the French Foreign Office, stating that war could not possibly be averted, wound up with this remarkable peroration: "Don't put so much horse-flesh in your next consignment of sausages." It turned out afterwards, so the story went, that in the hurry and scurry of overwork at the German telegraph office a purely commercial communication from a German pork-butcher named Benedict had got mixed up with, and tailed on, to the telegram from Count Benedetti.

The scenes at the Eastern Railway terminus were throughout the day and nearly throughout the night of a most animated and excited description. I remember walking home one morning at daybreak after a very grand entertainment at which there had been much dancing and supping, and many gorgeous uniforms, and many beautiful ladies blazing with diamonds; and meeting a regiment of Cuirassiers at its full strength, the men with bundles of forage artistically made up in globular form secured to their saddles

who were on their march to the terminus. While I
was gazing at them a ragged old woman, employed by
the municipality as a street sweeper—why do not our
London parishes employ poor but valid old females
as what I may call "outdoor charwomen" in summer
weather?—was inspecting with evidently affectionate
interest the several squadrons of Cuirassiers. She
waved aloft her broom in patriotic approbation, whereupon the colonel in command brought his drawn sabre
to the salute. When the regiment had passed, the
old lady with the broom uttered a sigh of gratified
relief. She took a pinch of snuff and offered me one ;
saying, at the same time : "*J'ai toujours aimé la grosse
cavalerie.*"

Yet another curious and pathetic sign of the times
was the strong manifestation of religious feeling
among the female population of Paris. Every church
in the great city, from Notre Dame to St. Germain-
des-Prés, from the Madeleine to St. Philippe-du-Roule,
was thronged from matins to vespers by women of
every class, not so much for the purpose of attending
the services as for that of burning votive tapers to the
Virgin and to their favourite saints, while the *Dames
de la Halle*, after kindling their candles at their favourite church of St. Eustache, used to lie in wait for
regiments on the march, and press sausages and fruit,
and packets of tobacco on the soldiers.

I repeat that for a time the war with Germany was
a thoroughly popular one. Had not millions of
French peasants denoted "*Oui*" in response to the
question asked at the plebiscitum of May, 1869, to ascertain whether the entire French people were content
with the Imperial rule or not? Had not Marshal
Lebœuf declared that the equipment of the French
soldier was altogether complete and perfect to the last
button of the last gaiter? Had not the Prime Minis-

ter, M. Emile Ollivier, announced in the Legislative Chamber that he entered on the war with a light heart; and, finally, was not the second in command of the Imperial Legions to be Marshal MacMahon, the hero of Magenta and Solferino? So everything wore a roseate aspect. The theatres were crammed; the hotels were full of wealthy English people; the *cafés* and restaurants did a roaring business; the boulevard *badauds* gaily expressed their opinion that the French army would only have to make a military promenade in the Prussian capital to the music of military bands playing at intervals "*Partant pour la Syrie*," and "*La Marseillaise;*" while at night the great line of boulevards exhibited, so soon as the playhouses had closed their doors, a procession of open carriages filled with ladies in dazzling evening toilettes rivalling those of the historical *Promenade de Longchamps* were preceded and followed by gangs of genuine or fictitious working people, mostly clad in white blouses, who waved aloft lighted torches and shouted in deafening unison: "*A Berlin! A Berlin! A Berlin!*" I did my best to send home day by day faithful narratives of the things which I saw; and then having received a letter from Fleet Street that I was to venture on the war-path, I packed up a valise of very modest dimensions, and started by rail for Metz. Midway, our train, although an express, was shunted. We very soon knew the reason why: for first there dashed by a pilot engine and next came a train of saloon carriages, the panels painted the Imperial green and bearing the Imperial cognisance in gold. Napoleon III. and his young son Louis, full corporal in the Grenadiers of the Guard, were in that train.

The fortress of Metz was swarming with soldiers of every arm of the service; and the Imperial Guard, in particular, made the most grandiose of shows. The

city was not strong in hotels, and those there were
were full to repletion with guests, including many
newspaper correspondents — English, French, and
American. We tried at first to engage furnished lodgings; but the people to whom we applied with that
intent manifested a strange reluctance to receive us.
I ceased after awhile to be surprised at it, when I
learned that the inhabitants of Metz were desperately
afraid of harbouring Prussian spies, with whom the
town was said to be infested. Luckily for the contingent of English journalists, I happened to know M.
Pietri, whom I had met in Algeria, and who had shown
me much courtesy; so I referred the landlord of the
principal hotel first to the police, and next to the Emperor's private secretary. These references, together
with the exhibition of our passports, soon satisfied the
landlord, who provided fairly comfortable accommodation for at least three of our number, while to me he
obligingly gave up his wife's own pretty little private
salon, which an agile chambermaid very soon converted into a bedroom.

I remember that sleeping apartment well, through
the circumstance that my next-door neighbour being
a corpulent French Colonel of Artillery, who, while
making his toilette in the morning, used to troll out a
song, the burden of which was " *Vive la gloire! vive
la gloire; la gloire de la France et des Français!* " I
must own that this martial ditty became, after four or
five days, somewhat wearisome in its monotony; but
one morning, when the news had arrived of the first
reverses which the French arms had sustained on the
German frontier, the colonel's refrain was curiously
varied. He got through the first verse very neatly,
but he broke down over the " glory " burden, and after
ejaculating " *Au diable la gloire, je me fiche pas mal de la
gloire,*" subsided into moody silence. He came out,

however, very strong that evening at the absinthe hour at a table in the hotel garden, adjoining the table where the English press representatives were accustomed to meet. He was especially hot in denouncing Prussian spies to the corpulent staff officers, his friends; and loudly expressed his determination, if any such *gredins* were brought before him within the limits of his command, to give them such a short shrift as twelve rifle balls would expeditiously furnish. "*Douze balles, messieurs! Douze balles! Rien que ça pour ce tas de coquins;*" and as he spoke he scowled malignantly at the harmless necessary representatives of the English Fourth Estate.

The journalists assembled at Metz were a band of brothers; and lengthened experience leads me to the conclusion that travelling special correspondents when they meet are almost invariably on terms of cordial friendship, and help one another so far as they are able, in every possible manner. Perhaps it is the knowledge that they are discharging a common duty, and frequently incurring a common danger that tightens the bond of good fellowship among them. At Metz we had Nicholas Woods, who had been in the Crimea for the *Morning Herald*, who had afterwards done good service for the *Times* and the *Pall Mall Gazette*, but who, on the outset of the Franco-German War, had been commissioned by an important Glasgow journal, to enlighten North Britain as to the conduct of the campaign, which few failed to foresee would be momentous. Nicholas Woods died far too early, but not too prematurely to have gained the love of a large number of friends. His journalistic masterpieces I hold to have been his description of the great prize-fight between Sayers and Heenan; his diary of the laying, by the storm-tossed *Agamemnon*, of the Atlantic cable, and his narrative—in the *Pall Mall*, I think—of

what befel him while having assumed a ragged garb,
he got himself locked up with the connivance of an
inspector of police, who was, in the joke, in the cells
attached to the Grand Stand at Epsom, on the Derby
Day.   Another very noteworthy correspondent at
Metz was that Henry Mayhew, of whom I have already spoken, and who brought with him his son
Athol.   Both father and son had long resided in Germany, and were finished Teutonic scholars.   For the
Standard, had come out Mr. John Augustus O'Shea,
the most versatile and the most courageous of Hiber-
nian journalists.   He had been everywhere and seen
everything, north, south, east, and west, in both hemi-
spheres ; and I rejoice to say that, although I see him
very rarely, he is still altogether fit and valid.   Our
little party was completed by the presence of two distinguished artists.   Mr. Simpson, who had served the
Illustrated London News literally from China to Peru,
was there; as was likewise that prince of rapid sketch-
ers, and master of impressionable effects, Mr. Sydney
Hall, who held a commission from the *Graphic.*

Although we had all plenty of money, and there was
a great deal to see at Metz which was amusing and
picturesque, our position was not in all respects a comfortable one.   The authorities sternly refused to allow
us to go to the front; although Henry Mayhew and his
son, at great personal risk, did contrive to push on to
the frontier, where they witnessed, on July 30th, the
repulse of a French force, at Saarbrück.   But we
fretted at being condemned to a condition of comparative inactivity ; and our restlessness was aggravated by
the setting in of a violent Prussian spy mania at Metz.
I was not suspected of being an "*espion*" by the people
at the hotel where I lived, but the gendarmerie and the
detectives kept the sharpest and the most malevolent
eyes upon us; and one night the correspondent of a

Scotch paper, whose name I forget, was incautious enough to wander about the camp, and seek to pick up information by talking with the soldiers at the canteens. At once he was denounced by a vigilant corporal as a Prussian spy; since the poor gentleman spoke French very badly, and his accusers were unable to discriminate between Teutonic and Caledonian Gaelic; so he was hauled away into captivity. Then, three or four days afterwards, Mr. J. A. O'Shea managed to get, quite innocently, into trouble with the police, and made his appearance at the Hotel de l'Europe, between two gendarmes, to inform us that he was at once to be delivered over to the tormentors.

I have omitted to state that the ranks of our little press-gang were swelled by a clever French gentleman, whose real name was Nicolas Thiéblin, but who, for some reason best known to himself, had adopted the *nom de guerre* of Azamat Batouk, and passed himself off as a Turk. He wrote English with perfect fluency, and was the correspondent of the *Pall Mall Gazette*. Some ten years afterwards I came across him in New York City, where he was on the staff of some influential local journal. "Azamat Batouk," who was an extremely shrewd individual, suggested that, looking at the fact of the arrest of Mr. O'Shea, was clearly the stupidest of blunders on the part of the police, proposed that the foreign journalists should, in a body, wait upon the Provost-Marshal, General Saint Sauveur, and state our case to him. We informed the two gendarmes of our intention; but these military bobbies, who were quite as thick-headed as the two immortal gendarmes in *Geneviève de Brabant*, could not deprive themselves of the pleasure of marching Mr. O'Shea between them to the Provost-Marshal's quarters, accelerating his pace now and then by a stern "*Plus vite que cela!*" I feel persuaded that one of these worthy fellows fumbled at least three times in his coat-tail pocket to make sure that he was furnished with the handcuffs with which he hoped to decorate the wrists of the supposed *espion prussien.*

We found General de Saint Sauveur, an elderly gentleman, with grey moustaches, with many crosses and medals on the breast of his undress uniform, and in spotless white trousers, and varnished boots, the most courteous and the most obliging of *Grands Prévôts.* He heard our story with a succession of deprecatory shrugs of the shoulders, alternating by conciliatory smiles. "I know very well, gentlemen," he said at length, "that you are no more Prussian spies than I am one ; *mais que voulez-vous ?—les temps sont si durs.* I have the highest respect for the intelligence and the integrity of the English Press. I served in the Crimea, and had the honour to know Monsieur Rousselle. *Mais que voulez-vous ?* I want to let everybody out. *J'ai envie de relâcher ce pauvre Monsieur.*" He was alluding to the gentleman with the Scotch name, which I forget. "Captain," he continued, turning to a young and handsome aide-de-camp, "supposing you step over to the Commandant de Place, and ask him to sanction the liberation of Monsieur, and M. Oshie." To my amazement, the young and good-looking aide-de-camp folded his arms and said : "*Mon Général,* I refuse respectfully, but categorically, to obtemperate to your demand. Whenever I wait on the Commandant de Place he treats me as *le dernier des derniers. Il menace de me flanquer à la porte ; il m'appelle chenapan.* I am willing *d'aller au feu,* and to die for the Emperor ; but to the Commandant de Place I will not go." Surely the recalcitrant aide-de-camp must have been the General's nephew ; or he would never have ventured to oppose the orders of his superior officer. Again the *Grand Prévôt* shrugged his shoulders ; but his smiles grew more frequent, and at length he said, " I think ; nay, I am sure, that I have the power to liberate these three gentlemen.   The Scotch one was certainly a little imprudent ; but Monsieur Oshie has evidently been the victim of excessive zeal on the part of the gendarmerie." So Mr. J. A. O'Shea, alias " Oshie," was at once set at liberty, the General signing an order for the immediate discharge of the Scotch journalist, much to the disgust of the two gendarmes, who would have dearly liked to clap the " darbies " on him, and march him off to gaol.

We tendered our thanks and made our bows to the *Grand Prévôt*, and left his quarters : not without, however, a protest from the ill-conditioned representative of a Belgian newspaper, who loudly expressed his opinion that Henry and Athol Mayhew must be Prussian spies, because they spoke German so well, and that Mr. O'Shea ought to be placed in the same category, in consequence of his fluent French.   The intelligent Flemish correspondent added that no Englishman could ever make himself fully understood in the French tongue.   To this Mr. O'Shea aptly made answer that he was not an Englishman, but an Irishman ; and that to all natives of the Emerald Isle, French came naturally.   So we " sat," figuratively speaking, on the cantankerous correspondent of the Belgian journal ; and Athol Mayhew told him that if he interfered with us again, he would get a good beating.   He gave us after that the widest of berths.

But worse remained behind.   The Emperor's headquarters were at the Hotel of the Préfecture ; and one morning, the Imperial equipages and their horses being exercised in the Grande Place, Mr. Simpson thought that a sketch of the Emperor's travelling carriage would be highly acceptable to the readers of the *Illustrated London News ;* and he forthwith jotted down his pictorial impressions of the vehicle.   He was pounced upon by the gendarmerie, and haled, not before the Provost-Marshal, but the terrible Commandant de Place himself, and a most ferocious personage he proved to be. His name has escaped me ; but it was that of one of the most prominent and sanguinary of the Terrorists in the first French Revolution. I think that his potential ancestor figures in the " Poetry of the Anti-Jacobin."

The Commandant bullied us all round, and seemed to be particularly wrathful with me, apostrophising me as " *l'homme au muscau rouge.*" " Let him know," he thundered forth, "and know all of you, if I hear anything more about so-called artists sketching, *je ferai leur affaire* in the course of two hours. Carriages forsooth !—it may be a carriage to-day ; but it will be sketching the fortifications to-morrow." How long he would have stormed at Mr. Simpson and ourselves, and what he would have done with the luckless special artist is uncertain ; but one of our party, ere the proceedings commenced, had cautiously written a note to the Emperor's private secretary, and M. Pietri lost no time in sending a message to the incensed Commandant, telling him that he knew the artist of the *Illustrated News* very well. So we were hustled out of the Commandatorial presence.

I was destined to meet the fiery-tempered gentleman once again. I was at Cologne, at the Hotel du Nord, and on my way to Berlin. The war was over, and at the *table d'hôte* of the hotel I met the ex-Commandant de Place, a prisoner on parole. I called for a pint of champagne, filled a glass, and sent the remainder to the once terrible swashbuckler, telling him that I should like to drink his health. I fancied that he recognised my incarmined proboscis, since he grinned a most horrible grin, preceded by a darksome scowl. Jules Mumm, however, is a vintage not to be despised under most circumstances; and the gentleman with the Terrorist name gulped down his spuming chalice, and made me a would-be gracious bow, when I pledged him and said, "*Honneur au courage malheureux.*" "*Ein verrückter Engländer*" (a mad Englishman), quietly observed a German civilian with blue spectacles, two or three removes off.

We were not troubled by the gendarmerie after the Simpson incident. The authorities were kind enough to send to us as a guide, philosopher, and friend, a certain Count De la ——, who, before we had been acquainted with him twenty-four hours, we knew perfectly well to be a French spy. I do not think that he got much out of us; but he was very agreeable, and full of anecdote about the Court of the Tuileries. The main business of this politic gentleman was to get the English newspaper correspondents out of Metz, and to send them back to Paris; and in this, ere long, he succeeded. On the 4th of August the battle of Wörth was fought; and after the desperate and long-continued engagement, the Crown Prince of Prussia defeated Marshal MacMahon, and almost completely crushed the French army of the Rhine. On the same day the battle of Forbach took place; Saarbrück was recaptured, and Forbach taken by the Prussians. Metz was utterly demoralised; and the narrow streets of the city were crowded by *bourgeois* and farmers, who had flocked in from the neighbouring country, bringing, in many cases, their cattle and their goods and chattels with them. It was a scare, a panic, a universal spasm of terror. The Germans were in France, and the Emperor Napoleon had left Metz for the front. Nothing remained for us but to fall back on Paris, which we most unwillingly did, the friendly Count De la —— telling us that we should be sure to find a great many things of interest well worth chronicling in the French

capital.   The affable Count was telling, unconsciously
—and for once in a way—the truth.   The railway for
many miles was held by the military authorities, as
fresh contingents of troops were being continually
pushed into Metz, in case of the virgin fortress being
besieged by the Germans; and already there was a
talk of Marshal Bazaine being appointed to the command of the already immense garrison.   So we set off
in an open carriage and pair, for which we paid a most
extortionate price; but eventually finding the railway
open, got, under circumstances of much discomfort, to
Paris.

CHAPTER XLVI

I SHALL never forget the remaining weeks of that month of August. Lord Lyons was British Ambassador, and showed me his usual kind hospitality; but even the ordinarily tranquil hotel in the Rue du Faubourg St. Honoré was, as the month wore on, the scene of ever-increasing anxiety and perturbation. Queen's messengers were continually coming and going; and the Chancery was thronged all day by English residents in Paris who wished to leave their plate and jewels in the vaults of the Embassy. There was a universal feeling that the city would be besieged. Strasburg was being bombarded by the Germans; and on the 2nd September came the final collapse of Sedan, so graphically described in the *Daily News* by my admirable colleague, Archibald Forbes.

But I must not forestall matters. Throughout August, supplies of grain and live stock were pouring into Paris, and in the Bois de Boulogne thousands of cattle and sheep were pastured. I do not know anything about the bovine or ovine race myself; but a member of the Smithfield Club would have watched with the deepest interest this gathering of live stock, in which every breed in France was represented. The spy mania, of which I had had a foretaste at Metz, was raging with much greater fury in Paris. My friend Parkinson, whom I found at the Grand Hotel, told me that for four long hours he had been tracked by an elderly individual, who, he felt assured, was a *mouchard* from the Préfecture of Police. The man persistently

" shadowed " him, as the Americans would say; but
fortunately for Mr. Parkinson, the detective, who was
elderly, had gouty feet, and my friend at last eluded
his attentions by ascending the tower of Notre Dame.
The podagrous detective did not care to follow him, and
gave up the pursuit in disgust; at least my friend did not
find him waiting for him when, half an hour afterwards,
he emerged from the west door of the cathedral.

There was something ludicrous in this widespread
panic; all the Germans in Paris suddenly discovered
that they were not natives of the Fatherland, but
that they were either Austrians or Alsatians; and to
be an Alsatian was to become for the time a popular
idol; for every day the emblematical statue of Strasburg on the Place de la Concorde was heaped with
wreaths of flowers. There was a German tailor in
the Rue de Rivoli to whom I owed, in 1867, a small
account. When I returned to Paris in July he began
to dun me, and I promptly settled his demand. In the
second week in August this worthy *Schneider* called
on me at the Grand Hotel. I did not receive him
very effusively, and contented myself by remarking
that I supposed he did not want to have his bill paid
over again. It was not that, he replied in faltering
accents, addressing me as High, well-born Herr.
Would that he had never asked me for a *sou;* I was
welcome to any number of suits of clothes on terms
of indefinitely protracted credit. But would I, as a
well-known English *Schriftsteller*, write him a testimonial stating that I had known him well for more
than three years, and that I could vouch for his thorough respectability and political harmlessness? I
wrote him the testimonial for what it was worth, and
he went away rejoicing. Whether it did him any
good or not I know not.

The acuteness of the Prussian spy-fever did not

abate one jot. The papers were full of the most ridiculous stories detailing the discovery, and in many
cases the arrest, of alleged secret agents of Bismarck.
One *gobemouche* wrote to the *Presse* to say that while
standing at a *bureau de correspondance*, he had seen
enter an omnibus an individual dressed in the garb of
a Sister of Charity, but as the individual raised her
robe to mount the step, there was plainly discernible
beneath, the extremities of tightly - strapped blue
trousers with gold braid, and spurs. Obviously, according to the *badaud*, the seeming Sister of Charity
was a Prussian spy in disguise; although why a spy
should wear trousers with gold lace down the seams,
and spurs, puzzles my comprehension. Another story,
as preposterous, was to the effect that the Hanoverian
Legion who had entered the service of France, not
because they were disloyal Germans, but because they
preferred their own king to His Prussian Majesty,
were, to a man, composed of Prussian spies.

Concurrently, however, with these myths, came a
number of incidents more momentous; they were
tragic. A valiant Marshal of France, full of years and
glory, was brutally maltreated by the mob on the es-
planade at Vincennes, on the grounds that he was an
espion prussien ; and a more than half-crazy German,
who had formerly been a lieutenant in the Prussian
army, and who had babbled some silly political rubbish at a *brasserie*, was positively tried by a court-mar-
tial, and shot as a spy in one of the courtyards of the
École Militaire. Long ago, Voltaire had said that the
character of his countrymen was a combination of
the traits of the tiger and the monkey; only he omitted to say that, on occasion, one of these qualities became, for a time, altogether dormant. At the end of
August, 1870, there was very little of the monkey visible in Paris: the tiger was everywhere.

Of this verity, I became personally and very unpleasantly aware. On the night of Saturday, the 3d of September, I was at the Café du Helder, in the saloon on the first floor, in company with an artist who had just returned, not from the seat of war, but from South America, and who was showing me some sketches which he had made in Chili and Peru. He had been absent from Europe for more than a year; and naturally our conversation turned on the stirring events of the last two months: and the words Metz, Strasburg, Nancy, Verdun, Mans, Latour, Gravelotte and Sedan, frequently turned up, together with the names of Napoleon, King William, Bismarck, and MacMahon. It was about midnight; I bade my friend farewell, and was preparing to descend the rather steep staircase of the Café du Helder, and, crossing the boulevard, return to the Grand Hotel, when I was surrounded by a mob of excited Frenchmen, who loudly denounced me as a Prussian spy. With their arms they barred the door of egress; a Commissary of Police was sent for; and I was dragged by police agents to the Central Station, which was somewhere about the Boulevard Montmartre. My captors flung me into a large cell, or rather lock-up room, saying to the inmates of the place " Here is a Prussian spy for you." There may have been five-and-twenty ruffians in this abominable den—swindlers, thieves, *souteneurs, rôdeurs de barrière*, pickpockets and mendicants. They set upon me, and did their best to kill me. I was knelt upon, buffeted, scratched, and my hair was torn out by handfuls. One villain in a white blouse, possibly one of the patriots who had howled " *A Berlin!* " on the boulevards in July, tried to bite me; while another devoted his energies to kicking my ankles with his wooden *sabots*. The hurts he gave me have not thoroughly healed, even to this day.

I found one protector, however, in the shape of a huge fellow from the *abattoir*—a slaughter-man, who was only locked up for being drunk and disorderly, and who, fortunately for me, having slept off his debauch, woke and shielded me with his powerful body; telling my assailants that they were a "*tas de gueux et de gredins.*" About four in the morning I was taken to the Central Police Station, somewhere near the Bourse; and the *sergents de ville* who had me in custody said that they had not the slightest idea of the crime of which I had been accused. The Central Station was full of police officers: each couple having in charge their particular prisoner or prisoners; and here I remained, without bite or sup, until eight in the morning, when I was taken to the office of the Commissary of Police in whose district the Café du Helder was situated. As I entered this magistrate's office there were leaving it a couple of Frenchmen, one of whom, from the thickness and blackness of his beard, I thought that I recognised as one of the excited crowd at the *café*. He looked at me narrowly; and I looked at him, and without exchanging a word, he and his friend departed. Doleful as were the straits in which I found myself, I could not help recalling that strangest of jingles in the " Devil's Walk "—

> " He passed through Tottenham Court Road,
> Either by chance or by whim;
> And there he saw Brothers the prophet;
> And Brothers the prophet saw him."

I was kept waiting exactly one hour; and at the expiration of that time the Commissary emerged from his private room, and informed me that I was accused of having held, the previous evening, certain *propos injurieux à la France;* and that I was, moreover, suspected of being a Prussian spy. I asked who were

my accusers ; he declined to furnish me with any information on the point ; but said that out of regard
for my apparent respectability — I was wearing, as I
have done for many years past, a white waistcoat,
which had got sadly smirched in the affray in the den
of human wild beasts, on the Boulevard Montmartre
—he proposed to send me to the Depôt of the Préfecture of Police, not in the ordinary cellular van, but
in a cab, if I had the means of paying for such a convenience. I put my hand in my pocket, and found
that I had a considerable sum in gold and silver about
me. My watch and breast-pin had, however disappeared. How my assailants missed rifling my pockets,
I could not for the life of me understand. I was given
over to a couple of plain-clothes detectives, who were
very decent fellows, and who already spoke of my misfortune as " the Affair of the Café du Helder." They
said that the two Frenchmen, one of whom had such
a very thick beard, whom I had met on entering the
office, had had a long interview with the Commissary ;
and it was on their "informations" that I was charged.
They had also, I was told, early in the morning, gone
to the Grand Hotel, and asked permission from the
manager to take away my papers ; but as they had no
authority to do so, the manager—who was a German,
by the way—had declined to gratify their wish. The
friendly detectives bade me be of good cheer. The
law was the law, they pointed out ; and if I could
prove my nationality and my professional status, the
juge d'instruction before whom I was brought, would
most assuredly, after a brief examination, set me free.
So we hailed an open victoria, one detective sitting by
my side, and the other mounting the box, and crossing
the Seine drove to the Préfecture hard by the Palais
de Justice.

Extensive structural alterations were in progress ;

and much more was visible in the way of boardings
and scaffold poles than of the architectural features of
the structure in which I was to be confined. We
passed through divers dark corridors, and emerged at
last into a spacious hall with a very high roof, and
with spiral iron staircases at intervals leading to at
least three tiers of cells. Presently, I was ranged
with a number of other real, or imputed, malefactors,
in a long row, but the inspecting officer consulting a
memorandum book, directed a warder to bring out
" the man in the white waistcoat." I was taken to the
greffe, an office where my designation, Christian name
and surname, my place of birth, my profession, my
age, and *état civil* generally, were all entered in a huge
book ; and then the inspecting officer, a grey-headed
gentleman in plain clothes, summoned me into his private room.

He was courtesy itself—as courteous as General
Saint Sauveur had been at Metz : observing that there
must be some mistake in my case ; and that after a day
or two I should probably be summoned before the
juge d'instruction, and the affair would be cleared up.
Had I any political enemies in Paris, he asked. I
replied that I was not aware of having done anything
to acquire any enemies at all, either at home or abroad.
Oddly enough, the refrain to all his questions and
remarks was identical to that with which we had
been favoured by the *Grand Prévôt* at Metz. " There
was," he said, " *un fâcheux état de choses ; et les temps
étaient très durs.* I am," he continued, " myself only
here provisionally ; I am the director of the female
penitentiary of Saint Lazare—a nice quiet place, where
discipline is admirably maintained by those good nuns,
les Sœurs Grises ; and where, although there is a break-
out now and again among the younger prisoners, one
may say that, as a rule, you never hear one word

spoken louder than another. But the Director of the Dépôt is ill, and I have been sent for temporarily to fill his place; and *ma femmes et mes enfants sont là-bas qui pleurent.*" Fancy a man expressing his sorrow at being temporarily divorced from his home in a penitentiary! Then he went on to tell me that I was to be kept in a cell *au secret;* but that I should find solitary confinement more a comfort than a hardship; inasmuch as I should not be in the company of the scum of humanity congregated in the common day-room and dormitories; and then, he added, "you can smoke and have books to read, and you will be put *à la pistole*"—which last meant that I should be able to order my meals from a neighbouring restaurant, instead of partaking of the usual and revolting prison fare.

All this while I was mechanically holding in my hand a large loaf of bread, which had been given me on entering the Central Hall. The Director was so polite as to conduct me himself to my cell, which was on the first floor. It was now half-past ten. He gave me over to the gaoler; a tall, meagre man, of about fifty-five, with a grizzled moustache, the military medal on his breast, and honesty written in every line of his gnarled visage. I have met with so many rogues in my time, that I fancy that I do not need the aid of Diogenes's lantern to discover an honest man. Presently a prisoner entered, dragging a mattress and some bed furniture with him; for as I was *à la pistole*, I was to be privileged, for a daily payment, to sleep softer than the ordinary *détenus.* When the prisoner had made the bed, the gaoler, setting his back against the door, asked me in a gruff, but not unkind voice, whether I could not eat my bread. I replied that I had no appetite. " No wonder," said he, " you have been terribly mauled. One lapel of your coat has been torn off, and your white waistcoat is smeared with blood. We don't often have people with white waistcoats here."

He was silent for half-a-minute, and then said, " Have you got any cigars?" I put my hand in my side pocket; my cigar-case had disappeared. " Like a pipe?" he asked. " I should like one," I replied, " dearly." He produced an old, blackened, short, wooden pipe, and, screwed up in paper, some of the strongest *caporal* tobacco—it is stronger than our shag —that I ever tasted. " Smoke," he said, " it will do you good." I sat down on the bed ; and after a few whiffs, he continued, still gruffly, " Can I do anything for you?" Yes, thank Heaven! he could. The benef-icent fairy, Nicotine, had suggested to me a happy thought. I had my card-case about me. The *porte-chefs* gave me a pencil ; and I hastily scribbled on the back of a visiting card these few words in French. " Lord Lyons, British Embassy. In prison, Préfec-ture of Police, Prussian spy. Please get me out." I handed the card, together with a gold louis, to the gaoler, saying, " Will you promise me to have this card conveyed to the British Embassy? The napo-leon is for the messenger." He looked at me very fixedly ; took the card and replied, " *Tenez, mon bour-geois*, I am an old soldier : after eight campaigns one does not go about *faisant des cochonneries*. Your card shall be at the Embassy in twenty minutes ; and I won't take a *liard* for it ;" whereupon he threw the piece of gold on the bed ; left the cell ; and locked me up, very securely indeed.

It was now eleven. Precisely at a quarter to twelve, the " Judas " trap, or inspection-hole, in the door of the cell was opened: and through the aperture I dis-cerned the rugged face of the veteran of eight cam-paigns. " There is an English captain," he said, " who has come to see you." He unlocked the door ; led me down one of the spiral staircases, and guided me, not towards the *greffe*, but through seemingly endless corridors and bureaux, and up and down staircases, to the private cabinet of the Préfect of Police himself; and with him was one of the secretaries of the Embassy, Mr. De Saumarez. The Préfect was profuse in his apologies. A lamentable mistake had been made, he said; and he could not help thinking that my arrest had been due to denunciations prompted by private malice. Then shaking me cordially by the hand, and telling me that I was free to depart, he handed me over to the secretary and bowed us out.

In the next room, however, the long pent-up sensations of the horrors which I had undergone, found vent. Although I never dreaded danger, and have been in peril of death over and over again, I am as nervous as a cat; and in one of the waiting-rooms we were passing through I had a violent fit of hysterics. I had another, even more violent, in the carriage into which we entered to cross the Seine, so Mr. De Saumarez very sensibly took me into a chemist's shop, where the *pharmacien* administered to me some restorative, of which I suspect the ingredients were sal volatile, opium, and gentian, for the draught was as bitter as gall; but I could taste the ammonia, and smell the vapid odour of laudanum. At all events the "pick-me-up" set me on my legs again. Mr. De Saumarez told me that my card had arrived at the Embassy while Lord Lyons was at church; but as the case seemed urgent, his private secretary, Mr. Sheffield, had sent the billet to His Excellency, who at once wrote instructions for one of the gentlemen of the Embassy to proceed to the Préfecture of Police, and explain who I was, and that I had been personally known for many years to the British Ambassador.

When I reached the Grand Hotel I broke down

again, not into hysterics but with sheer bodily pain ;
for I was bruised from head to foot, and in more than
one place, especially about my arms, my skin was lace-
rated.   At once my friends sent for the physician to
the Embassy, the Hon. Allen Herbert, who tended my
physical hurts, and prescribed complete rest in bed for
at least three days.   As a matter of fact I was a week
in bed ; but I had plenty of friends who came up to
condole with me and club their dinners with me.

But please to mark this.   It was about noon when I
left the cabinet of the Préfecture of Police—noon on
Sunday, the Fourth of September.   At one o'clock the
Revolution had broken out.   Before nightfall the
Second Empire was dead.   At two o'clock the mob
raided the Préfecture of Police; but the Prefect escaped their fury by flying through the garden, in the
wall of which there was a door.   Had the exasperated
populace, inflamed equally with loathing for Napoleon
III. and hatred for the Prussians, found me in my cell,
and registered at the *greffe* as being incarcerated as a
person suspected of being a spy, they would most assuredly have butchered me.

One droll incident marked the close of a drama
which to me, since midnight on the 3d, had scarcely
been of a festive nature.   From my bed, where the
next morning I was lying, tossing and tumbling about
in agony, there was visible a portion of the façade
of the Grand Opera, which in 1870 bore the inscription in large gilt letters " Académie Impériale de
Musique ;" and I could see, perched very high, a
workman, who was busily employed in scraping and
digging out the word " Impériale," and substituting
for it " Nationale."   The change had been decreed by
that Provisional Government, the members of which
were somewhat unhandsomely defined by Prince Bismarck as the " gentlemen of the pavement."

The German hosts were closing up, and every day the Parisians expected to hear of the Prussian outposts being visible at the suburbs. All kinds of wild tales were in circulation touching that notable trooper, the Prussian Uhlan. He was described as riding about quite alone, with his long lance, to the spear-end of which was attached a white pennant resembling, so the irritated Frenchman called it, *un mouchoir sale*. He would ride boldly into a village; halt at the door of the principal inn, and demand food, drink, and tobacco. And if he noticed any movement on the part of the local gendarme, the *garde-champêtre*, or the *pompiers*, to capture and hold him as a prisoner of war, he would coolly observe that seven hundred Uhlans would enter the village at noon next day, and that he had merely come prospecting for quarters for them. The rustic folk took him at his word; and this boldest of bold dragoons would ride away with German phlegm and self-possession.

CHAPTER XLVII

BESIDES Felix Whitehurst and myself, we had an ex
tra special correspondent in Paris, the Hon. Francis
Lawley; and, as it was thought inexpedient on our
part that three representatives of the *Daily Telegraph*
should be locked up in Paris during the siege, it was
agreed that I should go out of the city and proceed
to Geneva, which was on neutral territory, and wire
for further instructions to Peterborough Court. I was
nearly at the end of my tether in way of money, but
I had just sufficient to pay my bill at the Grand
Hotel, and my railway fare to Geneva viâ Lyons.
When, however, I arrived at the terminus to take the
night express the railway authorities refused to book
any heavy luggage, and, much to my disgust, I was
constrained to send the bulk of my *impedimenta* back
to the Grand Hotel. What became of it I never
knew; for just as one reads in the epigram in the
Greek anthology that Lycon set eyes on Nemestrinus's
cushion, but that Nemestrinus never set eyes upon his
cushion again, so were mine destined never again to
behold my trunks and portmanteaus, and I departed;
"travelling light," as the Americans say, with only a
small handbag of needments.

I broke the journey at Lyons: a city which had
been magnificently improved in an architectural sense
through the initiative of the much calumniated Napoleon III. When I first knew the great city of the
silk manufacture it was almost as dirty and as un-

sanitated as Marseilles, and there was scarcely a decent inn in the place; but I found the Lyons of September, 1870, adorned with streets as stately as the Avenue de l'Opéra, and possessing hotels as sumptuous as the Grand, or the Louvre, in Paris; but all that the fallen Emperor had done for the Lyonese was forgotten. The Red Flag was waving over the city; the abhorrent *tocsin* was jangling; and in the public squares, platforms covered with scarlet baize were erected, from which Republican orators, with stentorian lungs, inveighed against the iniquities of the Second Empire, and implored all good citizens to walk up and volunteer for the National Defence. It only needed a man in a fancy dress and a Roman helmet, beating at intervals a big drum, to make the spectacle twin brother to the show of a travelling dentist. More than all this, Garibaldi was expected to arrive to take the command of a Legion specially enrolled to act against the Germans. *Que diable allait-il faire dans cette galère?* Lyons, moreover, was infested by hordes of volunteer riflemen, who were called, in the slang of the day, *francs-tireurs*. The principal duties which they performed did not, so far as my experience went, go beyond loafing in the *cafés* and *brasseries*, or smoking and drinking at the little tables outside.

Re-embarking in a convenient train, I arrived at Geneva with exactly six francs seventy-five centimes in my pocket. I drove at once to the principal hotel, an excellent one; and having, fortunately, my professional card with me, in which I was described as *Correspondant Spécial du Daily Telegraph*, I went to the landlord and told him plainly the state of the case, and that, considering the disturbed state of the postal service in France, it would probably be a week or more before I could receive remittances from England. The landlord scratched his head, and looked puzzled. "But the luggage?" he said. "Monsieur has no *baggages*." I explained that my luggage had been laid under an embargo at the Paris terminus. The landlord cogitated for a while; and then went to consult his wife. He speedily returned; and said that of course I could remain as a guest at his hotel until remittances arrived, but would I be so very good as to oblige him by speaking a little English to his wife. So he introduced me to the landlady, a plump, buxom personage, who, after the exchange of a few phrases, expressed her belief that I was *tout ce qu'il y avait de plus anglais*. Her own English, by the way, was rather feeble.

I did not spend an altogether agreeable ten days at Geneva. The hotel *table d'hôte* was a very good one, and the morning *café au lait* delicious; the honey was most delectable. I drank nothing but *vin ordinaire*, which was dear, and not nice. Vevay cigars are extremely cheap, but I very soon came to the end of my few francs in purchasing these inexpensive "weeds." Finally the climax of my catastrophe was reached—as the Western farmer remarked when the caterpillars succeeded the Colorado beetles and the Hessian flies —by a cruel attack of toothache. The neighbourhood of a snow-capped mountain always gives me toothache; and I suppose Mont Blanc had something to do with my *mal de dents*. I wanted some creosote badly; but I had not a coin available for the purchase of any medicament whatsoever. However, I screwed my courage to the sticking-place; and, entering a druggist's shop described as a *Pharmacie Anglaise*, I candidly told a decidedly British individual behind the counter how I was situated, and what I wanted. He simply put his hands in his pockets and burst into a fit of genial laughter. "Why, bless my heart, Mr.

Sala ; who would think of your being hard up ? Don't you remember me ? Why, when you were last in Rome I was keeping a chemist's shop in the Corso. Here," he continued, pulling open his till, " help yourself to what you like, and welcome. I'll make you up something much better than creosote for your toothache." Without any hesitation I availed myself of the chemist's friendly offer, and borrowed five louis from him ; and he gave me something which in a short time alleviated my dental agony.

Next morning a letter of credit arrived from Peterborough Court, Fleet Street; and a day afterwards came a telegram saying : " Go to Rome. Something up." There was something very much " up " indeed in the Eternal City. So early as the last week in August, Rome had been evacuated by the French garrison, but the Imperial Government was kind enough to leave the Pope a *buona mano*, in the shape of eight thousand rifles and a few hundred shells. On the 21st, the French troops were also withdrawn from Civita Vecchia ; and all the defence that poor Pio Nono could reckon upon was that afforded by the faithful Pontifical Zouaves, and by his Swiss Guards and gendarmerie. On the 11th of September the Pope, to whom Victor Emmanuel had written a conciliatory letter, refused the terms offered him : namely, sovereignty over the Leonine City, and a splendid income. The Leonine City, so called from its having been founded in the ninth century, by Pope Leo IV., is popularly known as the " Borgo." It comprises the Castle of St. Angelo, the Hospital St. Spirito, the Vatican Palace, Museum and Gardens, and the Basilica of St. Peter. If His Holiness had had a free hand it is just possible that he might have acceded to the not unreasonable convention proposed by the King of Italy ; but everybody conversant with the affairs of modern Italy is aware that behind St. Peter's Chair there is a " Black Pope "—the General of the Jesuits. Nine-tenths of the citizens of Rome were enthusiastically in favour of union to Italy ; even in the Leonine City fifteen thousand inhabitants voted for union, but the Pope behind St. Peter's Chair, vaguely paraphrasing M. Rouher's memorable " Jamais," said " No."

I call the assumed utterance vague, because the Jesuits all astute and *rusés* as are the chiefs of that wonderful organisation, could only have indulged in a dimly speculative hope that something might turn up to lead the European Powers to oppose even by force the complete unification of Italy. There was the chance of the Republican *régime* being overturned in France, and of Monarchy being restored, either in the person of the Prince Imperial, the Comte de Paris, or the Comte de Chambord. There was the chance of an alliance between Catholic Spain, Portugal, and Austria, and even semi-Protestant Germany, to prevent the consolidation of the Kingdom of Italy. Thus, founding their hopes merely on chance, the advisers of the Pope said " No." On the 15th September the Italians occupied Civita Vecchia without resistance ; and on the 17th General Cadorna, at the head of the Italian army, crossed the Tiber at Casale. He at once sent flags of truce to General Kanzler, the Commander of the Papal Zouaves ; but that brave, if wrong-headed, German-Swiss, refused to surrender the city. On the 19th the Pope wrote to General Kanzler, directing that a merely formal defence should be made, and that bloodshed should be avoided. But the Commander of the Zouaves apparently thought it indispensable that a little gore should be spilt, for the honour of the Vatican, and his own temporary glorification. It did not seem to strike him that the odds were enormously and hopelessly against him ; and that he had no right to sacrifice the lives of even a few of the brave fellows who, for love of Mother Church, were resolved to fight under the Pontifical banners to the death. On the 20th September, Cadorna assaulted the city, and made a breach in the wall of Rome close to the Porta Pia; which, tourists will remember, is within a few paces of the garden of the British Embassy. The encounter that took place can scarcely be described as a battle; it was a scrimmage. The Italians lost about twenty-two killed, and a hundred and seventeen wounded. Of the *Papalini*, there were about fifty-five killed and wounded—in short, the Italian troops were in a thoroughly good temper at the conviction that they were bound to enter Rome triumphantly; and abstained so far as ever they were able from harming the devoted adherents of the Pope. That triumphant entry they did make; and, with the rear of the army, your humble servant came through that historic " Hole in the Wall " by the Porta Pia.

I had pleasant company with me. First, there were two gentlemen of semi-clerical mien in charge of a large barrow, drawn by a fine, strong Newfoundland dog, which vehicle was heaped high with Bibles and Prayer Books, printed in the Italian language, and sent out by the British and Foreign Bible Society. These pious gospellers made the best of their way to the Piazza di Spagna, forthwith hired a shop—they have changed their quarters since then—and the next morning the windows were one mass of open copies of the Authorised Version. The majority of the Romans were rather pleased at this display of Protestantism, which they associated with Liberalism; the majority of the women, however, averted their gaze from the, to them, detestable display of literature, which their priests assured them was composed half of downright atheism, and half of witchcraft and sorcery.

My other pleasant companion was good old Mr. Thomas Cook, the founder of Cook's Tourist Agency: an institution which, in my humble opinion, has done within the last thirty years, an immensity of moral and social good. The organisation has opened up, not only to the London middle-class Cockney but to the remotest provincial, countries and cities which, but for the " personally conducted " tour, they would never have dreamt of visiting. The devout have been able, by means of Cook, to make pilgrimages in the Holy Land; the humble student of archæology has had Italy and Egypt thrown open to him ; and Cook at present pervades the whole civilised world. I do not know when the agency, on very humble lines, was first established; but I first became aware of Mr. Thomas Cook in 1865, at Venice, to which he had " personally conducted " a troop of about fifty tourists, male and female. I was taking my wife over the Ducal Palace ; and in the cell, traditionally pointed out as the dungeon of Marino Faliero, I found, among a number of eager sightseers, a gentleman whom I had known twenty years previously as the box book-keeper at the Princess's Theatre.

" Rather surprised," he remarked, after mutual greetings, " to meet me here, eh ? " " I should not be surprised," I replied, " to meet a box book-keeper anywhere, or to see him do anything." " Ah," he rejoined, " you have got the old prejudices against our class ; you're thinking of W. R. Copeland, the manager of the Theatre Royal, Liverpool, who used to say that he was the only manager in England who could boast of having thoroughly honest money-takers, but that they all built freehold houses out of salaries of fifteen shillings a week." My ex-boxkeeper, however, was like Cæsar's wife, altogether beyond suspicion ; still I scarcely think that it would have occurred to him in his modest retirement at Walton-on-the-Naze to make a tour in North Italy had it not been for the friendly assistance of Mr. Thomas Cook.

This gentleman introduced himself to me on the common ground that we were both public servants; and he proceeded pathetically to complain of the attacks then being made on himself and his excursionists in *Blackwood's Magazine*, by a writer who assumed the *nom de guerre* of "Cornelius O'Dowd." Among the amiable things said by this censor was the expression of an opinion that the English tourists whom he saw trotting about were escaped convicts. "Cornelius O'Dowd" was, as a matter of fact, my friend Charles Lever, the author of the delightful "Harry Lorrequer," "Jack Hinton, the Guardsman," "Charles O'Malley," "Tom Burke," and a host of other vivacious novels, which, I am afraid, in this frivolous and yearning-for-sensation age, are not half so frequently read as they used to be, and who, in 1865, was Consul-General at Trieste.

He had sent me his photograph some short time before; and his countenance in the album carte bore such a haggard and woe-begone appearance, that I was justified in assuming that he was in the worst of health. Perhaps that circumstance had soured his temper, and incited him to vilify Mr. Cook, who, I believe, was so irritated by the undeserved strictures, that he made a formal complaint to the Foreign Office. Poor Charles James Lever died in 1872, at the comparatively early age of sixty-three. I do not know whether he was the originator of the droll story of the Italian hotel-keeper, whose heart leapt up when he saw no less than two omnibuses disgorging passengers at the door of his establishment; but who was reduced to a condition of extreme depression when his head waiter came mournfully to him and exclaimed that the new arrivals were "*tutti Cucchi.*" The story first appeared in the *World* newspaper; it is certainly *ben trovato*, but I doubt its entire veracity, seeing that Continental hotel-keepers who have made treaties with Cook's Agency always know when contingents of excursionists may be expected.

To make an end of my experience of Cook, I may say, that when I was in Australia, one of his agents called on me at Sydney, to ask for some information with regard to New Zealand, to which fair country he proposed to organise excursions from India; and again, so soon as I arrived in Calcutta, Cook's agent met me on the steamer in the Flûgh, found an English-speaking *baboo*, or body servant, for me, and procured me a series of railway tickets for a progress through the Three Presidencies.

All this I am perfectly aware is a digression, but occasional digressions are inevitable in a work of this nature. I have never kept a continuous diary; and it is impossible to remember everything in exact sequence; consequently when a name of an individual to whom some public interest attaches occurs to me, I tell my readers what I know about him. Farewell, Mr. Thomas Cook, now defunct! If there ever was a public benefactor you were one. I have never joined a "personally-conducted" tour; but when I travel abroad I always provide myself with Cook's railway tickets, which save you a large amount of trouble; and, moreover, Cook's money-changing offices give you, as a rule, much better exchange than you can obtain at the local *bureau de change*.

Exciting, but wholly pacific, weeks did I pass in Rome, after the entry of the Italian army. Some of the Papal Zouaves had taken refuge in the nunnery of the Trinità di Monte, where they were hospitably sheltered in the church by the good Sisters; but Gen-

eral Cadorna and his men had not the slightest animosity against these brave men, who, although they
were in a certain sense mercenaries, had mostly fought
purely for conscience sake. On the 22d September
the foreign Legionaries were suffered to march out of
Rome, with the honours of war: an act of courtesy
which I am sorry to say they did not reciprocate, since
they gibed, jeered, and swore at the Italians in their
passage through the streets. The Austrian soldiery,
I remember, behaved much better when they evacuated Verona, in 1866. The populace did not insult the
Tedeschi; they seemed to have a premonition of the
subsequent saying of a well-known Italian statesman,
that the Germans had only got to go away for the
Italians to discover what good fellows they were, and
at this day much of the trade in Venice is in Austrian
hands. At Verona, as the Croats and Magyars and
the Austrians marched by, the crowd contented themselves with shouting, " *Viva Italia !* " whereupon one
stalwart grenadier, holding ùp a birdcage containing a
canary, which he was carrying away as a souvenir of
sunny Italy, shouted, " *Viva la bella famiglia !* "—a
conventional cry, meaning, " Long live everybody,"
to which the many-headed responded by a shout of
" *Viva il canarino !* "—" Long live the canary bird."
So all things went off smoothly and pleasantly.

But what would you have? Circumstances alter
temper as well as cases. In 1864 I was riding with a
Federal General and his staff through the streets of
Culpepper Court House in Virginia, nine-tenths of the
inhabitants of which were sympathisers with the Confederate cause. We were received by the ladies of the
town, who, arrayed in the oldest and shabbiest of costumes they could have collected from their wardrobes,
stood confronting us on their doorsteps, or " stoops."
First they made the most hideous faces at us, and then

they turned their backs upon us, and re-entered their houses. The Confederates did worse than that at Baltimore ; they used to have miniature union flags sewn into the " hinder stomachs " of their pantaloons, and open their " claw hammers " wide while a Federal regiment marched past.

I went straight in Rome to the good old Hotel d'Angleterre, in the Via Bocca di Leone. The Silenzi family, to whom this admirably conducted house, as well as the Hotel de Russie, close to the Porta del Popolo, and another large hotel in the Piazza di Spagna belong, are " black "—*nerissimi*—I mean ultra-clerical. Monks and priests and *monsignori* are continually looking in at the Albergo d'Inghilterra and a couple of years since I was honoured by a visit there from His Eminence Cardinal Vaughan ; yet the bulk of the guests at the " Angleterre " have always been, within my experience, Protestants. Now and again an Irish Roman Catholic priest, or a Secret Chamberlain of the Pope has made his appearance at the *table d'hôte,* and during the winter seasons certain suites of apartments are occupied by noble Spanish families, necessarily Catholics. For the rest, I could enumerate at least a dozen Anglican bishops and archdeacons, and I know not how many rectors and curates, who have taken up their quarters at an hotel, the *cuisine* of which is the best in Rome ; while in its smoking-room you hear the best talk in Europe—and I have heard some very good talk in my time.

As I have said, the period of my stay in Rome in 1870 was most exciting ; since, every day, from the Italian point of view, there was something to be enthusiastic and jubilant about. On the 22d of September a mass meeting was held in the Colosseum — which, thenceforward, was to be given up to archæological explorations, *vice* the Stations of the Cross—to choose some forty eminent citizens to form a junta, or Provisional Government, the President of this body, approved by General Cadorna, being the Duke Gaetani. On the 30th, to the intense delight of the Romans, a proclamation from General Masi, the Commandant de Place, was headed by the anciently historic "S. P. Q. R." It must not, however, be thought that the four magic initials had even, when the Papal crown and the cross-keys appeared on all official documents, wholly vanished from public Roman ken. If you looked at the official journal, you would mark from time to time notices from the "Senator of Rome," a cloudy personage, having his office in the Capitol, and headed, "S. P. Q. R." These announcements, however, did not usually contain matters of any more importance than the regulation of the prices of beef and bread in the public market.

On the 2d of October took place the plebiscitum. Out of the total number of votes, 233,681 were cast for union with the Kingdom of Italy, and only 1,507 were against. How many oaths of allegiance did Talleyrand, in 1830, say that he had sworn? Thirteen, I think; but then Charles Maurice de Talleyrand-Périgord was seventy-six when he pledged his allegiance to Louis Philippe. I am not a diplomatist, I am not a wit, and I never had Carême for my cook, yet, before I was forty-two I had witnessed five plebiscita :—one for the election of Louis Napoleon as President of the French Republic ; a second one for his election to the French throne ; a third one in confirmation of the desire of the French to remain under Imperial rule ; and two in Italy : one at Venice and the other in Rome.

The Pope issued a protest about once in every forty-eight hours ; and when His Holiness was not protesting, Cardinal Antonelli kept the ball rolling. On the 9th of October, General La Marmora made his public entry into Rome as viceroy; and proclaimed that Pio Nono should be confirmed in his sovereign rights as Head of the Church; but, naturally, the Papacy behind St. Peter's Chair were not satisfied with this statement. The Pope was advised to refuse acceptance of the annual dotation of fifty thousand crowns, voted him by the Italian Parliament, nor has that dotation ever been accepted; and a fresh protest was made by Cardinal Antonelli, when it was announced, that on the arrival of Victor Emmanuel, His Majesty would occupy the whilom Papal Palace of the Quirinal.

Soon after the arrival of La Marmora, there was a grand review of the Italian army, in the Campo di Marte, at which the populace shrieked themselves hoarse with cries of "*Viva Italia! Viva Vittorio Emanuele, Rè eletto in Campidoglio;*" but these exultant cries were, to my mind, altogether surpassed by the utterance of a little Roman street-boy, aged, I should say, about nine. When the horse artillery came trotting by, this brat, capering and scampering to keep pace with the horses, yelled "*Viva la nostra artigleria!*"— his artillery, forsooth! But after a few repetitions of the patriotic cry, habit was too strong for the urchin, and he concluded his antics by turning a rapid succession of "cart-wheels."

Soon after this imposing spectacle, I was recalled to England. The siege of Paris was still in progress; the Franco-German War almost entirely absorbed public opinion; and beyond the mere fact that the Italians had entered Rome, and that Victor Emmanuel was literally, as well as theoretically, elected King in the capital, the British public did not care much about Roman affairs.

It is not my business to be a moralist, and I have studiously endeavoured, in the course of this book, to avoid bombasting my pages with reflections on the political events which I have witnessed. But as I happen to have a considerable infusion of Italian blood in my veins; as the language and the literature of Italy are as familiar to me as those of my own country; and as I once remarked, in the speech of my father's language, at a banquet of the Italian Chamber of Commerce, at which the Duke of Aosta was present, that I had personally known Italy in her darkest season of degradation and slavery :—when the infernal foreigner was in Lombardy, in the Dominio Veneto, and at Ancona; and the Papal Legates and the Papal soldiery were at Bologna and in the States of the Church—I think I may be pardoned if I say a very few words about the ethics of the occupation of Rome by General Cadorna and his troops, on September 20th, 1870. In strict morality, perhaps, the act was indefensible. Victor Emmanuel was not at war with the Pope, nor had any Italian subjects been subjected to ill-usage by the Papal Government. Again, by the withdrawal of the French garrison, Rome was practically defenceless, since it was obvious that the small contingent of Ultramontane mercenaries were utterly incompetent to make head against the prodigious forces which could be brought against them by the King of Italy.

They say that all is fair in love, war, and electioneering; perhaps the same may be said of politics. The Cabinet of Victor Emmanuel saw that they had a fine opportunity before them; and the coast being clear, they availed themselves of that opportunity, lest the action they must have so long contemplated should be impeded; and perhaps wholly frustrated, by the jealousies of other great European Powers. Furthermore, they might have pleaded that by the prompt occupation of Rome, they prevented the outbreak of insurrection in the city, and consequent effusion of blood. You must remember that 233,000 Roman citizens voted at the plebiscitum for union with Italy. Those two hundred thousand and odd supporters of Victor Emmanuel would not certainly have long remained quiet under Papal rule; they would have broken out in revolt; they would not have been spared by the Papal Government; and after a certain amount of slaughter, the Italian Government would have been absolutely compelled to intervene.

Perhaps after saying this, I had best refer the ethics of the question to some English Debating Society. It would not be by any means an uninteresting topic for discussion. After that our budding Gladstones and Beaconsfields might inquire as to what right William of Orange had to invade the United Kingdom of Great Britain and Ireland. He was not at war with King James II., to whom he was bound by the closest family ties; he was not called to invade us by the people of England as a body. He only came at the request of an association of powerful Whig families; and his coming was eminently distasteful to the majority of the Anglican clergy, and to the two great Universities. He was hailed as a Deliverer by the Scotch Presbyterians; but the Highlanders were almost unanimously against him; and he was certainly not wanted by the great body of the Irish people; but he saw his opportunity and availed himself of it.

When they had disposed of this question, the Debating Society might discuss whether Napoleon the Great was justified in returning to France from Elba. The Allied Sovereigns in their manifesto, in which they delivered him over to public vengeance, *la vindicte publique*, insinuating thereby that they would be very much obliged to anybody who would murder the invader, declared that his claim to existence had been nullified by his violation of the compact into which he had entered at Fontainebleau. It so happened that the compact had already been violated by the Government of Louis XVIII., which, with scandalous dishonesty, had omitted to pay him the stipulated revenue settled upon him. It was also a matter of notoriety that the diplomatists assembled at Vienna were contemplating the kidnapping of their dangerous neighbour, and his deportation to the island of St. Helena, or to some other far remote spot. Finally, Napoleon was kept constantly alive to the facts that the Bourbons were desperately unpopular in Paris; that the army were almost to a man enthusiastically favourable to him; that the judiciary and the bureaucracy were as willing to serve under Imperial as under Royal rule; and that, save in the South, the mass of the people, in spite of the repeated decimations of the Conscription, preferred his rule to that of the priest-ridden Bourbons, with their haughty emigrant aristocracy, and their swarms of Jesuit missionaries. This I hope is the last digression on which I shall venture.

CHAPTER XLVIII

THERE was plenty to do in my old line of leader-writing directly I got back to London; and the recent experience which I had gathered both in France and England was of great service to me in my articles. Of public events in England, requiring special narration, there were but few. Early in 1871, I went, for the first time in my life, to law; quite unwittingly, but, strange to say, with a quite unexpected amount of success. One day, a near and dear friend, whose advice I have always valued and generally followed, came to me and said, " George, look here; you must bring an action for libel against the publishers of this book." He handed me a little volume entitled " Men of Letters Honestly Criticised," the author of which was a certain Mr. Hain Friswell. I turned to the article relating to myself, and found so many pages of attenuated " skimble-skamble," which, although sufficiently ill-natured, did not strike me as being at all libellous from a legal point of view.

Here and again were innuendoes that I had squandered very large sums which I had gained; and that I had been repeatedly held up to odium as a sensational, foolish, and ungrammatical writer by the *Saturday Review*, and other influential journals. With regard to the manner in which my income had been expended, I am not aware that I had been very lavish in any respect, save buying a great many more rare books and china than I wanted, and giving away a good deal of money to people, the majority of whom naturally have requited me by the basest ingratitude; and besides, what I had done with the income which I had laboriously earned was my business, and not that of the author of "Men of Letters Honestly Criticised." Touching my being a "sensational, foolish, and ungrammatical writer," I have over and over again criticised myself much more harshly than any of my critics have done. I know perfectly well that, as an author, I belong to the second class; but I thank God that I have always been ready to recognise and to acclaim authors of the first class.

The most malevolent, and withal the drollest, of the aspersions contained in Mr. Friswell's book, had reference to that unfortunate nose of mine. How it got split open with a diamond ring, I have already told my readers; but that nose has been since a Slawkenbergian one, and has brought me alternately good and evil fortune. The doctor of a Life Insurance Company once refused to pass me in consequence of my nose; but I once made a little capital out of it at a crowded public meeting at which I was presiding at St. Martin's Hall, Long Acre. "Where did you get your blooming nose?" asked an unfriendly member of the audience. "That organ," I replied, "is permanently blushing at the vices of the age;" upon which the meeting gave me three cheers. But my nose became to Mr. Friswell a permanent worry and matter for discussion. It was to him as King Charles I.'s head was to Mr. Dick in the celebrated Memorial. He insisted, by imputation, that it was a Bacchanalian nose, a dissolute nose, a depraved nose, and perhaps a seditious one.

"Is it worth while?" I asked, laying down the book with a laugh. "Yes," replied my friend, "it *is* worth while. You must go to George Lewis at once." So off we went to the offices of Messrs. Lewis and Lewis, in Ely Place, Holborn ; where I was cordially received by Mr.—now, and worthily so, Sir—George Lewis, who said that there *was* something in the case, and that he would at once issue a writ against Messrs. Hodder and Stoughton, a most respectable firm of publishers, who certainly were not in the habit of issuing libellous productions :—their commercial staple being theology. I may here mention that I had long been acquainted with Mr. James Hain Friswell, a gentleman of about my own age, a most voluminous writer, who is chiefly remembered by a work called " The Gentle Life," a republication, I believe, of certain essays which he wrote in the dear old *Family Herald*—that joy to scores upon scores of thousands of innocent English households. " The Gentle Life " was an especial favourite with the lamented Prince Leopold, Duke of Albany.

Mr. Friswell was a lucid, and sometimes incisive, writer, and if his style was built on any model, it was, I should say, on that of Thackeray. When I first knew him, he had been an engraver on gold and silver plate, and was an assistant of Messrs. Howell and James, in Regent Street. He had, at the same time, a decided capacity for literature, and drifted into that uncertain and delightful profession. On more than one occasion, I had been enabled to do him some slight service—in particular, having to go abroad on some *Daily Telegraph* mission, while I was writing my weekly gossip in the *Illustrated London News*, I made over my " Echoes " to him ; and he wrote them, I have no doubt, in a very sprightly and amusing fashion for a good many weeks.

In the interval between the commencement of the litigation and the trial, I repeatedly puzzled myself as to what reason I can possibly have given Mr. Friswell to bear me any ill-will. Ultimately, two or three re-

mote causes for such malevolence dawned upon me. I
remembered that he was very much piqued when I
once inadvertently told him that Hepworth Dixon, the
editor of the *Athenæum*, always, but, I believe, quite
innocently, persisted in calling him " Mr. Frizzle."
Then the guiltier consciousness arose in me that I had
once suggested in private conversation that Hain Friswell had acquired his knowledge of the Latin language
by engraving the heraldic mottoes of the nobility and
gentry on spoons and forks. Finally I remembered,
that when I was in Spain for the first time, my library
had been sold by auction, and that possibly Mr. Hain
Friswell, who was my near neighbour in Great Russell Street—I living at the time in Guildford Street—
had been present at the sale, and had turned over the
leaves of my copy of " The Gentle Life." I have a
craze for annotating my books; and it is just within
the domain of likelihood that, on certain pages of Mr.
Friswell's masterpiece, I may have pencilled such dis-
courteous remarks as " ineffable donkey," "atrocious
cad," "sciolist," " humbug," " rot," and the like ; but
I had never borne the gentleman any malice ; I rather
liked him than otherwise, for his manner was smooth,
and his conversation agreeable.

Not more than a month elapsed before the case came
on for trial, which took place in the Court of Queen's
Bench, Guildhall, before Lord Chief Justice Cockburn
and a special jury. Mr. Montague Chambers, Q.C.,
was against me—the name of his junior I forget. My
counsel was the late Serjeant Parry ; and his junior
was Mr. Montagu Williams. Lawsuits, in those days,
rarely reached the calamitous length which, at the
present day, is so common. My case came on at ten
a.m., and it was finished just before one p.m. The
Serjeant, after the case had been opened by Montagu
Williams, made a brilliant and witty address to the

jury, but somehow or another he could not keep clear of my unfortunate nose. He said that its discolouration was due to exposure to many foreign climates. Would that Mr. George Lewis had inserted in the Serjeant's brief a note to the effect that the nose had been bifurcated " in a fite." There were not many witnesses. For the plaintiff—myself—my solicitors had thought fit to call Mr. Charles Dickens, Junior, who could only testify that he had known me ever since he had been a boy at school at Eton. Next came Mr. Edward Lawson, who gave evidence to the fact that I was an old and zealous member of the staff of the *Daily Telegraph*, that I had been half over Europe on their service ; that I had written thousands of articles for them ; and that, as one of the proprietors and editor of that paper, he could vouch for my undeviating punctuality, and for my financial integrity. Mr. Montague Chambers, for the defence, was not a very bitter opponent. His *cheval de bataille* was the reading of a long passage from an essay of mine in *All the Year Round*, which the *Saturday Review* had inveighed against as sensational rubbish. But the jury, to my amusement, seemed to be rather pleased at my essay, and laughed heartily at some of the paragraphs.

Mr. Serjeant Parry having replied, the Lord Chief Justice summed up, as I thought, somewhat in my favour, and then the jury retired to consider their verdict. " You'll get a hundred and fifty pounds for certain," whispered George Lewis to me, sitting by my side in the well of the Court. " You'll get two hundred pounds," said my neighbour on the other side, Mr. John Maxwell, the husband of Miss Braddon. Maxwell had wished to be called as a witness, because he wanted to say that in the numerous and heavy pecuniary transactions he had had with me, he had always found me exact to a pound, exact to a shilling, exact to a penny. But Mr. Edward Lawson's evidence in this particular was so straightforward, and apparently so satisfactory to the judge and the jury, that my counsel had not thought it necessary to put Maxwell in the box. At the expiration of twenty minutes the jury returned into Court. " Verdict for the plaintiff. Damages Five Hundred Pounds."

Why I should have got such a large sum I have always been unable to determine. Perhaps my white waistcoat, and a rose in my button-hole—it was winter, but my florist, now of forty years' standing, good Mrs. Buck, of Covent Garden, always took care that I should have a fresh button-hole every morning—had something to do with the favourable judgment of the jury. Sometimes I have fancied that I made a favourable impression on the foreman, who to my thinking was a merry man, and on whom I kept my eye throughout the trial ; but probably my success was mainly due to the eloquence and impartial summing up of the Lord Chief Justice, whose silver voice in polished periods I can hear now. Meanwhile, the unhappy Mr. Hain Friswell was tearing his hair—so at least I was told—in the adjacent Guildhall library. I say unhappy, because Messrs. Hodder and Stoughton were, not unnaturally, of opinion that, as they had not written the libel, Mr. Friswell, and not themselves, ought to pay the damages and costs. They were paid, however, but by whom I know not. Mr. Friswell was afflicted by continuous bad health towards the close of his career, and he died in 1878.

Five hundred pounds damages! Confound them ! They never did me the slightest amount of good. First a firm of solicitors discovered that I was in their debt for a bill of costs for £80, contracted some years previously, and not with respect to any matter of litigation, and this I paid with resignation. Then a worthy tradesman, who had supplied me with a large quantity of china, earthenware, and glass when I furnished my house in Guildford Street, remembered that I owed him £150, and that the debt was within a very few weeks of annihilation by the Statute of Limitations. Him also did I pay. On this followed even more irritating, though not pecuniarily afflictive, applications from all sorts and conditions of people, imploring, and sometimes bullying, me to lend them large or small sums of money. Blackmailing had not then reached the dimensions of a fine art; or perhaps I should have been the victim of a little *chantage*. These wretched damages so preyed upon my mind that, to relieve me, the *Daily Telegraph* sent me to Berlin to witness the opening of the German Parliament.

The function was to me a deeply interesting one. The session was opened in the famous White Hall of the Schloss, and I had the advantage of hearing a speech from Prince Bismarck. The delivery of the ex-Chancellor seemed to me extremely rapid; but, indifferent German scholar as I have always been, I could understand almost all he said. In particular did I notice the occasional shrillness of the Chancellor's voice, all the more remarkable from the massive frame of the orator. We had, of course, a resident correspondent in the Prussian capital, and, under his auspices, I saw a good deal of manners and customs in Berlin. Specially do I remember a *Tabaks Collegium* and Beer Symposium of students of the University. Considering the amount of smoke from porcelain pipes, by which I was surrounded for four hours, I only wonder that on the following morning I did not find myself transformed into a kippered salmon or a Yarmouth bloater.

As for the beer, which they drank incessantly by the *Seidel*, I may say that I consider beer to be one of the most delicious of beverages, but that I have never been able to drink it with impunity. The courteous *Burschen*, however, recognised, although they may have secretly reprehended my infirmity in this respect; and I was regaled with hock and allowed to smoke cigars instead of a pipe. They told me what "Philistine" meant, together with much more student lore; and then, about eleven by the clock, we began to sing songs. First came the "Wacht am Rhein;" next "Prinz Eugen, der alte Ritter;" then Körner's "Gebet," and his "Song of the Sword," and then a young fellow full six feet high, with auburn hair, sang with great solemnity the exquisitely humorous Studenten Lied about the bibulous party who, for three whole days, did nothing but drink beer at a tavern at Ascalon; until at length he lay stiff and stark as a poker on a marble bench. I was asked to sing. I did not venture on the Teutonic; but I gave my friends, in English, Mrs. Abdy's beautiful song, "The Rhine," founded on the anecdote that when the German armies, returning victorious, from the occupation of Paris, in 1814, arrived at the bridge of Kehl and beheld their beloved river, they uttered one tremendous and unanimous shout, "Der Rhein!—der Rhein!" and rushed forward at the double quick to salute the historic stream.

Another interesting social service did our resident correspondent in Berlin render me. He obtained a permit to visit the fortress of Spandau, where there were confined as prisoners of war, some thousands of French soldiers, most of them belonging to the unfortunate, and, perhaps, betrayed, garrison of Metz. I found these brave men comfortably housed in light and cheerful day-rooms, and spacious and well-ventilated dormitories, and was present at their dinner, which was abundant in the way of boiled meat, suet pudding, and vegetables. I was informed, however, that breaches of the regulations were visited by confinement in the casements of the citadel, and by restricted rations. Some hundreds of the captives, after dinner, took to card-playing ; and, as most of them were penniless, the loser paid his indebtedness by receiving a certain number of playful pats on the cheek from the winner. Their principal want was tobacco ; and my friend and myself had come provided with a good stock both of tobacco for pipes, and cheap cigars, which were almost rapturously received when they were distributed.

CHAPTER XLIX

RETURNING to London, I went "into collar again," and did not again leave England, save for my usual autumnal vacation at Homburg, during the rest of the year 1871. I was present professionally at the opening by the Prince of Wales, of the first International Exhibition at South Kensington, and at the opening, by Her Majesty the Queen, on the 21st of June, of the new St. Thomas's Hospital.

Everybody knows what took place towards the close of the year 1871. At the opening of St. Thomas's Hospital, Mr. Ernest Hart, by whom I was seated, close to the throne, observed that the Prince of Wales was not well; he was continually sneezing. Some weeks afterwards it was reported that His Royal Highness was out of health, and then, for many weeks, he was afflicted by a dreadful illness, somewhat resembling that which had carried off his illustrious father. The death of the Prince Consort had been altogether a surprise, but week after week did the whole British nation tremble lest a fatal end should come to the illness of the beloved heir to the Crown ; and one great sigh of relief and joy arose from the national heart when the crisis was successfully passed, and when the news ran like wildfire through the land that the Prince, sitting up in bed, had asked for a glass of Norfolk ale. I was present at the memorable Thanksgiving Service in St. Paul's Cathedral, on the 22d of February, 1872. The Dean considerately set apart for

the representatives of the press a spacious gallery,
whence we could witness the entire proceedings,
which I refrain from describing in detail, seeing that
they can be found in the " Annual Register," or in any
file of London newspapers. It was, so far as costume
went, a superb spectacle, and the Judges in their scarlet, the Lord Mayor and Corporation in their robes,
the clergy in their canonicals, with a plentiful admixt-
ure of naval and military uniforms, made the bravest
of brave shows : to say nothing of the crowning
glories of the presence of the Sovereign, the Prince of
Wales and the Royal Family, and a stately Court.

Still, the environments of this gorgeous array were
cold and devoid of an essential element of splendour—
bright light. St. Paul's can never be anything more,
so far as its interior is concerned, than a frigid and
poorly-illumined edifice. Dr. Johnson likened it to a
" sun-dial in a grave." The architecture and the statuary are alike chilly, and lacking in the picturesque,
and although a good deal has been done within recent
years in partial mosaic decorations, it is not probable
that in our time, at least, sufficient sums will be obtain-
able for completely garnishing the superb structure,
that is to say, by covering the whole of the walls by
mosaics, gilding the capitals and the flutings of the
columns, draping the side chapels with handsome
tapestry, and laying down handsome Oriental carpets
on the floor of the nave. This is a dream, of course;
but what is life but a dream, with a good many night-
mares *par dessus le marché?*

I saw a good deal of the Claimant during 1872. So
far back as May, 1871, his pretensions having been re-
sisted on behalf of Sir Henry Tichborne, a minor, and
son of Sir Alfred Tichborne, an action of ejectment
was brought by the Claimant in the Court of Common
Pleas, presided over by Lord Chief Justice Bovill.

The Claimant was examined during twenty-two days. It was adjourned on the fortieth day and resumed in November, and the case on behalf of the Claimant was closed just before Christmas. He was constantly at Watts Phillips's house, and at Mr. Bloxam's; and I remember once dining with him and the late Mr. Serjeant Ballantine at the house of Mr. Labouchere, who then resided in Bolton Street, Piccadilly. The senior Member for Northampton had, upon occasion, a curious way of directly putting things; and over the walnuts and the wine—of which our host was not a partaker—he startled us all by coolly asking his obese guest, "Are you Arthur Orton?" "Good heavens! Mr. Labouchere," exclaimed the stout litigant, "what do you mean?" "Oh, nothing in particular," quoth Mr. Labouchere; "help yourself to some more claret."

On the 17th March, 1872, things in this extraordinary lawsuit came to a crisis. A great meeting of the Claimant's supporters was held at a fashionable hotel in Jermyn Street, where he had for some time resided; and I was present, but in an altogether neutral capacity. I never clearly understood the rights or wrongs of this Tichborne case, and probably I never shall. About two o'clock a messenger arrived with the alarming intelligence that the Jury in the Court of Common Pleas had expressed themselves satisfied that the Claimant was not Sir Roger Tichborne, and that he was consequently nonsuited. The perturbation among the gentlemen who had assisted the Claimant, not only with advice, but with pecuniary means for carrying on his action, was intense. Tichborne bonds for very large sums of money, and redeemable when the Claimant should be placed in possession of his title and estates, had been freely taken up; and one of the largest holders of these bonds was, I remember, an Italian gentleman, engaged in some mercantile or financial business in the

City. It was edifying to watch his countenance at the recital of the news from Westminster Hall. First he turned very white, and then very blue. There was a refreshment buffet in the room ; and the investor helped himself to two bumpers of sherry, remarking that that was probably all he should ever get for his investment. The generous vintage of Xeres brought at least some crimson to his cheeks, and made him look for the moment quite warm and comfortable.

Presently the Claimant joined us. The mysterious personage did not look in the least discomfited ; nor did his speech betray the slightest trace of agitation. He spoke quietly, composedly, and even cheerfully ; and commenting on some of the hostile evidence which had been adduced against him, chatted about " his brother officers," and how he and they used to fish " our Hampstead waters." A remarkable person, and the coolest of cards, anyhow! On the following day he was arrested and lodged in Newgate, to be tried for perjury ; and on the 9th of April he was indicted as Thomas Castro, alias Arthur Orton, for perjury and forgery, and his trial in the Court of Queen's Bench before Chief Justice Cockburn and Justices Mellor and Lush, began on the 23d of April. Up to the 27th of June, above a hundred witnesses had sworn that the Claimant was not Roger Tichborne, and about forty that he was Arthur Orton.

But I was not to see him again—and then only once —for a very long time. Throughout 1872 I had been in painfully ailing health, and was sickening, so I had mournful reason to augur, for some great malady. I continued, however, to work with dogged perseverance ; and there is nothing to record touching the daily tale of bricks, which, in the way of leading articles, I had to construct. The year dragged itself out in physical pain and mental misery ; and the New Year brought no amelioration in my condition. On the 9th of January, Napoleon III. died, at Chislehurst, and had I been at death's door—that is to say, if I had only been able to crawl in and out of a carriage—I should have thought it my duty to my proprietors and to myself to attend the funeral of the ex-Emperor. It was settled that Edward Dicey and myself should drive down to Camden Place in a brougham and pair early in the morning, as a tremendous rush on the railway train was anticipated. Dicey had already been down to the house of death to see the lying-in-state of the deceased monarch, whose embalmed corpse—the moustaches duly waxed, and the cheeks slightly rouged—lay in the coffin, visible to all who passed through the mortuary chamber, which had been converted into a *chapelle ardente*. Throughout the day, which was one of the most arduous I ever passed, we had all of us to be grateful to the good offices rendered to us by Father Goddard, the chaplain of the little Roman Catholic Church at Chislehurst, and by a most energetic and intelligent officer of police, the late Superintendent Mott.

The ceremony in the church was exceedingly simple: indeed, it might have been the obsequies of a private gentleman. The church was draped in black, and there were many lighted candles in tall candelabra; but there was no heraldic or Imperial display ; nothing to remind you that the deceased had been Emperor of the French, and that he was a Knight of the Most Noble Order of the Garter. The young Prince Imperial was in plain evening dress; but he wore the broad red riband and star of the Grand Cross of the Legion of Honour. Looking at the poor bereaved lad, I could not help remembering the quiet rebuke given by his father when he was a captive at the Luxembourg, awaiting trial after the Boulogne attempt, to a pert *juge d'instruction*, who asked him by what right he was wearing the insignia of a Grand Cross of the Legion of Honour. " The founder of the Order," replied Prince Louis Napoleon, "gave them to me when I was in my cradle." The founder of the Order was Napoleon the Great.

But how difficult, nay, how almost impossible, it is to exclude droll images from the most solemn scenes, and banish irreverent thoughts from the mournfullest cogitations! I really was sorry for Napoleon III., who had been kind to me, whose career I had followed with abiding interest, and who, notwithstanding all the errors which he committed, did, in his time of supremacy, an immensity of good to the French people. It happened while the service was being performed that a colleague sitting next to me asked the name of the particular function of the Roman Church which was being celebrated. I replied that I did not exactly know; whereupon I heard a voice, with a pronounced German accent, just behind me saying, " Why, of course, it is a Low Mass." I turned round and beheld my old acquaintance Herr Meyer Lutz, of the Gaiety Theatre, to whom the musical part of the arrangements had been confided. Imagine a momentary vision of Toole in *Wat Tyler*, and Miss Nellie Farren as Sir Reginald Plantagenet rising before me, even while the choir were chanting the awful strophes of the *Dies Iræ !*

My presence at the funeral of Napoleon III. was my last appearance in public for many months. It was a raw, bleak January day, and I went home with a chill; and on the next day some slight touches of fever supervened. Then I fell ill in right earnest with a dreadful malady called erythema. The doctors know well enough what it is; to the laity I need only say that I turned from head to foot a reddish purple, and that I wore from January to July the shirt of Nessus. I tried hard to go on with my work; and, at my urgent request, my friends in Fleet Street sent me to Brompton, one of the leading members of their Parliamentary reporting staff. He took down in shorthand a review, which I dictated to him, of Lord Lytton's posthumous novel, "Kenelm Chillingly." When I had finished that article, it was decided by my medical attendants that I must have for some time complete rest from intellectual employment. They could not, in my judgment, have arrived at a more imprudent decision. I was helpless enough physically, Heaven knows; but the machine of my mind had not run down. The doctors arbitrarily stopped the driving-wheel; and the cessation of literary work did not give me that relief which they hoped and expected that I should enjoy. I did not go mad; but I had frequent fits due alike to bodily pain and mental anguish, and what with my howlings and shriekings, and the need I was in of constant help and supervision, I am really astonished that I did not drive my poor wife and my faithful servants out of their senses.

My friends in Fleet Street wanted to send Sir William Gull to me; but another friend, Dr. J. P. Steele, then one of the sub-editors of the *Lancet*, and who had been a staunch ally of James Hannay, when the latter was editing the *Edinburgh Courant*, brought me Dr. Anstie, the editor of the *Practitioner*, and a physician who was then steadily rising to eminence in his beneficent profession. Large as my acquaintance with doctors had been, I never met a more resourceful man than Dr. Anstie, who died, you will remember, of blood-poisoning while he was attending to the sanitation of an orphanage in the suburbs of London. Nothing discouraged him; nothing made him lose hope or heart. I was the most troublesome of patients

—a sick leopard, plentifully spotted, would have been about the fittest image for me;—but he did not mind my cries and objurgations at all; and when one experiment had failed, very cheerfully set about trying another. To exclude the air from my burning body was, in his opinion, the grand desideratum; and for that purpose I was successively painted all over with collodion *flexile ;* with flowers of sulphur; with white of egg, and with Canada balsam. Ugh! no more of my aches and pains!

The mental trouble was the greatest. The nerves of my mind, so to speak, were continually on the stretch; and this tension resulted in a protracted attack of insomnia. Thousands of lines did I recite night after night, week after week, from Scott, from Byron, from Spenser, from Virgil, and from Victor Hugo; but no sleep came. Dr. Anstie essayed hypnotic after hypnotic; he tried the old French remedy—musk pills taken every quarter of an hour; he tried chloral; syrup of poppies in old ale; and how many hundreds of drops of laudanum in Batley's solution of opium I took in one dose I do not care to tell, because many of my readers, I have little doubt, would think I was not telling the truth. A kind lady sent me a hop pillow, but that did no good; then we tried Dr. Franklin's device of changing from bed to bed—useless. At last Dr. Anstie came with a little golden syringe and injected morphia into my left arm. The hypodermic *pharmakon* did not give me sound sleep, but it sent me into a feathery, painless, and almost balmy state. Everybody was very good to me. Dr. Anstie came every morning; and Dr. Steele was with me three, and sometimes four, times a day. Watts Phillips was constant in his visits, nor did Mr. Labouchere forget to come to see me.

I was so bad at the beginning of the summer that

Dr. Anstie, for the first time almost reduced to despair, thought it best that I should try the soft air of St. Leonards; so the railway company sent the invalid carriage for me; and my miserable self, together with the whole household and loyal Dr. Steele, who had resolved to see us installed, went down to a pretty furnished house which we had taken on some high lands above the charming watering-place of St. Leonards. How I hated the lovely place! The sight of the pretty shops of the Marina was horrible to my view, and the little lambs skipping about in the pastures called Bo-Peep, looked to me like so many small wolf-cubs. Why? I had lost the use of my limbs. The continual bedevilments to which my frame had been subjected, had ended in partial paralysis of the vaso-motor nerves; so when I took carriage exercise, I had to be placed horizontally on a mattress laid on a plank; then they covered me up with bed-clothes, and I had as literally a bed-room on wheels as though I had been a passenger on board a Pullman sleeping car.

This agreeable state of affairs went on to the end of July, and as the enthusiastically affectionate Steele persisted in publishing weekly bulletins of my health, or rather the lack of it, in the *Lancet*, a large number of my friends must have been expecting my speedy decease. In fact, an esteemed brother journalist attached to an influential Conservative daily paper, told me that, after reading one of the bulletins, he had pigeon-holed a concise memoir of myself, which would have duly appeared had I gone to the bad. " It is at the office still," he said artlessly, "and it is not likely it will ever be lost; since I wrote it in a penny washing book with a red cover, with a nice white label and your name on it." I am sorry to say that the single gentleman who lived in his own house next door to our furnished one, was so disturbed by my daily and

nightly groans and shrieks, that he actually had to
shift his quarters to South Kensington, London. I
verily believe that the single gentleman thought that
his next door neighbour was a lunatic. However, I
was sane enough to appreciate the services of Dr. Bagshaw, to whose care I had been made over by Dr.
Anstie. Dr. Bagshaw thought that he could do something with me by means of galvanism, and thrice a
week he used to operate on my extremities with an
apparatus of which I could make neither head nor tail,
but which, in about a month gave me back the use of
my lower limbs.

Growing gradually stronger, I was despatched to
Brighton. I could walk, but with great difficulty; and
proceeding to the Grand Hotel, I deliberately engaged
a room in the very topmost storey; so that I might
painfully crawl up and down stairs, resting on occasion
and then resuming the crawl, in order that my mus-
cles might be gradually strengthened. I wholly ab-
jured the use of the lift and kept my pledge. Luckily
enough, one afternoon, looking through an open window on the hotel staircase, I became aware of a gentleman in a short jacket, black silk continuations, white
stockings, and half boots, who was walking round and
round a paved area which had been laid out for the
purposes of a skating rink, a site now covered by the
Hotel Metropole. I recognised the "walkist" as
the well-known professional American pedestrian, Mr.
Edward Weston, of whom I had some slight knowledge; in fact, he might have claimed some journalistic
friendship with me, inasmuch as he told me that he
had begun his career as a news-boy at New York. I
resumed my acquaintance with him, and he very
kindly gave me some most valuable lessons in walking. I could get about tolerably well on my feet now,
but I have never been able to walk steadily; and woe

betide the lady who is imprudent enough to accept the arm which I sometimes proffer to a member of the fair sex: forgetting what a stumbling creature I have become.   Lord Sandwich used to say that he knew a man who walked on both sides of the street at once. Can you understand the process of walking over your own feet?   That is what I have done for many years.

Nothing remarkable happened to me in 1874; and I had no adventures.   The *Daily Telegraph* did not think I was strong enough to go to St. Petersburg for the marriage of the Duke of Edinburgh with the daughter of the Emperor Alexander II.; but I was present at Guildhall on the 18th of May, when the Tsar was entertained with magnificent hospitality by the Lord Mayor.   I had a good deal to do with the International Exhibition at Kensington, which closed in October; but my work was simply so much mechanical business; and I should say that by this time, placable reader, you have had enough of the descriptions of exhibitions, international and otherwise, from my tedious pen.   I should also mention that in 1873 my illness prevented me from exercising my usual functions as art critic to the *Daily Telegraph* at the Exhibition of the Royal Academy; but in 1874 I returned with great glee to that particular branch of my employment as a journalist.

CHAPTER L

I HAVE said that nothing of an adventurous kind befel
me in 1874; but a tremendously remarkable adventure
was, on the 28th of February in that year, the lot of
the stout Sphinx of whom I have more than once
made mention in these pages. The case for the prosecution of Castro, or Orton, or whoever the strange
man may be, had closed late in January. He had
been liberated on heavy bail; but the end was coming; and there were very few intelligent people who
entertained a doubt as to what the verdict could be.
On February the 27th, Edward Lawson wrote to say
that he would call for me in Thistle Grove early the
next morning, in order that we might go down to
the Law Courts at Westminster and see the last of
the Claimant. Accordingly, by ten o'clock we gained
admission to the crowded court. I was not to see the
face of the defendant until some hours afterwards. I
was behind him on one of the benches reserved for
counsel; but I could see his broad back looming large
in the offing like some huge man-of-war hulk moored
in ordinary. Close to him sat two or three gentlemen
in private clothes, whom I easily recognised as super-
intendents or inspectors of police; then I could make
out the handsome countenance of Sir John Duke Coleridge, afterwards Lord Coleridge, Chief Justice of
England; and in particular, could I descry the gold-
rimmed spectacles and abundant whiskers of that sin-

gularly able, wrong-headed, and unfortunate advocate, Dr. Kenealy.

I call him unfortunate; because Edward Kenealy was a man of immense scholarship, of profound legal erudition, and wide ranging general attainments, which should have gained him the highest professional rank, and the admiration of his contemporaries; but there was, I should say, a moral "kink in his cable," which led him into extravagances and aberrations, and eventually wrecked the life which should have been valuable to himself and his contemporaries. I had first become aware of him when he was a young barrister in Gray's Inn, and when he wrote in *Fraser* a noble article on that great Irish scholar, journalist, and wit, William Maginn, LL.D. About 1848 or 1850, Kenealy got into trouble for having chastised, with reprehensible severity, a young boy, his son. The matter was settled somehow without his suffering any imprisonment; and as time wore on the incident was forgotten, and Kenealy did his utmost, by unflagging industry, to redeem the past. He rose steadily in the ranks of his profession, became a Q.C., and was chosen a Bencher of his Inn, one of the Temples I should say. It happened, however, on his promotion to this honourable post, that some evil-minded, ill-conditioned, cantankerous, and of course anonymous, scribbler, raked up the old story of his having mercilessly beaten the boy at his chambers in Gray's Inn. I took up the cudgels in defence of a man who was clearly entitled to claim the benefit of a moral Statute of Limitations; and pointed out in an article published I forget where, how much the new Bencher of his Inn had done, not only in his own vocation, but by his brilliant writings, to increase the sum of knowledge and culture. Kenealy expressed himself as deeply grateful for my defence of him ; and he sent me a copy of a work he had just published, entitled " Goethe ; a new Pantomime," which, so far as I can recollect, was a violent attack on the ethics of the author of " Faust." On the title-page of his book, he wrote an inscription to myself, full of flattering expressions ; but as the Claimant's case wore on, and Kenealy had accepted the position of counsel for the defence, I had to write somewhat strongly in the matter in the *Daily Telegraph*. Dr. Kenealy became aware that I was the writer of the articles ; and for some months he pursued me, whenever he had the chance, with the most virulent abuse, his favourite allusion to me being to call me " Sala the Spotted Dog." Why he should have coupled me with the highly respectable tavern in question—which, by the way, to the best of my knowledge I never set foot in—troubles my comprehension ; but in all probability he confused the interesting hotel in Holywell Street, the " Old Dog," with the " Spotted Dog " in the Strand hard by. Abuse never ruffled my temper for more than ten minutes, nor did me, as I have already hinted, a half-penny worth of harm ; and at present I can very deeply sympathise with Dr. Kenealy's family ; nor have I lost one iota of my thorough appreciation for his great natural capacity, and his equally grand scholarly attainments. The Tichborne trial—I have no reason to believe that he had himself the slightest doubt that the Claimant was really Sir Roger Charles Tichborne—was the ruin of Edward Kenealy. His intemperate utterances led to his being cashiered as a Bencher of his Inn, and to his being ultimately disbarred. He got into Parliament for some borough in the Potteries, and it should not be forgotten, as an illustration of the singularly noble and high-minded character of John Bright, that when the new M.P. came to the table to be sworn, the only Member who came forward to act as his sponsor was Mr. Bright.

His action was, I take it, as courageously dignified as that of Horace Greeley when he offered to stand bail for Jefferson Davis.

We heard the last of Sir Alexander Cockburn's summing up. I can see the great Judge pushing his wig a little off his high forehead, when, turning to the jury, he asked them with just a tone of irony in his beautifully musical voice, what they were to think of a defendant who did not even know the name of his own mother. The jury retired. I have not the least idea as to the length of time they were absent from the court; but I remember the dead silence which all at once succeeded the buzz of conversation when the " twelve honest men " resumed their places. The foreman rose and read their finding : " That the defendant did falsely swear that he was Roger Charles Tichborne; that he seduced Catherine M. N. E. Doughty in 1851; and that he was not Arthur Orton." The sentence, which was one of fourteen years' penal servitude — seven years for each allegation of perjury—was not pronounced by the Lord Chief Justice. That task fell to the lot of Mr. Justice Lush, a diminutive Judge with a somewhat rosy countenance. No sooner had the last words of doom fallen from the lips of Mr. Justice Lush than the individuals in plain clothes, whom I knew to be police officers, quietly environed the Claimant, now the prisoner. In American parlance, they " froze " to him, and as they dexterously piloted him out of the well of the court, he reminded me yet more strongly of the dismasted hulk of an old line-of-battle ship, being towed by a brace of smart tugs to some wharf, there to have her timbers broken up. The Claimant was to be broken up very small indeed, at Dartmoor or some other convict prison, where he was to be delivered over to the tormentors.

The Judges tucked up their skirts and departed;
and the jury dispersed in great glee, since they were
informed they would not be summoned again to serve
during their life-time. Thus ended the longest trial
ever known in England. Of course there immediately
ensued a violent rush out of court for luncheon. Edward Lawson had thoughtfully provided himself with
a case of sandwiches and a flask of sherry; so when
the tramping and scuffling of the emerging crowd had
somewhat abated, we tranquilly seated ourselves on
the stone bench running round the central lobby,
whence branched the two lengthy corridors leading
respectively to the Houses of Lords and Commons.
We were pleasantly discussing the merits of chicken
sandwiches compared with others made from *pâté de
foie gras*, and debating whether *Vino di Pasto* was a
preferable vintage to *Amontillado*, when to our surprise we heard a loud, resonant noise in the western
corridor. The old Law Courts were, you will remember, on the side of Westminster Hall adjoining
the House of Lords. What did that noise mean?
I remember the anecdote of the death of Louis
XV., out of whose body the breath had scarcely departed when there was audible, throughout the vast
saloons and ante-chambers of the Palace of Versailles,
a sound as of thunder. It was only a mob of courtiers hastening from the bedside of the dead monarch
to pay homage to the new King and Queen. The
central lobby might, perhaps, be considered as the
œil de bœuf of the Palace of Westminster; but of a
surety no Louis *le Bien-Aimé* had just expired. Speedily did we become cognisant of the cause of that noise
in the western corridor. There came onwards, with
a steady swinging tramp along the marble pavement,
a great body of police-constables; and in the midst of
this phalanx walked Castro, or Orton, or "the Jab-

berwock," as Shirley Brooks used to call him: borrowing an epithet from " Alice in Wonderland." He was between two inspectors in plain clothes, but I cannot remember whether he was handcuffed. That circumstance does not matter much. As he passed me, proceeding towards the eastern corridor, he gave me *one* look of recognition—a look which I shall not forget till my dying day. They got him safely, I was afterwards told, into the courtyard of the Speaker's house, where the " Black Maria " was waiting for him. The Home Secretary of the day was Mr. Cross, now the Right Honourable Viscount Cross : and this high functionary was, I understand, strongly in favour of the bulky captive being put into a police-galley, and conveyed to Blackfriars by water, thus avoiding the crowds which filled Parliament Street and Whitehall ; but the detective department undertook to get him to his destination without any friction or fuss. They just put him into the van, which was driven first over Westminster Bridge, and then along the York Road and Stamford Street, over Blackfriars Bridge into Middlesex again ; whence the transit to Her Majesty's gaol of Newgate was brief and easy.

CHAPTER LI

THE year 1875 was to me a most eventful one, and
fruitful in adventure. In the second week in January
I made my second journey to Spain. A journalistic
colleague of mine once, I believe, either wrote a book
or delivered a lecture entitled "Monarchs I have
Known"; or, "Kings I have Hobnobbed with," or
something of that nature. I have never been on terms
of familiarity with Royalty; yet it has so chanced that
I have been acquainted with three Kings of Spain—
one of them it must be admitted an extremely titular
one. Of him I will speak first. While I was living in
Guildford Street, Russell Square, there came to me
one forenoon a foreign gentleman, of slight stature and
dark complexion, who brought with him a letter of
introduction from the late Mr. Peter LeNeve Foster,
then secretary of the Society of Arts. At the same
time my visitor handed me his card. I had asked him
to take a chair; and I may add that the interview took
place in my study; that I was clad in a very ragged
silk dressing-jacket, and that I was smoking a short
pipe.

I looked at the card and found that it bore the name
of some Spanish grandee—*Conde* of something or another. Would I look, asked the foreign gentleman, at
the other side of the card? I turned over the paste-
board and read " Don Juan de Borbon." Of course I
stood up and made the gravest of reverences. My

interlocutor was the son of Don Carlos, the grandson
of Ferdinand VII., and consequently the legitimate
King of Spain; but the heir to a phantom crown only
smiled, and saying, "It is such a very little matter,"
made me resume my seat. He wanted me to render
him some newspaper service ; and I was, fortunately,
able to meet his wishes. After that he used to call on
me three or four times a week, and talk about books,
and pictures, and photography—of all of which subjects he had considerable knowledge. In politics he
seemed to me to be a thorough-going Liberal ; and frequently regretted that his son, Don Carlos Number
Two, who signs himself Duke of Madrid, and pretends
to be King both of France and Spain, had been brought
up by the Jesuits, and was full of reactionary tendencies. My wife, womanlike, was naturally a little
pleased that I should be visited by so illustrious a personage ; and, as naturally, she told her maid who the
little dark foreign gentleman was. At all events, coming home to dinner one evening, I asked the parlour-
maid—" Anybody been here to-day, Jane?" " No,
sir," she replied ; "*only that King's been bothering here
again.*" The idea of a King, even a discrowned one,
bothering anybody !

Ten or twelve years afterwards, taking my annual
holiday at Monte Carlo, I had a constant neighbour at
the tables in the shape of a comely gentleman with a
full glossy beard, who apparently had scarcely reached
middle-age. We used to meet not only at the Casino,
but on the terrace, in the gardens and the concert-
room. At first we used to converse in French ; but
having incidentally remarked one day that I could
speak Italian, our parley was thenceforth in the Tuscan tongue. I had not the slightest idea as to who he
was ; and if I hazarded a conjecture, it may have been
that he was either an operatic singer, or a secretary of

the Italian Embassy at Paris. He was fonder of that gay enchantress *roulette* than of the austerer *trente-et-quarante;* and as at the former game he persistently backed the numbers—he generally lost his money. One day, however, he made a *coup;* it was not a very large one : only thirty-five five-franc pieces, which he had won by putting a single piece *en plein* on the number mentioned. As he laughingly gathered his gains together—to lose them five minutes afterwards—he showed me one of the pieces, saying, " I think that I have seen that face before." In those days they took all kinds of money at the Monte Carlo gambling tables —French and Belgian five-franc pieces, American, Mexican, and South American dollars, and Italian five-lire pieces, and Greek five-drachmas ones. I looked at the piece which the gentleman with the glossy beard had handed me. It was a Spanish dollar ; on the reverse the Pillars of Hercules and the proud device, "*Plus ultra ;*" on the obverse the profile of the comely gentleman with the glossy beard, with the inscription, "*Amadeo, Rey de Espana y de las Antillas.*" Only a few months before he had disdainfully refused to rule any more over a people who hated him because he was an *estranjero,* and who insulted his wife. He had become once more the Italian Duke of Aosta.

I shall now proceed to deal with Spanish Royalty Number Three. A civil war was raging in the North of Spain, where the Carlists were in full force. By the end of the year they had bombarded Pampeluna, and were committing shocking barbarities in the way of devastating whole districts, and butchering their prisoners by the score. Long before, Doña Isabella de Borbon, forced by circumstances over which she had no control to resign her crown, abdicated in favour of her son Don Alfonso, then a cadet at our military college at Sandhurst. In December, 1874, Marshal Serrano, commanding the Loyalist army in the north, the army at Murriedro pronounced in favour of Alfonso; and, on the 29th of December, the youthful Prince was proclaimed King by General Martinez Campos; he was again proclaimed by General Primo Da Rivera, at Madrid. At once my friends in Fleet Street gave me, what in journalistic technology is known under the collective term of a "travelling ticket"—passport, letters of introduction to influential people, letter of credit, and so forth. My own travelling equipment I always kept in a room especially set aside for the purpose; one trunk packed with a view to a hot climate, the other to serve one's need in a cold one. I knew the winter at Madrid to be a very keen one, but as I hoped to cross the Sierra Morena and go south before I returned, I provided myself with a summer as well as a winter equipment. So I sped to Marseilles, whence I took a Messageries steamer for Barcelona: my instructions being to reach the Spanish capital before the arrival of the new King.

As I anticipated, the weather was bitterly cold at Madrid; and a walk up the wide and windy Calle de Alcala was more trying even than the perambulation in the month of January of the Nevskoi Perspektive at St. Petersburg; since the Russian cold is, if I may so call it, a non-tempestuous and almost gentle frigidity. You have only to wrap yourself up in your fur *skouba* and pull the wings of your beaver or sealskin cap well over your ears, and you will scarcely suffer any inconvenience; whereas in Madrid there blows throughout the winter a horrible wind from the Guadarana, which seems bent on cutting your throat, and makes the general temperature so penetrating as to be almost unbearable. It is a crafty wind, moreover, that blows without making much noise, and has been aptly defined in the following couplet—

" El aire de Madrid es tan subtil,
    Que mata a un hombre y no apaga a un candil."

" The air of Madrid is so subtle that while it kills a man it will not blow out a candle."

I found plenty of friends in the capital; to say nothing of the usual crowd of "mooners" in the Puerta del Sol, clustered round the fountain; wearing apparently the same ragged cloaks and the same battered slouched hats, and smoking the same *papelitos* which they had worn and smoked when I first knew them, ten years before. I had not been two days at the Fonda de Paris, or the Fonda de los Principes—I forget which—when I received a visit from my old friend, Colonel Howsomever—there is no need to mention his real name—who had been an Anglo-Madrileño ever since the time when Mr. Henry Bulwer, afterwards Lord Dalling, had been Minister at the Court of Queen Isabella: if not for many years previous to that period. We used to call him, jocularly, " Colonel Howsomever" because he generally began conversation with that adverb, and as plentifully garnished his subsequent utterances with it. He was a wonderful storyteller; and used to tell an extraordinary yarn of having ridden on horseback from Madrid to Gibraltar, with the despatches for Sir Robert Wilson, at the period when that distinguished officer was Governor of the Rock. " You're a dead man, Colonel," was, according to his showing, the Governor's remark when, with his saddle under one arm, and his bag with despatches under the other, the Colonel presented himself at Government House, the Convent. " Pursued by guerillas; all but captured by the Carlists; three horses killed under you—you'll never get over it, Colonel!" "Howsomever," added His Excellency, "let him have a warm bath and a bottle of champagne immediately."

He was equally great in describing the attitude of George IV., when the news arrived of the surrender of Napoleon I. to Captain Maitland, on board the *Bellerophon;* only it is but justice to the Colonel to admit that he did not claim to have heard the Royal *dicta* himself; but said that they were transmitted to him by his worthy father, who was always about Carlton House. "Bonaparte taken!" the First Gentleman in England is said to have exclaimed, "Dash my wig, Colonel!"—my friend's sire must likewise have held His Majesty's commission—"What are we to do with the scoundrel?" "Send him to the Tower of London, Sir." "The Tower, be blowed! He would corrupt the Beefeaters. Howsomever, we will pack him off to St. Helena." What Colonel Howsomever had been doing at Madrid all these years I never had any means of ascertaining. I heard that he rendered some service to the English colony in the Spanish capital by successfully negotiating with the Government for permission to establish a Protestant cemetery in the suburbs. Perhaps he was employed in some sub-diplomatic capacity, and had a small income from the Secret Service Fund. At all events, he was a kindly, courteous, and obliging old gentleman, and if he did draw the long-bow occasionally, the shafts which he shot never did anybody the slightest harm. He was good enough, unasked, to get me elected a member of the principal club; but confessed somewhat ruefully that he had been occasionally gently reproached by the committee for introducing so many of his English friends as candidates. "Howsomever," he would console himself by remarking, "there's a *rouge-et-noir* table in one of the rooms of the club, and a *monte* table in

another; and most of the fellows whom I have introduced are fond of sitting up gambling till three in the
morning—which is good for the club."

To my great joy, I found dear Antonio Gallenga in
Madrid. When we renewed our friendship the special
correspondent of the *Times* must have passed his sixtieth year. Was there ever a more valiant and indefatigable journalist and *littérateur* than Antonio? In
the interests of the great journal of Printing House
Square, he had repeatedly travelled through Spain and
Italy, through the Spanish Antilles and South America; and he had been in the United States when the
great Republic was in the midst of war. He had been
a Deputy of the Italian Parliament; he had been, I
fancy, mixed up with a good many political conspira-
cies; and in addition to all this, he had led two lives;
for in his youth he had been a teacher of languages in
England under the *nom de guerre* of Luigi Mariotti. I
picked up the other day, at a second-hand bookstall, a
copy of " Mariotti's Italian - English Grammar " —
fifteenth or twentieth edition. Somebody must have
made a mint of money out of that grammar. I was
destined to meet my dear friend again in 1877 at Constantinople; and I rejoice to say that, although in his
old age he had suffered a bitter bereavement in the
death, by a cruel accident, of his beloved and accomplished daughter, he still lives, a substantial country
squire, at The Falls, near Monmouth. He has written a
small library of books of travels, and of political essays.
He served the *Times* for a quarter of a century, and
must have written thousands of leaders on foreign
subjects, and columns of special correspondence from
abroad. For many years he has been a member of the
Athenæum Club; and yet not very long since, when I
was asked by the pert young editor of a weekly paper
to give him a list of eminent journalists whose por-

traits he might have engraved, and I mentioned the name of Antonio Gallenga as that of one of the most gifted and most distinguished members of my craft, the pert young editor stared at me, and said that he did not know who Antonio Gallenga was.

Archibald Forbes had come out as representative of the *Daily News*. I was, at that time, only slightly acquainted with him: having met him cursorily at a few Volunteer Reviews, and once on the Ladies' Lawn on the Cup day at Goodwood. He had already, however, achieved European fame, by the splendid services which he had rendered to his journal in the Franco-German War; and I had heard much of the amiability and geniality of his private character from Edmund Yates, who had been intimately associated with him at the Vienna Exhibition. Finally, at the house of Señor Salamanca, the millionaire banker, I found Mr. Roger Eykyn, of the firm of Eykyn Brothers, the well-known stockbrokers. I am sorry to say that Roger Eykyn was, to all appearance, desperately ill of pleuro-pneumonia, the result, I should say, of that detestably insidious Madrileño wind, which kills men while it cannot puff out a candle.

At length arrived the great day of the entrance of young King Alfonso into the capital of his kingdom. He had been received with rapturous enthusiasm at Barcelona; but the haughty Madrileños made light of that incident. "The Catalans are very well," they remarked; "but they are not Spaniards. *Madrid es sola Corte;* it is the Eye of Spain; and when Don Alfonso has been installed at the Palacio Real, His Majesty can make a tour through Castile and Aragon, and make the acquaintance of Juan Español, the real Spaniard." The entire city was decorated in profusion with the national colours; and the grandees followed the picturesque Latin custom of hanging out their carpets from their windows. One possessor of the *sangre azul*—the Duke of Medina Sidonia, I think—displayed his ancestral tapestries, which had been woven, indeed, in Flemish looms from the cartoons of Raffaelle. For once the "mooners" evacuated the Puerta del Sol; and in their stead the great Place was crammed with a multitude of people of all sorts and conditions, including large bodies of peasantry, who had come up by rail to see the show, and who, in most instances, were clad in the picturesque national costume. The day fortunately, although cold, was an extremely fine one. The military cavalcade was splendid; and it culminated in the appearance of the King, who, while the cannon thundered, and the bells of all the churches were ringing joyful peals, rode, mounted on a superb charger, into the Puerta del Sol. The sun's rays caught the leaping waters of the fountain, and there was a great shout from the crowd of "*Mira el fuente !*" followed by another cry, which to me, for the moment, was a little perplexing: "*Es hijo de su madre !*" *Es hijo de su madre !* was repeated over and over again, from one end of the Plaza to the other. I was subsequently made to understand that the remark made was a proverbial one; and that it implied that there could be no rational doubt that the young Don Alfonso was the son of Doña Isabella de Borbon—it being a matter of comparative indifference as to who his papa may have been.

On the day following the Royal entry, Antonio Gallenga and I went to Court. Unless you have naval or military rank, or belong to the diplomatic service, it is not necessary to assume any kind of Court dress, when you wait upon a Majesty of Spain at an ordinary reception. You are simply bound to don ordinary evening attire and a white cravat; white kid gloves are also considered *de rigueur*. I think Gallenga had

some difficulty about buttoning his gloves, of which
he split at least three pairs before we reached the
Palace. In any case he was in a very ill temper when
we arrived there ; and when we had passed the hal-
berdiers in the marble vestibule, and had ascended the
grand staircase to the landing, which is adorned with
two enormous Venetian mirrors, my colleague, still
struggling with a refractory white kid, first scanned
himself in the glass, then looked at me, and observed
in an accent in which facetiousness was mingled with
ferocity, " By Jove, we are two dashed ugly fellows."
" Speak for yourself, brother," I replied. Of my own
facial shortcomings, I have been long and good-
humouredly aware. We were playing once at Pope's
Villa, Twickenham, a game of similitudes, at which all
the players had in succession to name the animal
which his or her neighbour was like ; and the verdict
of the majority decided whether the similitude was
accurate or the contrary. The lady who had to reckon me up, took some time to examine my countenance ;
and at last said, rather hesitatingly, that I reminded
her of a baked bull-dog ; but I am glad to say that her
summing-up was not endorsed by the majority of the
ladies and gentlemen present, who agreed that I more
closely resembled a seal.

The young King was to leave Madrid almost immediately for Zaragoza, where he was to review a large
body of troops ; and then he was to march at the head
of his army to raise the siege of Pampeluna, which for
many weeks had been held by the Carlists. We correspondents were in a state of great perturbation as to
the day and hour of the Royal setting forth ; but at
length I was able to tell them, " from information
which I had received," that the King would leave at
seven on a given morning by special train ; by which,
however, in addition to His Majesty and his staff, only

persons connected with the Court would be allowed to travel. There was to be an ordinary express leaving at six o'clock ; and by that the representatives of the English press agreed, not without some sullenness, that they would journey to Zaragoza. As it turned out, my colleagues did get to the city in question before I did ; but somehow, in the way of " seeing the show," I fared better than they did. Late in the evening, kind Roger Eykyn, who was rapidly approaching convalescence, sent for me, and told me that Señor Salamanca, who was to have accompanied the King, had been called away by most important business to Seville ; but that he had placed his own private saloon-carriage at the disposal of Gallenga and myself. Evening dress was indispensable, " But mind," added Roger Eykyn, " take your thickest great coat and plenty of railway rugs with you."

One did not mind rising at six in the morning ; breakfasting on the eternal cup of chocolate without milk, and the greasy slice of something which was half bread and half pastry ; and dressing by candle-light in a big, comfortless bedroom, imperfectly heated by a *brasero* or pan of incandescent charcoal ashes : the carbonic acid gas evolved from which is " killed " by oil or by the lees of wine. We drove to the terminus ; and fortunately there was nothing the matter that morning with Antonio's white kid gloves. The platform was crowded ; naturally there was a bishop with all his clergy ready in waiting to give the young Sovereign his benediction ; and then the King was effusively greeted by several ladies of the highest rank, all, of course, wearing the national mantilla. The queerest incident occurred just as the King was entering his saloon. An old man, bent nearly double, leaning on a staff, and dressed in the most astonishing conglomeration of rags and tatters that ever I beheld, hobbled up to the door of the Royal carriage, and extending one attenuated and skinny palm, begged. Yes, begged! No *Guardia Civil* collared the audacious mendicant; no *aide-de-camp* drew his sword to punish the shameless tatterdemalion. Everybody seemed to take the thing quite as a matter of course ; and the King laughingly gave Lazarus something. I asked him how he had dared to approach the Sovereign and solicit alms from him. He tried to draw himself up to his full height ; he surveyed me with an air of wrathful dignity, and he replied that things were going " *muy mal á casa* "—that things were going very badly at home.

Señor Salamanca's saloon-carriage proved to be a most sumptuous conveyance. In addition to the saloon there were two handsomely furnished bedrooms, a comfortable dining-room, and an elegant boudoir. There were plenty of mirrors in massive gold frames, and gorgeously upholstered chairs and sofas ; and in particular there were console tables, and at least five-and-twenty wax tapers in massive gilt candelabra. We reached Zaragoza in time for lunch, which was provided for the King and all his suite, including ourselves, at the municipal palace ; all the livery stable-keepers in the city had been laid under contribution to supply conveyances for the visitors coming with His Majesty ; and a barouche with a pair of white horses had been placed at the disposal of the occupants of Señor Salamanca's saloon carriage. Very cheerfully, after we had partaken of a bounteous repast, moistened with some excellent champagne, we drove down to the Fonda, which had been agreed upon as a *rendezvous* for ourselves and our colleagues. We found them sitting over the national dish, *puchero*—fresh boiled beef—accommodated with garlic and other vegetables, among which *garbanzos*, or chick pease, predominated. They could get nothing to drink but Val de Peñas ; and, on the whole, I do not think that they received us with any exceptional cordiality. They had, in truth, arrived five-and-twenty minutes before the Royal train; but there were no cabs to be had at the Zaragoza Station; and they had been fain to walk through the snow to the Fonda, where their demands for luncheon had been met by the reply commonly used by Spanish hotel-keepers in the provinces, *no hay nada*. Whether Archibald Forbes had to produce his revolver before the inn-keeper would consent to supply *puchero* for six, I did not learn. They fancied that Antonio and I had lost the train; and received, not precisely with good grace, the tidings that we had not only witnessed the departure of the King from the Madrid terminus, but had been allowed to couple Señor Salamanca's saloon-carriage to the Royal train.

But man should never boast of good fortune. For aught he can tell, when he deems himself most felicitous ill-luck is dogging his footsteps, and, in a moment, may spring upon him. The train halted at a town called Alhama de Aragon, which, in summer time, I believe, is an inland watering-place, extensively patronised by the flower of Madrid society. On the 14th of January, however, its leafless trees and blast-swept garden walks presented a most woe-begone appearance. The train was to stop, we were told, twenty minutes; and, after a brief stroll, timing ourselves by our watches from five minutes to five minutes, we returned to the station, out of which, to our horror, the Royal train was just moving; while, to add to our discomfiture, the station-master politely informed us that there would not be any more ordinary trains passing through until the next morning. This did not matter to our colleagues, who had not intended to go any further than Zaragoza; but to us who wished to accomplish another day's journey with the King, the mishap was almost tantamount to journalistic death. The station-master pondered; he was, under the circumstances, as polite as a French *chef de gare* would have been rude. At length he was able to tell us that a train full of troops would be going through in about two hours, that he would wire for this train to be stopped at Alhama de Aragon; and that he had no doubt the officer in command of the military would allow us to take passage with them. In due time this train in question drew up to the platform, and we reached our destination where the King was to pass the night. We were unmercifully chaffed by some of the officers of the Royal staff; but we contented ourselves with expressing the wish that everybody might live a thousand years; and so *papelitos* were handed round, and cups of black coffee, and everything went merry as a marriage bell. Gallenga and I slept each in our well-appointed bedroom. We laughed heartily when, at six o'clock in the morning the train resumed its march, at the trifling misadventure which had occurred to us on the preceding day.

Woe is me !—worse, much worse was to come. The cold during the night had been intense; the water in the *cabinet de toilette* was frozen as hard as a stone, and there we were in evening dress, with a good deal of coal dust on our white shirt-fronts and cravats, and with our faces and hands in a general condition of griminess. To make matters worse, at half-past nine one of the Royal *aides-de-camp* made his appearance at the door of our saloon with a gracious invitation from His Majesty to breakfast with him at ten a.m. What was to be done? To put the matter as mildly as possible, Antonio Gallenga, Esq., and your humble servant looked a great deal more like two sweeps than two reputable journalists. We did not presume, while accepting the invitation of His Majesty, to ask for a basin of hot water from the kitchen of the Royal train. Archibald Forbes, I feel confident, would have asked for a gallon at once ; but we had not sufficient muscle of mind to proffer such a request.   What, we repeated, was to be done ?   I remember once at a gala-day at the Crystal Palace, and after a very hard day's work, being suddenly pounced upon by a friend, who told me that I was to join, then and there, a dinner-party, given by some Brahminical personage, whom my friend defined as a " howling swell."   I said I should be very glad to avail myself of the invitation ; and only asked for a few minutes' time to wash my hands.   " Oh, bother your hands !" exclaimed my friend, who was rather of an impetuous temperament; " come along at once ; " and he literally dragged me away to the hospitable board of the howling swell aforesaid.   Fortunately, when I took my seat I descried by the side of my plate a beautifully crusty loaf, of Viennese make.   I seized the precious bread, and, remembering that when Mohammedan pilgrims in the desert are unable to find water they perform their ablutions with sand, I slipped my hands under the tablecloth and practically washed my hands with the nice, fresh bread.   But in that abode of splendid misery, Señor Salamanca's saloon-carriage, there was not a crumb of bread.

Suddenly a happy thought seemed to have struck Gallenga.   " Did you ever try candles ? " he asked. "Candles for what?" I repeated in amazement. " Why, to wash with," he replied; and, suiting the action to the words, he took one of the Salamanca wax candles from its gilt metal socket and gravely proceeded to roll the taper backwards and forwards over his face and hands.   I followed his example, and I believe that, with the aid of a couple of waxen cylinders, we did manage to get off a considerable quantity of our grimi-ness, and even to endue our skin with a slight veneer

of wax.   At all events, we did the best we could with
the dry polish.   Then we entered the Royal saloon;
were most graciously received by His Majesty, and
partook of a truly Royal breakfast.   The condition of
our complexions did not excite the slightest notice;
for, during the meal everybody was fully occupied
with his knife and fork; and, directly breakfast was
over, the saloon was filled with a blue haze, emitted
from some thirty lighted Havanas and *papelitos*.   But,
as the temperature grew gradually warmer and
warmer, " Tears, such as Tender Fathers Shed," began
to trickle down my face: *the thin veneer of wax had
melted.*   I have never had occasion since then to try
candles as a means of washing; still, Gallenga's device
was certainly an ingenious one, and may be found
worthy the attention of travellers placed in the pre-
dicament in which we were.

CHAPTER LII

DOWN SOUTH

AT some town, the name of which I forget, we left the
Royal train about two o'clock in the afternoon. I had
no instructions to describe the siege of Pampeluna;
and thenceforward, I was to have for six weeks longer,
a free hand in the way of my wanderings. So I thought
that I would return to Barcelona, of which I had seen
but little when I landed there, and explore that large
and most interesting city. After two or three days'
strolling about the Rambla and visiting the two prodigiously spacious theatres, I bade farewell to Gallenga,
who was returning to England, and took the train for
Madrid. It was not an express, but a train with first,
second, and third class passengers. I started at the
usual unholy hour of seven in the morning; when, just
as we were entering a deep cutting, the train slack-
ened speed; and, to our extreme uneasiness, we could
hear the repeated discharges of rifles, and a pattering
of bullets against the side of the carriage. At once I
stood up on the seat; and bade the only other occupant of the compartment to do likewise. I knew that
the Mexican *guerrilleros*, when they fire into a carriage,
always aim low when they wish to maim the passengers
and not to kill. My companion, who sat opposite to
me, told me that he was a silversmith in a large way of
business at Barcelona; and the number of patens,
chalices, and candlesticks, and silver which that worthy
tradesman vowed to the Virgin, and to a whole host of
saints during that extremely *mauvais quart d'heure,*

passes my power of computation. I heard him murmuring also to himself, " To die so young, to leave my wife and babes. Oh! it is sad, it is sad ; *and I haven't even had my breakfast.*"

In a short time the train came to a dead stop ; and we could see the sides of the cutting swarming with armed men, who, from the red caps, or *chapelgorris*—the word is Basque, I believe—which they wore, we knew, at once, to be Carlists. The door of our compartment was opened ; and the conductor of the train made his appearance, accompanied by a tall man in a *chapelgorri*, whom, from a sabre at his belt, I took to be the commander of the Carlist band. He straightway hauled the Barcelona silversmith out of the carriage, and handed him over to two of his men, who proceeded to relieve him of his purse and his watch. They only exacted, however, from him five gold Isabelinos—a sum equivalent to about five pounds sterling—and then the tall man with the sabre at his belt asked me in Spanish who was my King. I heard the conductor say to him, in an under tone, that I was *un estranjero*, a foreigner ; but on my remaining mute he repeated his question more sternly, adding, " Carlos or Alfonso, which?" I rose ; made him a low bow; and replied in the best Castilian that I could muster, that my King was Her Most Gracious Majesty, Queen Victoria, of Great Britain and Ireland, Defender of the Faith, whom might God long preserve ; and then I offered him a cigar—a real Havana, which is a rarity in Old Spain. Once more I heard the conductor mutter to the Carlist chief that I was an Englishman, and *un poco loco*—all Englishmen, he was so obliging as to say, were a little mad. Whereupon the man with the sabre shrugged his shoulders; smiled grimly; lighted my Havana, and departed. The conductor, when the train was allowed to proceed, told me that the remainder of the passengers had not been so lucky as to get off scot free as I had done; the Carlists having exacted five Isabelinos from every first-class passenger; ten dollars from every second-class one, and, from the third-class, anything they could get—cabbages, onions, and other garden produce; tobacco, a silver peseta now and again, and a considerable quantity of copper money.

At the next stopping place, which fortunately was a garrison town, we took on board a body of sixty infantry of the Line. We travelled all night; but the next morning, between eight and nine, the train was again surrounded by another band of Carlists, who began firing upon us. The tables were at once turned; and with a vengeance. Our military escort returned the fire of the insurgents; and then, sallying forth from the train, they charged the marauders with fixed bayonets; and the adherents of the elder branch of the Spanish Bourbons being completely routed, ignominiously took to flight. They left a few wounded behind them, and the soldiers took about half-a-dozen prisoners. I hope that the wounded were removed to some neighbouring hospital or monastery for medical treatment; but I know and remember with awful distinctness that the prisoners were all shot, and that their corpses were hung *in terrorem* to the telegraph poles. *À la guerre comme à la guerre.* When the French were in Mexico they used, after shooting the *guerrilleros* whom they captured, to cut off their right hands, which they nailed to the telegraph poles. Swollen and blackened by the heat these severed hands presented a sufficiently ghastly appearance.

There was nothing to detain me in Madrid, save to pay a few more visits to the magnificent museum of pictures, and the equally splendid armoury. I went to the Opera two or three times, and to a number of

minor theatres, where the staples of entertainment are
zarzuelas and *saynetes*, corresponding with the French
opéras bouffes; then I wended my way, without further
adventure, over the Brown Mountains down to Cordova and Seville, and other cities of interest in the
south. I saw another carnival at Cordova; and my
guide to the inner mysteries of the festival was a most
intelligent and good-natured Englishman, who I am
afraid has joined the majority. It was Sir Henry
Layard, who in 1875 was Her Britannic Majesty's Minister at Madrid, who gave me a letter of introduction
to the gentleman in question, who was known as Don
Juan Rutledge, and was traffic manager on the Southern line of railway. From Cordova I went to Seville,
and thence to the *Nave de Piedra*, or Ship of Stone—
the title which the Andalusians give to the delightful
city of Cadiz.

At the *table d'hôte* of the principal fonda of the city
immortalised by Byron in "Don Juan," I made a
transitory but altogether amusing acquaintance. My
opposite neighbour at luncheon and dinner was a
chubby little boy,.who, I should say, was about five
years of age. He had, strange for a Spaniard, a fair
complexion, large blue eyes, and auburn hair, which
curled like the young tendrils of the vine. "He is a
Goth," whispered my next-door neighbour. "Sit with
me at any *mesa franca* throughout Spain, and I will
point out to you, quite apart from the foreign guests,
three races of Spaniards—the old Iberian, the Arab,
and the Gothic." The little fellow opposite invariably
wore a huge coach-wheel hat, profusely adorned with
white ostrich feathers. A servant in livery stood behind his chair; on his right was a major-domo, in
dignified black, with a silver chain round his neck; to
his left was a matronly female, also in black, who
was-the child's *ama*, or waiting gentlewoman—a do-

mestic whom English people often erroneously call a duenna.

The small party in the prodigious hat and feathers, after staring at me intently for two or three evenings, began to be very friendly. " *Yo soy Don Arturo*," he said, emphasising the rarely used personal pronoun: " *Yo soy Don Arturo; Y Tú ?* " All the company burst out laughing at this, which tickled me immensely; and they laughed louder when I told him that I was Don Jorge Augusto Enrique, and that I kissed his hands and feet. That evening I went to the theatre; and in a private box on the pit-tier was the little darling in the hat and feathers, attended as usual by his major-domo, his *ama*, and his liveried lacquey. I was in the stalls, he beckoned to me, and for some time was most affable in his artless conversation; but, after a while, I fancy he had enough of me, for he had fixed his eyes on a ragged little urchin about ten, who was in the pit, where there was only standing - room. Nothing could please him, till the footman went and fetched the ragged, unwashed boy, who was not, however, for easily comprehensible reasons, permitted to enter the box. The tiny hidalgo contented himself with leaning over and stroking and patting the urchin's most suspicious-looking head. He subsequently presented him with a dollar; and the unwashed boy went away rejoicing.

I only saw my affable young friend once more. I was on my way to Granada; and on the train halting for a few minutes at some station, I became aware of the diminutive hidalgo, attended as usual by his suite, but tranquilly reposing in the arms of a railway porter, who was apparently delighted with his young burden, and whose head the child from time to time affectionately patted. He had a passion, I should say, for stroking people's heads, and was not very particular in his choice. The footman hurriedly advanced to say that the carriage was waiting; so away they carried Don Arturo, who, I hope, was conveyed in a coach drawn by six fat mules to his ancestral castle. When the porter came back, I asked him who Don Arturo was. "Who is he?" echoed the porter, "who should he be, but the Lord of all the orange groves of Bobadilla." But the train started; and I had no time to ask whether of Bobadilla Don Arturo was the Duke, the Marquis, or the Count.

I went to Granada; renewed my acquaintance with the Alhambra; then took a trip to Valencia; returned to Cadiz, and thence took steamer for Gibraltar, where I enjoyed the customary cordial welcome from many of the officers in garrison.

A queer place, Gibraltar! My stay there in 1875 was marked by a sufficiently droll incident. On the 15th of April, H.M. steamship *Serapis* put into Gibraltar, having on board His Royal Highness the Prince of Wales, and a numerous suite, including an additional private secretary, Dr. W. H. Russell. In her wake there was another steamship, on board of which were several of my journalistic colleagues, who had accompanied His Royal Highness on his tour to India. Among these were Archibald Forbes for the *Daily News*, and George Henty for the *Standard*, while the *Daily Telegraph* was represented by Mr. Drew Gay. A satirical journal called *El Mono* (The Monkey), published at Gibraltar, in commenting on the joyful event of the Heir to the Crown being in Anglo-Spanish waters, incidentally remarked that there was one drop of bitter in the cup of delight, one rift in the lute of gladness, in the circumstance that there was on board the *Serapis* the notorious enemy of Spain in general, and "*Los hijos de Gibraltar*"—the sons of Gibraltar— Jorge Augusto Sala, who had cruelly, maliciously, traitorously and mendaciously insulted the sons of Gibraltar in question, by calling them *Escorpiones de roca*—rock-scorpions. Clearly I had not followed the Prince to India, and I was not honoured by a passage on board the *Serapis;* and it so chanced that I was not the inventor of the term " rock-scorpions ;" which, as all travellers in the Levant have known for goodness knows how long, is a term often applied to the Spanish-speaking people of Gibraltar. The epithet occurs more than once in Captain Marryat's novels, and I am almost certain that it finds a place in " Peter Simple." Talking of the *Mono*, I may mention that the King of the Monkeys which inhabit the summit of the Rock died while I was at Gibraltar ; and the population—I speak in the human and not in the simian sense—were anxiously awaiting the arrival of a new monkey monarch. I say arrival ; because at the demise of the Jocko Crown at Gibraltar, the new Sovereign does not ascend the throne by hereditary descent ; nor is he elected by the apes of the Rock itself. The new King arrives from the African coast, somewhere near Tarifa, where there is also a mountain of monkeys ; and nearly universal is the popular belief that the potentate with the tail travels by way of a tunnel passing under the Straits.

Having yet some weeks at my disposal, I crossed from Gibraltar to Oran, in Algeria, my travelling companion being a son of the late Sir Gilbert Scott, R.A., the distinguished Gothic architect. Thence I took a run by rail to Algiers; whence I crossed to Carthagena in Spain, and so made headway to Marseilles; but we were nine days accomplishing the short voyage, in a succession of positively horrible storms.

CHAPTER LIII

I SHOULD have said, some pages back, that on the day
when the Claimant was sentenced to his double dose
of penal servitude, took place the funeral of my old
friend, Charles Shirley Brooks—he dropped his first
name in signing his letters; and was always known
among his friends as "Shirley." He was the third
editor of *Punch:* having succeeded Tom Taylor in that
prominent, if somewhat invidious, position. He was
verging on his sixtieth year, when he was with apparent suddenness snatched from a host of friends. Shirley Brooks had not been a member of the original
staff of *Punch:* in fact for a considerable time he was a
militant member of the opposite camp. He had always been friendly with Thackeray and with à Beckett; but he had some kind of grudge against Douglas
Jerrold, who returned the inimical feeling with interest. Shirley was the son of an architect well known
in his day, who was the designer of the London Institution in Finsbury Circus. I think that his son was
bred to the law, whence he drifted into literature and
journalism. So early as 1845, he was writing short
humorous stories in *Bentley's Miscellany*, and in 1847, I
first made his acquaintance, as I have already set forth,
in connection with the *Man in the Moon*, to which he
was a copious contributor.

He was also one of the staff of the *Morning Chronicle ;*
and when Henry Mayhew suggested that his great
work on "London Labour and the London Poor"

should be extended by cognate researches into the conditions of labour and poverty in continental countries, Shirley Brooks was despatched on a mission of inquiry in the provinces of European Russia. Some of his observations, full of brilliant description and witty comment, were embodied in an entertaining book called " The Russians of the South." On his return he was appointed to write, during the session, the Parliamentary summary in the *Morning Chronicle*, and eventually made up his quarrel with *Punch*, or rather with one or two of the Punchites, and contributed to the pages of that periodical, in which in the course of fifty years, not one unseemly word or impure thought has found a place, a vivacious tale of modern life, called "Miss Violet and Her Offers." He was also the author of a novel, not published in *Punch*, but in three-volume form, called " The Silver Cord," which was illustrated by Sir John Tenniel.

As an editor of *Punch*, Shirley Brooks was perhaps not quite so diplomatically opportune as Mark Lemon, but he was a much more brilliant man at the helm in Whitefriars than Tom Taylor had been. Tom Taylor was a ripe, classical scholar, and an admirable playwright; he was essentially clever, just, and upright, but he was not very much gifted with either wit or humour in the true sense of the term. Beyond his exceedingly droll " Adventures of an Unprotected Female," I cannot recall any *Punch* contributions of his which were absolutely comic; and, being altogether bereft of an ear for music, the poetry on which he occasionally ventured was, as a rule, deplorably cacophonous. Shirley Brooks, on the other hand, was a born poet. Whether the brilliant verse with which he copiously enriched the columns of *Punch* has ever been reprinted in a form even approximating to completeness, I am not aware; but he was the author, to my knowledge, of scores of graceful lyrics, which, to my mind, posterity should not willingly let die. I had known his pleasant and naturally humorous wife ever since I was a boy. She was a Miss Walkinshaw:—one of two good-looking sisters, who, from their marked divergence in complexion, had their miniatures painted about 1843, as "Night" and "Morning," by that Mr. Carl Schiller, of whom I was at the time a pupil. As a further illustration of the world being after all not such a very big village, I may mention that about 1864 I found Carl Schiller engaged in the comparatively humble, but useful, task of converting photographic portraits into miniatures at the studio of a well-known photographer in Regent Street. He was overjoyed to meet me again, and painted, in miniature, a little portrait of myself, to fit into a gold locket, which I gave to my wife.

It would be unjust were I to omit to put on record another instance of the constant and thoughtful kindness invariably shown to men of letters by the Earl of Beaconsfield. When Shirley Brooks died, Lord Beaconsfield was Prime Minister. The editor of *Punch* did not pass away in absolutely straitened circumstances; he left a policy of insurance, the realisation of which placed a considerable sum of money at the disposal of his widow; but she had only attained middle-age, and she had two sons growing up, the completion of whose education was indispensable. One day, passing through Cavendish Square, I met Alderman Sir Benjamin Phillips, some time Lord Mayor of London, the worthiest and most generous of Hebrews, who had shown very many kindnesses to Shirley. In the course of conversation, he asked confidentially how the widow and her sons were getting on; and I told him frankly the whole state of the case, so far as I knew it; explaining to him how sorely difficult it was for a modern Englishman of letters, even with an income amounting to £2,000 a year, to save anything substantial for those whom he left behind. The prominent literary man of the existing era, now that Bohemia has become, so far as literature is concerned, an almost mythical land, does not find it so very easy to lay by a competence for his widow, even if he enjoys an income larger than that I have set down. He is largely asked out into society ; and, unless he be a curmudgeon, he must himself occasionally entertain in partial requital of the entertainment which he has himself received.

If he be a journalist as well as an author, and writes on a great variety of topics, native and foreign, he must needs keep a secretary, and a secretary must be not a mere clerk, but an intelligent and accomplished person. If he be stricken in the vale of years and is slightly infirm, or has suffered from bronchial trouble, he cannot well get on without a brougham ; which he will find in the long run not much more expensive and a great deal safer than a hansom cab, in which, other-wise, he would be forced to be continually careering ; and this brougham he keeps, not for show, but for use, just as a medical man does. In addition to his incidental expenses, he is chronically the prey of all the begging letter writers, the secretaries of hospitals, refuges, asylums, and other charitable institutions in London and the provinces. He is expected to sub-scribe to a memorial statue of that great philanthropist Sqybob, or to become a member of the committee for purchasing the birthplace of the Poet Podgers ; and if his donations to these doubtless deserving objects are in amount less than those given by a Member of Parliament—I do not say anything about Peers, because, as a rule, they have, or say that they have, nothing to give—he is looked down upon and sneered at as a miser. Finally, the more he earns, the more does the Imperial Government tax him for being industrious; and every spring a sum which would pay half his house-rent is extorted from him in the shape of the unjust and iniquitous Income Tax.

Naturally I did not say all this to Sir Benjamin; but I gave him a sketch of what was passing through my mind; whereupon he nodded his good old head, and told me to enlarge on what I half hinted in a nice long letter, which he would show to Disraeli on the ensuing Sunday afternoon, when the statesman almost invariably paid a visit to the Rothschild mansion, in Piccadilly. A very few days afterwards I had occasion, on some matter of business, to see Sir Benjamin Phillips again in the Venetian Parlour at the Mansion House, where he was acting as *locum tenens* for the then Lord Mayor. "It's all right," he said to me, after the customary greeting had been exchanged; "Disraeli has read your letter, and Mrs. Shirley Brooks's name is down for a pension:" which pension was presently allotted to her. In concluding this parenthetical notice of my old and valued friend, I may mention that Shirley Brooks was a very handsome man—prematurely white as to hair and beard; he had the clearest of complexions, and a lustrous, speaking eye. In politics he was a staunch Conservative; and although in the days when I had not any politics at all, we were at the very opposite poles of political convictions, there was never any discord between us on public topics.

There is no need I trust for me to apologise for having written the above lines. I am not aware of any living man of letters who was sufficiently the contemporary and the intimate of Shirley Brooks, to be able to write even a fragmentary Memoir of him, to say nothing of an exhaustive Life.

The year 1876 was to me one of the usual journalistic activity and industry, but it was not, so far as I can remember, marked by any noteworthy adventures. It was signalised, however, by a curious little social victory, won after hard battling by the *Daily Telegraph*. For years we had advocated as forcibly as ever we could, the demolition of old Temple Bar. I am sure that, if I wrote one, I wrote forty leading articles, impetuously demanding the removal of the disreputable old structure: first, because it did no honour, but rather discredit, to the memory of its illustrious designer, Sir Christopher Wren. The design in question is not an original one—there is at least one church in Rome, the architectural outlines of which closely resemble those of the old Bar, *i.e.*, a basement composed of one central arch and two side arches, or posterns, and an attic storey with niches for statues, and a central window, flanked by two ugly, cumbrous, carved stone scrolls. Sir Christopher was never in Rome, but there is a counterpart of Temple Bar in a gateway in one of the courtyards of the Palace at Fontainebleau, which the great English architect is known to have explored.

Next, I objected to the Bar as a grievous obstruction to metropolitan traffic, and as the chief reason of the permanent congestion of locomotion in one of the busiest arterial thoroughfares of the Metropolis. A wag of the last generation used to say that a block in Fleet Street was generally due to one of two causes—either there was an old lady who had stopped her brougham at Child's Bank, and was unable to find her cheque-book ; or large quantities of soda-water and bottled-beer were being delivered from a wagon at the shell-fish shop, higher up. Finally, the detestation we experienced for the Bar was intensified by the remembrance that, historically, it was associated with nothing save that which was gloomy, deplorable, and disgraceful in English history. For a hundred years the grimy architrave had been defaced by poles surmounted by the skulls of gallant Jacobite gentlemen, who had sacrificed their lives in a cause which they believed to be that of religion, loyalty, truth, and justice, and whom the merciless behests of the bloody-minded law of high treason had doomed to be butchered in front of Newgate, or on Kennington Common.

This view of the question was, I am glad to say, more effectually taken up by the late Mr. Godwin, the architect, who published a powerful pamphlet, entitled " Temple Bar, the City Golgotha," but public opinion had become fully ripe for the removal of this foul and hideous old anachronism, before the City Fathers could be persuaded to yield to the popular demand, and cart away the crazy old nuisance. The City surveyors, as early as March, 1868, reported the structure to be dangerous; the façade cracked soon after that, and it began to sink, so that by the end of July its rotten masonry had to be shored up with unsightly beams of timber. Still the Court of Common Council hesitated and vacillated. There was an idea at Guildhall, that Temple Bar somehow symbolised the municipal supremacy of the Corporation of London; since the Lord Mayor and Aldermen were empowered to shut the old oaken gates of the Bar in the face even of Royalty, and not to throw them open until Garter King of Arms, or some other dignified delegate of the Crown had asked permission to enter. At length, on the 27th September, the removal of the Bar was voted by the Court of Common Council, and early in the ensuing year, the work of demolition was commenced. The stones were numbered, and were eventually given to Sir Henry Meux, Bart., to be re-

erected at his seat, Theobald's Park, near Cheshunt;
but with the knowledge that the bogey in question has
vanished from the Metropolis, it matters but little, I
should say, whereabouts it is now exhibiting its dimin-
ished head.

When the wretched old thing had been entirely
cleared away from Fleet Street, the incurably obsti-
nate civic authorities were permitted to mark the site
of Temple Bar by another semi-obstruction, that is to
say, they set up, between the branch offices of the
Bank of England and the banking house of Messrs.
Child, whose firm had for two hundred years kept their
old ledgers and cash books in the windows above the
archway, a kind of stone sandwich, in which were inserted indifferent statues of the Queen and the Prince
of Wales. The design also comprised a couple of
panels filled with absurd tableaux in high relief, supposed to represent the Lord Mayor in his state coach,
and a number of the Aldermen on horseback; while
the entire monstrosity was crowned by the bronze
effigy of some fabulous creature which the City people
declared to be a griffin, but which experts in apocryphal zoology announced to be a dragon. The stone
sandwich and its plastic disfigurements cost nearly
£12,000; whereas not more than £1,500 had been spent
on the architectural admiration of Sir Christopher
Wren.

I must do the City Fathers the justice to say that
they exhibited just one touch of sly humour ere Temple
Bar altogether disappeared in the leafy shades of Theobald's. It was pretty well known that I had been
active in bringing about the demolition of the whilom
Place of Skulls. The Common Council caused a number of medals commemorative of the Bar to be struck,
from the lead which covered the superstructure; and
one of these medals was sent to me from Guildhall,

with a polite note expressing the civic appreciation of the solicitude with which I had sat at the death-bed of a venerable relic of the past. I replied as politely: stating that I had not only sat by the death-bed of Temple Bar, but that I had been humbly instrumental in pulling the pillow from under the head of the scandalous old moribund. I took a rubbing in heel-ball from the metal disc, and then presented the medal itself to a valued friend at Baltimore, Maryland, U.S.A. Perhaps at Baltimore that leaden lump may, in process of time, be really regarded as an historic relic.

The close of 1876 was politically tumultuous, and to me professionally exciting. War had broken out between Turkey and Servia; and the Servians were favoured with the active sympathies of Russia. It is true that early in November the Tsar made a pacific declaration of his intentions to Lord Augustus Loftus, the British Ambassador in St. Petersburg; but on the 10th November His Imperial Majesty, in an address to an assembly of nobles at the Kremlin, Moscow, said that if sufficient guarantees were not given by the Ottoman Government he would act independently. This portentous announcement was held in England to be tantamount to a threat that the Emperor Alexander II. meant to go to war with Turkey; and that in all probability Great Britain would be, as an ancient ally of Turkey, very speedily embroiled in the quarrel. At all events, affairs in general in South-Eastern Europe were deemed, by the authorities in Fleet Street, to be in a sufficiently troubled condition to warrant my being sent to Russia to see how things were going on there. It took me only a few hours to pack up; and, furnished with letters from the Foreign Office to Lord Augustus Loftus, I was soon on the road, by way of Berlin, to the Muscovite capital.

The scare was not quite groundless; the air was full of bellicose rumours, although I am bound to admit that, socially speaking, there did not seem to be the slightest ill-feeling existing in Russian society against Englishmen. I was most cordially received by the Ambassador, who, among other favours, introduced me to a clever gentleman named Horn, who was the editor of the *Journal de St. Petersbourg*, a daily paper shrewdly suspected to be the organ of the Russian Foreign Office, and published in the French language. It was in this journal, just after I arrived in St. Petersburg, that Prince Gortschakoff published his memorable manifesto, denying that Russia had formed any schemes for territorial aggrandisement at the expense of Turkey, and sneering at the notoriously apocryphal will of Peter the Great, as one of the "*Contes de la Mère l'Oie*," or tales of Mother Goose. All experts in continental politics are aware that this so-called testament of Peter Veliké was concocted by August von Kotzebue, a hack political pamphleteer and subordinate diplomatic agent in the service of Russia, who is just faintly remembered in England as the author of that mournful and mawkish drama, *The Stranger*. Peter the Great no more declared in any will he ever made that the ultimate mission of Russia was to seize Constantinople, than that his successors were bound to take possession of the Scilly Islands and the Peak of Derbyshire. Still it is as likely enough that Kotzebue had his cue to the line of Russian politics which he was to indicate in this bogus testament.

Mr. Horn was kind enough to hold at his residence a couple of receptions at which I had the honour to meet, so I was given to understand, the flower of intellectual Russian society. One gathering was composed exclusively of university professors and medical men. In 1876 I had, apparently, hopelessly—but such turned out not to be the case—forgotten all the Russian which I had acquired in 1856; so the " medicos " and the professors all talked to me in French. I mention this trifling circumstance for the reason that soon after my departure from Russia, there appeared in a leading St. Petersburg paper a lengthy leading article in which I was accused of being, not an English journalist but a Turkish spy. It happened, to be sure, that there was, at the time, a Count Sala in the diplomatic service of Turkey; and the writer in the Russian newspaper made the very best he could of the, to him, damning circumstance that at several dinner parties and receptions in Russian society at which I had been present, I had never been heard to speak a word of English. I can only deferentially say that I did not make use of my vernacular tongue, because nobody I met outside the walls of the Embassy ever spoke English to me.

I had, apart from political complications, a right merry time; although my unfortunate name was two or three times the cause of some trifling embarrassment to me. I resided at the Hotel d'Angleterre, in the Izaak's Ploschad, or Great Square of St. Izaak's Cathedral; and it chanced that in the same hotel there was staying a French *prima donna* called Mlle. Sala, or Salla; and we were continually getting hold of each other's letters. I think that I was sufficiently judicious not to unseal any of the missives addressed to Mademoiselle; but she invariably opened the letters addressed to me, and would come down in a towering passion to my room, and shrilly insinuate that I was not an " *homme comme il faut*," that I was " *malhonnête*," that I was a "*goujat*," a "*cancre*" and the "*dernier des derniers*," because my paternal designation happened to be identical, or nearly identical, with hers. However, she gave a benefit concert during her stay, and I took a couple of stalls for it ; and she became partially placated.

I had as an interpreter, and ultimately as a courier, one of the oddest fishes that I ever came across; he was an Englishman of originally "horsey" tendencies; and had come out to Russia as a stud groom to some wealthy Boyard, whose service he had quitted to become a *valet de place* at the Hotel d'Angleterre. He had a settled idea in his mind — first, that English people knew nothing whatever about Russia ; and next, that journalists were despicable and degraded beings, who never had any money. I went out to dinner one evening, in the Mala Millionnaia ; and on my return I asked him, casually, if he knew who my host was. "He is a gentleman," he replied, in a tone of dogged disdain. "Yes, certainly," I said ; "I knew that before I went to dine with him ; but who is he?" "He is a gentleman," he repeated ; "a real gentleman, the proprietor of extensive mills for making rape-seed oil, in the government of Tomsk." By-and-bye, when he found that I was receiving constant invitations to dine, not only at the British Embassy, but at the other Legations, and at great Russian houses, I used to hear him muttering that he really must charge me an additional fifty kopeks a day. I had evidently risen, not in his moral, but in his financial estimation. Add to these pleasing traits that he had a morbid hatred of the Jews, and an abiding terror of the police, and you have a tolerably comprehensive picture of this remarkable *cicerone*. Stay ; if he was interrupted in his cut-and-dried descriptions of the rarities at the palaces and museums which we visited, he would grow absolutely livid with rage, clench his fists convulsively, and breathe hard.

For example, in the Palace of the Hermitage there is an extraordinary collection of works of gold and silver *repoussé*, discovered in certain ancient sarcophagi at Kertch; so he would begin—" Tombs of the ancient kings of Scythia; four thousand years old. Tomb of the Master of the Horse of the ancient kings of Scythia; four thousand years old. Observe the hosses; observe the ornaments in gold and silver—four thousand years old." I took the liberty of interrupting him to observe that the processes of horse-taming, exhibited on a splendid shield of gold, precisely corresponded with the methods employed by Mr. Rarey, the noted *dompteur* of refractory steeds; whereupon he flew into a rage, as before described, and proceeded to indulge in some broken utterances in Russian, to me incomprehensible, but which I do not think I am wrong in assuming to have been vehement curses, invoked on my head, and on that of the transatlantic horse-tamer.

One day I had taken, in his company, a jaunt in an open droschka to the very extremity of the Nevskoi, even to the historic monastery of St. Alexander, of that ilk. It happened that a Russian friend had told me the exact fare for such a journey. It was eighty kopeks, which I duly handed to the Ischvostchik. To my amused astonishment, the Jehu, with the long beard and the proportionately long caftan, immediately proceeded to fall on his knees, and sprawl across the cushion of the droschka; occasionally raising his hands to heaven and uttering a series of piteous ejaculations. " What the deuce is the fellow doing?" I asked impatiently of my interpreter. " He is praying," he made answer; " that Heaven will be merciful to the person who has given him an insufficient fare; and a gentleman," he added, with bitter sarcasm, " would give him a rouble." For once I put my foot down; I knew enough Russian to bid the driver "go to the devil," and I told the *valet de place* to behave himself.

You may ask how it came about that I brooked so long the man's insolence and forwardness, but he amused me while I was riding with him; I had only to mention, apparently inadvertently, the name of Trepoff, who was then Chief of Police, to make my guide start up from his seat in a spasm of consternation; and a sure way of arousing his ire was to say something kindly about his much loathed foes the Jews. There were times when he was placable, and even amiable : that was when he had had a thorough skinful of *vodka*, or corn brandy.

Now and again the ill-tempered *valet de place* would become civil, and for a short time, almost amiable. It was when he had partaken somewhat too freely of the just-mentioned *vodka ;* under which circumstances he would tell me confidently that he was madly, and hopelessly, in love with a young person of Icelandish extraction, who was lady's-maid in the family of a Russian Minister, Plenipotentiary at the Court of Stockholm. Once a year His Excellency came to St. Petersburg, on leave of absence ; but, according to the showing of the crusty *cicerone*, the young person of Icelandish extraction was as cold as the country of her birth, and only gave him, metaphorically speaking, so many penny ices in return for the burning embers of his passion. Poor man ! somehow or another he diverted me, and I bore with his disagreeable peculiarities : chiefly, I should say, because Russia, notwithstanding the slight savour of Orientalism which you enjoy while rambling through the bazaars, especially in Moscow, is a miserably monotonous country. There is no middle-class ; there is no medium between a luxurious and sensuous life made up of champagne, *sterlet* balls, *soirées*, operas, French plays, and the ballet, and a squalid existence, the distinguishing features of which are cabbage soup, salted cucumbers, ryè-bread, red-hot brick stoves, grimy sheepskin *touloupes*, and the mingled odour of tallow, coarse tobacco, fiery *vodka*, and unwashed moujik.

I had the honour of enjoying, during my stay in Petropolis, the friendship of the American Minister, who, in addition to being a diplomatist, was a dramatist and poet of no mean repute; and I shall never forget a remark once made by his bright and observant spouse. " St. Petersburg," she used to say, " is the grandest of capitals; the diplomatic corps are surrounded by a galaxy of diamonds, stars, crosses, ribbons, and splendid uniforms. But all the while you feel that you are in a cage. The bars are gilded, I freely grant; but a golden cage is, nevertheless, a prison; and I'd rather be at the Continental Hotel, Philadelphia, in the State of Pennsylvania."

I went down to Moscow in quest of rumours of war, and I found plenty of indices pointing to a proximate outbreak of hostilities between Russia and Turkey. One morning I received a despatch from Fleet Street, saying, " Go to Warsaw ; instructions awaiting you." The winter had set in with its accustomed keenness; but you suffer less from intense cold in Russia than in any country with which I am acquainted. I have felt cold in Canada, in New York, and even in Vienna, in winter time; but in Russia the natural asperity of the climate has led the ingenious Moscovites to adopt a multitude of devices which almost completely ward off the onslaughts of King Frost. Your rooms are always kept warm at a temperature of at least 70 degrees ; and in most drawing-rooms there is a kind of vivarium of flowering plants, with ivy and Virginian creeper clinging to a mural trelliswork. Nearly one side of the apartment is occupied by an immense stove, covered with white enamelled tiles, often of so ornate a pattern that it might be a monument to the memory of some eighteenth century Landgrave of a petty Russian principality; and, from November till March, the icy air from the outside is only admitted by the servants at early morning, while you are still comfortably in bed, through a small square Judas trap, in one of the window-panes, called a *vasistas*, a term, obviously a corruption from the German *was ist das*—what is it? You never venture out unless you are swathed in a huge furred pelisse; and even the carriage in which you ride contains a small stove, and the doors and windows of the vehicle are shielded from the external blast by strips of list. -

It was thus with a light heart that I left Moscow on my way from St. Petersburg *en route* for Warsaw: a somewhat circuitous mode of travelling, I confess, but I had to get some money from my bankers in St. Petersburg. During my stay in Warsaw, Madame Adelina Patti was singing at the Great Theatre; and she was so kind as to send me for one of her performances a couple of stalls, by the hands of one of the most alarmingly imposing *chasseurs* that I ever saw. An American essayist has somewhere observed that the two most "spanglorious" creatures of which he is aware are a cock turkey and the captain of a British man-of-war in full rig; but I will back Madame Adelina Patti's *chasseur* against both. His whiskers and his cocked hat and plumes made an immense impression on my ill-conditioned *cicerone*, whom I had now taken into regular employ as a travelling courier; and I used to hear him muttering to himself that if gentlemen had letters brought to them by such heavy swells as the party with the cocked hat, he must certainly demand an increase of salary.

A pleasant acquaintance did I also make in the city of the Kremlin, in Mr. Leslie, Her Britannic Majesty's Consul, who turned out to be the brother of Mr. Henry Leslie of musical renown. The friendly Consul came to the railway terminus to see me off. The only other occupant of the well-warmed compartment in the corridor train was a Russian general officer, tall, stalwart, and middle-aged, with the usual grey great coat over his full military uniform. He was very courteous — the Russians next to the Mexicans are the politest people in the world. We exchanged cigars; and for about an hour we conversed in French, which of course he spoke with perfect fluency and purity. Suddenly, as he was lighting a fresh Havana, he said in English, " You're an Englishman?" I bowed, and owned the soft impeachment. " I knew it," he continued, " because I heard you talking English to Mr. Leslie, the English Consul, at Moscow, just before the train started; and now," he added, " might I without giving offence, ask what is just at this moment the predominant thought in your mind concerning my humble self?" I felt slightly embarrassed at the directness of this question, and was stammering out some conventional banality about my gratification at having the honour of—and so forth and so forth, when the middle-aged General stopped me. " Let us be frank; you were thinking that I was speaking with a broad Scotch accent." I replied laughing, that that was precisely the impression produced on my mind. " I'll tell you how it is," he resumed, " I am General Greig, a descendant of Catherine II.'s Admiral Greig, and I am an *aide-de-camp* of the Grand Duke Constantine. We are at present Russian subjects, and members of the orthodox Greek Church; but from father to son the boys of our family are always sent to be educated at the High School, Edinburgh." After this explanation we relapsed into French, and parted very cordially at the St. Petersburg terminus.

On the same evening I dined at the British Embassy, and among the guests was the General's brother, Admiral Greig, who, at that period, I believe was Minister of Finance. He was highly amused with my account of my rencontre with his brother; but I had no opportunity of ascertaining how His Excellency pronounced English, seeing that the party was a very small one, and that one of the guests was the French Ambassador, General Le Flô, who did not speak the language of John Bull; and it would have been a grave breach of one of the strictest rules of Russian etiquette to converse in a tongue of which any lady or gentleman present was ignorant. I remained only twenty-four hours in Warsaw, where, however, I had the pleasure of meeting Colonel Maude, V.C., who was then British Consul-General in the Polish capital. In what remote region of the world that gallant officer may be at present, I am unaware, but I should say that in the way of adventures his career has been of a nature to make my own petty record of life quite humdrum and uneventful.

The instructions that I found waiting for me were, as usual, terse and business-like. "Go to Odessa; see mob: go Constantinople." I knew well enough what "see mob" meant; it signified, "Take notice of the mobilisation of troops in the southern provinces of Russia." My proprietor's behests were simplicity itself, but it was not quite easy to obey them. It was a desperately hard winter; and in many districts the railways were blocked by immense masses of snow, kept in slow motion by the wind, and called by the French-speaking Russians "*chasse-neiges*." However, I persevered, as it was simply my duty so to do; and with tolerable ease I reached Kieff, which may be defined as the ecclesiastical capital of European Russia. Here are painted and framed, and partially gilt, an innumerable multitude of *Ikons*—scriptural and other pictorial representations of the Panagia, and other varieties; Virgins, white, pink, coffee-coloured, and pea-green for aught I can tell; Virgins with three hands, and it may be with two heads; ecclesiastical vestments, censers, votive lamps and candlesticks—are all manufactured at Kieff.

Beyond this sacrosanct city, the railway was available for only about fifty miles; and then for a couple of days the ill-conditioned courier and I were fain to travel in a sledge, with three horses abreast, over the snowy steppes. We only travelled by day; and our driver could tell to a verst the hour at which we should reach a Government post-house, where we were sure to find at least hot tea, biscuits, brandy, and repose, such as it was, on sofas upholstered in black leather, and haunted to an unpleasant extent by insects known to the Americans as " chintzes," clearly a corruption of the Spanish " *chinchas*," and which by polite English people are termed " Norfolk Howards," or " gentlemen in brown." " They may well call this place Stony-Stratford," remarked the traveller in the well-known *non sequitur* anecdote, " for I have been most terribly bitten by fleas." I may hint that I was most terribly bitten—but not by fleas—at a good many Government post-houses on my way South. About three hundred miles from Odessa we found the railway again, and I reached that city in safety. I may just add that my nose did not get frost-bitten while I was sledging it through the snow, as I had adopted the very sensible American practice of covering my whole face with a thick layer of cold cream; nor did I make the acquaintance *en route* of any packs or pack of wolves. Had I come within measurable distance of those normally famished brutes, I might, it is true, have propitiated them by throwing out to them, as a peace-offering, the ill-conditioned courier, who was, like most horsey individuals, short of stature, and slight of frame.

The man's temper between Kieff and Odessa was simply diabolical; he was continually grumbling that "a gentleman would chuck the whole blessed thing up" and go back to the Hotel d'Angleterre. How would he have looked, I wonder, if I had chucked him out to the potential wolves? As it was he further nourished his spleen by continually asking whether I really thought that I could get any money from the banker at Odessa on whom I had a letter of credit. "Real gentlemen," he added, "always carried with them a pocket-book well lined with rouble notes." Confound his impudence! Yet the man made me laugh and was useful; he was an adept at slanging extortionate post-masters and sledge-drivers, and was always able to conciliate subordinate officers of police, who were perpetually bearing down on me, and who professed to be dissatisfied with the wording of my passport, possibly because they were incapable of reading the document in question. The Crusty One had an infallible method for quieting these gentry. I happened to have some *carte de visite* about me, which I had had taken at Moscow, and in which I was depicted in full travelling costume, in a fur pelisse, jackboots lined with lambs' wool, seal-skin gloves, a courier bag slung at my left hip, and a beaver *kalpak* as big as the busby of a horse artilleryman of the last generation. The Crusty One borrowed one of these photographic effigies; and whenever a sub-sub-deputy assistant inspector of gendarmerie was troublesome, he used to exhibit the *carte de visite* as proof positive that it precisely corresponded with the description of my features and general aspect given in the passport ; he would place the cardboard close before the eyes of the *polizei*, and strange to say the official would at once, with many bows and smiles, take his departure. When I asked the Crusty One to account for the apparently magic effect of these graphic displays, he replied, " I took blessed good care to put a rouble note in front of the *carte ;* and an hour afterwards I'll go bail that the beggar will be as drunk as I should like to be now."

Kind Lord Augustus Loftus had given me a letter of introduction to the British Consul-General at Odessa, a gentleman whose name has escaped me, but who proved to be politeness itself. He was a bit of a wag ; for so soon as he had read my letter he proceeded to remark, in a grave, business-like tone, that the instructions issued by the Foreign Office for consuls in foreign countries did not entail upon them the obligation of showing any hospitality to persons provided with official letters of recommendation. I bowed, and said that the honour of making the acquaintance of Her Majesty's representative was amply sufficient for me, whereupon the Consul-General bowed again, and altogether dropping the business-like tone, went on to say that his dinner hour was half-past seven, and that his wife, he was sure, would be delighted if I would favour them with my company that evening. I was only too glad to accept the invitation, and spent a delightful evening : one of the guests being the Ottoman Consul at Odessa, a highly-educated Turkish gentleman, who had been educated in Paris and at Vienna.

Gilbert à Beckett, in the " Comic History of England," defined the character of Lord Chancellor Bacon as " streaky." Of the climate of Odessa, at the beginning of December, I may say that it struck me as being of that degree of streakiness which the Americans call " a little mixed." In the daytime the sun shone brightly, and at noon the temperature was broiling hot; whereas the evenings were chilly, and the nights piercingly cold. I saw all the sights of the city, which owes its handsome architectural features almost entirely to the energy and good taste of the French Duc de Richelieu, who was Governor here in the early years of the present century. I went to the Opera House, a really splendid theatre, but with a rather poor company. As for the crusty courier, he was in ecstasies with Odessa. " It's a love of a place," he exclaimed ; "grapes as big as gooseberries for breakfast, and real, red wine at twenty kopeks a quart." But this dream of some tropical warmth was rudely interrupted by the fact that the port of Odessa was slowly beginning to freeze, so I made all haste to take passage on board a Russian *pyroscaphe*, or steamer, bound for Constantinople.

The ill-conditioned courier was agreeably surprised, or professed to be so, when he found that my bankers made me an advance of a thousand roubles on my letter of credit ; but these astute financiers paid me in Russian notes, of various denominations : telling me, when I protested against paper money, that there was absolutely no gold at all in Russia. My friend, the British Consul-General, got me, however, out of this difficulty ; and, for a very slight commission, he obtained from a money-changer about the most remarkable collection of coins that ever came under my notice. There were golden ducats of Catherine II., hundred-franc pieces of Napoleon I., twenty-dollar American eagles, Mexican doubloons, Friederichs d'or, louis, Turkish pounds, and Belgian twenty-franc pieces. I have always had the instinct of a collector, and I should dearly have liked to bring this curious assortment of coins home, and garner them in one of the drawers of a cabinet of rarities; but, as it happened, I had to pay the wages of the cantankerous courier, and his journey back to St. Petersburg, together with my passage to Constantinople. So, as Charles Keene's Scotchman would have said, " Bang went," not " saxpence," but Mexican doubloons and the golden ducats of the Semiramis of the North.

CHAPTER LIV

WE had a tranquil passage across the Black Sea, the hue of which struck me as really approximating to its name; since its waters in winter are a dark opaque grey; whereas the Red Sea, when I traversed it, was as blue as the Mediterranean. The submarine coral certainly does not give rubescence to the waters above. We coasted for a while along the shores of the Crimea, where perfect summer seemed to be reigning, but it grew raw and chilly when we were off the mouths of the Danube. The captain of the steamer was a most intelligent Russian, who had been second officer on board an East Indiaman, and who was continually deploring the accursed earth-hungering spirit which was urging the Government of his country to force a war upon Turkey. There were very few passengers on board; and among them I only remember a young Russian, of noble family, who was a lieutenant in the Imperial Navy. He was in the last stage of consumption, and was on his way to Naples "to die," as he quite composedly put it.

It was happily a sunshiny, bracing morning when the *pyroscaphe* entered the Bosphorus. The gloriously enchanting view, both of Europe and of Asia! You know that I am a Cockney; you know that I have not one grain of poetry or imagination in my composition —I have said so fifty times—and thus I am not ashamed to say that when we reached Buyukdere, and the marvels of Stamboul were revealed to me, with its domes and minarets, all pink and gold in the morning sunshine, they reminded me of nothing so forcibly as of the panoramas that Grieve and Telbin used to paint at old Vauxhall Gardens.

It was about eleven when we made Pera. The examination of my baggage at the Custom House was a pleasant farce; since I had no sooner landed than I engaged a Greek Dragoman, who spoke Italian fluently, and was to do all I needed for a Turkish *medjidié*, equivalent to about five francs a day. I gave him my passport, and instructed him to distribute a moderate amount of piastres in official quarters when such distribution was expedient; and, in half-an-hour after landing, I was safely housed at the Hotel de Byzance, in the Grand Rue de Pera, a Greek *Zenodocheion*, kept by a most obliging descendant of Miltiades. As for my dragoman, I believe his name was Constantine Fenerli; but, for convenience, we called him the descendant of Alcibiades.

I say we; for in a few days I was joined by my brilliant colleague, and old friend, Campbell Clarke, who, for many years, had been the resident correspondent of the *Daily Telegraph* in Paris. He had come out as political special correspondent of the *Daily Telegraph* to gather up all available intelligence from day to day, and transmit telegrams to Fleet Street; while I was to write special articles, of two or three columns each, descriptive of life and manners at Stamboul and Pera. Campbell Clarke had come from Paris, through Italy to Brindisi; whence he had taken steamer to Corfu, and had so steamed through the Sea of Marmora to Constantinople; his travelling companion from the Ionian Islands being a Turkish Pasha, whose main object in life appeared to be to smoke, quaff dry champagne, and play écarté, at which game he was keenest of hands.

Constantinople has become during the last few years a place of habitual resort for trippers; and I almost wonder that the globe-trotter has not long since abbreviated the name of the City of the Sultan into "Con" or "Stan." At all events I am not about to weary you with descriptions of the mosques, the bazaars, the Valley of Sweet Waters, the Atmeidan, the palaces, and so forth. I wrote a good many letters in the *Daily Telegraph* about the lions of Constantinople, but I have never cared to republish them; cognisant as I am of their immense inferiority to the description of Stamboul in the " Pencillings by the Way " of the American, Nathaniel Parker Willis; to " The City of the Sultan " of Miss Pardoe; and in especial to the " Constantinople " of Théophile Gautier. I find, however, a few memoranda in my note-book which may not be wholly without interest. On the tramway running from Pera to Galata, I was much amused by the circumstance that there was a harem on board each car for the accommodation of the Turkish ladies. Next I find that on the occasion of my first visit to the mosque of the Divine Wisdom, commonly called St. Sophia, the Turkish janitor, for the consideration of a *medjidié*, obligingly, with a long stick, knocked down from the walls a handful of the original Byzantine mosaics, which I carefully placed in an envelope and brought home with me. It was most Vandalic on my part to make such a purchase, but what would you have when one has a craze for collecting? Most of us are from time to time Vandals, Goths, Visigoths, Ostrogoths, and Huns into the bargain. When I reached England I went to a chemist and druggist and bought sixpennyworth of " jujubes," which in size and colour—abating the gilt obverse— closely resembled the *tesseræ* of dull glass, with which the Emperor Justinian the Great adorned the walls of the Agia Sofia. I placed the " jujubes " in one pill-box, and the *tesseræ* gilded, faces downwards, in the other. I asked a succession of lady-friends to tell me which set of cubes were thirteen hundred years old, and which were made the day before yesterday. In five cases out of six the ladies declared the jujubes to be the antiques; but the accurate guesser was a widow and consequently crafty. She shook up the *tesseræ* in the box and said "glass," and then she felt the jujubes and remarked "gum."

As regards the Dancing Dervishes, I look upon them simply as a gang of teetotum-like humbugs; but I remember that, as Campbell Clarke and I emerged from their mosque, we were fiercely scowled upon and even rudely hustled by groups of *softas* or theological students in long caftans and voluminous white turbans. It was these young gentlemen who were mainly instrumental in fomenting the discontent which culminated in the deposition of the hapless Sultan Abdul Aziz. The Howling Dervishes interested me a little more than the dancing ones had done: first because at least two of these professors of ululation appeared to have a genuine epileptic fit during the performance; and next because it was with the very greatest difficulty that I could restrain myself from howling with might and main, "Amalaïaoo! Amalaïaoo! Amalaïaoo! Oo! Oo! Oo!" Try it yourself—not in your bath—but rocking your body backwards and forwards in a rocking-chair. If you are nervous I will go bail that you will begin to howl involuntarily before you are a quarter of an hour older.

The dogs of Stamboul interested me mightily. The vagrant curs that hung about the Legations in the Grand Rue de Pera were almost invariably mangy, but that was due not to starvation but to overfeeding; those in the neighbourhood of the British and Russian Embassies being the mangiest and the plumpest. No little sensation was caused during my stay by an incident which would have delighted that eminent friend of the canine race, the *Spectator* newspaper. A French Consul-General and his wife both died within a few hours of each other of fever. The Consul's effects were sold by auction; but nobody cared to buy a poor little white poodle, whose woolly frills and tufts, pink barrel, and coal-black muzzle I had often admired while his master was in the flesh. The unfortunate little beast was left homeless to wander about in shiftless misery; and he fell among a pack of pariah dogs. Had they followed the established canons of their race, these four-footed *gitanos* would have immediately proceeded to tear the little white poodle to pieces and devour him; but it singularly and beautifully happened that the bow-wow *zingari* adopted the homeless waif and stray, scouted for food for him, and made much of him, generally.

He was pointed out to me one day near the Swedish Legation, quite unshaven and unshorn, as grubby as a sweep, but looking quite happy and comfortable. This act of toleration, however, must be considered as wholly exceptional and almost phenomenal on the part of the pariah dogs. I think that Messrs. Pickford had an agency at Pera; at least, I remember some parcel-van belonging to an English company, which in its perambulations was " bossed," so to speak, by a little black-and-tan English terrier, which from the summit of a mound of merchandise used to bark with genuine terrier impudence impartially at Turks and Greeks and Franks alike. The vagrant dogs of Pera would go half crazy when they caught sight of this bumptious little animal; they howled, they yelled, they yelped, they threw themselves on their backs and rolled about with their paws in the air in impotent rage; while the little terrier, from his proud eminence, looked down upon his poor relations, yapping contemptuously.

At the northern extremity of the Golden Horn, beyond the Port of Commerce and the Port of War, there is a suburb called Eyoub, famed for an ancient mosque of that name. An English friend of mine was very curious to see the mosque in question, but he was warned by a Turkish acquaintance that the outcast dogs of Eyoub, not being pensioners of any foreign Legation, were as exceeding fierce as those humans who used to come out of the tombs, of old. The Eyoub dogs, added the Effendi, were supposed to be able to detect a Frank at the first sniff, and might prove very troublesome customers. However, my friend was not to be deterred from his purpose by the reputed ferocity of the dogs ; so with an English companion he hired a caique and was swiftly rowed to the place of his destination. He had no sooner landed than he was surrounded by a herd of angrily barking dogs. It happened that he was an expert in canine characteristics ; so, seeing either a post or the trunk of a tree, I forget which, standing conveniently close by, he coolly sat down and looked at the dogs, which immediately followed his example by squatting on their haunches in an irregular semi-circle and looking at him. He then rose and composedly walked to an adjacent baker's shop—the dogs quietly following him —and cleared out the baker's stock at an expense of about half-a-crown ; then he and his companion broke up the loaves and distributed them among the hungry pack ; after which act of hospitality the two English-men, quite unmolested, went about their business. " *A beau mentir qui vient de loin*," says the proverb. I don't think that my friend in telling me this story drew a longer bow than is from time to time drawn by travelling toxophilites ; and I own, myself, that the simper of incredulity has sometimes trembled on my lips when I have heard the pilgrim to the mosque of Eyoub de-clare that when he and his companion returned to the landing-stage they were followed by a friendly escort of pariah dogs, who, as the caique pushed off, wagged their tails sympathetically and uttered a succession of amicable barks, as if to say, " Come again soon, Giaour, and Allah be good to you."

I found Antonio Gallenga, as representative of the *Times*, installed at the Hotel Royal with his wife and daughter. Mrs. Gallenga, who was passionately fond of dogs, had taken one particular colony of pariahs under her protection; and one of the female vagrants being in an interesting condition, the kind English lady fitted up quite a comfortable little dormitory in a tomb in a disused cemetery close to the hotel, where the poor beast could lie soft and warm, and bring forth her young in peace.

Special correspondents of the newspapers abounded at Constantinople just then. Mr. Pearce, an English barrister, was the resident correspondent of the *Daily News;* and as a colleague he had a distinguished American journalist, the late—alas! the late—Alexander Mac Gahan. A brilliant, various, indefatigable writer, a thorough cosmopolitan, and as thoroughly a prince of good fellows was Alexander Mac Gahan, who in his capacity as a journalist had been almost everywhere and seen almost everything. He was an admirable type of the travelled, unprejudiced gentleman. Courtesy was to him not only a duty and a habit but a pleasure; hotel waiters bustled gaily about to do his bidding; and at the villanous music-hall at Pera (it was a variety show combined with a gambling-house) the eyes of the German leader of a band composed of two cracked fiddles, an asthmatic cornet-à-piston, and a stammering piano, the keys of which had turned yellow like the teeth of an old horse, used to sparkle with gratification when Mac Gahan, addressing him as Herr

Kapell-Meister, would beg him to let his clever artists —who also grinned with satisfaction at being so qualified—play the air of the " Sire de Framboisy " over again.

Mac Gahan had only one fad, or crotchet, or " lune " —call it which you will. He did not care for the Turks; he did not like the Greeks, and he scouted the proposal of one of us that the Eastern Question might be settled if Constantinople were made a federal city, to be garrisoned in equal proportions by the troops of the Great Powers, just as Frankfort was to a limited extent before the divorce of Austria from Germany, and the subsequent establishment of a united German Empire. Mac Gahan's solution was formulated in just four words: " Alfred, King of Byzantium." He yearned for the Padishah to be relegated to his Asiatic dominions, and for European Turkey, including the Principalities, to be erected into one monarchy under the rule of the then Duke of Edinburgh. " Alfred, King of Byzantium," was his pet watchword.

I am like the Friar in *Romeo and Juliet*. These old feet stumble at graves. I call to mind, among our Constantinople friends, another brilliant American, Eugene Schuyler, journalist, author, and diplomatist. In 1876 he was the United States Consul-General at Pera, and was afterwards to fill important diplomatic missions. That he was a versatile linguist was only one of his many attainments; and he will be remembered I hope on both sides of the Atlantic for his scholarlike and impartial life of Peter the Great. Staying with Schuyler was a young American gentleman who had come to Constantinople in order to study Byzantine archæology; but I am afraid that in our merry set less attention was paid to researches into the architecture and iconography of the Lower Empire than to holloaing and singing of anthems, and playing the fascinating but fatal game of poker. One day it occurred to Schuyler to get up a *narghilé*—smoking party. Now the *narghilé*, the pipe with the convoluted tube, and the smoke from the bowl of which passes through a cut-glass vessel containing perfumed water before it reaches the lips of the smoker, has almost entirely gone out of fashion in Constantinople. Even the *chibouck*, the pipe with the long cherry-stick stem and the bowl of porous terra-cotta, has practically vanished; and when you call nowadays on a Turkish pasha you are regaled, not with coffee and pipes, but with coffee and cigarettes. Schuyler had the octagonal hall of his house fitted up as a divan; and about half a dozen of us sat gravely on our haunches *à la turque*. The *narghilés* had been duly " cooked " in the kitchen —I mean the servants had filled and lighted the tobacco and tested the free passage of the smoke through the agate mouthpieces. I always abhorred the taste of the nastily-sophisticated tobacco with which the Turkish *narghilé* and the Indian hookah are fed; so I contented myself with puffing out the smoke as soon as it reached my lips; the others inhaled the so-called " aromatic " fumes.

I noticed that the complexion of my friend, the student of Byzantine archæology, had undergone in the course of about eight minutes several changes. First he turned very red, then a pale yellow, then a dull lead colour—the hue which the countenance of Napoleon III. was wont to assume at critical moments. Then his features were suffused by a tint in which green strove for mastery with blue, and eventually he turned a pasty white. " How are you getting on, old chappie ? " asked Eugene Schuyler encouragingly. " Oh! splendidly," replied or rather gasped the young American. " It's delicious, it's entrancing, I feel in Heaven *and I don't think I shall live five minutes*," mur-

muring which last words he tumbled off the divan
and rolled on to the marble pavement. The young
gentleman being an American citizen I felt that it
would be, as a British subject, *ultra vires* on my part
to interfere with him; but Mac Gahan and Schuyler,
not being troubled by such scruples, did their best to
assist him by kneeling on his chest and pumping the
fumes which he had inhaled out of his mouth, his ears,
and his nostrils, and by dashing cold· water over his
face, and administering judicious " nips " of Bourbon
whiskey within.

Another old ally—I need scarcely say that he has
also joined the majority—turned up in the person of
Frank Ives Scudamore, late of the General Post Office,
St. Martin's-le-Grand, from which service he had retired on a pension; after having with astonishing success carried out the extension of the postal telegraph
system throughout England. He was an intimate
friend of Edmund Yates; and besides his great official
capacity he possessed a great deal of literary culture,
and used to write many of the diverting Anglo-Latin
macaronic verses in *Punch*. Scudamore, in 1876, had
been commissioned by the Turkish Government to
superintend that department of the Ottoman Post Office which dealt with the reception and transmission
of the European mails; but in this position he somewhat resembled the fifth wheel to a coach; or, to put
the case more precisely, he might have been likened
to a wheel without any coach at all attached to it;
seeing that the English merchants and bankers at
Constantinople laboured under the singular impression that the Turkish Government had a *cabinet noir*
attached to their General Post Office, and that the
English mails were systematically opened and read
before they reached the proper recipients thereof.
Thus being warned of this sportive practice on the

part of the True Believers, I used to take my letters
to the office of a certain English agency at Galata,
where I also received such correspondence as came
out for me. I hope that the Turkish Government
punctually paid Scudamore. He would certainly
have earned his salary if he had had the opportunity
of earning it to any appreciable extent.

I cannot pass by in silence three notable Englishmen
who joined our little circle at the club in the Grand
Rue de Pera. First there was Hobart Pasha—blunt,
burly, and bearded, some time a post-captain in the
British navy ; afterwards in the American Civil War,
the boldest of blockade runners ; and in the winter of
1876 holding high rank but a somewhat phantom command in the Turkish fleet. Secondly, I may mention
Baker Pasha, who had commanded the Turkish gendarmerie, and had also held an important command in
the Turkish army. Poor Pasha ! He had been that
Colonel Valentine Baker, known to all military men as
one of the most brilliantly efficient staff officers in the
British army. He had lost everything—grade, repu-
tation, social status, and some seven thousand pounds
sterling which he had paid for his commissions,
through one solitary miserable act of indiscretion,
which might well have been punished by a fine of
£50. In recalling the story of the woeful collapse
of this brave, honourable, injudicious, and most unfortunate gentleman, there is only one bright ray to
illumine a tale of otherwise unmitigated darkness.
That ray shines on his true wife, who adhered to him
in his misfortunes and comforted him in his captivity.
The third distinguished Englishman whom I met at
Stamboul was the late Colonel Fred Burnaby, a pala-
din in arms, and Admirable Crichton in his knowledge
of languages, handsome, highly bred, and a charming
conversationalist, but who always seemed to me to be

somewhat of a disappointed man, and to be weighed down by some hidden sorrow. He joined Lord Wolseley's force in Egypt as a volunteer; put himself in the forefront of the battle and got killed. I believe that my friend Mr. H. W. Lucy first made the acquaintance of Fred Burnaby in a balloon; I had the pleasure of meeting him for the first time at the mess of the Royal Horse Guards Blue at their barracks in Albany Street. When I came to Constantinople he was on the eve of starting on one of his equestrian Central Asian expeditions; and we saw him off from his hotel at Scutari, accompanied by the trusty trooper who had been his henchman in former journeys.

But you may well ask by this time what the object was of my sudden Hegira from the north to the south of Russia and appearance at Constantinople. It was all on account of that confounded Eastern Question. I had seen the Russian army organising in their thousands; and I knew, so far as a journalist liable to error could know, that war between Russia and Turkey would inevitably break out in the early spring. To avert, if possible, this war the British Government had despatched to Constantinople the Marquis of Salisbury as Ambassador-Extraordinary; and His Excellency arrived accompanied by the Marchioness, and attended by a numerous and brilliant staff of Foreign Office officials and attachés. The resident Ambassador to the Sublime Porte was Sir Henry Elliot; and at his table I met a remarkable functionary, Mr. William White, who, at the time I speak of, was Consul-General at the capital of one of the Principalities. Lord Salisbury, indeed, had summoned to Constantinople the *élite* of the British consular body from South-eastern Europe and those portions of the Levant which bordered on the Ottoman dominions; and among these I especially remember Mr. Blunt—he was afterwards knighted—

who was Consul at Salonica, and Mr. Reade, who had been Consul at Tunis.

This last-named gentleman, to my agreeable surprise, received me in a most amicable manner. I subsequently learnt that he was the son of Sir Thomas Reade, the military secretary of Sir Hudson Lowe while Governor of St. Helena. I have been a hard student of the Napoleonic legend and the Napoleonic history to boot ever since I was a lad; and although I have read Mr. Forsyth's " Captivity of Napoleon," over and over again, I have never been able to conquer my dislike for the character of Sir Hudson Lowe, who seems to me to have been, although a strictly just and conscientious man, something very like what the Americans call " a mean cuss." The late Sir Emerson Tennant, who knew him well, used to say that on first meeting Sir Hudson he reminded him of the etching by "Phiz" of Ralph Nickleby. At the same time, I am ready to grant that Napoleon was the most troublesome and quarrelsome of captives, and that he outrageously abused and vilified the Governor, who certainly showed great forbearance in not resenting the insults of his vituperative charge.

It chanced that for several years I enjoyed the friendship of Sir Hudson's eldest son, General Edward Lowe, who had been at Lucknow during the Mutiny; and this gallant gentleman told me many stories of Sir Hudson's amiability in private life. I think the Governor had " Bonaparte on the brain," and that it was his carking apprehension that he should wake up one morning and find the caged bird flown that made him worry his captive with petty restrictions and regulations.

Again, I was a frequent correspondent of good old Colonel Basil Jackson, who had been an aide-de-camp at large at Waterloo, and who, by the caprice of fate, was afterwards in garrison at St. Helena when Napoleon was at Longwood. He, too, was a staunch advocate of Sir Hudson. Some time before I went to the East there appeared in some London magazine an article full of the idlest tarradiddles about Napoleon's imprisonment, and, as I thought, reflecting most unjustly on Sir Hudson Lowe. I answered that article and exposed its unveracity, either in *Temple Bar* or in *Belgravia*. It happened that my article came under the notice of Mr. Reade while he was Consul at Tunis. I had more than once mentioned his father's name not unfavourably in the paper in question, and which he had reprinted at Gibraltar; hence his friendly welcome when I met him at Pera.

CHAPTER LV

THE TURKISH CONSTITUTION

THESE notes of our little society at Constantinople would not be complete did I not mention that the journalistic section thereof also comprised a young, handsome, and clever Frenchman, who spoke English quite as fluently as he did his native tongue. His name was Barere; and at the time he was a proscribed Communist, under sentence of death *in contumaciam*. His Excellency Monsieur Barere is now Minister-Plenipotentiary of the French Republic at some European Court. So we all have our ups and downs, and as Mr. Thackeray used to say, " It's the lot of one man to be handled by the hangman, and of another to be High Sheriff and to ride in a golden coach." The *Journal des Débats* was also represented at Constantinople by a tall, dark, somewhat bald gentleman, who was a confirmed misanthropist, and whose views and opinions as regarded the Eastern Question, the city of Constantinople, and the *cuisine* of the Pera hotels was summed up in the single but expressive word *pourriture*. Hamlet discovered long ago that there was something rotten in the state of Denmark, but what were you to do with a gentleman who, when you talked of the last dinner at the English Embassy, or the last reception at the Russian one, or the last news from Paris or London, or the humours of the Bezesteen, or the gossip of the Pera and Galata clubs, merely replied, " *Monsieur, c'est une pourriture !* " I do not know exactly to what section of our coterie belonged Mr. Hormuzd Rassam, whom we sportively called the Heathen Chaldee, and whom I always associated with that blessed word Mesopotamia. At all events, we got him to admit that he knew a great deal about Nebuchadnezzar, and that he was aware that that monarch during his salad season was the first epicure who discovered that asparagus was edible. Mr. Hormuzd Rassam, as most people know, had rendered most valuable services to Mr. (afterwards Sir Henry) Layard in the course of his great explorations at Nineveh; he had also been one of the captives of King Theodore of Abyssinia, and, with the missionaries, had spent some months in a dungeon, and in chains; but, as he put it, his fetters caused him no great inconvenience: he always had enough to eat and drink, and was, as a rule, in favour with Theodore. Whether he had come to Constantinople in a journalistic or a diplomatic capacity, I know not; but he was always ready and alert; he knew all the Turkish shopkeepers in the bazaars, and rendered us considerable services when we were curio-hunting.

He seemed to be in correspondence with all manner of Oriental folk, and one morning he showed us a telegram which he had just received from a correspondent, a merchant at Lake Van in Armenia. The despatch ran somewhat to this effect: " Turkish Bashi-Bazouks raided bazaar. Murdering women and children. Collect all debts." The next morning he brought another telegram, worded: " Governor of Van quite powerless. Troops threaten to burn the town. Pay nobody." From these data Campbell Clarke thought that he could construct a very telling political telegram ; so he sat down and began somewhat to this effect: " Turkish irregular soldiery have committed great excesses at Lake Van." " No, no ! " exclaimed a crafty Levantine Consul when Campbell read out the telegram. " That will never do. It should run,

'Turkish irregular soldiery, instigated by Russian intrigues, have,' etc., etc."

Among the diplomatists who day after day met in conference at the Turkish Ministry for Foreign Affairs, most conspicuous, after the Marquis of Salisbury, was the Russian Ambassador-Extraordinary, General Ignatieff, who in society was a most affable and pleasant gentleman, with somewhat weak eyes. I ventured to remind him that I had had the honour to have an interview with his father, who in 1856 was Governor of St. Petersburg. The ambassador evinced some curiosity to know what was the purport of the interview in question. "Well, Excellency," I replied, "it certainly did not amount to much." In the days of which I speak it was compulsory for a foreigner who wished to leave the Russian capital first to advertise three times in the official *Gazette* his intention of going away; so that if he owed anybody any money his creditors might at once demand their due; then he had to present in person a petition to the Governor of St. Petersburg for leave and license to depart; and this being accorded, he was referred to the Grand Master of Police, who eventually granted him the coveted passport.

All this meant a sad waste of time, and the distribution of a considerable number of rouble notes among hungry employés. My interview with the Governor lasted precisely one minute. All petitions had to be handed in by two o'clock; and I arrived at three minutes to two: a circumstance which the General tacitly noticed by pulling out and consulting his watch. Then I made him the profoundest of bows and presented the petition, which His Excellency received with a slight and stately inclination of the head. Then another fifteen seconds passed, leaving me in comic uncertainty as to what was to come next. When the minute was up the General said, "*Eh bien; vous l'avez présentée,*" the English equivalent of which was, I at once inferred, "Go about your business." I went about it, but the *dvornik* in the hall "had me" for a rouble before I left the gubernatorial bureau. When I told the story to General Ignatieff at St. Petersburg, he smiled, and said that foreigners often found it somewhat difficult to understand Russian manners and customs.

The General had one of the most diplomatic voices that ever I listened to. I mean that it was curiously capable of inflection. Talleyrand's voice, we are told, was harsh and strident; but the Prince of Beneventum had a diplomatic eye, a diplomatic smile, and a diplomatic shrug: all three being very valuable factors in statecraft. In society at Constantinople General Ignatieff was continually saying, "*Ma mission est terminée;*" and precisely as the tone of his voice seemed grave or gay, satisfied or discontented, so did the quidnuncs of Constantinople interpret his utterance to mean either that war between Russia and Turkey was inevitable, or that a satisfactory solution of the difficulties between the two Powers had been arrived at.

I spoke just now of Mr. Consul-General William White. Possibly that lamented gentleman, when he was summoned to Constantinople by Lord Salisbury, had no more notion of being one day Her Britannic Majesty's Ambassador at the Sublime Porte than he had of becoming Sheikh-ul-Islam. It was simply through his vast natural capacity, his long experience of affairs, and his familiarity with the Slavonic languages that he rose to the exalted position which he held at the time of his death. Lord Salisbury must have been a rare judge of character and abilities when he thus promoted, *per saltum*, as it were, Mr. White to the much-coveted position of ambassador.

Sir William White—whom I afterwards met in Rome, at the Royal Garden Parties in London, and at the house of Sutherland Edwards, who had known him when he (Edwards) was special correspondent for the *Times*, when Poland was in a state of insurrection, and Mr. White was British Consul at Danzic— was a tall, massively built, rugged-looking gentleman, with something of a North of England accent. He dressed very plainly; his hat had an abnormally broad brim, and altogether, abating the fact that he did not wear a red waistcoat and top-boots, he reminded me of the portraits which I had seen of William Cobbett. He lived, as most of us journalists lived, at the Hotel de Byzance; and I could reckon on most mornings on a visit from him, just after the mail from the West came in. Noon was our time for the *déjeuner à la fourchette*; and, odd to say, when we came to compare notes it was tolerably sure to turn out that every representative of an English or foreign newspaper in the house had received a visit between the hours of eight and ten a.m. from Mr. William White.

The Christmas of 1877 I spent at the picturesque suburb of Buyukderé at the house of Mr. Fawcett, then Judge of the Consular Court Pera; and who now, as Sir George Fawcett, fills a much more important post. His kind and clever wife made Campbell Clarke and myself heartily welcome; although the good lady was fain to apologise for what might possibly be some slight shortcomings in the plum pudding. "You see," she remarked, "that I had a Greek female cook. I quarrelled with her this very morning; paid her her wages and told her to go; whereupon she cursed Mr. Fawcett and myself, the gardener's baby, and my little toy terrier. She departed, as I hoped, for good; but in ten minutes she returned to curse the plum pudding, which was already tied up for boiling ; and she repeated the malediction three times and with the greatest solemnity." Nothing, however, turned out in the long run to be the matter with the pudding ; and after a capital dinner we sat down to play whist, a game at which I have taken a hand exactly three times in the course of my life — once in Paris, once in New York, and once on the shores of the Bosphorus. I do not thoroughly understand any one of the rules of the pastime at which Charles Lamb's Mrs. Battle was and Mr. James Payn is so consummate an expert; and I ascribe it simply to the kindness of a sometimes placable Destiny that I have never revoked nor have had the cards thrown at my head by an exasperated partner.

Before I left Constantinople I witnessed a truly singular ceremony. This was the proclamation of the new Turkish Constitution, devised, I should say, by the wily Ottoman diplomatists in order to throw dust in the eyes of the Giaour by leading him to believe that Turkey meant in right earnest to adopt the liberal political institutions of the West. Prior to the ceremony, which took place at the Old Seraglio, we had some business to transact at the Ministry of War; and as a student of Oriental manners I found it somewhat edifying to watch the way in which His Excellency Somebody Pasha partook of luncheon. A servant brought him a small black leather valise, which, being opened, disclosed some scraps of meat, a loaf of bread, some cheese, and a liberal allowance of dates and dried raisins. After rapidly consuming these modest viands, the Pasha clapped his hands ; and another servant brought him a basin of water to wash in. Then, having carefully dried his hands with a gold-embroidered napkin, His Excellency lighted up another cigarette and tranquilly resumed the business which he was transacting. But the part of the affair which most reminded you of the Arabian Nights was that, while the Pasha was busy with his luncheon, the heavy curtain of the room was drawn slightly aside and a brown and skinny palm was protruded through the cleft; while a voice outside whiningly implored alms in the name of the Most Merciful Allah. Surely it must have been the beggar who had solicited charity from King Alfonso on the railway platform at Madrid transported on some magician's carpet to Stamboul! The Pasha took no notice of the solicitation; and the hand suddenly disappeared as though its owner had been dragged back by the scruff of the neck; but as I did not hear any subsequent yells, I do not think that they administered the bastinado to the beggar.

Shortly after noon the Constitution was formally promulgated in the presence of a host of officials in resplendent uniforms, and a large body of Ottoman troops, who, when the Grand Vizier had finished reading the prodigiously lengthy document, raised a unanimous shout of "*Amin!*" and grounded their arms with a thunderous clang. Then the vast assemblage of grandees in gold-embroidered tunics and fezzes somewhat tumultuously dispersed; but I was sorry afterwards to learn that it had not fared so well with our dragoman Constantine Fenerli as it had done with the mendicant who begged of the Pasha at luncheon. "They have beaten Fenerli," piteously exclaimed the descendant of Miltiades; "men with large sticks have made Fenerli's back sore. How could Fenerli help accidentally treading on the heels of an Effendi?" He always spoke of himself in the third person. Thus, he told me once: "Fenerli's family was rich once; he had a house in the Fanarl; his sisters were richly dowered. But a great fire broke out, and sparks fell on the roof of Fenerli's house, and in half an hour he was ruined."

About the beginning of March I left Constantinople. All things considered, I should not care about returning to it, even in early spring, at which season the climate is said to be enchanting. The city in many respects is interesting, but it is desperately uncomfortable—so, at least, it was in my time. When you went out to a dinner or a reception you were forced, there being no hackney-carriages, to hire a sedan-chair, a quaint but horribly uncomfortable conveyance. Except at the Legations and at the houses of a few British merchants, there was nothing fit to eat at Pera; and I grew so weary and nauseated with the *cuisine* of the *table d'hôte* that, to the horror of Campbell Clarke, I used two or three times a week to cross the Bridge of Boats into Stamboul and dine at a Turkish cook-shop—pilaf kebobs, pastry, fried fish, and so forth; moistened with the contents of a flask of sherry-and-water which I brought with me. The Moslem frequenters of this " slap-bang " knew that I was an Unbeliever, but they never interfered with me; they would even point out in a dish the most succulent bits of mutton or fowl which they thought I should find to my liking. Every Turk, as regards good manners, is a born gentleman; and although he has his occasional outbursts of fanaticism, he is, as a rule, toleration itself when compared with the barbarous Moor.

An American missionary at Constantinople told me a story pleasantly illustrative of the usual placability in theological matters of the Osmanlis. He and his wife were at their work in some small town in Asia Minor; and, with the permission of the authorities, had opened a day-school for girls, but these proceedings raised the wrath of a Turkish *santon*, or Holy Man, who dwelt in a disused tank opposite the school;

and who manifested his disapproval by inciting the ragged boys of the town to launch volleys of stones at the missionary's windows and follow and yelp at him and his wife in the streets. Forthwith the chief of the Ulema or Mohammedan priesthood convened a meeting of the principal inhabitants and addressed them somewhat to this effect: "I know this Frank: he is not a follower of the prophet; but I also know that he acts up to the precepts of his own creed; that he prays diligently, and is always ready to succour the sick and relieve the poor. Therefore, perceiving him to be a man of God, I purpose to lead him round the town this afternoon on my own donkey; and woe be it unto all of you if a hair of his head or that of his wife is harmed." A good many Christian clergymen might take a lesson in toleration from this Turkish Mollah.

Just before we left there came into harbour a splendid American corvette, which, sad to say, was totally wrecked two or three years ago in a storm at Apia, in the Samoan Islands. Eugene Schuyler took us on board, and the captain regaled us with ample hospitality, put the crew through gun-drill, and in every way showed us politeness. Schuyler asked him how he had managed to get so large a vessel of war through the Hellespont. "Oh," he replied, laughing, "I got the thing off well enough. Of course, the Governor of the Dardanelles remonstrated and pointed out that under the Capitulations we can only bring a gunboat through the Straits; but I quietly said, '*It's the smallest we've got;*' so he shrugged his shoulders, and we had coffee and cigarettes, and I came up here right away."

Bidding our friends in Constantinople, not forgetting Mr. Wrench, the British Vice-Consul, and Mr. Whittaker, the editor of *The Levant Herald*, a hearty farewell, we left Pera on board an Austrian Lloyd for the Piræus, where, had my mind behaved properly, I ought to have thought of all the wise things that Socrates said to Plato. As a matter of fact, I did not think about the son of Sophroniscus at all, my attention being principally occupied by the incessant demands of the boatmen and luggage-porters for gratuities, and the exceptionally impudent extortion of a Greek *amaxelates*. As there was something the matter with the Piræus and Athens Railway, we were compelled to take a carriage ; being very careful before starting to make a bargain with the coachman, who drove a pair of spavined, shoulder-shotten steeds which reminded me strongly of Homer and La Marmora, my old equine friends in Garibaldi's campaign in the Tyrol. We had not, however, reached half-way before the crafty *eniochos* drew up his horses and insisted on having more drachmas in addition to the sum stipulated for. We had nothing to do but to accede to his demands. But when the rascal—I feel sure that he had been a brigand in his youth—had landed us at the door of the hotel at Athens, his first act when I handed him the supplemented fare was to fling the money on the ground and, folding his arms, deliver an oration so long-winded and so voluble that I felt convinced that the race of rhapsodists to whom the author of the " Iliad " is said to have owed so much was not extinct. The hotel people, however, made the graceless Automedon pick up his money and bundled him off.

Haunted by a wholesome fear of inflicting guidebook talk on my readers, I shall say very little indeed either about ancient or modern Athens. The new town, built in the reign of the Bavarian King Otho— *Ho skouphos*, the Night-cap, his subjects, for what reason I know not, used to call him—is neat and clean ; and might, but for a queer little old Byzantine cathedral in the middle of the city, be the capital of some small German principality. As for the Acropolis, it looked

to me, at first sight, small, and the ruins the reverse of
imposing. I had been told by Constantine Fenerli to
expect the most wondrous sights in Athens; but that
which most struck me during my first ascent of the
Acropolis was the sight of a Greek, in a white fusta-
nella much in need of washing, shaving a large French
poodle, which for the purpose was perched on a block
of Pentelican marble, while another Helline played the
guitar to him to keep him quiet. On the whole I felt
a sneaking sympathy with the American tourist who,
when he first beheld the remnants of the Parthenon, remarked, " They may well call this place a Necropolis;
for I never saw so many tombstones in my life." I dare
say that these honest first impressions of mine have
been experienced by unnumbered travellers from the
West who have lacked courage to confess the disappointment which came over them on their arrival at
Athens—Milton's " Eye of Greece." But, I am glad
to say, in my own case slight disillusion was soon followed by intense admiration and affection for the unique
city. " You must learn to love me," Mr. O'Smith used
to say, as the Bottle Imp in the old Adelphi melodrama.
You learn to love Athens: it takes some travellers a
week and some a month to appreciate the place, but
sooner or later the appreciation will surely come, and
grow more enthusiastic every day.

We had a most intelligent Greek as a guide on
several successive days. He took care at the outset to
warn us that we should say " *tragoudia* " instead of
" tragedy," and that Aristotle should be pronounced
Aristotéles, with the accent on the fourth syllable;
but he was also full of anecdote and lucid information.
With one morsel of Greek folklore with which he
favoured us I was much entertained. He told us that
when the Elgin marbles were removed from Athens
to be shipped for England, the removal, in order to

avoid the popular commotion which was expected, took place at night; but that, as the labouring wains were rumbling through the streets on their way to the Piræus, the statues which Phidias had graven were heard to moan and shriek for grief at their expatriation. He also related to us, as a modern Greek Joe Millerism, the story of a lawsuit in which a deaf plaintiff sued a deafer defendant before the deafest judge in all Hellas. The plaintiff claimed so many hundred drachmas for rent that was due. The defendant pleaded that he never ground his corn at night; whereupon the judge, in giving judgment, observed, " *Well; she's your mother, after all; you must keep her between you.*" When I got home I found this apparently up-to-date triad of ludicrous *non sequiturs* in a collection of ancient Greek epigrams. Is there any new joke under the sun? I doubt there being one, very gravely. There used to be told a story of Sheridan Knowles, the dramatist, who was a first-rate hand at Irish bulls, meeting one of twin brothers, and asking him, " Which of ye is the other?" Compare the story of that very ancient jester Hierocles—"Of twins, one died; Skolastikos, meeting the survivor, asked him, ' Was it you who died or your brother?'"

There was a squadron of British ironclads at the Piræus during my stay at Athens; and my visit to the city of Theseus terminated very agreeably with a dinner on board the Admiral's flagship. Campbell Clarke took his departure for Corfu, *en route* to Paris; but I, having a few weeks' leave of absence, enjoyed a brief spell of idleness at the Greek island of Syra, a most interesting and exceedingly dirty place. Then I went to Nice, where I abode for full two months, making, I need scarcely say, occasional visits to Monte Carlo, with the usual results. I was, however, more than usually unlucky in the spring of 1877. The idiotic idea occurred to me of purchasing a miniature roulette wheel with a cover to it, and carefully noting down the result of each "spin," comprising the number, the colour, the pair and impair, the "*passe*" or the "*manque.*" Then I went to Monte Carlo and played precisely the contrary game at roulette to that which I had played at home with my private wheel. The provoking result was that the private little game almost exactly repeated itself in the gilded saloons of "Monty," and I was nowhere. At home I only staked my haricot beans; "at Monty" I played louis.

They say that gambling is an incurable vice. Do not believe anything of the kind. That little game of haricots *versus* louis practically cured me of the passion for play. I have been to Monte Carlo at least a dozen times during the last fifteen years; and although I have won or lost a few pieces at *trente-et-quarante* or at roulette, I have never experienced the slightest yearning to play high. To use a haughty metaphor, I no longer answer to the whip of the croupier. On one occasion, on my way to Corsica, the steamer put into the old port of Nice; and the weather being very stormy, she remained there the whole day. I landed; took a walk on the Quai Massena, and dined at the restaurant of the Hotel des Anglais; but no thought of taking a trip to the once irresistible *tripot* of the Prince, whose coat-of-arms, so far as I can make out, is the Nine of Diamonds, came into my head.

I note two rather droll incidents as having occurred during my stay at Nice. In the way of gambling capital I was perfectly cleared out within a fortnight of my arrival; but the manager of the hotel considerately cashed my cheques for board and lodging. He asked one day whether I got other cheques cashed anywhere else. I told him that, beyond the drafts I had given him for his bill, I had not drawn a *sou* from home.

"That is strange, very strange," quoth the manager—
he was a most friendly soul—meditatively. "Why
strange?" I asked. "Well," he continued in rather a
hesitating manner, "you know that we Nice hotel-
keepers have to keep a rather sharp look-out as regards
our much-respected guests; and I need scarcely tell
you that we have agents in the salons at Monte Carlo
who keep us *au fait* with the luck or ill-luck of the
ladies and gentlemen—especially the ladies—who honour us with their patronage. When Monsieur had
been here about a fortnight he was completely *décavé*;
and yet he is continually smoking twenty-five-sou
cigars. He frequently lunches and dines at the Hotel
de Paris, Monte Carlo; and before he begins to play
he always changes a crisp note of the Bank of England for ten pounds." I laughed and told him that I
had learnt alchemy in my youth, and that I sometimes
practised the occult art of the adepts.

If the manager was puzzled touching the secret of
my resources, my friend Captain Cashless was more
than puzzled : he was simply amazed. Most of us have
met Captain Cashless during our travels—middle-aged,
good-looking, well-preserved ; a linguist, a dancing,
fencing, boating, racing, pigeon-shooting gentleman ;
late of the Heavies. Spent most of his money before
he came of age ; lived for several years on the credit
of his credit; is a widower, and spent every penny of
his wife's fortune. Has tried unsuccessfully to get a
berth as governor of a gaol, chief constable of a county,
manager of a hotel, or secretary of a co-operative
store. Desperately and continuously vexed for lack
of pence; save that he contrives, somehow, to pay up
his subscriptions to the two military clubs to which he
belongs.

Captain Cashless was a chance acquaintance ; but
our acquaintance soon ripened into friendship—a trav-

elling friendship. That ten-pound-note business was, I feel confident, a source of continual bewilderment to the captain. He was a gentleman, and forebore from asking me whence I obtained my funds; but upon one occasion I heard him mutter, " No; he hadn't any diamond rings when he came." I was too much amused with his chronic state of astonishment to enlighten him as to my ways and means. But I may as well let my readers into the secret at once. At a pretty little villa at Mentone there resided a very old business friend of mine, the late Mr. John Dicks, proprietor of *Reynolds's Newspaper*, of *Bow Bells*, and of many other popular publications, for which I have written in my time a large number of short stories. Mr. Dicks's appetite for novelettes was insatiable ; and whenever I wanted cash I had only to scribble for a few hours ; take the copy over to Mentone ; and receive from the hands of my friendly publisher a crisp ten-pound note and two louis and a half in gold. Was not this, practically speaking, alchemy?

I note in my diary that the *table d'hôte* at the hotel was honoured by the presence of a lady, who, although of a matronly aspect, possessed a fair residue of her former surpassing comeliness. She was Madame la Baronne Unetelle, and had been one of the beauties of the Court of the Second Empire; in fact, I think that her portrait figured in Winterhalter's two pictures— one is rather " risky "—of the Empress Eugénie surrounded by her ladies of honour. Madame la Baronne, who was nothing if not voluble, and was charmingly affable to boot, was never tired of talking of the ridiculously awkward and clumsy manner in which the majority of English people pronounced French—when they could speak that language at all. Some malicious imp prompted me to play into the hands of the ex-*dame d'honneur* of the Court of Napoleon III. ; and

I let her have every day at luncheon and dinner an un-stinted allowance of Anglo - French of the Stratford-atte-Bowe character. You know the sort of French I mean. "*Aow yes; eel est tray bow.*" "*Commong voo portay voo?*" "*Garçong, donnay moy ung morsow de pang.*"

The Baroness's sides used to shake with suppressed merriment while I held forth; and one evening, as she was entering the *salle à manger*, I heard her say to two French ladies whom she had invited to dinner, "You shall enjoy yourselves; you shall hear the Englishman talk French; it will be *ravissant*." As luck would have it, two old friends of mine, a French general and his wife, whom I had known in Spain, came on to Nice; and I had to speak French not at all of the Stratford-atte-Bowe order. I shall never forget the expression of astonishment mingled with indignation which came over the well-cut features of Madame la Baronne Une-telle, when she heard us conversing. I met her the next day in the reading-room; when, casting upon me such a glance as Cleopatra might have bestowed on the messenger from Augustus, she said, "*Monsieur! vous êtes un traître!*" swept out of the apartment, and never spoke to me again. But was I so very much to blame? At least, I had amused Madame la Baronne Unetelle twice a day for at least a week; and in this very dull and monotonous world of ours some slight guerdon of gratitude is due to those who amuse us. I have nothing more to say about the year 1877, save to mention that it was one of unremitting journalistic work. I had long since ceased to write books; in fact, I think that full ten years had passed since any new book with my name upon it had been published; and I, to say nothing of the public, had practically forgot-ten that I had ever been an author at all. Toiling for a daily newspaper is scarcely compatible with the

composition books. At the end of your day's work
you feel—at least, that is the case with myself—an un-
conquerable loathing for the production of any more
"copy;" and you turn, as a pleasant recreation, to
nocturnal study: a practice not immediately remun-
erative, but which I take to be of inestimable service
to the elderly man of letters. At all events, it keeps
his memory green; and he must learn something new
every night. Never mind what it is that you study:
dead or living languages; art or archæology; science
—if you have a predilection that way, which I have
not—theology, Blair's "Preceptor," Colenso's "Arith-
metic," Miss Acton's "Cookery," or Patterson's "Book
of Roads;" you will get something out of any one of
these books which you did not know before, or knowing, had seemingly forgotten.

CHAPTER LVI

IN 1878 I had acquired the lease of a good old-fashioned Cubitt-built house in Mecklenburgh Square: my next-door neighbour to the left being poor dear Lewis Wingfield. Although in the heart of London and within pistol-shot of that not very savoury thoroughfare, the Gray's Inn Road, I lived in Mecklenburgh Square with eye-refreshing greenery on three sides of my house. Before me was the good old square itself, with its velvet sward and its tall trees; just beyond Wingfield's house stretched the back-garden of the Foundling Hospital, the children of which noble charity soon became great allies of ours; while in the rear was my own garden and beyond that a green burying-ground long since disused. I lived in Mecklenburgh Square in happiness and prosperity for some years; but I shall only trouble my readers with one little story touching No. 46. We used to go every autumn to Brighton: taking a furnished house for a few weeks prior to our eventual exodus to Rome after Christmas. We took our servants with us: leaving our house in charge of a care-taker. One year we engaged an elderly female, very highly recommended for integrity, sobriety, and cleanliness. I used to come up to town every Monday morning for a few hours: and for about a month all went well in the square; the elderly care-taker seemed to be exemplarily pious, and was always reading good little books of her own bringing. I think she once incidentally mentioned that she had seen better days, and that her deceased husband had been a sexton.

One Monday morning—it was a sunny, early autumn one—I made my appearance in the square about half-past eleven a.m. But, to my perplexity and consternation, I knocked and rang repeatedly and violently at the door of No. 46 without obtaining any response to my summons. Lewis Wingfield was out of town, so that it was no use in knocking him up; but the noise I made had attracted the attention of my next-door neighbours to the east—two kindly ladies, mother and daughter. They sent out word to say that their housemaid had seen the elderly care-taker emerge from No. 46 at about half-past ten a.m.; and that she had remarked that she was going to Guildford Street to buy a little meat for the cat. It was useless to knock or ring any longer, and at last my good-natured neighbours suggested that I should pass through their house and clamber over the wall of their garden into mine own. My climbing days had long been over; but with the assistance of the housemaid, a pair of steps, and a broom-handle, I managed to get over the wall, somehow.

The door leading into the back part of the house was open; but so soon as I had entered the passage I was encountered by a most fearful, searching, monotonous stench—the never-to-be-forgotten stench of a field of battle when the fray is over. Goodness gracious! what had happened? Evidently the elderly care-taker had not died suddenly some two or three days previously, and it was not the odour of her decomposed remains that I was scenting; since the housemaid next door had seen her an hour before and heard her say she was going out for some meat for the cat. A horrible suspicion passed through my mind. Had she invited another elderly female to tea with her; and had the two ladies, like Sairey Gamp and Betsy Prig, quarrelled over their cups, with the possible and tragical result that the sexton's widow had brained her friend with the kitchen-chopper, and that it was the corpse of the murdered female which was evolving the dreadful smell? I searched the coal-hole; I explored the dust-bin; I rummaged the upper and the lower chambers; but no dead body did I find: the stench meanwhile growing louder and louder. I had some writing to do; but I could not possibly accomplish it in the midst of that charnel-house perfume. My good-natured neighbours permitted me to use their back drawing-room, where I wrote without intermission until nearly three in the afternoon. I was just sealing my packet of manuscript when the housemaid entered the room, and said, " She's a-coming, sir." " Who's coming?" I asked. " The care-taker," she replied; and as she spoke the broadest of grins, culminating in a giggle, was developed on her features.

She opened the street-door for me; and, to my horror, I beheld, in the red, golden afternoon, the elderly care-taker just turning the north-east corner of Mecklenburgh Square and staggering towards No. 46. As she neared the house we noticed that she held the latch-key in one hand and a black bottle in the other. When she reached my door-step a sudden lurch caused her to drop the bottle, which fell on the pavement and was broken into many pieces. The liquid which flowed from it was certainly not water; for it was a dark red—rum, possibly. She contrived to let herself in and close the door. I slipped back into No. 45 and got over the garden-wall again; but as I had taken the precaution to place another pair of steps on my own side the feat was accomplished without much difficulty. I had thrown up every window, back and front, in the house; so that the stench, although still terrible, had lost something of its sickening strength. As for the elderly care-taker, the effort of turning the key in the door had been too much for her; she had succumbed to excess of alcohol and was lying prostrate and speechless in the passage. Poor woman! I sent at once for a doctor, and suggested when he arrived that the unfortunate creature, who seemed to be at the point of death, should be at once conveyed to the Royal Free Hospital. "Nonsense!" replied the medical man; "she's only dead-drunk. Do you know where she lives?" I replied that I did, and that she had lodgings in the not far distant district of Pentonville. "Very well," went on the doctor; "then the best thing you can do is to put her in a four-wheeled cab and pack her off home; care-takers have a weakness that way." The elderly female was removed with the aid of the housemaid from 45 and a sympathetic cabman, who observed that the "old lady had had her load and no mistake."

But that dreadful, that searching, that noisome stench remained: somebody was lying dead in that house for certain. All at once the housemaid from 45 exclaimed that she saw something white under the form in the hall. She knelt and tried to drag the object out; but fell back almost swooning from that pestiferous smell. Then I helped her, and I succeeded in lugging out a wooden box, which I at first thought to be a child's coffin; but at the other extremity the box turned a corner and was continued for a short length at an oblique angle; and children's coffins are not obliquely angular. A journeyman carpenter was sent for; he opened the box and made visible that which had been a splendid haunch of venison, but was now one festering mass of maggots. The lid of the box bore a parchment label with my address; the date of its expedition a fortnight since; and the compliments of Colonel Farquharson of Invercauld. It was that gallant Highland chieftain familiarly known as " Jim," but now, I am sorry to say, deceased, who had sent me some venison of his own stalking. I had to pay the journeyman carpenter five shillings to bury, at dead of night, that awful carrion.

Voltaire has somewhere said that men of letters who go into society superior to their station are like flying-fish. They flap and flutter for a time between air and water; and then they fall on the deck of the ship and the sailors knock them on the head for venturing to move out of their proper habitation. I have been knocked over the head by the flat of a sabre of a French dragoon; but I am alive to tell the tale, and, figuratively, my sconce is still intact. I am reminded, nevertheless, of Voltaire's remark by the circumstance that when I was living in Mecklenburgh Square I began to mingle again in that society in which, through the position of my dear mother, I had mingled in my boyhood. I had never lost the friendship of the Baroness Burdett-Coutts and of the Viscountess Combermere; and I shall always remember the happy days I have spent at the Baroness's house in Stratton Street, and at Holly Lodge, Highgate, and at Lady Combermere's residence in Belgrave Square. But late in the 'seventies came other distinguished friends, among whom I hasten to mention the Earl (now Duke) of Fife and the Earl of Rosebery and his late deeply regretted Countess, a lady of varied attainments, and one of the sweetest and noblest-minded of women.

At Lord Rosebery's house, then in Piccadilly and afterwards at Belgrave Square; and his country seat at Mentmore, Leighton Buzzard; and at The Durdans, near Epsom, I met the best of all good company in the way of rank and talent—among others, the Rothschilds, Sir William Vernon Harcourt, Sir Charles Dilke, and, last but not least, Mr. Gladstone. The Earl of Beaconsfield I never had the honour to be presented to; but he was so kind as to introduce himself to me on the occasion of a number of journalists going up to Downing Street as a deputation on some question affecting the laws of copyright. Mr. Disraeli was then Chancellor of the Exchequer, and when the business part of the proceedings was over, he crossed the room; said that he ought to know me, and shook hands cordially. A minute or two afterwards he as affably requested me to introduce him to Miss Brad-don, who was present. It was not precisely a case of *Bertrand et Raton;* still I confess that the fable touching some chestnuts and a certain fire *did* occur to me when I introduced Mr. Disraeli to the authoress of "Aurora Floyd." Lord Houghton I had known for years; and of Robert Browning and Abraham Hay-ward I had made the acquaintance at Lady Comber-mere's. Finally, at the well-remembered marriage of Mr. Leopold de Rothschild with Miss Perugia, at the Synagogue in Great Portland Street, Lord Rosebery was so kind as to present me to the Prince of Wales: telling His Royal Highness that I had written an ac-count of his wedding with the Princess Alexandra, in St. George's Chapel, Windsor. A few days afterwards I received a letter from the distinguished surgeon the late Sir Oscar Clayton, reminding me of old Princess's green-room days, and asking me to dine in Harley Street to have the honour of meeting the Prince. I have subsequently often enjoyed the hospitality of the Heir to the Crown at Marlborough House and at the Garrick Club. Of the gracious notice taken of me by other members of the Royal Family it is not necessary that I should say one word; and in this, I hope not too lengthy, paragraph, I have honestly and, I think, modestly liberated my soul with respect to the illustrious and noble personages whom I have met, and who have been invariably good and courteous to me. I have never flattered nor toadied the great: I never asked anything from them, and I don't want anything; but I am justifiably proud, as a working journalist of no celebrity but of some notoriety, to have come in amicable contact with the flower of English society.

To Mecklenburgh Square days likewise belongs my earliest remembrance of the Grosvenor Gallery in New Bond Street, which was built by Sir Coutts Lindsay, who adorned the façade with a portico brought from a palace at Venice, and who opened the gallery as an annual exhibition of high-class pictures selected by himself, with the assistance of his directors, Mr. Comyns Carr and Mr. C. Hallé. Mentioning only the circumstance that Sir Coutts showed me much attention, and that I preserve to this day the esteemed friendship of Lady Lindsay, I will adhere to the law which I have laid down to myself not to say anything more touching the grand folks whom I have met in England; although I could say a good deal of perhaps an interesting nature touching the " Grosvenor Sundays "—splendid convocations as they were of all that was worth seeing and talking to in London. Without indiscretion, however, I may mention that these " superlative afternoon teas " brought me in friendly fellowship with such painters of renown as Alma-Tadema, Edward Burne-Jones, W. B. Richmond, Holman Hunt, G. F. Watts, and T. Woolner. There are no Grosvenor Sundays now. *Foyers éteints.*

The year 1878 was marked by another Paris International Exhibition. My proprietors wanted me in London, and were loath to send me abroad; but in the middle of the summer they thought that I might as well go over to Paris and write some letters, less about the Exhibition itself—it did not materially differ from preceding displays of the kind, save that it was bigger and was the primary cause of greater rapacity on the part of the Parisian hotel and restaurant keepers—than that I should say something descriptive about what was going on in the Gay City generally. I was to stay a fortnight; but at the expiration of that time Mr. J. M. Levy suggested that, as my letters had been received with some approval by the British public, I might as well remain another week or so. The end of it was that I did not return to Mecklenburgh Square until the eve of my birthday, the 24th November; and I was able to collect and republish in book form a portion of my letters, to which I gave the title of " Paris Herself Again." The book passed through seven or eight editions and I made a great deal of money by it. Thus, although I had thought that my days of book-making were over, my case was that of an author *malgré lui;* and, as things stand at present, I do not care to enter into any mental recognisances that I will not write any more books.

The year 1879 dwells in my memory through two, to me, most interesting experiences. Archibald Forbes, the valiant and brilliant War Correspondent, had come home from South Africa; a little broken in health but covered with literary laurels. It was resolved by a committee of his many friends, among whom the guiding spirits were Edmund Yates and J. C. Parkinson, that a congratulatory dinner should be given to Archibald; and I was asked to take the chair on the occasion. It was in all respects a splendid and memorable banquet, the guests being exclusively composed of military men and personal friends of Forbes. He sat, of course, on my right hand; and to my left was the late Duke of Sutherland, who had put on his star and riband of the Garter to do honour to the brave correspondent of the *Daily News*. Next to the Duke was Lord Houghton. The speeches, after the ordinary toasts had been disposed of, were admirable; but those who expected a set oration from Archibald Forbes were drolly disappointed. When the tumult of applause which followed the proposal of his health had subsided, Archibald rose and quietly said, " I am no orator, as this old Brutus is, so I must content myself with thanking you for the great honour you have done me." Then he sat down. Why he should have alluded to me, being the chairman, as " Brutus," I have not the remotest conception; but I believe that the man's heart was simply full to overflowing; and that was why he did not say more.

IN December, 1879, my wife and I paid our second visit to the United States. I was pretty well fagged-out with continuous hard work; and my friends in Fleet Street thought that a few weeks' change would do me good. Why I selected the bleak, wintry month for the journey I shall tell my readers ere long. The authorities in Fleet Street only contemplated my making a trip to New York, Boston, Philadelphia, Baltimore, Washington, Cincinnati, and Chicago; but I had ulterior views of a voyage of a far more ambitious nature. We crossed the Atlantic in a Cunard in a succession of storms — I never *did* cross that ocean save in winter and in tempestuous weather—and found plenty of old friends in Manhattan to welcome us. I had a brief attack of illness at Christmas; but was soon convalescent, and after passing a week at Boston, we went to Philadelphia, where we were the guests of that most munificent and hospitable of hosts, the late Mr. G. W. Childs, the proprietor of the *Public Ledger*. At Washington we were received with much kindness by the British Minister-Plenipotentiary, Sir Edward Thornton; and soon afterwards my ulterior views as to travelling began to be developed. We determined to go down South; and made the best of our way by rail to Richmond, in Virginia. I took but one letter of introduction with me: it was to the Governor of the State. His Excellency at once asked us to dinner, and invited a large party to meet us; and the next day we were free of the best society in the whilom Confederate capital—a society equally hospitable and refined. I believe the Southerners had some inkling of the fact that twenty years before I had stood . their friend in their gigantic struggle with the North; but in this connection let me say that in New York I was not subjected to any kind of newspaper hostility owing to my bygone Copperhead tendencies. These tendencies were, indeed, humorously alluded to by an Irish journalist at a reception offered me by the New York Press Club. "And," said the speaker, "if Mr. Sala (pronounced "Sailer") *did* sympathise with the Confeds, it was only the sympathy which one ought to feel for the under dog."

From Richmond, after a sojourn of some three weeks of unmingled pleasantness, we journeyed to Augusta, in the State of Georgia; to Charleston, in South Carolina; and ultimately to New Orleans, where I found the Carnival "in full blast." Again I had brought but one letter of introduction with me. It was to General Randall Gibson, one of the senators for the State of Louisiana; and through his prompt kindness every door of note in the Crescent City was thrown open to us. "Rex," the occult king of the Carnival, was most attentive to us: sending us day after day cards of invitation to balls and gala performances at the Opera and other theatres; and one day my wife received a magnificent bouquet of flowers with "Rex's" compliments. The Carnival was a very splendid one; but that which enchanted me most in New Orleans was the perfectly Parisian society which one found on one side of Canal Street and the as completely American community that existed on the other. In the French quarter you found French milliners aud dressmakers, *confiseurs*, libraries full of

French novels and newspapers, French restaurants,
cafés, and *guinguettes*, and in the old French market
on Sunday mornings we used to have an irreproachable French *déjeuner à la fourchette*, followed by the
renowned "drip" coffee, which is so strong that
it is said to stain the saucer into which it is poured.
All over the city you find excellent French restaurants, where the claret is better and cheaper than that
which you drink at hotels and restaurants in France;
while at a place of entertainment on the way to Lake
Pontchartrain they not only give you *bouillabaisse* as
good as any that you can obtain at the Reserve by
Marseilles; but show you an autograph-book, in
which there is a terse eulogium of the fish stew in
question, in the handwriting of Thackeray and signed
by him.

I have one sad confession to make with regard to
New Orleans. I went to a cock-fight; and the contest, I grieve to say, took place on a Sunday. Well, I
had been a spectator, years before of gallomachia at
Algiers, at Seville, and at Granada; and the combats
were always held on the Sabbath. With great reluctance did we leave New Orleans. It was mid-February,
but sunny and sultry in the Crescent City; but we
had not forgotten that we were going back into winter; and had so provided ourselves with a good stock
of warm clothing; but we brought away with us a
large branch of an orange-tree with six ripe oranges
upon it; and carrying that golden bough, after a
weary two or three days' journey, did we enter the
city of Chicago to find it enveloped in a mantle of
snow. The great metropolis of pork and grain was
then, as it is now, a wonderful city; but I should say
that the majority of my readers have heard enough
about Chicago in connection with its World's Fair to
enable me to dispense with any prolusions on the sub-

ject. I may just remark that at the Chicago Club I met Mr. Robert Lincoln, the son of the murdered President, and who was subsequently Minister-Plenipotentiary to England. I should have mentioned, too, that at Washington we were indebted for much graceful hospitality to Senator Bayard, now United States Ambassador at the Court of St. James.

Leaving Chicago, we paid a visit to Cincinnati, which seemed to me to be almost as much a German as an American city; and there we made the acquaintance of a prominent Western journalist, Mr. Murat Halstead. I had still ulterior views; and to carry them out it was necessary that we should return to Chicago, where we had left our heavy luggage; indeed, we did leave much of our belongings at the luggage-room of the Grand Pacific Hotel when we started on a journey still further west. Travelling by the Chicago and North-Western Railway, we reached Council Bluffs, once the home of Mrs. Amelia Bloomer: the lady who invented the peculiar feminine costume of which, in the modified form of knickerbockers, the English public is now witnessing a revival. Crossing the bridge over the river, we " detrained," as the French say, at Omaha, which, in 1879, was an insignificant town, with a few thousand inhabitants, and with only one habitable hotel—The Planters' House. We only stayed a day at Omaha, and then took the Central Pacific Railroad for Ogden, in the territory of Utah. We had a drawing-room car, splendidly furnished, and with two comfortable bed-rooms and a kitchen; and so well stocked were our larder and cellar that beyond fresh eggs in the morning we had no occasion to purchase anything at the refreshment-rooms on the line. Crossing the Rocky Mountains was rather tedious; as the speed sometimes does not exceed fifteen miles an hour. But it is a long lane that has no turning ; and in due time we found ourselves at Ogden; and then availed ourselves of a branch line to Salt Lake City, the Mormon capital. I have described all the incidents of this expedition in a book called "America Revisited." Coming back to Ogden, we began the descent of the Pacific Slope ; found ourselves one morning at Sacramento City in glorious spring weather, with the birds singing and the camellias growing in the open air, and a few hours afterwards we were comfortably installed at the Palace Hotel, San Francisco.

This huge caravansary seemed to me the largest American hotel I had ever seen : it cost I know not how many hundreds of thousands of dollars to build ; and thoroughly to decorate it would cost, I should say, a good many more hundred thousands. The proprietor of the amazing pile in 1879 was Senator Sharon ; and when we asked for a modest sitting-room, bed-room, and bath-room, there was placed at our disposal a suite of about twelve or fourteen spacious apartments. Whether these rooms were on the tenth or the sixteenth floor of the hotel it does not in the least signify ; seeing that the lifts or "elevators" appeared to my dazed sense to be as capacious as the old ascending-room at the Colosseum in the Regent's Park. I knew, as I thought, absolutely nobody in the modern El Dorado ; but before we had been a week in 'Frisco we had a host of friends—millionaires, artists, journalists, lawyers, and what not. The whole place seemed to me the realisation of some brilliant but somewhat bizarre vision. The hospitality which we experienced knew no bounds ; but the millionaires who fêted us, and whom we found in gilded saloons hung with lustrous fabrics, and sparkling with plate, crystal, pictures, and statuary, resided for the most part in houses built entirely of wood—San Francisco being, as I was warned, a town chronically subject to the infliction of earthquakes. When I asked whether by dwelling in palaces of timber the residents on " Nob Hill "—the popular name for the fashionable quarter of 'Frisco—did not expose themselves to the perils of fire, I was informed that the wood of which the edifices were built was of a practically uninflammable nature.

The streets of San Francisco were to me a source of never-ending delight. There I saw for the first time the electric tram-cars, the capacity of which was pithily summed up by a Chinese critic as " No Pushee ; no Pullee ; go like Hellee." Of the Celestials themselves, in their own picturesque and indescribably filthy district known as Chinatown, I saw a great deal both by night and by day. The rejoicings consequent on the Chinese New Year were in progress. We dined one evening at the house of a wealthy merchant from Canton ; and the next evening we visited a Chinese restaurant. Of many strange, and to me, incomprehensible dishes did we there partake. Still, mysterious as was the *menu*, I continue to nourish the fond hope that the bill of fare comprised neither puppy nor kitten ; neither stewed rattlesnake nor skunk *au gratin*. We went to two large Chinese theatres ; at one there was an afternoon performance and the house was crammed ; at another at the evening performance there was scarcely standing room, and my olfactory memory yet retains a lively impression of the aroma of that pigtailed audience. At one theatre the company were playing a comedy ; I am not aware of how many acts it was in, as it had been going on for six weeks and was not half concluded. At the other house an historical tragedy had been unwinding the scaly horrors of its folded tail for full four months. That perhaps need excite little surprise. The Acts of

the Bollandists are not yet within measurable distance
of completion; and what letter of the alphabet, I may
ask, has as yet been reached by the compilers of the
dictionary of the French Academy? I completed my
investigations of life in Chinatown by a nocturnal
visit, under the auspices of a captain of police, to the
gambling-houses and opium-smoking dens of the yellow people.

I spoke rather hastily when I said that I knew nobody on arriving at 'Frisco. I was destined to meet
there a very old, old friend. I had often heard of a
weekly periodical called *The San Francisco News Letter*,
a kind of transatlantic *Truth*, only a little more personal, and a little livelier—not to say more libellous—
than Mr. Labouchere's amiable sheet. I was aware
that the *News Letter* had been owned and edited for
many years by Mr. Frederick Marriott, the whilom
proprietor of *Chat*; but a great gulf of time yawned
between 1848 and 1879; and I scarcely even surmised
that Mr. Marriott, who was middle-aged when he left
England, was still living. I sought information re-
specting him from Mr. George Smith, the polite chief
clerk of the Palace Hotel, who immediately made
answer, "Living, indeed! I guess that Fred Marriott
is altogether a live man! Go and see him." So I
went to the office of the *News Letter*; sent in my card,
and a moment afterwards was grasped by the hand by
my ancient friend, grown very old and somewhat
feeble, but still alert and vivacious. I recognised his
features and his voice at once; but he owned that he
would have failed to do so had he met me in the street.
He introduced me to his son—a fine, handsome young
fellow, who on the morrow, after the pleasantest of
dinners at the house of Mr. Marriott senior, drove me
in a vehicle to which I would not have the hardihood
to give a definite name, but which was drawn by a fast

trotting mare, through the Golden Gates Park to the Gates themselves, which the Australians would call "heads," and which form the entrance to the harbour of 'Frisco. There is a capital hotel here overlooking the blue Pacific ; and close to the balcony of the room where we lunched rose from the waves the great Seal Rock, on and around which hundreds of seals were disporting themselves, barking and splashing, romping and turning somersaults, as it is the manner of those jocund mammals to do. Charles Kingsley's "Poacher's Widow" saw the Merry Brown Hares come Leaping ; but I will back the Golden Gate seals for downright whole-hearted fun against any inarticulate creatures that I have come across. They are, one and all, the most festive of " cusses."

Another English friend did we meet at the Golden Gates Hotel. This was Edward Sothern, the inimitable Lord Dundreary, who was fulfilling an engagement at one of the San Francisco theatres ; but who seemed to me an utterly worn-out and broken-backed man. He was so exhausted before the middle of luncheon that he had to lie on a sofa for full two hours before he could be driven back to San Francisco. We went to the theatre that night to see *Our American Cousin*. The house was full, and I think that the occasion was the four-thousandth one of Sothern's enacting a part with which he will be ever as closely identified as Joseph Jefferson will be with that of Rip Van Winkle. Some fifteen months afterwards, at the Princess's Theatre, London, I saw Sothern in a private box opposite our own, and went round between the acts to greet him ; he looked more lamentably ill than he had done in 1879, and a few weeks afterwards he was dead. Poor Lord Dundreary !

CHAPTER LVIII

I CAME home in the spring; and I do not find that anything of sufficient importance to merit record here occurred during the year 1880. It was different in 1881. One Sunday, in the second week in March, I was present at a dinner-party given by the Earl of Fife, who then lived in Cavendish Square. Prince Lobanoff, the Russian Ambassador, was to have been one of the guests; but His Excellency was detained at the Embassy by affairs of a gravely serious nature. Early in the afternoon Lord Fife received a telegram from Chesham House stating that an attempt had been made on the life of the Emperor Alexander II. at St. Petersburg; and that His Majesty was grievously wounded. The first course of the dinner had not concluded when another despatch arrived from Belgrave Square saying that the Tsar was dead. Naturally this terrible tragedy formed the principal subject of conversation throughout the evening; but I myself was for personal reasons uneasily preoccupied by the shocking catastrophe at St. Petersburg. I reflected ruefully that, in all human probability, ere many hours were over I should be on my way towards the snow-clad plains of Russia. I dreaded lest a messenger from the office should be waiting for me on my return home with instructions for me to proceed Due North by Monday morning's express from Charing Cross. I dreaded that messenger as much as the naughty boy dreads the advent of the schoolmaster.

I thought that at least I would tire the juvenile
Mercury from Fleet Street well out. It was nearly
midnight when the party at Lord Fife's broke up;
and I wandered from club to club till three in the
morning. No messenger had been in quest of me, so
I learned when I returned to Mecklenburgh Square;
and my wife did not even know of the horrible crime
which had been perpetrated at St. Petersburg. Of
course the morning's papers were full of news about
the latest Nihilist atrocity, but it was a private and
not a public communication which I was nervously
awaiting. The communication arrived, sure enough,
just before lunch; it came from Mr. Le Sage, the man-
aging editor of the *Daily Telegraph*, and was to this
effect:—" Please write a leading article on the price
of fish at Billingsgate, and go to St. Petersburg in the
evening." My duty was before me, and I had to do
it; and my wife understood quite as well as I did what
course of action to adopt under the circumstances. I
merely said: " Office; passport; money," lighted a
cigar, and went to work on the fish leader. By four
o'clock she had returned with my Foreign Office passport, *viséd* by the Russian Ambassador; with a letter
of credit, and a large supply of rugs and fleecy hosi-
ery. I had no fur pelisse; but I thought that I could
easily buy one so soon as I arrived in the Russian capital; and that meanwhile a great coat of stout beaver,
wadded and lined with quilted silk, would keep out
the cold well enough.

So I hastened, if not precisely like a " Tartar's bow,"
as directly and expeditiously as ever a Channel steamer
and express trains would carry me, through Brussels
and Cologne, and Berlin and Königsberg, to Petropolis.
It was an exceptionally cold winter; but Russian railway compartments are rather over- than under-heated;
and I suffered little from the cold until I found myself

settled down in a large hotel, kept by an intelligent Frenchman, in the Nevskoi Perspektive.

I cannot exactly settle in my mind whether it was this hotel or another one in the Izaak's Ploschad where one of the most pleasing features of the *table d'hôte* was the appearance there, once a week, of several mighty tureens of splendidly made Irish stew. Whence the landlord had got the recipe for this grand dish I am uncertain; but its *ensemble* would, I am convinced, have excited the enthusiastic admiration of every son of Old Erin. The proprietor told me that once a week he had a live sheep sent up by railway from Finland. At once, when I heard this, did my mind revert to the live turtles which, nearly fifty years before, I used to see stolidly crawling about the floor of a pastry-cook's shop in Old Bond Street, with a little flag labelled "Soup to-morrow" stuck in the centre of their cara-paces. That doomed mutton from the Gulf of Finland ought to have had hung round his neck an equivalent to the Greek "*Thanatos*"—"Irish stew on Saturday." Officers of the Imperial Guard, merchants and bankers and *tchinovniks*, used to flock to the hotel at the close of every week to partake of that delicious dish; and a murmur of approbation would arise from the guests at the dinner-table when the stew, in a good-sized bucket, was carried by two sturdy blond-bearded moujiks into the *salle à manger*, to be afterwards more elegantly served up in tureens. The great charm of the suc-culent preparation was that it thoroughly warmed you. As Jane Welch Carlyle used to say of a glass of sherry, "it made all cosy inside."

But unfortunately there was the outer as well as the inner man to be considered; the cold out of doors was excruciatingly intense; and my well-padded paletôt was, comparatively speaking, no more a defence against the frost than a race-course dust-coat would have been.

To my dismay, I found that in consequence of the assassination of the Emperor all the shops, with the exception of those where articles of food were sold, had put up their shutters, and would not reopen until after the funeral of the Emperor. So I continued to shiver. The ill-conditioned courier who had been a stud groom turned up again in as chronically snarling a condition as ever. " There's a new English Ambassador here," he remarked; "Lord Augustus Loftus is gone away; and you don't know the new one." I told him I had had the honour to know the Earl of Dufferin for many years, and that I proposed to wait on His Excellency at once, and bade him accompany me. I fancy that the Ill-Conditioned One was rather pleased than otherwise when he noticed that I had no *schouba*—not even a sheep-skin *touloupe* with the woolly side in. The varlet knew very well, so I was afterwards told, that I could have sent for a furrier and hired a pelisse by the week or month; but it was evidently the ex-stud groom's mission to gloat over the misery of people who were good to him.

Lord Dufferin was kindness itself; and I was also glad to meet at the Embassy young Lord Frederick Hamilton, the brother of the Duke of Abercorn. I only mention his name because in his case I am able to recall an odd instance of aural memory on my own part. I have often said that I have a most treacherous memory for names; and that, owing to imperfect vision, my recollection of faces is wretchedly uncertain; but as the old saying truthfully reminds us, when Heaven closes one door it opens another, and I have a singularly retentive memory for people's voices. Quite recently, coming up from Brighton for a day or two, I dined at the pleasantest of London clubs, " The Beefsteak." During my repast I noticed that a good-looking gentleman opposite to me was eyeing me intently and smiling meanwhile. His countenance did

not present the slightest purport or significance to
me ; nor did there even come over me the dim impression that I had seen him at some time in some part or
another of the world. He was simply a " swell," and
only impressed me as one. Presently, however, he began to talk ; and remarked that I did not know in the
least who he was or where I had last met him. " Yes,
I do," I replied quickly; " you are Lord Frederick
Hamilton, and I saw you at the British Embassy at
St. Petersburg twelve years ago." It was by his voice
that I had recognised him.

Lord Dufferin has gone through life, so it has seemed
to me, with the main object of rendering gentle services to those who needed assistance. He helped me
to a material extent in March, 1881, by obtaining for
me an invitation to the house of a wealthy English
merchant whose windows commanded a near and clear
view of the Winter Palace, whence the corpse of the
Tsar was to be borne across the bridge which spans
the Neva, to be interred in the chapel, or rather the
cathedral, of the fortress of St. Peter and St. Paul. I
could have procured from the Russian Minister of the
Interior, or from one of the Imperial Chamberlains, a
card of admission to the church ; but I should have
had to wait two or three hours in the crowded edifice,
and should only have witnessed the funeral ceremony
itself, whereas from the merchant's residence I could
see the whole stately procession winding its way from
the palace to the fortress. I called at the Embassy
early on the morning of the funeral ; and Lord Dufferin, who was in diplomatic uniform, and who intended to witness the first part of the mournful pageant, and then to make his way to the fortress and join
his brethren of the *Corps Diplomatique* in the church,
drove me in his sledge from the Embassy to the close
neighbourhood of the Winter Palace.

I had by this time provided myself, through the
intermediary of an old friend, then British Consul at
St. Petersburg, with a very comfortable furred pelisse; but I had gone through some dire tribulation
before I obtained my *schouba*. Constant driving about
the streets, both by day and by night, had half killed
me with cold ; and one day, when it was snowing almost without intermission, I had constantly to throw
into the roadway masses of frozen snow which had ac-
cumulated on the cushion at my back. The consequence was that three days before the funeral I awoke
in the morning utterly prostrated by an attack of lumbago. The pain of the ailment was excruciating ; but
the worst of it was that I was physically unable to
stand, or sit, or dress myself. I sent for a Russian
doctor, who as usual spoke French fluently. He told
me that the attack was not constitutional, and would
pass away. " There are three ways," he continued,
" of treating you. First, I could take the case medic-
inally—that would last, perhaps, three weeks. Two
alternatives remain. We might send for the four Dale-
carlian women." He explained to me that the four females from Dalecarlia were as tall as grenadiers and
as strong as farriers; and that their vocation was to
kneel upon, punch, pinch, smite, and buffet the bodies
of persons afflicted with lumbago, sciatica, and rheu-
matism. In brief, they were professors of a rude kind
of *massage*. I declined their services, as I did not wish
to become a mass of bruises. " Then there is the last
alternative," said the doctor; " we will try *Yod*."

I had not the remotest conception of what " *Yod* "
might be, but the medico proceeded to tell me that
the medicament was iodine. " Would its effects be
immediate ? " I asked. This was Tuesday morning,
and if I was not well by Wednesday evening I should
consider myself, journalistically speaking, an irretriev-

ably ruined and disgraced man. " You will be cured in twenty-four hours," quietly replied the dóctor. He brought his specific; and while two friends held me down, he painted my veins with four coatings of iodine. Possibly I shrieked with agony during the operation, and it was certainly as well that my friends were muscularly strong ; else I am afraid that I should have " gone for " that doctor, iodine, paint-brush and all ; as it was, by noon on Wednesday I was "as fit as a fiddle ; " but my flesh was horribly raw ; and I did not care to tell the Ambassador that beneath my garments I was girt with cotton-wool soaked in oil. When I got to England again I looked up Dr. Tanner's " Index of Diseases ; " and found among the local applications for lumbago, " iodine paint," which is composed of iodine, iodide of potassium, and rectified spirits of wine. This was the compost with which I had been *badigeonné;* but it did its work, with a vengeance ; and I should strongly advise all ladies and gentlemen suddenly attacked with lumbago to try " *Yod.*" If they would prefer a different treatment, they will find that the obliging Dr. Tanner gives them a choice of blisters, or belladonna and aconite, or acupuncture, or ironing the part, a piece of brown paper being placed between the skin and the hot iron ; but I pin my faith to " *Yod.*"

The thoroughfares through which we drove were densely crowded ; while the route of the funeral *cortége* was lined on each side by troops, including several batteries of artillery. A special police permit had to be obtained before a window in a house in the line of procession could be opened, since there was no knowing from what casement a murderous shot might be fired. The pageant was magnificent in the extreme ; but the most touching part of the spectacle was the illustrious group which followed on foot on the snow-

covered roadway the funeral car of Alexander II.—
the young Emperor Alexander III., a numerous body
of the Princes of the Imperial family, and our own
Prince of Wales supporting the Chief Mourner. It
was awful to think when the procession had entered
the fortress, and the minute-guns were sullenly firing
at the close of the ceremony, that the dull roar of the
cannon must have been audible to the accomplices of
the assassin of the Tsar, who were immured in the
stone casements of the citadel.

As I have said, the funeral itself I did not see, but
on the Sunday following the deposition of the body I
witnessed the lying-in-state of the dead Tsar in the Cathedral of St. Peter and St. Paul. The coffin was placed
on a daïs, forming an inclined plane, in the middle of
the church, which was hung with rich sable draperies, while on either side the bier were lighted wax
candles in towering candle-sticks of silver-gilt. The
lid of the coffin had been removed, and as the spectators passed in single file they were expected to incline
themselves and kiss the right hand of the corpse,
which hand was covered with a piece of yellow silk
gauze. The remains of him who a few days before
had been Autocrat of All the Russias were clad in full
military uniform, and with a constellation of stars and
medals on the breast. The body had been embalmed,
and the injuries in the face skilfully plugged and
painted over; below the waist, I was told, the limbs of
the victim of the devilish bomb outrage were only so
much padding, cloth, and leather. "Oh, eloquent, just
and mighty Death! what none have Dared thou hast
Done. . . . . . . Thou hast taken all the Pomp,
Pride, and Ambition of Man, and Covered it over with
the two Narrow Words, *Hic jacet*." Thus wrote, in
his dungeon in the Tower, Walter Raleigh more than
two hundred and fifty years ago.

Lord Dufferin was so good as to procure for me a ticket for the trial of the Nihilist conspirators, whose chief, the actual assassin, had been mortally wounded by his own murderous petard simultaneously with the death of the Tsar. But my attending the trial of Sophie Perofskaja, Hersie, Heljmann, Risakoff, Ribaichick, and Michailoff might also have involved the necessity of seeing those culprits hanged ; and since that dismal private execution at Maidstone in 1867 I had made up my mind not to be present at the judicial strangulation of any of my fellow-creatures. So I re-turned home, after having attended a deeply interesting memorial service for the dead Tsar, held at a mosque close to the Nevskoi—the Russians tolerate every religion except the Jewish one—which service was attended by many officers and soldiers of the Tartar regiments of the Guard, and by half the hotel and restaurant waiters in the capital, who are Mohammedan Tartars, and whom the landlords preferred to Christians, as the Tartars are all teetotallers.

CHAPTER LIX

IT was a very different Russia that I paid a flying visit
to in May, 1883. The Tsar Alexander III. was to be
crowned with the utmost pomp and magnificence at
Moscow. I received my usual instructions to depart
Due North; but on this very special occasion I was to
be accompanied by Mr. J. M. Le Sage, who was to
undertake the onerous duties of despatching a number
of telegrams which would certainly fill a formidable
array of columns in the *Daily Telegraph*. We had some
few difficulties to surmount ere we started. We were
politely but firmly informed that all newspaper correspondents who proposed to be present at the Imperial
Coronation would be expected, as a preliminary, to
forward their *cartes de visite* to the *Chancellerie* of the
Russian Embassy—a very sensible precaution—and I
improved on the idea by gumming on to my passport
half-a-dozen little portraits of myself of the exact size
of a postage-stamp, which had been taken by a friendly
photographer in San Francisco. Again, it was conveyed to us that we could not possibly be permitted to
enter the Kremlin on the eventful 27th May unless we
were in uniform or in Court dress. Fortunately for
Mr. Le Sage, he had long been a member of the Court
of Lieutenancy of the City of London; a proud position which entitled him to assume a scarlet tunic with
silver epaulettes, a sword with a gilt scabbard, and a
cocked hat and plumes.

But I had never been to Court; and as regards uni-

form I was not even a member of the Ancient Order
of Foresters. The obstacle, I am glad to say, soon
vanished; the then Lord Chamberlain—Lord Sydney,
I think—permitted me to wear *levée* dress, with the
understanding that I was to be presented at Court
directly on my return home; and it was consequently
in the highest spirits that about five o'clock one sunny
May afternoon we started for the Continent by the
London, Chatham and Dover Railway. At Berlin we
found our resident correspondent, who made much of
us; and without any obstacle we reached the Russian
frontier. The tin cases containing our gala costumes
proved of considerable service to us at the Custom
House; the sight of Mr. Le Sage's scarlet panoply and
plumed cocked hat apparently induced in the mind of
the *douaniers* the impression that he was not a deputy-
lieutenant but a major-general at the very least; while
an equally favourable opinion of myself was entertained by the officer who examined my paraphernalia.
" I can see what you are," he remarked, turning over
quite gingerly my *levée* dress, " captain of an English
gunboat going to join your ship at Cronstadt." I did
not precisely own the soft impeachment, but I bowed,
and, of course accidentally, placed three or four choice
Havanas on the lid of the tin case, which—the cigars,
not the case—the officer as accidentally pocketed.

I found Russia considerably altered from the country that I had visited in 1856 and 1881. The most notable change that I observed was what I may call the
Sclavonification of military costume. In the days of
the Emperor Nicholas and of his successor German
uniforms, both in the Russian army and in the police,
were almost slavishly copied. In 1883 the German
helmet or *Pickelhaube* had entirely disappeared, and the
cocked hat had almost as completely vanished; the
substitute for this head-gear being the Circassian bon-

net or busby of black Astrakhan wool. Another curious innovation was visible in the general discarding of
metal buttons; in place of which you now saw only
hooks-and-eyes; and the third remarkable social revolution was visible when we reached Moscow. The hotel-
keepers professed not to understand a word either of
French or German ; and although I had not quite forgotten my Russ, we had hard work to do before we
could find the hotel to which we had been directed. I
must here mention that the Russian Government behaved with the greatest liberality towards the foreign
representatives of the Press, who had free quarters
assigned to them at a splendid and exclusively Muscovite hostelry. Nay; the Imperial generosity went so
far as to offer each special correspondent a considerable sum of money to defray his travelling expenses ;
and, finally, after the Coronation we were each presented with a decoration of silver and gold enamel,
embellished with the Imperial crown, the double-
headed eagle, and two crossed swords. I thought,
however, that my proprietors might think it rather un-
dignified on my part if I played the *rôle* of a " dead-
head ; " so, while gratefully accepting the decoration
—which, of course, I never wore—we politely declined
the free quarters and the travelling expenses ; and,
thanks to the assistance of a Dutch gentleman to
whom we had been recommended for business purposes, we obtained a billet at a very comfortable German hotel in the heart of the city. I could never cor-
rectly gather the name of our Batavian friend, but it
was something like " Oysterbank," by which appellation we usually called him. He was, I believe, in some
way connected with a department of the Imperial
Master of the Ceremonies; at all events, I know that
for a consideration he obtained for us, four clear days
before the Coronation, an exhaustive programme of the

ceremonial; which schedule enabled me to despatch
to London at least three columns of readable matter
before the pageant itself took place.

Readers inexperienced in the ways of the great
newspaper-world might open their eyes with astonishment, or smile the smile of incredulity, if I told them
the amount of pounds sterling which we disbursed
every day at the telegraph office. I know that my frequent recourse to the bank on which I had a letter of
credit seemed wholly to perplex the amicable cashier
who handed me the required cash. "What!" he
would say, "another thousand roubles! Is it baccarat
or *écarté?*" I would reply, with a smile, that it was
chess.

The Duke of Edinburgh was staying at the Kremlin; and His Royal Highness sent for me and promised
to render me any assistance that was in his power to
extend. At the Imperial Palace, also, I found Lord
Wolseley; and another British visitor of distinction
was Lord Clanwilliam, as representing the Royal
British Navy. Among the English newspaper correspondents was my old friend Alfred Thompson, artist, dramatist, and journalist, who had been sent out
to Moscow to represent the *Daily News.* Alfred had,
in his youthful days, been a subaltern in a crack cavalry regiment, the Carabiniers; so that he was all
right as regarded the wearing of uniform. The name
of the correspondent of the *Standard* has escaped me;
but I remember him through the perfect fluency with
which he spoke Russ. He told me that it was the
practice in modern journalism, as regarded Russia, for
special correspondents at St. Petersburg to spend at
least six months in a village; boarding either with the
pope or priest, or with the *starosta* or mayor; so as to
acquire a colloquial familiarity with the soft-flowing
but grammatically thorny Muscovite speech. Finally,

I made the acquaintance of a most capable and amiable journalist, Mr. Lowe, who was acting as correspondent of the *Times*.

We witnessed the solemn entrance of the Tsar into Moscow. We had come provided with letters of introduction to Count Woronzoff Daschkoff, who had courteously handed us over to an exalted *Tchinovnik* named Waganoff, at whose office we called every forenoon, and who kept us pleasantly *au courant* with everything of note that was going on. M. Waganoff put us in communication with the Military Governor of the Kremlin; and this dignitary gave us permission to witness the spectacle of the Imperial entry from the ramparts of the palace-fortress; where our companions were a crowd of officers of the Imperial Guard, whose views were not exclusively Sclavonic, and who chatted with us very cordially, telling us a number of things worth listening to and remembering. The *cortége* itself seemed to me to be of interminable length. It was not the first time that I had seen the Imperial state carriages. I had witnessed their preliminary exhibition in 1856 prior to the Coronation of Alexander II. Many of them are sufficiently antique vehicles, a few of them even dating from the reign of the Empress Elizabeth — heavy coaches and chariots, brave in carving and gilding, with their panels profusely adorned with sham diamonds, and drawn by tall grey Holstein horses. But what most struck me was the magnificence of the costumes of the Oriental potentates who had come to Moscow to do homage to the White Tsar. The Khan of Khiva and the Ameer of Bokhara were both there, attended by a numerous escort of Oriental magnificos; and they and the housings of their steeds were one mass of brilliants, rubies, emeralds, pearls, and precious stuffs. It was not then my fortune to have witnessed an Indian Vice-regal Durbar—I was to see one in 1886—and my breath was almost taken away by the superb display, a little barbaric in some of its details, which was visible from the ramparts of the Kremlin.

Two or three days afterwards the Coronation took place. It were useless to dwell in detail on a ceremonial which was described at fullest length in the newspapers of the time. I could have swollen these volumes to thrice their size had I distended them with excerpts from my writings as a newspaper correspondent; but my object, throughout, has been to place my readers behind the scenes of my life, and not to parade myself behind the public footlights. I will just hint, however, that the Tsar, who is, like Melchisedec, Priest as well as King, and is thrice anointed, entered the *Ikonostast*, or altar-screen; received the Imperial diadem from the hands of the Patriarch; consecrated it on the altar, and crowned himself, and subsequently the Empress. To me the most interesting scene in the pageant took place immediately after the Coronation. I had a Russian friend who was a correspondent of the *Journal de St. Petersbourg;* and he got me a huge green-and-white card of admission to the palace of the Kremlin itself. Our object was to see the Tsar at dinner.

We were frequently stopped by the police. But, to begin with, we were both in Court dress; and then, in accordance with the advice of my companion, I continually waved the big green-and-white ticket above my head and shouted "*Billet! Billet!*" so that at length, pushing through a crowd of courtiers and officers, we reached the foot of the grand staircase of the palace. My companion knew the topography of the edifice well, and eventually we reached a gallery, looking down from which we could just descry His Imperial Majesty sitting alone at a table not much bigger

than the stand of a sewing-machine. The Tsar wore
his crown ; but a great officer of the household held
his sceptre, and another the orb. The courtiers who
served him knelt as they placed the dishes on the
table ; and my companion told me that the repast was
a normally Muscovite one, beginning with the national dish of *stchi*, or cabbage-soup. On the whole,
it struck me that the Tsar of All the Russias looked
slightly uncomfortable at his repast.

I experienced a slight disappointment before I returned to the hotel. Lord Wolseley had promised to
give me some inner details of the banquet ; but when I
strove to find him in his quarters at the Kremlin my
progress was impeded by a gigantic sentry of the
Preobajianski Guards, who absolutely refused to let
me pass. That check, however, did not so very much
matter. Before even the Coronation was over I had
finished another column of matter, hastily pencilled
in the most abbreviated longhand on slips of paper ;
my cocked hat serving as a writing-desk. I handed
my manuscript to Mr. Le Sage, who quietly rose from
his seat, and with a grave and dignified manner made
his way through the crowd. I watched his retreating
figure narrowly ; and I noted that, when he had got
into the open, his slow and measured pace quickened
into a trot ; and that then, tucking his sword under
his arm, he ran as hard as ever he could in the direction of the telegraph office. I had about two and a
half columns to write after the banquet in the Kremlin ; so returning to the hotel and refreshing myself
with a meat-pie and a tumbler of hot tea without milk
or sugar, but with a slice of lemon in it, I sat down
and set to work. I have never been a rapid writer ;
and it took me three hours and a half to commit between three and four thousand words to paper. My
labours, as it turned out, were enlivened by the un-

conscious assistance of the *dvornik*, or porter, who occupied a little hutch in the courtyard of the hotel. Full of exuberant patriotism, this worthy wearer of a greasy caftan and a red cotton shirt began about six o'clock to sing a loyal song in I know not how many verses; accompanying himself on the *balalaïka*, a kind of lute of triangular form ; and quaffing at short intervals copious draughts of *vodka*. Then his voice began to quaver ; then he hiccoughed ; then he was sick ; and then he went to sleep and snored. I had just begun my second column when Ivan Ivanovich woke up ; resumed his song ; again got tipsy, and was again indisposed. He was at his third "turn" when I turned down my lamp.

There was just one other little item in connection with the Coronation of Alexander III. I compute that altogether we sent home about seven columns of descriptive matter to Fleet Street. Upon my word ; the next morning, *the entire narrative appeared in Russian in the Official Gazette of Moscow*. Some astute *employé*, who knew English, had deftly translated my article slip by slip before it was placed on the wires. A smarter device of practical journalism I fail to remember. Into the ethics of the transaction I do not propose to enter. Ethics in Holy Russia are still in their infancy.

CHAPTER LX

FORBEARING reader, I am approaching the conclusion of, I hope, a not intolerably tiresome performance. For some years I had entertained a project of visiting the Australian Colonies, and I was told by many experienced friends that I should make much money there if I delivered a series of amusing lectures on my journalistic and viatorial adventures. Now, I have never been a good lecturer. In the first instance, I have too rapid an utterance to be easily followed by my audience; and for that reason, probably, although I have continually made speeches in public, my remarks have very rarely been reported at length. When I have been bent on making a lengthened speech on some matter of moment, I have sent for a Parliamentary shorthand-writer; paid him his guinea, and dictated the speech to him; then, when he has transcribed his notes in longhand, I have taken the manuscript down to the dinner or the meeting at which I was to speak, and handed the " copy " to the gentlemen of the Press, who have made use of it or omitted to use it just as they pleased. Another obstacle to my success as a lecturer has been the bad habit, of which I have never been able to cure myself, of cruising about the platform with my hands in my pockets; so that very often that which I had been saying has been quite, or nearly, inaudible to my hearers. Finally, I am obliged to speak extempore: first, because I am unable to learn anything of considerable length by heart; and next, because I am partially blind and cannot read even the largest type with ease by lamp-light.

However, I determined to make the attempt; and having arranged in my mind a general scheme for four lectures—one on Wars and Revolutions which I had seen; another upon Foreign Lands which I had visited, a third on British Journalism, and a fourth on the Statesmen and Politicians of my time—a gentleman named Bowden was enthusiastic and ill-advised enough to pay me £500 in advance for ten discourses, to be delivered in the United States; as it was by the transatlantic route that I had resolved to visit the Antipodes. And he further covenanted to defray my travelling and hotel expenses between New York and Chicago— stipulating, however, that these expenses were not to include any kind of intoxicating liquor. It was through the intermediary of my good friend and then solicitor, Mr. George Lewis, of Ely Place, that the agreement was concluded; and I remember distinctly the keen gratification which I felt when Mr. Lewis handed me a crisp Bank of England note for £500; remarking at the same time that cheques in early transactions were sometimes of a phantom nature.

Then came the question of who was to undertake the management of my lectures in Australia. I had had some embryo negotiations with Mr. Smythe, of Melbourne, familiarly known in Australia as " Little Smythe," and whom I have always regarded as the Napoleon of lecturing-agents. He had been the *entrepreneur* of Archibald Forbes on his lecturing tour in the Colonies; and had helped him to clear a sum of some £12,000 sterling. But Mr. Smythe wished to have personally a taste of my quality as a lecturer, before closing with me; and suggested that I should pay his passage home and back to Melbourne in order that he might judge of my style as an elocu-

tionist; to which I replied that I would see him in
the lowest pit of Tartarus before I parted with so
much as a guinea; whereupon the embryonic negotiations fell through.   It chanced, however, that there
was in England at the time a very able actor, Mr.
George Rignold, who, conjointly with a Mr. Alison,
was the lessee of the Theatre Royal, Melbourne.   Mr.
Rignold was an intimate friend of my next-door neighbour, Lewis Wingfield ; and he expressed great eager-
ness to come to terms with me for a course of lectures; the conditions were that I should receive half
the gross takings of every entertainment, he paying
all advertising expenses, the hire of theatres and
halls, and the salary of £10 a week of an agent-in-
advance.

These matters being settled, it was about Christmas-
time I bade adieu to my friends.   I shrank from expos-
ing my wife to the fatigue of a journey across the
American continent; so we agreed she should go to
Australia by long-sea; and I secured a state-room for
her in one of the steamships of the Orient Line which
touch at Naples.   I went down to St. Leonards to bid
farewell to my dear old friend, Viscountess Comber-
mere.   Then I dined with the Baroness Burdett-Coutts,
who gave me a letter of introduction to the King of
the Sandwich Islands, whom I had previously met at
her *villeggiatura* at Holly Lodge ; and finally Lord
Rosebery bade me God-speed, and furnished me with
letters to the Governors and Prime Ministers of all
the Australasian Colonies except New South Wales:
the Governor of which, Lord Augustus Loftus, I had
the honour to know.

My wife and I held our Christmas dinner, not in
Mecklenburgh Square, where all the furniture had been
laid up in ordinary, but at the Midland Hotel, St. Pancras; where among our guests were Mr. and Mrs.

Labouchere. On Boxing Day, 1884, my wife and I
went down to Liverpool, where I embarked on board
a big Cunarder bound for New York. The passage
was a horribly tempestuous one ; but I have been in a
storm, morally and physically speaking, for the best
part of my life ; and, fortunately, I am not subject to
sea-sickness ; although since my illness in 1873 I have
never possessed proper sea-legs. Off Sandy Hook Mr.
Bowden boarded us in a tender, and straightway conducted me to the New York Hotel, Broadway, where
I found a group of interviewing journalists awaiting
my arrival. They drank a great deal of champagne ;
smoked a large number of cigars, and published the
next morning articles varying in tone about my views
on all kinds of topics, my attire, and my Nose. I delivered my first lecture not at New York, but at Boston ; the audience was a large but not a crowded one ;
although the chair was taken by the genial " Autocrat
of the Breakfast Table," the late Dr. Oliver Wendell
Holmes. The next lecture was attended by an even
smaller gathering, and the third by a thinner one still.
Mr. Bowden was inclined to think that the presence
in Boston of Madame Adelina Patti, who was giving a
series of concerts there, had something to do with the
paucity of my patrons ; and then it occurred to him
that what was known as " The Week of Prayer " was
in progress in the capital of Massachusetts, and that
many seriously-minded people had been deterred by
devotional reasons from coming to hear me.

So back we went to New York, where I was splendidly entertained at dinner by the members of the
Lotos Club. Among the after-dinner speakers were
the facetious General Horace Porter, and the equally
humorous lawyer and orator Mr. Chauncey Depew,
who made a great point in his speech by saying that I
was going to Australia by way of Portland, in the

State of Maine: a city which I never had the pleasure of visiting; but he repeated the assertion over and over again, and every time he reiterated it the company laughed uproariously: — a circumstance which strengthened a long-existing conviction in my mind that in after-dinner speaking and "stage-gagging" you have only to continually repeat something —"What's o'clock?" or "That's the idea!" or "How do you feel now?" or "Still I am not happy!"—to excite the hilarity of your hearers.

My lectures at Chickering Hall, New York, were passably well-attended; but I had a very sparse audience at Brooklyn, where in the chair in the church where I discoursed was the well-known American divine, the Rev. De Witt Talmage. At Philadelphia I had an overflowing audience, chiefly due, I should say, to the exertions of Mr. George W. Childs. Washington, where the wintry weather was terribly severe, turned out a miserable failure; but I spent a pleasant time there as the guest of Eugene Schuyler, at whose house I met General Sherman and General "Phil" Sheridan. I had the honour, also, of being presented to, and holding a long conversation with, the President of the Republic, Mr. Chester Arthur; and I renewed my friendship with Senator Bayard. At the Capitol I was introduced to an American warrior, lawyer, and statesman, of whom I had heard a great deal, and concerning whom during the War of Secession I had written frequently, not altogether in a complimentary manner. This was General Benjamin Franklin Butler. He was most genial; and asked me whether I had ever been at New Orleans. I replied that I had sojourned for a considerable time in the Crescent City in 1879. "Ah!" he cheerfully remarked, "if you had been down at Orleans in 1864 I would most certainly have hanged you—Yes, sir!"

and I thoroughly believe that the General would have been as good as his word.

A most decided, uncompromising personage " Ben " Butler. It is true that rude people used to call out "Spoons!" when he appeared at the theatre: the derisive exclamation being founded on the clearly libellous calumny that when in command at New Orleans he had shown a *penchant* for appropriating the valuables of recalcitrant Southerners; but, be it as it may, General Butler struck me as being a born ruler of men. I remember his coming to take military command at New York late in '64, when political riots, fomented by the Democratic party, were apprehended. His very arrival inspired a wholesome terror. He was waited upon at his head-quarters at the Fifth Avenue Hotel by the Mayor and Aldermen of the Empire City. An American friend who was present on the occasion observed that when the deputation retired from General Butler's awe-exciting presence, "their socks were full of toe-nails." B. B., they knew, was not a man to be trifled with.

Worse luck in Baltimore; although my good friend Mr. Otho Williams and his accomplished daughter, Miss Susan Williams, did all they could for me. Still direr misfortune at Cincinnati. Here the hitherto cheery Mr. Bowden fairly lost heart, and wrote me a letter saying that there was no armour against Fate, and that he must " chuck the lectures up." He added that he had made arrangements for me to lecture at St. Louis and at Chicago; but that I must bear the expenses myself, and that he intended to go to Buffalo for a change of air. I have never seen him since, but I met a relative of his at San Francisco, to whom I related the story of his unsuccessful speculation in my brains and tongue. The sole comment of the gentleman at San Francisco was "Ah! just so; it's so like him." Why so like him? Was he always giving away five-hundred-pound notes in wild-cat schemes, I wonder? Henry Irving and Ellen Terry were playing at Chicago when I arrived there, and the presence of those admirable artists, who were drawing overflow houses every night, militated, of course, against my chances of success. The last straw that broke the camel's back was the circumstance that Mark Twain, who came to see me, was himself lecturing in the city.

However, I did my best. I gave away three hundred cards of admission to the clerks at the Grand Pacific Hotel. Henry Irving likewise consented to distribute another hundred passes, and I had a fairly well-filled house; while the money taken at the doors just paid for the hire of the hall and the cost of advertising. Lecturing, so the proprietor of the hall was good enough to tell me when he gave me a receipt for his charges, was " played out " in the States. I thoroughly agreed with him; and resolved to keep my mouth shut in public until I reached the Antipodes.

But the agent and I were both mistaken. I went to Omaha; crossed the Rockies, and descended the Pacific Slope in the usual adorable spring weather. At Sacramento I found the editor of an important San Franciscan paper, who had come to welcome me to the Golden State; and with him was an Italian gentleman, whose name I have forgotten, but whom I will call Risotto. He was of Semitic extraction, and he was most anxious that I should deliver a course of six lectures at 'Frisco. I frankly told him of my failure in the Northern and Western States, and warned him that to speculate in myself was a perilous venture. "*Accidente !* " he made answer. " Dese eastern folk, dey know noting, noting at all. You shall draw crowds efery night, or my name is not Risotto. *Corpo*

di Bacco!"   He offered me the usual terms of fifty*
per cent. on the gross takings.   I agreed ; and arrived
at San Francisco quite in a merry mood, and took up
my old quarters at the Palace Hotel.   My success as
a lecturer was triumphant.   The theatre in which I
held forth was crammed every night ; and my *impresario* was only disappointed at my declining—through
cautious apprehension that it might come to the ears
of the Australian Mrs. Grundy—to lecture on the Sabbath.

Punctually at ten o'clock every morning the energetic Neapolitan used to wait upon me with a long
rouleau of gold eagles or twenty-dollar pieces, and I
took about three hundred pounds' worth of these handsome coins to Australia and sold them to the Commercial Bank at Melbourne.   Whenever he handed over
the rouleau to me, my friend used to ask, " Are you
content?"   " *Contentissimo*," I would reply.   " Yes," he
would continue, "this is what Risotto de Neapolitan
Chew can do.   Dose eastern folk, dey know noting ;
dey have *teste di formaggio.   Accidente !* "   The members of the Bohemian Club, who are no more Bohemian
in their ways than the members of the Lotos Club at
New York are eaters of the *sizyphus*, entertained me
at a grand banquet, on the morrow of which I embarked
on board a steamer bound for Auckland, New Zealand.
My Italian friend saw me off ; and just as the ship was
starting he clasped me fraternally by the hand, saying, " Got bless you !   Risotto the Neapolitan Chew
bids you farewell.   Be happy, *carissimo*.   I have made
much more money than you."

The steamer had a right good English skipper and a
Chinese crew.   The Celestial stewards were continually winking and simpering, but they were civil and
attentive.   There was a dead calm on the Pacific ; and
for seven days we ploughed our way through what

seemed an unbroken sheet of molten glass. We did not meet a shark; but we saw several "schools" of porpoises and a few albatrosses. At the week's end we made the harbour of Honolulu, where everybody within hail seemed to be crying " Aloha !" Not being skilled in the Hawaiian tongue, I am quite ignorant as to what " Aloha !" may mean; but I take it to be a conventional exclamation equivalent to the English " All right," the American " Bully for you," and the Spanish " *Hombre !* " So soon as I landed I was bustled by some newly made friends into a wagonnette and conveyed to the Royal Palace, a handsome stone edifice, of architectural pretensions quite equalling those of the Schloss of a German Grand Duchy, and standing in tastefully laid-out grounds, rainbow-hued with tropical plants and flowers. There was a sentinel in a smart uniform on guard at the entrance gate; and a few more soldiers were lounging about at the door of the guard-room.

His Hawaiian Majesty was not residing at the Palace itself; he was dwelling in a commodious wooden bungalow in the grounds. I sent in my card; and in a few minutes I was ushered into the presence of the late King David Laamea Kalakaua.

The Royal sitting-room was simply but elegantly furnished; and behind the arm-chair of the occupant were two tall book-cases full of well-bound volumes. The King rose when I entered; gave me his hand, bade me be seated; and during a prolonged audience expressed, among other things, the hope that I was going to stop at least a month at Hawaii, and " visit the largest volcano in the world." I had to state, with regret, that the steamer was leaving at the expiration of four hours. I found His Majesty a stalwart and well-built gentleman, with an intelligent expression of countenance, and speaking excellent English. When in the afternoon the steamer left Honolulu, the King sent down his own private band, with a German bandmaster, to bid us farewell; and the friendly, chocolate‑coloured Polynesians pelted us with flowers and oranges. In another week we were at Apia in the Samoan Islands; and another seven days brought us safely to Auckland, always in unremitting sunny and windless weather. I forget at what stage of our voyage we crossed the Line; but I know that Neptune did not make his appearance on board; nor do I remember when it was that we lost a day; but I can vouch for the fact that on a certain Wednesday the captain caused to be affixed to the looking-glass in the saloon this brief notice, " To-morrow will be Friday."

It was on a Sunday morning that we arrived at Auckland. A party of journalists came off in a boat and boarded the steamer; and I was marched off to the principal hotel, the smiling landlady of which establishment informed me that Miss Geneviève Ward, the *tragédienne*, had been staying in the house, and had just left for the Hot Lakes. After luncheon, the steamer again took her departure, and on the fifth morning afterwards we entered the indescribably beautiful harbour of Sydney, and anchored at the Circular Quay. The Mayor of Sydney and Mr. Alison, one of my *entrepreneurs*, were waiting for me; and I was told that my first lecture was to be delivered in the Town Hall, Melbourne, on the morrow of St. Patrick's Day. After luncheon, I went to Government House; paid my respects to Lord Augustus Loftus; and was subsequently conducted to the Public Offices, where I was introduced to most of the Cabinet Ministers, including a great friend of Lord Rosebery, the late Hon. William Bede Dalley, who had been mainly instrumental in sending the New South Wales contingent to the Soudan.

Mr. Dalley was one of the most cultured gentlemen and the most fluent orators I ever had the honour to meet. The Postmaster-General presented me with a free railway pass available for some months for myself and my wife; and I may here mention that every one of the Australasian Colonies showed us similar courtesy, and it never cost us a penny for railway travelling during our stay in the Colonies. Before leaving for Melbourne the members of the Athenæum Club—a society in which Lord Rosebery during his stay in Australia took great interest—entertained me at dinner, the chair being occupied by Mr. Dalley. The railway journey from the capital of New South Wales to that of Victoria occupied from six in the evening until about eleven the following morning. But midway, at the frontier of the two colonies, there was an examination of luggage at a Victorian custom-house. The line of railway seemed to run principally through tractless forests of tall gum-trees. At the railway terminus at Melbourne I found my wife and Mr. and Mrs. George Rignold waiting for me on the platform; and we at once adjourned to Menzies' Hotel, then, and perhaps now, the very best hotel in Australia.

I found Melbourne a really astonishing city, with broad streets full of handsome shops, and crowded with bustling, well-dressed people. For two days we held almost continuous receptions at the hotel; and I wish that I had preserved the hundreds of cards of the ladies and gentlemen who were so kind as to visit us. The next evening I lectured for two hours at the Town Hall, which was crowded, and the receipts amounted to more than £300. At the second lecture the aggregate takings were only £80. I am afraid, to begin with, that the hall was much too large for my purpose, and that my voice was scarcely audible to

the occupants of the back seats. I remember at my
first lecture being struck by two very curious circumstances. First, that what I intended to be a glowing
eulogium on Mr. Gladstone was received in dead silence; and that every allusion I made to Lord Beaconsfield was responded to by a thunderous storm of hand-
clapping and cheering.

I went to Government House; was received by Sir
Henry Loch, and dined with His Excellency, who, with
Lady Loch, was present at my third lecture; but I
must frankly own that as a lecturer I was not particularly successful in Melbourne. I realised, however,
large sums in Australia. In Sydney I did remarkably
well; and in New Zealand even better in a financial
sense:—my agent there being the "Little Smythe"
with whom I had had the embryonic negotiations already mentioned. I earned, moreover, between March
and December, something like £100 a week by the
republication in the Melbourne *Argus;* the Sydney
Morning Herald; another journal at Adelaide, South
Australia, the *Auckland Herald,* and the *Calcutta Englishman,* of my letters under the title " The Land of
the Golden Fleece," for which I was receiving another
£20 a week from the *Daily Telegraph.* I got four per
cent. for my money on deposit in the Commercial
Bank of Australia, and, in fact, by the end of the year
I had realised a competence—which, for a literary
man, might be considered handsome—for my old age;
but within a year of my return to England I lost all
my laboriously acquired shekels in one great crash.

I had my ups and my downs during my lecturing
tour on the Australian continent; journeying, as my
wife and I did, into the remotest "back-blocks" of the
Bush. In some towns our success was magnificent, in
others the takings did not exceed £10. At Adelaide,
at Brisbane in Queensland, and indeed throughout the

last-named colony, the money rolled in gloriously. At one township where there was a rather handsome theatre, I peeped—as lecturers as well as managers will do —through the usual orifice in the drop-curtain to see what kind of a house there was; but to my dismay the pit—there were no stalls—was tenanted only by three men and a boy. It was a case, I thought, of Hull and Lieutenant Gale's lecture on " Aërostation " over again. But the case was pleasantly altered when the curtain rose. The most expensive seats in the house were in the dress circle, which had been invisible to me through the hole in the curtain; and I found the boxes crowded with the " quality " of the place—magistrates, clergymen, and wealthy squatters. We had hot roast fowl for supper that night.

Great financial success was also our lot at Wagga-Wagga, a really pretty town, with the name of which all those who remember the Tichborne trial will be familiar. The Assizes were on when we arrived ; and by good luck the Crown Prosecutor turned out to be an old friend of mine. I had a capital house on that and the succeeding night—the Judge came, the bar and the solicitors mustered in full force ; the prosecutors and the witnesses were all to the fore ; and I could almost have believed that the prisoners, escorted by friendly warders, were likewise present. It was at a place called Mudgee that I underwent one of the most serious snubs that I ever experienced, although I must admit that I have not unfrequently, while making a speech, been more or less "shut up" by an unsympathetic audience. Once, taking the chair at the Holborn Town Hall, in advocacy of a movement for establishing a tram-car system in the parish of St. Pancras, I began my address with—" Ladies and gentlemen. When I was last in the United States——" whereupon a gentleman in the gallery cried out:

"Why the devil didn't you stop there?" This was
not very encouraging, but my rebuff at Mudgee was
much more mortifying. It came from the lady who,
as I have elsewhere related, exclaimed " Rubbidge!"
when I had come to the end of what I thought was a
pathetic and picturesque description of the appearance
of Her Majesty Queen Victoria at her Coronation in
June, 1838.

It was at Brisbane, in Queensland, that I found
Miss Geneviève Ward, whose dramatic tour, in company with that excellent actor Mr. Vernon, had been
one uninterrupted triumph. She made, I apprehend,
as much if not more money than I did ; and she had
the sense, I hope and believe, to keep her winnings.
We afterwards had the pleasure of meeting her both
in Melbourne and Sydney. Of the many score of
places, many of them with wholly unpronounceable
native names, I took careful count in a ledger which I
kept, but which I have mislaid. I know, however,
that in the autumn, under the auspices of " Little
Smythe," I went to New Zealand, and lectured with
bright success at Auckland, Wellington, Christchurch,
Dunedin, Invercargill, and other places. At Wellington, the capital of the colony, I had the advantage of
meeting the Governor, Sir William Jarvis, whom I
had not seen since the old Canadian days in 1864.
Moreover, I received from an unknown source £100
as an honorarium for visiting the wonderful Hot
Lakes district and formally opening some of the
baths. I saw the marvellous Pink and White Ter-
races, since utterly annihilated by a succession of
dreadful earthquakes.

Returning from New Zealand early in December, I
lectured four or five times, but with indifferent success, at Hobart and other towns in the beautiful and
hospitable island of Tasmania—the sanatorium, the

Isle of Wight of Australia. In the third week of December my wife left me to go to Melbourne to pack up our things with the intent of departing for India; and three days after she left I crossed to Sydney to draw out some money from a banking-house there. I spent my Christmas Day at sea, not very convivially; there was no roast beef and there was no plum pudding, and I dined on boiled mutton and turnips, and a pint of Bass's pale ale. At Sydney I left my card with Lord Carrington, the newly arrived Governor, who at once sent down a trooper to the hotel where I was staying and asked me to dinner that same evening. At the end of the repast His Excellency, after proposing the Queen's health, told me that that was the only toast usually drunk at Government House; but that he meant to drink the health of my wife, which he did. We walked afterwards in the garden, and gazed at the blue velvet sky—not *Melaina astron* ("black with stars"), as the Greek playwright somewhat paradoxically puts it in *Electra*—but studded almost overwhelmingly with the dazzling luminaries of the Southern Cross. "What a beautiful country!" exclaimed Lord Carrington, "and what a happy time you must have had." Yes; I had had, all things considered, a happy and most prosperous time.

Next evening, having settled all my money matters, I took the train; and on the platform at Melbourne I found, not my wife, but Mr. Smythe, who told me that my dear partner had caught a chill at sea in Bass's Straits; that she was lying dangerously ill at Menzies' Hotel, where a consultation of three physicians had just been held. It was New Year's Eve; the weather was ferociously hot, with a hotter wind, and a "brickfielder," or dust-storm, blowing through Melbourne's broad streets. I found my wife inarticulate in the agonies of peritonitis; she only spoke once, when, pressing my hand, she said, " Go to India, dear, and complete your education." That night she died. At three o'clock in the afternoon of the next day I had to bury her. I had no mourning attire ; and I was obliged to borrow different articles of sable dress from different friends. Everybody was pitiful and kind to me. The Governors of every one of the Australasian Colonies sent me condoling telegrams ; and similar missives reached me from Lord Rosebery and from Henry Irving. The Bishop of Melbourne, now Bishop of Manchester, wrote me a touching letter. The Venerable Archdeacon of Melbourne, then nearly eighty years of age, and who died only a few days ago, came and prayed with me. Geneviève Ward was away ; Mrs. Menzies and her daughter were touchingly kind to me, but I fancy that during a full fortnight I was more or less off my head.

CHAPTER LXI

THE Chairman of the Peninsular and Oriental Steam
Navigation Company, so soon as the news of my sad
bereavement had been cabled to London, telegraphed
to Melbourne to the Company's agent there, instruct-
ing him to give me, if I wished to visit India, a free
passage to Calcutta, Madras, and Bombay, and back
to England. When I was well enough to travel, I
boarded one of the magnificent P. and O. steamers at
Williamstown; and three weeks later, after a brief stay
at Colombo and Kandy, in the enchanting island of
Ceylon, I arrived at Calcutta. Lord Dufferin was
away, in Burmah; but he had telegraphed to Calcutta
to say that I was to be asked to the Vice-regal country residence at Barrackpore, and on his return to the
City of Palaces he showed me all his usual goodness.
Sir W. W. Hunter, a Member of Council, too, to whom
I had been recommended by Génevième Ward, " put
me up" at a house which he had rented somewhere
on the Hūgli. We crossed the river one night to witness some religious ceremony at a Hindoo temple. I
caught a chill on the water, and two days afterwards,
at a hotel in Calcutta, I awoke with a high fever.

When I grew apparently convalescent I was again
" put up," or entertained, at the house of Mr. J. O. B.
Saunders, the proprietor of the Calcutta *Englishman;*
and when, after a few weeks' stay under his hospitable
roof, I began to feel quite well and strong, I shipped
myself on board the P. and O. steamer *Ballarat*, and

returned home by way of Colombo—where I met Sir Edwin Arnold, who was revisiting India—Madras, Aden, the Red Sea, the Suez Canal, and Marseilles. I reached London just in time for the Queen's Jubilee, and of the ceremonial in the Abbey I wrote a long account in the *Daily Telegraph.* I had not, however, been more than three weeks in Mecklenburgh Square when the fever, or rather the fag-end of it, came back to me, and I believe that the malady is in my bones still. I was more or less an invalid for nearly a year.

I may here be allowed to say something about one of the last public transactions in which I have been concerned. In February, 1889, I was the occupant of a flat in Victoria Street, Westminster, and one Saturday, between one and two p.m., a knock came at my study-door, and I was handed a letter which had been brought in hot haste by a servant who was instructed to wait for an answer. The missive was of the briefest possible kind, and was from my near neighbour Mr. Henry Labouchere, M.P., whose house was then at 24, Grosvenor Gardens, and the note ran thus: "Can you leave everything, and come here at once? Most important business.—H. L." I told the servant that I would be in Grosvenor Gardens within a quarter of an hour, and, ere that time had expired, I was ushered into a large library on the ground floor, where I found the Senior Member for Northampton smoking his sempiternal cigarette, but with an unusual and curious expression of animation in his normally impassive countenance.

He was not alone. Ensconced in a roomy fauteuil a few paces from Mr. Labouchere's writing-table there was a somewhat burly individual of middle stature and of more than middle age. He looked fully sixty; although I have been given to understand that his age did not exceed fifty-five; but his elderly aspect was enhanced by his baldness, which revealed a large amount of oval *os frontis* fringed by grey locks. The individual had an eye-glass screwed into one eye, and he was using this optical aid most assiduously, for he was poring over a copy of that morning's issue of the *Times*, going right down one column and apparently up it again ; then taking column after column in succession ; then harking back as though he had omitted some choice paragraph ; and then resuming the sequence of his lecture, ever and anon tapping that ovoid frontal bone of his, as though to evoke memories of the past, with a little silver pencil-case. I noticed his somewhat shabby-genteel attire ; and in particular I observed that the hand which held the copy of the *Times* never ceased to shake. Mr. Labouchere, in his most courteous manner and his blandest tone said, " Allow me to introduce you to a gentleman of whom you must have heard a great deal, Mr. ——." I replied, " There is not the slightest necessity for naming him. I know him well enough. That's Mr. Pigott."

The individual in the capacious fauteuil wriggled from behind the *Times* an uneasy acknowledgment of my recognition ; but, if anything could be conducive to putting completely at his ease a gentleman who, from some cause or another, was troubled in his mind, it would have been the dulcet voice in which Mr. Labouchere continued : " The fact is that Mr. Pigott has come here, quite unsolicited, to make a full confession. I told him that I would listen to nothing that he had to say save in the presence of a witness, and remembering that you lived close by, I thought that you would not mind coming here and listening to what Mr. Pigott has to confess, which will be taken down, word by word, from his dictation in writing." It has been my lot, during a long and diversified career, to have to listen to a large number of very queer state-

ments from very queer people ; and, by dint of experience, you reach at last a stage of stoicism when little,
if anything, that is imparted to you excites surprise.
Mr. Pigott, although he had screwed his courage to
the sticking-place of saying that he was going to confess, manifested considerable tardiness in orally " own-
ing up." Conscience, we were justified in assuming,
had "gnawed" to an extent sufficient to make him
willing to relieve his soul from a dreadful burden; but
conscience, to all seeming, had to gnaw a little longer
and a little more sharply ere he absolutely gave
tongue. So we let him be for about ten minutes. Mr.
Labouchere kindled another cigarette. I lighted a
cigar.

At length Mr. Pigott stood up and came forward
into the light by the side of Mr. Labouchere's writing-
table. He did not change colour; he did not blench ;
but when—out of the fulness of his heart, no doubt—
his mouth spake, it was in a low, half-musing tone,
more at first as though he were talking to himself than
to any auditors. By degrees, however, his voice rose,
his diction became more fluent. It is only necessary
that in this place I should say in substance that Pigott
confessed that he had forged the letters alleged to
have been written by Mr. Parnell; and he minutely
described the manner in which he, and he alone, had
executed the forgeries in question. Whether the man
with the bald head and the eye-glass in the library at
Grosvenor Gardens was telling the truth or uttering
another batch of infernal lies it is not for me to determine. No pressure was put upon him ; no leading
questions were asked him ; and he went on quietly
and continuously to the end of a story which I should
have thought amazing had I not had occasion to hear
many more tales even more astounding. He was not
voluble, but he was collected, clear, and coherent ; nor,

although he repeatedly confessed to forgery, fraud, deception, and misrepresentation, did he seem overcome with anything approaching active shame. His little peccadilloes were plainly owned, but he appeared to treat them more as incidental weaknesses than as extraordinary acts of wickedness.

When he had come to the end of his statement Mr. Labouchere left the library for a few minutes to obtain a little refreshment. It was a great relief to me that Pigott did not confess anything to me when we were left together. There came over me a vague dread that he might confess his complicity with the Rye House Plot, or that he would admit that he had been the executioner of King Charles I. The situation was rather embarrassing; the time might have been tided over by whistling, but unfortunately I never learnt to whistle. It would have been rude to read a book ; and, besides, to do so would have necessitated my taking my eyes off Mr. Pigott, and I never took them off him. We did get into conversation, but our talk was curt and trite. He remarked, first taking up that so-often-conned *Times*, that the London papers were inconveniently large. This being a self-evident proposition, met with no response from me ; but on his proceeding to say, in quite a friendly manner, that I must have found the afternoon's interview rather stupid work, I replied that, on the contrary, so far as I was concerned, I had found it equally amusing and instructive. Then, the frugal Mr. Labouchere coming back with his mouthful, we went to business again. The whole of Pigott's confession, beginning with the declaration that he had made it uninvited and without any pecuniary consideration, was read over to him line by line and word by word. He made no correction or alteration whatsoever. The confession covered several sheets of paper, and to each sheet he affixed his initials. Finally, at the bottom of the completed document he signed his name, beneath which I wrote my name as a witness.

One day, not very long after my return from India, and while I was miserably ill, there came to visit me a tall, comely lady, who brought me a letter from dear old Antonio Gallenga. She sought my assistance in some matter of lady journalism. Eventually she became my faithful and efficient secretary. I mourned my dear lost Harriet for four dismal years. But time was good to me. I thought it wicked and ungrateful to Providence to continue to dwell in sulky solitude, eating my own heart when I had the means of making another person happy ; and four years ago I was married at St. Margaret's Church, Westminster, to Bessie, the third daughter of the late Robert Stannard, C.E., the tall and handsome lady whom Antonio Gallenga had sent to me.

THE END.

INDEX